THE CRYSTALLINE CRUCIBLE

ADAM ROWAN

Copyright © Adam Rowan 2024

All rights reserved.

No part of this publication may be altered, reproduced, distributed, or transmitted in any form, by any means, including, but not limited to, scanning, duplicating, uploading, hosting, distributing, or reselling, without the express prior written permission of the publisher, except in the case of reasonable quotations in features such as reviews, interviews, and certain other non-commercial uses currently permitted by copyright law.

Disclaimer:
This is a work of fiction. All characters, locations, and businesses are purely products of the author's imagination and are entirely fictitious. Any resemblance to actual people, living or dead, or to businesses, places, or events is completely coincidental.

Acknowledgments

Special thanks to my mother and father, David Lugo at Spinning Monkey Press, and my editor, Robin LeeAnn.

CHAPTER 1

THE WOOLLY MAMMOTH THIEF

In the seven-decade-long existence of the Nottingham Natural History Museum, no break-in had ever occurred until five a.m. on one fateful Saturday. The trespasser's name was Maxwell Oscar Jacobs, a local retail worker. In his spare time, he enjoyed playing Tetris, doing crossword puzzles, and—his preferred pastime—a spot of treasure hunting.

With a stone he'd found on the pavement, Max had smashed the museum's back window and climbed into it by balancing on a rubbish bin. Shortly thereafter, he padded warily through the geology exhibit surrounded by models of Earth, not enjoying the experience in the slightest. Surveillance cameras mounted above on the wall scanned him, but he dearly hoped the authorities hadn't been despatched to arrest him. They shouldn't be. After all, he hadn't poured chocolate milk on the power box outside for nothing.

Max was twenty-one years old, rather tall with stick insect limbs. Bright blond hair and a poorly cut fringe topped his head. He wore a grey Cookie Monster hoodie, straight-legged jeans, Mickey Mouse socks and a cheap, half-broken children's watch with coloured numbers. He also wore blue trainers with the shoelaces undone and carried a Tony the Tiger rucksack in which to store the mammoth tusk he was after. To top it all, he had a scabbard that held a broadsword called Fleshrender, Max's favourite possession.

Pacing along, he thought passingly that he should have dressed the part more and put on a ski mask. His heart pounded as he passed by the dinosaur exhibit, unease assailing him. It was too late to go home at this point. He just had to find the mammoth tusk before daylight.

He gathered himself, drew his sword and focused on not tripping while he navigated through the dark, winding corridors. Even the smallest of noises made him jump—broadsword at the ready—as he crept through the empty halls.

With the lights off, the museum was practically a haunted house. While he tiptoed into the zoology section, glimmering rays of moonlight streamed in through the windows, falling gently over him. Shadowed model animals lined the walls, felt rabbits and plastic spiders sitting on table displays. A frightening bear stood with its paws raised and its sharp jaws wide open as if ready to pounce on him at a moment's notice. Max's eyes widened, but within seconds he discerned to his relief it was just taxidermy.

At last, the mammoth appeared behind a red security barrier not far away. With every muscle tensed, he gazed in awe at its gigantic figure. But his jaw dropped as he realised, despite how carefully he had planned this mission, he'd forgotten one crucial part: how to extract the mammoth tusk out of the skeleton. It looked like it'd been screwed in tightly. *Should've brought a screwdriver. Oh, bother.*

Pushing his shoulders back, he sheathed his weapon, strode right up to the mammoth and peered at the display label. It read:

This woolly mammoth skeleton was discovered in 1925 by a team of esteemed archaeologists in rural Devon. It was the first almost entirely preserved specimen ever uncovered in England. It is a relic of priceless historical value. DO NOT TOUCH.

Deciding to disobey and wrest the tusk out, Max stepped over the maroon rope that encircled the mammoth and wrapped his hands around it.

Like Arthur pulling the sword from the stone, there was nothing else to do but pull really, really hard.

After counting down from three, he tugged the mammoth tusk towards him with all his might. It took a few tries, but finally the tusk separated from the woolly mammoth skeleton with a nasty crack, and he fell on his backside. Yet before he could rejoice, he heard the sound of a creak.

A door opened across the room.

"PUT YOUR HANDS BEHIND YOUR BACK! LAY DOWN ON THE GROUND!"

Max turned around and scrambled to his feet, mouth wide open. Police with intimidating weapons emerged out of nowhere, swarming him. He gaped at the approaching horde before looking back down at the tusk. This couldn't be happening.

The thought crossed his mind to run. But what was the point? There were too many police. He was toast!

He dropped the mammoth tusk on the floor and unsheathed his sword. "Listen, this is all a b-big misunderstanding," he stuttered.

"NO MISUNDERSTANDING!" a second officer yelled, a woman in a navy tunic with a bulletproof vest. She inched over to him. "HANDS BEHIND YOUR BACK NOW!"

Max stared at the police, aghast. *They think I'm a criminal. How ridiculous. I'm just an innocent treasure hunter!*

"Let me e-explain. It's v-very, very important for you to let me e-explain," Max stammered.

He pointed his sword at them threateningly, before spotting a paunchy man who held what looked like a laser pointer and was aiming it at him.

Max swung the sword around as a warning. "Please. If you'd just give me a second to clear this up, I'm sure that—arghhh!"

His words cut out with a bloodcurdling scream. Electricity surged through his body. The red dot he'd seen on his chest hadn't been from a laser pointer at all, but a taser. Limbs spasming, Max fell onto the floor and crumpled into a ball as the police closed in on him.

CHAPTER 2

CONSEQUENCES AND CLUES

The officers at Nottingham Police Station didn't seem to like Max much, but then again, it was rare to find anyone who did. Of course, on the surface, they had a good reason to dislike him. He knew what breaking into the Nottingham Natural History Museum with a broadsword to steal a priceless relic looked like. But he would have never dreamt of doing something so strange unless he'd thought it through long and hard and had a good reason.

Unfortunately, nobody else seemed to appreciate that.

After being tasered, he'd been handcuffed, loaded into a police car and driven to the station, where he was swiftly locked in an interrogation room with a gruff fellow by the name of Constable William Tomlinson.

"Hold on, son," Constable Tomlinson said, scratching his grey stubbly chin. He was a tall, middle-aged officer with weathered skin, cold eyes and a bemused curled lip stitched onto his face. He was also the one who had so rudely tasered Max. "What is this Crystalline Crucible you keep mentioning?"

Max sighed. He longed to be comfy on the sofa at home and watching *Miss Marple*. "I could have told you that without the taser or these chafing handcuffs," he muttered, caustic spite in his voice.

"Well, you *did* break into a museum," the constable insisted. "And tried to steal a mammoth tusk, damaging it in the process! And threatened police officers with a sword! Answer my question."

Max scanned the dusty interrogation room, a crooked light fixture flickering overhead. This police station was new to him. He lived in

Stapleford, a town to the west of Nottingham. *That* police station he knew like the back of his hand. Although much like ice cream, pizza or chocolate, he didn't like it at all. This one was just as bad.

"The Crystalline Crucible is a treasure hunting competition or a puzzle quest, if you will," he grumbled. "I would've thought you'd heard of it. It *is* the most famous one in the treasure hunting community presently. The reason I broke into the museum is to find the next clue."

"A blimmin' clue? What are you talking about? Is this *The Da Vinci Code* or something?"

Max closed his eyes, frustration getting the better of him. *Am I brain-dead yet? Sure feels like it. I've been at this station for aeons.* "A few months ago, a mysterious organisation posted ads online saying that they are looking to recruit highly intelligent individuals. They reportedly devised a test to find them, a treasure hunt that is said to be the most difficult one the world has ever seen. They call it The Crystalline Crucible."

"I've never heard of it," Constable Tomlinson said with a thin frown. "I don't keep up with the treasure hunting community. I didn't even know there was one! Why did you think a clue was in the museum? And what's with the sword?"

"The previous clue's decrypted answer recently leaked, the words *woolly mammoth tusk*," he clarified. "Knowing that the closest mammoth tusk in the country is stored in the local natural history museum, I wanted to have a close look. Before breaking in, I sent over fifty email requests to the museum's director, Ms Smith, most of which were ignored. To be accurate, she replied to the last one instructing me to 'stop harassing me or I'll call the…'" He dropped the air quotes. "The point is that I had to get to the tusk *alone*. As for the broadsword, as well as moonlighting as a treasure hunter, I happen to be a self-trained swordsman. Indeed, I may well be the last true knight of England. I expect that explains everything."

It didn't.

"Blimey. Treasure hunting? Sounds like a waste of time," Constable Tomlinson chided, standing. "And a *swordsman*? You from the Dark Ages, Maxwell? You belong in a loony bin. I've got to speak with my colleagues to decide what's to be done with you. Back in a few."

Max yawned; his tongue felt drier than ash. "Am I going to be allowed to go home soon? If you'd like to continue asking me obvious questions, may I suggest a search engine?"

"You'll be here a long time if you continue speaking to me with that cheek," the constable snapped, and stormed out.

The interrogation room had a single barred window. Max approached it and looked out at the late afternoon sky over Nottingham's cityscape. They'd kept him at the police station all day. It was spitting with rain out there. He listened to the drizzle's relaxing rat-a-tat as he rested his chin on his arm. *I needed that clue to win. What can I do now? The lottery? But I'm banned from it for attempted fraud!*

"The winner of The Crystalline Crucible will be gifted riches beyond their wildest dreams. All their earthly problems will be rendered null, and the mysteries of the world answered," the contest had advertised on its website and in newspapers for the past couple of months.

The enigma of it all had taken the treasure hunting community—and even some of the general public—by storm. Rumours had begun to spread online that the winner would become a member of the Illuminati. Even more intriguing was the priceless crystal trophy, the Jewelled Chalice, which was said to be presented to the winner by none other than the director general of MI6.

Maxwell had been treasure hunting for *years*. All the same, the most he'd ever found was a limited-edition box of Jaffa Cakes from the eighties that offered free tickets to an arcade that was now regrettably closed. So, it was more important than ever that he win The Crystalline Crucible and make a success of his life's work. The thought of this all made him groan, as he dwelled on the decade-plus he'd spent hunting without finding any treasure.

Max had practically fallen asleep by the time Constable Tomlinson returned.

"It's decided: you're getting bail. One hundred pounds," the constable uttered grumpily. "Aren't you lucky? Turns out the prison is full."

"Huzzah," he drawled, forcing his head to stay upright. "But I've got no way to get home."

"We'll contact your parents."

"You might have trouble with that unless you have a Ouija."

Constable Tomlinson's eyes drooped pitifully. "Ouija board?"

Max swallowed. "My mother died in a car accident on slippery ice when I was a child. The car plunged off a bridge and into the River Trent. The coroner said it was drunk driving, but I blame friction—or the lack of it."

"And your father?"

"In prison. He's not the nicest guy. Tortured and killed three prostitutes. Or so I've heard."

Constable Tomlinson's face reddened slightly. "You must have a guardian. Or somebody to drive you home. I'm not doing it!"

Max thought hard, rubbing his eyes. "Not a guardian per se, but I have a best friend by the name of Rosie Shaw."

"Right. We'll give her a ring." The constable unlocked the handcuffs on Max's wrists. "But don't think you're out of trouble just because we're letting you go. Bail doesn't mean you're off scot-free. You'll have a court hearing. That's a little thing called consequences."

Bail? Consequences? A court hearing?! Max stiffened. *Oh, no. Am I gonna end up in prison for this? I swear I was gonna return the tusk eventually!*

Constable Tomlinson brought him into the waiting area to pay his bail while he rang Rosie. As he waited, Max grimaced and put his head in his hands as he anticipated how she would react. He couldn't imagine a good outcome. It was never a pleasurable thing to be called by the police to pick up a friend.

The moment Rosie set foot inside the station, Constable Tomlinson started to explain what was going on in an incredibly biased manner. She bit her nails, glancing disapprovingly at Max.

"Your friend is quite a character," the constable said, pointing at Max as if he were a naughty schoolboy. "He may well face serious charges for this in court. And if he does anything else like this again, he could end up in prison. If it were my choice, he'd be in the clink right now."

"I'm so sorry," Rosie said briskly. Luscious brown hair flowed over her shoulders, and she wore her favourite bead necklace as usual. "Only a total man-child would be stupid enough to do something like this."

"A man-child?" Max interrupted, which caused them both to raise their eyebrows. "You do realise I haven't gone deaf."

"What? I think it's pretty accurate," Constable Tomlinson said.

After they returned his Tony the Tiger rucksack, the police station let him go. Yet there was one notable absence.

"Wait. Where's my broadsword?" Max asked, rifling through the Rubik's Cube and Game Boy games in his rucksack.

"You're not getting that back, son. No way!" the constable sneered. "You're too dangerous to have such a weapon. Not to mention, it'll be evidence in your court hearing. I didn't even know they still make swords."

"How totally and utterly ridiculous!" He flounced out, mouthing the word, "Scoundrel."

Once Max and Rosie were in her car, she did not seem at all pleased to see him, as expected. She drove him home with a furrowed brow and gripped the steering wheel so tightly her knuckles were almost white.

Max supposed her name was something of a misnomer, as Rosie was certainly not rosy in any way, shape or form. Only once in a blue moon did he hear her say anything positive. She loved horror films, wouldn't be able to see the genius of Miss Marple if it sucker-punched her and was writing a children's book about a talking tabby. Still, they had known each other since secondary school.

"Did you hear I was tasered?" Max revealed as he threaded his fingers and crossed his legs in the passenger seat. "Agonising. But another box ticked on the bucket list, I guess."

"So traumatic for you," Rosie said, still not looking at him.

This might have been one of those incidents where it was better to keep his mouth shut. He analysed her body language: taut muscles, jaw clenched. He had read about those signs of anger in *Body Language for Dummies*, a book his caretaker, Ms Kensington, had given him at the Children's Society, the institution in which he'd been raised.

"What did you think of that Constable Tomlinson fellow? I wonder if he's related to Lucas Tomlinson. You like him, don't you? Or is that just Henry Styles?" he continued.

"It's Louis Tomlinson and Harry Styles, and I liked him when I was about sixteen. Glad to see you care so much about my interests. You're distracting me from driving."

"Let's address the elephant in the room: you're angry."

"Well observed, Sherlock," Rosie barked, simmering as her nose twitched so violently that it might have been covered in spiders. "I had to come from school. I was working late, tutoring some boys who are struggling."

"Ah, I see. And how are the kids at Kiddy Winks? Can they do fractions yet?"

"It's a nursery. They can barely count."

Max stifled a breath, speculating whether the length of her grudge would beat his previous record: twenty-four days. "If it means anything, I can assure you it was absolutely not my intention to get in trouble. It was the whole getting arrested thing that really threw a spanner in the works. My faith in the English police system has been shattered."

"If you insist on talking, let me pull in somewhere first."

Rosie steered into a petrol station car park with such speed that her air fresheners were practically doing ballet. Truckers had parked around them, filling up their vehicles with diesel. It had been an unsympathetically glacial January day, the sky a van Gogh of oranges and greys framed by the setting sun.

After the car came to a stop, she turned to Max with down-turned lips. "I don't know what's wrong with you! Did you really think that by breaking into that museum, even with the remote chance you succeeded in stealing the tusk, there was going to be some magic clue hidden inside?"

"No, not at all. I simply thought it would've been written on the tusk in invisible ink."

"This could've been so much worse. Count your blessings you got bail," she said, her voice irate. "And besides, isn't…"

Max opened his mouth, half tempted to interrupt her and defend himself. But truthfully, for the first time in a while, he thought that she *might* have a point. This was quite abnormal. He had rarely experienced being wrong in his life, although he had thought elephants were a fictional animal until he was eighteen, and also briefly believed he'd been growing horns and was a centaur.

"I've been saying this for a long time, but this time, it's for real: you *need* to give up this damn treasure hunting business!" Rosie castigated. "The Crystalline Crucible…or whatever it's called. Sorry to break it to you, but you always enter these types of contests, year after year, and never win. Even if you somehow *did* win, the prize would surely be a complete let-down."

"Hmm… This pill is incredibly bitter to swallow," Max mumbled in a regretful tone. "But maybe you're right. Maybe I need to stop."

"What?"

"You heard me. Maybe I got carried away. It's a feasible possibility."

"You're not going to fool me."

"Ever heard of a Damascene conversion? Perhaps I'm having one of them."

"Or you're just saying what you think I want to hear." She exhaled. "All this drama is making me hungry."

On the spur of the moment, they decided to get a bite to eat at the roadside Burger King.

"Brad and I may move someday, and then I won't be able to save you," Rosie warned him as she dug into her double cheeseburger. "These days, I feel more like a babysitter than a friend."

Max's fist coiled at the mention of Brad. He had despised her boyfriend since the moment he'd met him almost a year ago. Brad owned a tattoo parlour called Nottingham Ink Factory and did "wicked" and "sick" tattoos, including his own. Ironically, all his tattoos looked like the scribbles of an infant.

"This contest has been distracting you from the Stapleford Quiz Championship. Don't you want to do well this year?" Rosie added, glancing around at the neighbouring tables. "Last year, we came *so* close to the final three. This year, maybe we can really do it. But only if you focus on studying."

"That's your thing," Max grumbled, swallowing a tiny draught of his Coca-Cola. "The prize money for the quiz championship is nothing compared to The Crystalline Crucible's. I need enough so that..."

But he didn't finish. Instead, he rubbed his chin and evaluated their prospects in the championship. They were members of a local quiz team called Agatha Quiztie, along with two others who never showed. Yet they were aiming to win the Stapleford Quiz Championship, a one-day event in May where all the quiz teams of Stapleford competed to win first prize: five thousand pounds.

"Come on, Max," Rosie pleaded with a worried glint in her eyes. "Please just tell me you're quitting."

He was not one to bow to pressure, so much so that he had once been suspended for refusing to wear a tie. Nevertheless, even though she often seemed to hate him, Rosie was quite possibly Max's favourite person in the entire world, and he hated disappointing her.

"FINE. I'll quit treasure hunting," he gave in. "Should I get in any more trouble, you have my full permission to do whatever you want with me: lock me in a padded cell, put me in a straitjacket and throw away the key."

"I'm not sure that's what I want, but thank God," she said, fiddling with her necklace. "I mean, breaking into the natural history museum... What's next? The Louvre?"

With their meals finished, they soon left Burger King, and she drove him back home to his apartment complex. Meanwhile, Max tapped his foot and wondered if he'd truly meant what he had said about quitting treasure hunting.

Norman Court was a working-class tenement at the centre of Stapleford, characterised by its unfinished brickwork, missing shingles and the stench of nicotine. It was the only place Max could afford to live. It also sat across from the half-collapsed, unfinished Poolway Shopping Centre, where everyone knew drug dealers lurked. He had often heard strange noises coming from it and had seen shady figures heading in and out.

"Don't forget practice is on Monday," Rosie reminded him as she dropped him off on the curb.

"Sure," Max said through the window. "I'll be revising my Greek myths as planned; funny, I feel much like a modern Prometheus tonight. You're doing American presidents?"

"I thought Fred was revising presidents. Or was it genera of flowers?"

"Presidents, as he has been for months... And Bob was studying taxonomy."

"Right. I've almost forgotten what Bob looks like!" she said dryly. "Well, see ya."

Rosie drove away into the dark.

Max walked up the steps to Norman Court two at a time, going his usual route around the cigarette butts, gum and vomit stains on the floor that hadn't been cleaned in years. He opened his front door and went to turn on his Wii to log in to TreasureNet and shut down his account. He didn't have a computer because he couldn't afford one, so he always browsed the internet on his Nintendo Wii. Sitting in his best, comfy wingback armchair, he flicked the Wiimote, loaded the forum and spotted the top post for the day: *Lunatic Breaks into Nottingham Natural History Museum in Attempted Woolly Mammoth Robbery.*

He frowned, and hovered the cursor over the post. A surge of adrenaline told him he had to see what people were saying about him.

The post led to a *Daily Mail* article. The writer was sparse on details, yet speculated that the break-in was linked to the latest The Crystalline Crucible clue. Thankfully, the TreasureNet commenters didn't know Max's name, though they were full of rumours and insults about his theft skills.

As Max scrolled down, a far-fetched idea came to him.

What if, somehow, The Crystalline Crucible clue could be hidden on the museum website instead of in the building?

He bit his lip in thought. Treasure hunting clues were usually cryptic, often requiring savant-level knowledge of ancient languages and decryption skills. Could it possibly be so simple? He went on the museum website and saw that the home page had a picture of the mammoth skeleton. He clicked on the tusk.

A pop-up appeared: "Congratulations! You've just solved a crystal clue! The next one is loading."

He gasped. At that instant, the Wii browser froze, and he couldn't get it to work again. He fiddled with the remote. It didn't help.

"Oh my God..."

Max stared at the pop-up and the rotating loading symbol. An image of the contest's trophy flashed through his mind. He *had* to see what was behind that link. The only computer he could access was in Stapleford Library. It would be closed now, but luckily he knew where the spare key was thanks to being friends with the management.

"Treasure beckons," he said under his breath, as he got up and dashed straight for glory.

CHAPTER 3

STRANGERS IN THE NIGHT

Less than a mile away from Norman Court, a photographer with a white bag slung over his shoulder strode down Stapleford high street while taking pictures of the River Trent. This might have been a regular situation, except that the bag he was carrying happened to contain several thousand pounds worth of stolen jewellery.

The photographer's name was Khalil Ahmed, and unlike Max, he looked like a relatively normal person in a plain raincoat and tattered jeans, along with a silver bracelet on his wrist. Nervous of being spied on, he put his camera away and tightened his grasp on the bag as his onyx curls fell over his eyes. He hastened his pace through the night.

Breath laboured, he passed by the Stapleford Community Centre, trying his best to avoid the evening crowd. Winter's harsh chill made his skin erupt in gooseflesh.

I just need to get rid of the jewellery, and then I'm out of Aaron's business forever. He glanced at the gunmetal sky. The stars blinked while the wind whistled by his ears. *Nobody will know a thing. Unless he's a copper. Let's hope not.*

Several nights ago, Khalil had found an anonymous man on the dark web who'd agreed to take the jewellery—diamond rings, mostly. He'd been trying to get rid of this bag for weeks. Every minute he still had the jewellery was another that the Black Dog Disciples, the most notorious modern drug gang in England, was surely using to track him down and get it back. The only reason he had it was that he was originally supposed to be holding it for the gang's leader, Aaron, but that was before he'd threatened Khalil's life if he didn't become his new dealer. The anonymous man had agreed to give Khalil a decent sum for the jewellery, yet he mainly just wanted to be free of it as soon as possible.

As he paced along, lusting for the sweet burn of alcohol in his throat, he briefly checked his whisky flask. *Oh, shit. It's all gone. Just what I bloody needed on such a fun evening.*

Soon enough, Khalil found the anonymous man in their agreed meeting place: the alley by the Co-op, which happened to be where he would start work tomorrow. In the dark, he could barely see the man's face, other than his prominent moustache. He seemed to be avoiding the street lamps and wore a fedora that concealed much of his countenance, no doubt for anonymity's sake. He held a black duffel bag.

"You got the jewellery?" the man asked in a rough, working-class voice.

"Nope. This is just imaginary jewellery, mate," Khalil said, squinting at him.

"No need to be like that," he grunted. He reached over, grasped the bag from Khalil and checked the contents. "Looks good. Here's the payment. I trust it's satisfactory. So, where are you from? New around here or something?"

"Illicit deals aren't a great place to make new friends in my experience," Khalil replied, taking the man's money and slipping it into his pocket.

"Come on. Humour me. My name's Gerald, by the way."

He kept quiet.

"Okay, fine. Don't tell me anything personal, then. What do you do for fun? Strip clubs? Brothels? You a drug dealer too?"

"I'm a, er, photographer. So, no, I'm not a drug dealer or a mule. This is just some jewellery I happen to have and needed to get rid of."

"Photos? That's not much fun…unless they're a certain *type* of photo." Gerald cackled. "Well, how about you do me a favour while you're here? I've got this black bag I need someone else to dispose of. The River Trent would be ideal."

"And why the hell would I do that?" Khalil asked snidely.

Gerald shrugged, holding the white bag in one hand and his own in the other. "Because it's a tiny favour, and I'll pay you extra. Besides, it seems to me like you're hiding from something or someone, and I know an awful lot of people who might be *real* interested in that."

Khalil's phone rang, and he withdrew it. The caller ID said it was Fatima, his sister. *Great. How did she get my new number?* He resolved he would have to block her, at least for the short term.

With his phone back in his pocket, he took a breath, thinking the offer through. Maybe there was something to be said for making an ally and getting some extra rent money. Yet at the same time, it sounded somewhat like he was being threatened.

"Um, okay. Fine," Khalil said. "I'll do it." He gingerly took the bag, followed by a few extra fifty-pound notes. "But what's in it?"

"Oh, just daffodils and sunflowers," Gerald quipped, turned and strode away. "G'night, Khalil!"

Khalil jumped as the man uttered his name, but words caught in his throat before he could ask how he knew it.

Weighing the bag, he decided against peeking inside. What if it was something he was better off not knowing about? Instead, he strode away in the direction of the River Trent. Yet as he walked down the road and neared the river, he heard footsteps pursuing him. He was not alone.

Despite his rapid pace, the steps behind him only grew louder. Was it the moustache man? Turning the corner into an ill-lit backstreet, he attempted to throw off his pursuer. The stranger's steps continued to beat on the pavement like a crescendoing snare drum.

Panting, Khalil speed-walked faster and faster, certain somebody was following him. *Click, clack,* the footsteps went, accelerating much like his heart rate.

I gotta bounce. He broke out into a run.

Returning to Stapleford high street, he sprinted past the greengrocers and the butchers. The figure chasing him was right on his tail.

"Watch out, buddy!" a stranger yelped as he leapt over their feet and elbowed them to the side.

Running in the night-time streets was not so much about being fast as it was about not colliding with lampposts. Though Khalil was not in a good position to assess his lead, he could sense his stalker gaining ground. He also knew that he couldn't outrun him for long with the bag weighing him down.

He had to do something, and he had to do it *now.*

Entering a local park, he leapt into a bed of roses and lay down as low as possible. He couldn't tell whether it was the thorny flower stems or his anxiety prickling him. Exhaling so heavily it made his lungs ache, he watched from behind the flowers as his pursuer sprinted ahead, oblivious to his hiding place.

Khalil stayed there for several minutes, letting the sweet scent of the roses soak into his every fibre. He clutched the wet grass and gazed at the inky sky as he waited for silence. From here, it would only be a five-minute walk to the River Trent, and he would be free of this mysterious black bag. *Shouldn't have agreed to this. My stay in Stapleford hasn't exactly started swimmingly.*

When he was more or less certain his chaser was gone, Khalil got to his feet, slung the black bag across his back and bounded off towards the river. Once he was there, he leaned over the railing and chucked the black bag as far as he could manage. He watched it sink into the river like a boulder.

It was gone.

He sighed and wiped his hands on his jeans—beads of sweat dripping down his forehead—when a rustle sounded behind him.

"Excuse me, sir," someone said admonishingly. "You're not supposed to dump rubbish in the river according to the Environmental Protection Act of 1990. I happen to know that as I once memorised all the laws of the country when I was considering starting my own sovereign nation."

Khalil jumped out of his skin and whipped around. There stood an ungainly fellow who wore a Cookie Monster hoodie and had hair as bright as the sun.

"A sovereign nation?" Khalil croaked in confusion.

The peculiar man nodded. "Yes. The Republic of Crosswordia, in which all are united in devotion to the crossword gods. It never came to be because I lost the constitution I had made. And the flag. But I still have the national anthem. I could hum it if you're interested."

Baffled, Khalil stared at the young man. *What is this weirdo talking about?* "Uh, I don't care," he said gruffly. "Mind your own business, mate."

"Fair enough," the fellow said, looking askance. "I can see you would certainly not be welcome in Crosswordia. Valedictions."

He trudged away.

Putting all that had just transpired to the back of his mind, Khalil headed back to his apartment, careful to keep out of sight. Though he seemed to have lost his stalker, as well as that crossword fanatic, he knew he wasn't in the clear just yet. He might be free of the stolen jewellery, but if somebody knew he was here in Nottinghamshire, they weren't just going to go quietly. And if it was the Black Dog Disciples who had found out, then they wouldn't be at all pleased with what he'd just done.

CHAPTER 4

A CLEAN SWEEP

"I need to speak with you in my office right now."

It never bodes well to hear those words first thing upon entering one's workplace, but that was the very sentence that Maxwell Jacobs was presented with as he set foot in the Co-op Monday morning.

Slouching, he followed his manager, Ms Mary Johnson, in what felt like a funeral march. She was a short septuagenarian with wavy grey hair who regularly wore a pashmina. Much like Rosie, she largely lacked the ability to form a smile. Max had been working at the Co-op for years and had not once been fired by her, a near miracle considering how poor he was at his job.

As he trudged into her office, nerves swept over him like a tidal wave. Was this going to be his last day? Had he finally, as it were, cooked his goose?

Ms Johnson's files sat in yellow folders in alphabetical order on her office cabinets. A picture of her son was sensibly positioned in an expensive purple frame on her desk, along with one of the late Mr Johnson, who had originally owned the shop. The point of the meeting became clear as soon as she slapped today's *The Stapleford Herald* on the table. It was right there on the front page, beside an article on a scandal about Lovell Unlimited stealing funds from a cancer fundraiser to manufacture their new vacuum.

"This is you, is it not?" Ms Johnson asked, the lines on her forehead creasing. She tapped her ring finger on the article. "The man who broke into Nottingham Natural History Museum on Saturday works at the local Co-op…and carries a broadsword."

Max picked up *The Stapleford Herald* and paged through it. "Huh. He does have a lot in common with me," he remarked. "Either someone has undertaken a nefarious case of identity theft, or I must have a doppelgänger."

"As you kids say, do you think I was born yesterday?" she snapped, eyebrows arching. She snatched the newspaper out of his hands.

"I guess the jig is up!" Max cried. He'd been trying to forget the events from the past weekend as much as possible, especially the taser part. Yet he couldn't afford to lose this job. "I just hope you don't overreact due to a high cortisol-provoked state of mind. *Semper anticus,* always forward—that's what I say!"

"Sampa Ant and Dec?" she barked. Her eyes flickered with annoyance. "Never mind. I have a question for you. Have you ever wondered why I haven't fired you after all these years? Even after you told a pregnant customer the caloric content of ice cream and that she might want to buy fruit instead? Or when you accidentally tripped over a disabled man and sent him to the hospital? Or when you warn everyone who tries to buy lottery tickets that their odds of winning are infinitesimal?"

He gazed up at the ceiling. "Uh… Not particularly."

Ms Johnson seethed, pacing back and forth as she continued. "I felt *bad* for you. My son told me your mum had passed away in a tragic accident, and everyone around here knows what your dad did, leaving you basically an orphan. Thanks to my son, I knew perfectly well who you were when I got your application. What I didn't know then was that in hiring you I would be employing quite possibly the worst employee in the history of—"

This sentence isn't going to end well.

"—England."

Oh, good! Much better than the world.

Max sighed. It had taken him years to get decent at running the Co-op cash register, and even though he was better at it now, he still gave customers the right change only about half the time. With that said, he felt he wasn't so bad at *everything*. He'd got quite good at washing the bathroom, for instance. Apart from that time he spilled three bottles of bleach and ended up fainting and having to be taken to the emergency room.

"Look, I'm sorry I'm not the best, but I'm trying for a clean sweep, Ms Johnson. Promise. Pinky promise. And I need this job," he asserted earnestly, joining his fingers as if begging her.

"A *clean sweep*? Do you mean a new leaf?"

He nodded. "One or the other."

Ms Johnson sat back at her desk and paused like she was weighing whether he had had enough chastising for the day. "Very well. I'll give you your clean sweep. But you should know that this is your final warning. I can't deal with my employees attracting such negative publicity."

"Thank you so much," Max said gratefully. "You will no doubt go to Heaven for this, in the incredibly unlikely event that such a place exists."

She glared at him, still cross. "But from now on, you won't be working with Poppy anymore. I don't think she's tough enough on you. I've swapped the shifts around, so from now on, you'll be under Khalil Ahmed, a *highly* experienced retail worker despite being a new hire. And I told him to tell me the moment he sees any funny business from you. So, you'd better be a sterling employee from today onwards."

"Khalil? Oh. I think I saw him by the cash register. You don't have to worry." He stood. "From now on, I swear I will be God's gift to cashiers, the ne plus ultra of the grocery store, the da Vinci of bagging and stocking."

"That's a splendid goal, Max," Ms Johnson muttered. "But I'd prefer if you just focus on not getting arrested. And—" Her face contorted, and she leaned over, looking pained and pale.

"Are you having a stroke, miss?"

She shook her head and regained her composure, clutching at her heart. "Cardiac pains. That happens when you get to my age. Forget it. Now off to work!" she ordered. "And no more swords!"

As he changed into his uniform in the bathroom, Max struggled to decide whether he really intended to change his ways as he had promised. A part of him didn't even know if he was telling the truth, both to Rosie and Ms Johnson. It often felt like words emerged out of his mouth with wills of their own. But he didn't have Fleshrender anymore, his sheath now sadly empty, so at least he wouldn't be rending flesh anymore.

The Co-op only had two employees per shift since it was a tiny shop on the corner of Shenfield Way, not far from Max's flat. He stepped behind the counter, set up the second cash register, and looked at the man who must be Khalil with a friendly smile. Perhaps the shape of the smile was a little off though, as Khalil glared at him out of the corner of his eye. To Max, Khalil looked to be in his mid-twenties. He had a long, tangled black thatch of hair and sunken eyes.

But Max's eyes popped out as he realised—Khalil was the same man he'd seen throwing the black bag away the other night! *What are the odds? Infinitesimal! I certainly hope he's nicer than he was then.*

As Khalil served an old man, he glanced over at Max again and his mouth fell open as if he'd finally recognised him.

Max decided to go ahead and introduce himself. Making as much eye contact as possible, he greeted, "Salutations. I'm Maxwell Oscar Jacobs, your new co-worker. Let me say, I do hope our professional relationship becomes one of conviviality and collaboration."

"Huh?" Khalil grunted. "Why are you standing so close? I'm serving a customer."

He stepped away to achieve better bodily proximity. "How ironic. In the past, I've been told that my proximity during social intercourse is insufficient. I may be overcompensating to lower the chance of a faux pas. Either way, good luck with the transaction. Cheerio."

Max waited for a customer. But the store was rather empty, and once Khalil finished giving the old man his change, a painful silence stood between the two men for a few minutes.

Khalil looked over and spoke with a slight accent. "So, Max, is it? The guy with the crossword nation. Have you been working here long, mate?"

Max nodded vigorously. "Surely that depends on how you define *long*."

"Uh, I just meant normal long," Khalil replied, running his fingers through his lion's mane-esque hair.

"Is any time span long in the context of the universe, over thirteen billion years? Or short in terms of an amoeba life of only forty-eight hours?"

"Amoeba?" Khalil rolled his bright blue, almost cyan, eyes. "Not sure. Well, how many days?"

Max beamed, having kept count. "Nine hundred and forty-five. And when I finish building my time machine, I'll be able to tell you down to the nanoseconds."

"Thanks so much."

The door chimed as another customer entered.

At this point, Ms Johnson doddered out of her office and murmured, "I'm off for my doctor's appointment. Have you two got acquainted?"

"We have indeed," Max said proudly. He got to work sponging the laminate floor.

"Yup," Khalil said unconvincingly. "I'd love a go at your time machine when you're done, mate."

"That doesn't sound much like a clean sweep to me," Ms Johnson grumbled, shot daggers at Max and grabbed her purse. "Remember to be on your best behaviour, Maxwell. I don't want to hear that you've been reading *or* juggling again during work hours."

She left.

Despite Ms Johnson's hearty efforts to improve it, Stapleford Co-op had always been a rather grubby shop with spiders lurking where customers could not see and with gum stuck under one counter or another. Ms Johnson usually preferred Max to do some form of cleaning or stocking, activities that lowered the chances of him interacting with customers, which a good percentage of the time resulted in complaints and threats of lawsuits. Yet the lunch rush quickly began, so he was obliged to be at the checkout for much of his shift.

Overall, he felt he did not do *too* bad during the first hours of his clean sweep. He made a couple of errors, such as when he charged a customer for a hundred chocolate bars rather than one and when he sold a bottle of vodka to a boy in school uniform. Though, as Ms Kensington said, you can't win them all!

By the time his break arrived, Max was acutely peckish for his white bread cheese sandwich, salt and pepper crisps and Owl-themed bottle of orange juice. Rosie had once gifted him the bottle as she used to call him a human embodiment of Owl from *Winnie the Pooh*. He retrieved them from his Tony the Tiger rucksack, along with his volume C–E encyclopaedia, and hurried to eat at his usual spot on the bench outside the Co-op.

Sitting on this bench for lunch was part of his well-maintained routine. He had done this for several years, always at one p.m. on the dot. As he tucked into the sandwich, relishing the sensual caress of buttered cheese melting on his tongue, he read over the encyclopaedia article on chlamydia with great interest. But bizarrely, chlamydia was slowly losing his attention: "Chlamydia is a common STD that can cause infection among both men and…" *treasure hunting, treasure hunting, treasure hunting...*

As Max digested the caseous molecules, he struggled to stop thinking about the Egyptian hieroglyphs he had found the other night. He'd discovered them at the library on the museum's secret link. Yes, his little evening trip to the library had been successful, but he remained conflicted about whether he should have done it to begin with. On all The Crystalline Crucible clues one could find a crystal symbol, the value of the crystal increasing as one progressed in the contest. The kind he'd found had a quartz symbol on it, which was almost the lowest type of crystal. So, there must still be an awful lot of clues left to go.

Max glanced through the shop window and realised he could see Khalil.

The man stood stiffly and looked around into thin air. While the shop was temporarily empty, he reached into the register, slipped a load of notes out and deposited them in his pocket.

Mid-bite, Max froze, his fingers loosened and the cheese sandwich escaped his grasp. It tumbled onto the pavement and was promptly enveloped by a mob of hungry ants.

He sat there for five minutes, chomping on his crisps and mulling over what to do. While he wasn't particularly a stickler for rules, even having stolen from the shop himself a couple of times when he was in dire financial straits, he knew Ms Johnson would actually notice anything more than a few missing coins.

An experienced retail worker, eh? Such a good judge of character, Ms Johnson. I'm sure Khalil lied on his CV too. To be fair, so did I, but still.

Max grunted, knowing he had to say something to Khalil. Binning his rubbish, he re-entered the shop and unsteadily ambled behind the counter. But he couldn't think of a good way to bring the stolen money up, so he stood there, staring wordlessly at Khalil.

"Can I help you?" Khalil asked, digging his hands into his pockets as if to make sure the money was not visible. "Or is there something on my face?"

"How do I put this? I just noticed you purloining from the cash register," Max said.

Khalil's eyebrows shot up. "Purloining?"

"Stealing," Max clarified. "Apologies. I do like my synonyms."

"Ah, that," he grumbled, peering down at the counter. "What about it?"

Max gulped. "I should warn you that Ms Johnson is quite careful with the books. If you are convinced it's necessary, I suggest you resign yourself to slipping out the odd coin, or you'll inevitably be caught in no time."

Khalil made a dismissive hand gesture. "I don't need you telling me what to do, mate. Just like the other night with that environmental act talk, it's none of your business."

As his desire to continue this conversation tapered off, Max shrugged. "As your colleague, it is."

With that, Khalil reached into his back pocket and pulled out a Swiss pocketknife. He flicked it open, stepped over and held it to Max's Co-op shirt so that the point was grazing the cotton above his navel. "I don't care, mate. I didn't take that much. Now, let's agree to not bother each other from now on, or Mr Knife here might end up getting wet. And not with butter."

Max looked down at Mr Knife and at Khalil's menacing eyes, resenting the fact that he didn't have Fleshrender to defend himself. But he rallied almost at once and stepped away.

"Well, uh, d-don't think you're going to be, er, using m-my time machine with that attitude," he stammered, backing off. *What a vile scoundrel. I should've guessed.*

He strode over to the *Daily Mail* stack and subsequently scarcely said a word to Khalil for the rest of the day.

Despite his intention to get on Khalil's good side, Max was pierced with the disappointment that by the end of his shift he had not only failed to do so but had failed so badly he had gained a new enemy. Like him, Khalil now worked at the shop five days a week.

How very unfortunate that was.

Free at last, Max left work, not bothering to say valedictions to Khalil, and headed to the local Costa Coffee for quiz practice. Yet even after he'd arrived and had been sipping his apple juice for five minutes and six seconds, he remained the only Agatha Quiztie member to bother to turn up. Daydreaming of duelling with Khalil over a lava bridge, he was on the verge of giving up when Rosie burst through the doors.

"Sorry! A kid ate some glue after maths class, and I had to take him to A&E." She dashed to order herself a Frappuccino before sitting across from Max. "Christ, working in that damn nursery must be more taxing than working in a coal mine sometimes."

"I feel similarly about my life-sucking job," Max commented.

"Let's get started. We need four members in total to compete in the championship." Rosie's cheeks were flushed, and her hazel hair swayed like freshly spun silk below her shoulders. "Well, we can find two more people in the next few months, right?"

"Possibly," Max said, thumbing his chin. "But unlike illegal drugs, competitive quizzing is not exactly undergoing a surge of popularity in Stapleford."

"Sadly true. Could you maybe put some posters up for new members? Doubt anyone will respond though. You can scarcely find quizzers under a microscope in this godforsaken town."

"Not that I particularly care about the championship, but I suppose I could go to the library after this and make some."

"Excellent. That would be...pretty nice of you."

Max noticed with Rosie's cynicism that she could not quite manage to say it would be nice of him. One would be hard-pressed to find her saying something positive.

Rosie dug into her baguette bag and retrieved the question cards. "Time for some questions. Who was the only British Prime Minister to be assassinated?"

"Spencer Perceval," Max answered at once, the crowd thrumming behind them. "Bullet to the chest. Shame the bulletproof vest wasn't invented till 1893."

"Correct." She shuffled to a new card. "What is the only English word that ends in mt?"

"Dreamt. Oh, and also daydreamt."

They carried on for half an hour.

"Boy, you're not bad today," Rosie said as she handed him the cards to test her. "I haven't had much time to practise lately. I've been reading this book on Grigori Perelman, the mathematician who solved the Poincaré Conjecture and won the Millennium Prize. But guess what? The madman turned down its award of one million dollars."

"Lunacy! Perelman could've easily given it to someone deserving. Like me."

"I have to confess that I had the same reaction," she admitted, cracking a reluctant smile. "If I had a million, I could finally pursue my childhood dream: going on a world cruise. But I suppose the government would no doubt take ninety percent of it in taxes. Ah, it's your turn to question me."

It felt like no time had passed since they had started doing this in the Stapleford Senior School quiz team. Rosie had always been a couple of classes ahead of Max, being a few years older than him at twenty-four. They had not really befriended each other properly till he joined Agatha Quiztie three years ago, which had been founded by her while she was at university. Their friendship had been a slow burn.

"Which Greek philosopher held that everything is constantly changing?" he asked, stifling a yawn.

"Um…" she said. Her answers had been getting slower, and now she'd taken to staring off into space. "Let me see..."

"ROSIE! It's Heraclitus, obviously. The guy who said no man steps in the same river twice."

"Sorry! My maladaptive daydreaming is acting up again," she said, embarrassed. She guzzled down the last dregs of her coffee. "Look, I have to run. Brad wants me to attend his football match. I wish you would come to one of them sometime. They're really pretty fun, but it's so boring to go alone."

"I'll be far too busy beginning my shiny new treasure hunt-free life for that."

Before departing, she turned back and added, "I'm sure you'll have time to go to the zoo this weekend? I hear they just opened a new hippopotamus exhibit. I have to book tickets for my class' school trip."

"I don't think so! Hippopotami can be incredibly violent creatures," Max said in a squeaky voice. "Did you know they have sharper teeth than lions and piranhas combined? Or was that lynxes… What if one escapes and attacks me?"

"I'll take that as a yes. I'll pick you up!" Rosie said, and rushed off before he could protest further.

Max groaned and went on his way to the library. It was a short walk from the Costa Coffee, one hundred and nine steps—or three minutes—according to his count. The sky above turned cantaloupe peach as he strolled along the River Trent, listening to the water purl and watching the geese swim along. To him, the River Trent was the only nice thing about Stapleford, a town otherwise rotting in decay. It was rare to find pavement that wasn't broken, a street with walls not strewn with graffiti, and, most of all, a person who actually enjoyed living here.

Entering Stapleford Library, he breathed in the heavenly smell of paper and ink, feeling at home. His mother had used to work here, which was a large factor in why he loved it so much. He'd memorised every secret of the library over the years, including the hidden aeronautics section and the comfiest red chair.

However, all was not well for the library. As he passed the shelves, he found something depressing about seeing this place filled with only a handful of visitors. The library was badly in need of volunteers.

The librarian, Sofia McLintock, fumbled among the shelves while pushing a book trolley. She was an overweight, middle-aged Scottish woman who always had headphones on whether someone was talking to her or not, and only ever wore tracksuits and trainers. She glanced around as she slotted *Lady Chatterley's Lover* into the bookcase and locked eyes with Max.

"How ya doin', pet?" she asked amicably. "Good day at work?"

"Abysmal, to be quite honest," he said. "In fact, abysmal isn't strong enough. Cataclysmic, disastrous, ruinous and terrible seem more accurate."

"Och. Yer kidding. It's not a good one for the library either. Mr Johnson told me this morn' that the Man is takin' away fundin' in a few months." She dropped *Pride and Prejudice* on the floor, and her knees nearly buckled as she picked it up. "Aye. It's not looking jammy!"

David Johnson's shared surname with Max's boss Mary Johnson was no coincidence. Mr Johnson was Ms Johnson's middle-aged son, her moody counterpart, and the one who had indirectly got Max the job at the Co-op.

Left motionless, Max exclaimed, "Oh, bother! How long do we have left?"

"'Bout August fifth. After that, all the bookies will be chucked like Kit Kat wrappers," Sofia informed him as rap music boomed through her headphones. "Pish posh. I cannae believe it!"

"*Thrown* away? My God. It's book genocide. *Fahrenheit 452.*"

His stomach churned as he looked around at all the beautiful bookies. It seemed lately that every time he came to the library, Sofia delivered worse news. Eight months wasn't likely enough time to come up with funds to save this place. He had been planning to do that with The Crystalline Crucible prize money. If the government was taking away funding, *he* would have to provide it. But he'd been informed that thousands of pounds per year were needed to keep the library open, and his lemonade stand fundraiser had just made things worse when he gave that diabetic lady food poisoning.

As he regarded the hundreds of spines peeking out from their shelves, from *Jane Eyre* to the *Textbook of Erectile Dysfunction*, compassion throbbed through him.

Max had read almost all the books; they were like friends to him. However, it was not the books themselves that affected him so emotionally but all the Stapleford orphans who relied on the library for knowledge. They were much like him and would now have absolutely nowhere to turn. *If Mum were still alive, she never would've let this happen. She took care of this place like it was her baby. I miss her.*

Defeated, Max collapsed into a beanbag. "That's terrible." His face crumpled up. "Say, do you happen to know any get-rich-quick schemes?"

"Dinnae worry too much about it, pet," Sofia mumbled, reclined next to him and patted his back. "Yer a thoughtful laddie, but this library ain't nobody's burden but Mr Johnson's."

"I know, but Mr Johnson doesn't seem to care much that it's going under. So, I'd like to help. The newest fundraiser hasn't raised anything much yet?"

"Nowt, really. You're always blethering on about treasure hunting. Could it contribute, pet?"

"I'm not doing that anymore. Rosie, my best friend, made me quit."

"Aye, I see. Maybe you could try marryin' into money," she suggested as he wrung his hands. "My friend Darcy from Edinburgh did that with a mint billionaire, and now she's class rich."

"I don't honestly think anybody would be interested, let alone someone rich. Besides, there is, uh, already someone I like," he said, trying to keep his composure.

"Who?"

He tapped his foot. "My…um, Rosie. But she is already taken by a pillock."

"Forget 'er. Getcha self on OkCupid and find some nice lass who will give ya lots of cabbage just to chew the fat. Lots and lots for nowt."

"I'm not sure," Max said, scratching his arm. "I'm no playboy. I learned the painful way in my teenage years that my romantic charms are not widely appreciated. That is, not with females of the human variety. I'm quite charming to pigeons. Excuse me. Pigettes."

"Hens? Don't be daft. Yer plenty interesting and propa dashing too. You don't need to be nae bloody Byron or Hemingway. I'll make ya a brill profile right now. I know what lasses like in a fella. At least, I met my hubby on OkCupid too, an' now I'm doin' awright, aren't I?"

He hesitated. "I dunno. Isn't this a bit manipulative?"

"Nah, not at all. Mint ol' lasses are always dead lonely, so it's a win-win. Trust me, pet," Sofia assured. "You cannae make an omelette without breaking a few eggs."

Although he didn't anticipate success, Max agreed to let Sofia help him make a dating profile. When she was done, he scrolled down his new OkCupid page yet remained less than optimistic about his chances of getting a date. *Waste of time. Unless someone doesn't care about social skills, money or three nipples…*

A ridiculously cute little boy ran up to them. "Ms Sofia, can you help me find *George's Marvellous Medicine*?" he asked in a high-pitched voice. "I've just finished *Matilda*. It was marvellous!"

"Thanks for that, Sofia," Max mumbled, and arose. "I'll let you work now."

At this point, a stern-faced David—aka Mr Johnson—appeared at his office door bearing a starched shirt and the trademark Johnson family frown. "Sofia, a cup of coffee. Two sugars. No milk."

"Pish posh. Make yer own damn drinks," she hit back hotly, turning around to face him. "I'm a librarian, not a secretary. Plus, this wee yin just asked me fer a bookie."

"I simply request you to do your job. Nothing more, nothing less!" he shouted, irritated. "Are you trying to lose it?" His eyes met Max, and he shot him a hostile scowl. "Oh. It's *you.*"

"Forsooth. How're you, Mr Johnson?" Max asked.

"I'm just splendid, Maxwell. Now, Sofia?"

"Go flip yerself," she rejoined impertinently. "I'm helpin' the lad. Laters, Max."

Sofia took the boy's hand and led him over to the children's section. In response, Mr Johnson swore and slammed his door.

Reminding himself of his reason for being here, Max made for the computers to create the Agatha Quiztie posters. But as he sat and logged in with his recently updated thecrystalhunter username—formerly thedreadnoughtchevalier—and imagoofygoober password, a mischievous idea occurred to him of which Rosie most definitely wouldn't approve.

Maybe I shouldn't have broken into the museum, but now I have got the clue. I would be foolish not to capitalise upon it. He attempted to suppress his recalcitrant thoughts for a fleeting instant, but he couldn't dam the flood. *You know what, Rosie can take her cynicism and shove it. I was born a treasure hunter and I'll die one.*

Max went back onto the museum's website and looked over the clue.

Of course, the hieroglyphs were completely meaningless to him. He entered them in Microsoft Word as best as he could, printed the page out and analysed them carefully. Within a few minutes, he glimpsed hints of a meaning and started to hyperventilate. He took out a book on Egyptian writing from the back of the library and began translating while consulting the ancient alphabet, his clean sweep getting filthier by the minute. Max's attention became so focused on the task at hand that it was like the world had halted entirely.

Before long, something remarkable happened. He cracked the code.

The hieroglyphs weren't random at all. There was a pattern! Astonished, he glanced at the clock. It had somehow reached eight p.m. He turned back to his work, and as he stared at the translation, he could scarcely believe what he was looking at:

Pleats, Cake, Wordsworth, Drowning, Cottage, Hilton, Saucer, Sues, Tiled, Ruined, Belly.

Another code. Max printed the deciphered words and left the library in a daze. At this rate, he was not only going to win The Crystalline Crucible, but was going to become the greatest treasure hunter the world had ever seen!

CHAPTER 5

AN UNWELCOME VISITOR

T*hat Maxwell guy was a complete nutter,* Khalil reflected as he drove home that evening.

Indeed, Max had turned out to be especially annoying after he had found Khalil stealing the cash. He kept telling customers that Khalil was new here and that he didn't know what he was doing. Then, in true cartoon fashion, Max fell flat on the floor he'd just mopped. Meanwhile, customers would say, "Glad someone competent is finally behind the till"; "Mummy, that man looks funny"; and "Put my curiosity to rest. Is that Max fellow all right in the head?"

Ms Johnson had said he was neurodivergent, so that explained things to a degree.

As the traffic light turned green, Khalil's mind moved on to other matters. After work, he had been out taking photographs of Stapleford and liked some of the shots he'd taken. Stapleford wasn't exactly the most photogenic town, but it was said a photographer's role was to look beyond the obvious. Now while he headed home, the talk radio guy wittered on.

"Next up, apparently there is a new 'treasure hunting' competition called The Crystalline Crucible that's gaining popularity," the host explained. "They say you have to solve a series of cryptic clues to win a crystal trophy, the Jewelled Chalice; a fortune beyond your wildest dreams; and the ability to join a secret institution, too. Welp, I'd like a new car this year, but I don't reckon it's worth all that effort!"

Khalil cocked his head. *A fortune beyond your wildest dreams. Boy, how nice that would be. I'd settle for just a regular fortune. Father used to say a fortune abounds within us.*

Gazing inattentively out the windshield, he turned the radio off. Somewhere along the way, he'd developed a pounding migraine, and he longed for the release of a cigarette and a cold can of beer. He hadn't been in Stapleford long and wasn't quite sure if he liked the place yet. Unlike central London, where he could scarcely go out the front door without being surrounded by landmarks and sightseeing spots, there was pretty much zilch to do here. That said, some parts of Stapleford did have somewhat of a quaint, small-town charm.

He wasn't sure if he liked his new job yet either. His first day had been a mixed bag. On one hand, retail work easily bored him to tears, and yet on the other, the boredom of it all was a great relief. Sure, it had felt a tad ridiculous threatening Max with Mr Knife. But he seemed to have got the message, and Khalil had only taken enough money to help pay rent until he got his first pay cheque.

Pulling into the car park of Hamlet House, his new tower block, Khalil got out, locked his car and promptly cursed the fact that the lift was out of order. He hastened up the grotty winding staircase. The building was a huge brown cube jutting out of the weedy grass—a total eyesore. The residents dreamt of leaving; that was his intuition from the pining, depressed faces he frequently saw.

As Khalil unlocked his door with his camera in his other hand, Mr Alfred Brooks jumped out of the next-door flat like he'd been waiting for him. He had a strong suspicion that the old man had been idling there for a while to complain about something new. Last week, Mr Brooks' latest complaint was that "lowbrow hoodlums" were hanging about his apartment. As if it were Khalil's responsibility where the locals went for a smoke break.

Saliva dripping from his chapped lips, Mr Brooks wore a tired-looking red woolly jumper and tea-stained trousers. His eyes always faced each other like magnets. He had the voice of someone for whom everything was a matter of utmost seriousness.

"What the gadzooks is wrong with you?" Mr Brooks exclaimed, banging his walking stick on the floor. "I've been going bonkers all day with the racket you've been making in there!"

"Really?" Khalil grumbled. He tucked his key into his pocket and prodded the door open with his foot. "That's odd because I haven't been here since this morning. I think you're hearing things again. Unless it's ghosts, or Borrowers."

The cheers of children playing football in the common area briefly distracted Mr Brooks.

"What was that?" Mr Brooks asked skittishly, his hand racing to his ear to turn up his hearing aid. "And why are you always carrying that camera out and about?"

Khalil groaned. "I'm a photographer. Is that a crime?"

"Don't talk to me like I'm two sandwiches short of a picnic! You must have left the TV on."

"Or maybe you just forgot to take your meds."

"I heard that, whippersnapper. Why don't you mind your tongue with a Falklands War veteran? I've been a proud Brit since Churchill. When did you get to this country? Last week, I bet." He scowled. "Humph. I've got to get back to this antique teapot sale in *Dickinson's Real Deal*. Keep it down."

He hobbled back into his flat and slammed the door shut, David Dickinson faintly jabbering behind him.

"I was born here," Khalil said to himself as he stepped into his flat. "Isn't that enough for you, old fogey, or do I need to have the Queen's blood too?"

His apartment was sparser than sparse. It had a small bathroom, a square bedroom, a TV-less living room, a dusty kitchen and a narrow hallway. The sole decorations were an *Only Fools and Horses* poster and a broken lava lamp, both of which the previous tenant had left behind.

Switching on the lights, Khalil proceeded to the kitchen to find himself some noodle soup for dinner, basically all he had. But while he opened his cupboards, two thumps sounded from the other side of the kitchen. He turned on his heels, and his eyes fell upon a figure lurking in the shadows beside the door.

His hand shot to his pocket for his Swiss Army knife. "Who the hell are you?" he demanded, raising the knife and whipping out the blade.

As the figure stepped forward, he realised it was not a stranger, after all. It was Aaron Casablancas.

"Put the knife down, Khalil. No need to act like a big man. It's just me," Aaron replied blithely. He had an aquiline nose, an uneven jawline and a balding head. "Boy, you really don't have much to eat. Shocking considering you work at a Co-op now."

"What are you doing here?" Khalil demanded, his heart racing.

"What do you think?"

"Just hanging about in my kitchen for fun?"

"Put down the knife," Aaron instructed, flashed his cleft lip and grinned. He munched on a half-eaten piece of salami. "Swiss Army knives aren't exactly intimidating anyway."

Khalil couldn't believe it. What a disaster.

Less than a month ago, he'd set foot in Stapleford with the hope of never seeing Aaron again, and already, catastrophically, Aaron had managed to track him down. Did this mean he would have to move yet again? Did this mean the second chance he'd fought *so* hard to build for himself was over?

Aaron's cufflinks glinted on his slim-fit suit. He pulled out a carton of milk and drank directly from it. "Now, calm down. I won't be staying for long. I just thought I ought to be here in person to deliver the message rather than send an email or something. I find modern communication so impersonal. You could say thanks, y'know. I mean, I did come all the way from London and managed to get a master key from the apartment complex owner on account of a little bribe."

Khalil groaned, all too familiar with Aaron. He was the head of the Black Dog Disciples and capable of giving someone the nicest compliment in the world before stabbing them in the back. All without breaking the act. Anybody who spent five minutes beside Aaron with his guard down would find the word *psychopath* fitting.

Khalil was certain that Aaron wouldn't have come without a means of self-defence. The reason his hand was hovering around his coat pocket was likely because he was concealing a pistol in it. "Unless you just want some of my last salami, tell me what you want and leave."

"Sorry. I was getting hungry waiting. But as you wish. I'll cut to the chase." Aaron's face hardened. "When you left London with no warning, I guess you thought you could just be free of your responsibilities to us without any due notice. Clearly, you were wrong."

"Was I? Foolish of me to think I could move without a goddamn maniac stalking me."

"Your sudden departure has cost us a lot of money, in no small part due to the jewellery that 'mysteriously disappeared'. We have been forced to accept that you've left our organisation, but I have a reasonable request: return all the jewellery."

"What jewellery?" Khalil snapped. "Maybe someone else took it. Besides, I never *joined* your organisation. I made that perfectly clear."

"Don't play the fool," Aaron said as he returned to the fridge for another slice of salami. "You were in possession of at least twenty thousand pounds worth of stolen diamond rings. I know it was you; I have it on my records."

"Maybe you're confusing me with Charlie Almond. We do have similar names."

"Don't think so. In any case, your absence has completely delayed our plans for territorial expansion. You also have outstanding uni debts, which I never officially let slide. In all, you owe us about fifty thousand pounds."

Fifty thousand? He's lost his mind!

Every muscle in Khalil's arm urged him to punch Aaron right in the jaw, but that certainly wouldn't end well if he had a gun. Maybe he should have left the jewellery in London, yet he'd needed a fresh start and couldn't achieve it with nothing to his name. Before anything, Khalil knew he *had* to get the crook out of his apartment. He could figure out what to do afterwards.

"This isn't fair," he pointed out. "I never wanted to work for you. I only held those rings for you so you'd stop harassing me and my family. I didn't rat to a soul."

"It's perfectly fair," Aaron snarled. "You cost us a lot of money, so you will pay it back and then some or pay the price in other ways. Of course, there's always the option to join the Black Dog Disciples."

"I'd rather jump off a cliff. But fifty thousand pounds? Do you really think I have that much lying around? That's way more than anything I could theoretically owe you."

Aaron beamed, teal pupils enlarging as his Adam's apple bobbed up and down. "Find it."

"And if I don't?"

"If you don't? Let's just say it'll be a pity when your mother doesn't make it through the year. And your sister."

Khalil sucked in a breath. "*What*? You wouldn't dare. I only ever did anything for you to support them in the first place."

"You underestimate me. Now, let's get down to how this is going to work. Thanks to my generosity, you'll be given the chance to pay us back in three simple instalments over the course of the year. I left a note on your bed with more info. How thoughtful of me, right?"

Khalil didn't respond as he evaluated his options. Sadly, he didn't really have any. He couldn't go to the police since he'd end up in prison too, and he couldn't run again, or Aaron would hurt his family.

He *had* to pay.

"You're evil," Khalil remarked. "Money is nothing to me. My dad used to say that a wealth you cannot imagine flows through the true-hearted."

"Evil's a social construct, so I do not mind being labelled as such," Aaron said, snorting. "Understand that, and you'll be much happier." He glanced at the door. "Thanks for the warm greetings. I'll be off now, as you clearly wish. But before I go, remember these words carefully: 'And if thy right hand offends thee, cut it off, and cast it from thee: for it is profitable for thee that one of thy members should perish, and not that thy whole body should be cast into hell'. Oh, and good luck with your photography."

Khalil shuddered. Aaron was notorious for the horrific habit of cutting off the hands of people he didn't get along with. It didn't take a genius to work out what he was hinting at.

As soon as the door slammed shut, Khalil put his knife back in his pocket and fell onto the kitchen chair.

The weird thing was that, despite the threats, he wasn't afraid of Aaron at all. He had spent too much time with the gangster over the years. Yet he knew full well that logically he *should* be terrified.

Khalil's chest tightened as he gazed at the landscape of Stapleford through the kitchen window—the dreary public parks, the lacklustre high street and the bland suburban houses—and deliberated where in the hell he could possibly find fifty thousand pounds.

CHAPTER 6

GREATEST ARCHENEMY

The dawn horizon of Stapleford bloomed with rosy, blazing sunlight. As morning arrived, Max mopped up bacteria on his kitchen floor in preparation for Rosie's arrival when a knock resounded from the door down the hall. His heart fell. Rosie. She was exactly four minutes and eighteen seconds early. How egregiously careless of her. Max wasn't nearly ready.

She called his name through the redwood door. Unnerved, he tripped over the mop, sending an open box of Coco Pops and a glass of chocolate milk flying. A panicked two minutes followed, in which he had to compete against time to clean up the spill with his Crystal vacuum cleaner. *Damn branding. You may be named after crystals, but you aren't the kind I desperately need!*

Max's flat looked plain and tidy at first sight. Although on further inspection, one could easily find certain alarming eccentricities and peculiar abnormalities. The fridge was full of a basic selection of foods that he ate constantly and rarely ventured far from, including cheese, bread, Brussels sprouts and a limited number of toffees. The cupboards were stocked with his favourite cereal: Coco Pops. The only drink he had other than tap water was chocolate milk. As a fishing enthusiast, he possessed a fishing rod which was propped against the fridge, but Rosie often mocked him for this since he had never actually gone fishing.

His careworn childhood stuffed bear, creatively named Benjamin the Bear, was keeping guard on his bedside table beside a beautiful poster of sunny Ithaca. In the living room were his extensive DVD and Blu-ray collections, his most expensive item being a rare box set of every single *Miss Marple* episode. He had a large bookcase, and by far his most read tomes were his treasured *Oxford English Dictionary* and *The Guardian Crossword Collection.* He possessed over fifty books about the Knights Templar, swordsmanship as well as areas of medieval history, such as the Crusades and the Thirty Years' War.

Besides his Game Boy, he had one other game console, his Wii. He only owned two games: *Wii Sports* and *Just Dance.* Eddie Tomlinson had stolen the rest when Max had moved out of the Children's Society. Max had trained himself in swordplay through the fencing minigame in *Wii Sports Resort.* As a self-respecting adult, he would never agree to play *Just Dance,* and when Rosie once asked why he had the high score on the Britney Spears hit "Oops!... I Did It Again", he explained that it must be some kind of unfortunate glitch.

But he also had something clandestine in his apartment that day: library books on secret codes. He'd taken them out a few days prior to work out what the next Crystalline Crucible clue meant. The books were now hidden under his bed by his list of phobias, which included thalassophobia, the fear of deep bodies of water and acrophobia, the fear of heights. Max didn't plan on letting Rosie see the books, as she was not stupid and would quickly deduce he was back at The Crystalline Crucible.

Once the spill was cleaned up, he opened the door.

"What took you so long?" Rosie asked as she strode inside. She wore a red plaid coat, her hair especially dark and glossy today. "And why are you dressed so formally?"

"Do you not like my new accoutrements?" Max questioned. "I am just *so* looking forward to the zoological park."

"You really dressed up for the zoo?"

"I thought the pandas might appreciate it." Max looked down at his well-cut suit; he knew he'd done a terrific job of appearing like a normal person, a Herculean task. "Bought it yesterday with my clothes budget for the decade."

"Pandas being such fashionistas..." She parted her lips and strolled over, fixing his bent collar. "It's better than the Cookie Monster hoodie. I'll give you that."

"As John Hammond said, I spared no expense. You don't look so bad yourself. Are you trying to imitate Princess Di or Kate? Or could it be the famous English fashion icon, Gemma Collins?"

"I was going for Coco Chanel, obviously," Rosie said, rolling her eyes as she caught sight of his bookcase. "Gosh, why do you have all of those classic stories about ghosts?"

"Someone once said there's a ghost in all of us," he mused, hoping to sound deeply impressive. "Besides, any self-respecting adult should peruse the English canon in their spare time in between filing tax returns and drinking aperitifs."

"Fair point."

She swivelled around and gazed at a poster of an impressive knight that hung on the wall.

"And that's Jacques de Molay, the last grandmaster of the Knights Templar. My favourite knight. He was burned at the stake for defending the order. The paragon of a true and chivalrous martyr!"

"Uh… Cool. Well, shall we go?"

Before they left, Max dashed to his bookcase and picked up a book to keep him company during the day out: *How to Win Friends and Influence People*. They exited Norman Court, breathing in the rich, pungent magnolia and maggot-infested rubbish bin scent.

"So, how're the posters going?" Rosie asked as they walked to her car.

"Badly," he replied, having made the posters the day after his clue discovery. "I must have put a hundred up all over the town, yet somehow, I've had zero calls so far."

"So it goes."

Interestingly, Rosie revealed that she was taking him for a "surprise" before the zoo. Yet as he regaled her with anecdotes from his massively successful life—his flourishing retail career and his endless crossword-related achievements—he neglected to look inside Rosie's Volkswagen before entering. If he had, he would've spotted that her car wasn't empty. In the passenger seat sat none other than Bradley Thompson, Max's greatest archenemy.

As he shut the car door, Max's mood soured.

"Y'all right, Grouch?" Brad asked, twisting the volume knob to louden the radio's football commentary.

"It seems I have been set up," Max said and gazed reproachfully towards Rosie. "If I knew *he* was going to be here, I would've outright declined your offer. Perhaps even fled the country."

He tried to open the door, but she'd initiated the child lock.

"At least I don't get in trouble like you do," Brad mocked. "Breaking into the Nottingham Natural History Museum last week? You're mental." He put his hand on Rosie's shoulder. "You all right, baby?"

She glared at the stereo. "I was listening to my Radiohead CD, Brad."

"You know I don't like that stuff. Just let me listen to this for a few minutes. West Ham is owning Manchester." He glanced back at Max. "So, how've you been, Oscar the Grouch? You two still planning on running in that big quiz contest thingamajig this year?"

Max put his seatbelt on before Rosie drove off. He frantically glanced around for getaway options. Perhaps he could crack the glass in the sunroof, but unfortunately, it seemed his best option would be to run for it as soon as they arrived at their destination and Rosie released the child lock.

"Of course. You think Rosie makes me come to practice every week for fun? And by the way, I look nothing like that muppet, you goddamn mothertrucker," he muttered.

"There you go again with that mouth of yours," Brad flared up. "No wonder you have no social life."

Max shot daggers at Brad's pomaded hair and his sports jersey. He was captain of Stapleford Men's Football League, a club largely created to make those who couldn't get into a real team feel less inadequate for not being good enough to compete professionally.

Sun Tzu said it best: if an enemy is annoying you by playing well, consider adopting his strategy.

Max opened his book as Rosie started the car and began to drive away from Norman Court. "I'll have you both know that my social life is going excellently," he said in a boastful tone, reading the preface. "I have a date tonight with Carol. We matched last week on OkCupid and have been chatting since. And that, you might be interested to know, is another reason why I am so dressed up."

"Really?" Brad asked as Rosie drove past the Co-op. "Does she know you've been on the front page of *The Stapleford Herald* for attempted theft?"

Max couldn't believe Brad's patent disbelief and jealousy, although he didn't care to mention to either of them that Carol, his date, was about forty years older than him.

Tiring of the conversation, he turned a page of his self-help book and read on. *Intriguing. So, to get people to like me, I must be genuinely interested in them. This is going to be more difficult than I'd thought.*

As it turned out, Rosie's surprise was that she wanted to take him to Brad's football game before going to the zoo, and she wasn't giving him a choice.

"I did *not* sign up for this," Max replied viciously, ripping off his seatbelt.

"Blimey, Grouch, will you just do something for others for once? Rosie wants you to come," Brad appealed. "Why do you have to make such a big deal out of everything? We're taking you to a football game, and you act like it's the dentist."

"I'll tell you what, Max," she added, subsequent to further failed attempts of persuasion. "If you do come, we can go get Brussels sprouts right after. Your favourite."

Left with no real choice, Max reluctantly agreed. Despite their negative reputation, Brussels sprouts were his favourite food, and he was starving.

Yet the game didn't go any better than he had expected. Indeed, it was much worse.

He sat beside Rosie in the front row. She was so distracted by the game, swooning over Brad's every kick, that they barely said two words to each other. The sound of the handful of cheering fans was far too many decibels for his liking, and all he wanted was to be at home, doing a challenging crossword or making schemes for world domination. He resorted to reading Dale Carnegie's wise words.

By the half-time interval, no goals had been scored, and he began to wonder if football could be used as a torture method. It was perhaps the least entertaining activity ever conceived. He decided to cut his losses and head home. The zoo would have to wait.

"Heavens me, this has been so much fun," Max said, and stood up. "Although I have to admit, I didn't expect the zoo to have quite so many balls."

Rosie folded her arms. "Typical Max. You expect me to help you when you get arrested, but you won't even stay for one of Brad's matches. All I wanted was for you to act like a good friend for *one day*! But you had to be all pretentious like usual."

"Sorry. I'm just not good at being interested in people…who are not me."

"And why is that? Because you are totally self-absorbed and never try anything mildly out of your comfort zone?" she barked. "You know what? You will be doing crosswords alone on your deathbed. You're surely the biggest killjoy, wet blanket on Earth."

As Max sidled away, he wondered once again whether Rosie might have a point. But it truly pained him to see her happy with Brad, and she had looked totally in love with the guy as she watched him play. That was the main reason Max had been so eager to leave.

He actually didn't mind football at all; he even quite enjoyed watching the physics of the ball and thinking about the tactical side of the game. The fact Brad loved it so much, however, made everything about the sport despicable. Likewise, if Brad took a shine to crosswords, he would instantly have to throw away his entire collection.

Stepping out of the stadium, Max experienced the insufferable misfortune of bumping into Brad.

"Hey, Grouch. Leaving early?" Brad clutched his arm and glowered at him. "How about you leave us alone while you're at it, too? I could easily beat you up."

Without thinking, Max struck Brad across the face with *How to Win Friends and Influence People* and shouted, "Stay back, you hellacious reprobate!"

And with that, he ran away as fast as his feet would carry him to the bus stop.

Unbeknownst to him, that awful weekend outing was an apt warning of the terrible week to come.

Soon after Max got back home from the stadium, Carol messaged him asking to delay their date until the next weekend and requesting to borrow his debit card number so that she could afford a chauffeur to Stapleford. She explained that she'd lost access to her million-pound bank accounts and needed his card details to pay a small fee and regain access to them. Apparently, she would reward him with a large payment as soon as this was done.

All the same, he didn't feel quite right about giving her his debit card number until they had met in person, not to mention he was perplexed why her profile showed her location as Nairobi when she had said she lived in Dorset. Her profile pictures had changed as well; now she looked more like nineteen rather than sixty-two.

Perhaps it was karma. He was starting to question whether there was something unethical about attempting to marry a woman for her money, but when he expressed his doubts to Sofia at the library, she assured him that there was absolutely nothing morally wrong with it. Still, he retained his misgivings.

To distract himself from his spiralling dread about his date and the total lack of replies to the posters, Max fell back into his old treasure hunting habits. As much as he tried, he couldn't forget the promise of riches and how the enigmatic crystal organisation would change his life forever. After winning, he could buy a plane ticket to Ithaca, where he had long dreamt of fishing by the ocean. He might not be fond of new places, but he hated

Stapleford more than anything, and he would have to stomach the aeroplane ride.

Every night, he found himself reading the mysterious code words…until at last, he realised their secret. All the words rhymed with famous British/Irish poets!

Thus, Pleats, Cake, Wordsworth, Drowning, Cottage, Hilton, Saucer, Sues, Tiled, Ruined, Belly became Keats, Blake, Wordsworth, Browning, Cottage, Milton, Chaucer, Hughes, Wilde, Ruined, Shelley.

In fact, *almost* all the words rhymed. All except for three: *Wordsworth, Ruined*, and *Cottage*, which happened to be a real poem, Wordsworth's "The Ruined Cottage." That must be the next clue!

The following day, Max headed out at first light and took out a Wordsworth poetry anthology that contained "The Ruined Cottage" from the library.

All the words in the poem became cemented into his nearly photographic memory:

'Twas summer and the sun was mounted high.
Along the south the uplands feebly glared
Through a pale steam, and all the northern downs
In clearer air ascending shewed far off
Their surfaces with shadows dappled o'er

He logged back into the TreasureNet forum with his trusty username, thecrystalhunter, having neglected to delete his account.

Unfortunately, the mammoth clue seemed to have leaked the other day, meaning his prior lead was already effectively useless. He worried it might have come about from when he had stupidly messaged a supposedly ginger girl, whom he knew only as boyzonefan42, on the forum and gave a hint away.

boyzonefan42: hey, have u made any progress on the latest clue, Max? Lol

thecrystalhunter: I may or may not have. Thank you very much for your curiosity, Madame Boyzone Fan.

boyzonefan42: what's that supposed to mean? commme onnn. you can trust me :)

thecrystalhunter: Let's just say woolly mammoths may not be

so extinct after all in Nottingham Natural History Museum. And now if you'd kindly excuse me, I have to get back to finishing my origami dog and renovating my igloo in Club Penguin.

boyzonefan42: kk. u don't have to be so formal, but thanks for the hint. and your knight profile picture looks cool btw. didn't u used to be thedreadnoughtchevalier? rofl

thecrystalhunter: Don't you dare share that hint with anyone, or I will report you to the moderators in short order.

It made Max spiteful to think that others were potentially profiting off his work. Even worse, somehow everyone on the forum had found out that he was the one who'd tried to rob the museum. Throbbinhood420 and wombraider69 were essentially cyberbullying him.

throbbinhood420: What a numbskull! Did you really think The Crystalline Crucible organisers were going to meddle with an ancient artefact just to hide a clue?

wombraider69: yer a nitwit

Max tried to ignore the comments by focusing his energy on the Wordsworth poem. Although he didn't used to read verse, now he did every day. "The Ruined Cottage" was about an old, derelict cottage in the countryside that a vagabond pedlar stayed at over the years. The poem suggests that the pedlar developed affection for a lady named Margaret. She, her husband, Robert, and their infant children lived together in the cottage originally. However, Robert disappeared during wartime, and Margaret was left with a tragic end in that era: to rot away in isolation, destitute, and to one day die of sickness.

The point of the clue must be to find the real ruined cottage that Wordsworth had been talking about, which he might well have stayed at too if *he* was the poem's pedlar.

In the meantime, Max and Khalil had been working together for the past two weeks, and it'd been simply dreadful. This very uneventful morning at the Co-op, Max was busy unpacking the new flavour of sour onion crisp packets from their boxes when something hit his back. He pivoted around and realised that Khalil had just thrown a chocolate egg at his back.

"What was *that* for?" Max asked crossly.

"Nothing," Khalil replied, standing by the till and sorting his freshly stolen cash. "It's just fun to watch you stress, mate. Plus, I can tell that something is on your mind."

It was not false. Max had been in a daze, his mind ensnared by two things: his upcoming date, which had been rescheduled for this evening, and Wordsworth.

"Are the contents of my cranium really of interest to you? By the way, how much have you stolen this week in your quest to piecemeal bankrupt Ms Johnson?"

"I'll repay her eventually. I just *purloined* what I needed," Khalil said, shrugging. "But don't change the subject. You can get whatever it is off your chest if you want, mate."

Max tapped his foot as he knelt down to pick up another packet of sour onion crisps. "Fine. I have a date this evening, and I'm determined for it to be a success. We're going to the Bottle Bureau. I've been practising my social cues in advance as I tend to forget them in high-stress situations. Perhaps you can tell what I think of you from my dilated pupils and flared nostrils."

Khalil pulled a flask out of his pocket and took a sip, fiddling with his bracelet. He had a rather heavyset, bull-necked figure and didn't fit all that well in his Co-op uniform. "I can bet what you're really thinking about: that crystal contest thing."

"You know about it?"

"I heard about it on the radio the other day. The prize sounds good, doesn't it? And is it true that you get to join some mystery organisation, too? Maybe I should have a go."

Max stopped himself from chortling. How did Khalil think he stood a chance at The Crystalline Crucible? Even he didn't believe he was smart enough most days, especially after the disaster of the museum break-in.

"Have a go?" he repeated. "Unless you have William James Sidis on speed dial, I wouldn't bother. It's said to be the most difficult treasure hunt in the world, and besides, you don't know anything about treasure hunting."

"Maybe not, but I heard that you're the lunatic who broke into the Nottingham Natural History Museum while looking for a clue. Ms Johnson told me a couple of days ago." Khalil grinned scornfully. "Good job on getting arrested, mate."

"Thanks so much," Max said, taken aback that Khalil knew about his arrest.

Throughout the rest of the shift, Khalil would not stop badgering Max about The Crystalline Crucible. As he finished stocking the crisps and moved on to gum, a strained quiet lingered between them for a few minutes before Khalil broke it again.

"I have an offer for you," Khalil said, scratching his stubble.

"Not interested," Max said at once.

"Just hear me out."

Trying not to fidget, he turned to Khalil with his right eyebrow raised. "Fine. What?"

"Let's team up in The Crystalline Crucible. We can split the reward fifty-fifty," Khalil proposed as he rubbed his hands together.

Max burst out in laughter, unable to keep it in any longer. "Sorry. I tend to be very literal. You're joking, right?"

Yet Khalil looked disturbingly serious. "I'll stop stealing and all. If you say yeah."

For a split second, Max was convinced this constituted some kind of attempt at comedy. But by the earnest glint in Khalil's eyes, he realised that he must be genuine.

"You must be completely gormless," Max said with a scoff. "I think the idea of being stoned to death by chocolate eggs sounds more appealing than teaming up with you. The mere notion of being around you at work makes me lust to drink Ms Johnson's bleach toot sweet."

"God. Aren't you a pleasure? Well, fuck you too," Khalil snapped as he picked up another chocolate egg and aimed it squarely at Max's head.

It hit the target painfully.

"Ouch!" he yelled, and grimaced. "You just killed a million brain cells. Murderer!"

"Good. You're such a know-it-all. And take this, too."

More eggs and even some ice cream cones rained down on Max. Not one to back down from a confrontation, he decided to retaliate by throwing crisp packets back. Within less than a minute, chocolate bars and soft drink bottles were being hurled everywhere. Several appalled customers looked on in dismay at the unfolding chaos.

"What the Lord in Heaven are you doing?!" Ms Johnson asked out of nowhere. She had just stepped out from her office, and gazed around in horror at the bedlam and the products littering the floor. "A food fight?! Pick these up! Now! To think, I've been running this shop for thirty years, and

I've never seen anything like this."

"Sorry, Ms Johnson," Max and Khalil said in unison.

They raced to pick up the products.

"Goodness gracious me. You boys are going to give me a heart attack!" Ms Johnson sounded faint as she clasped her heart. "Khalil, I hope Max isn't causing you too much trouble. I'm sure he instigated this."

"He's…all right," Khalil said ambiguously as they picked up the last chocolate eggs.

"Let's keep it that way." She returned to her office, highly outraged.

The week of build-up to his big date had caused Max's excitement to dwindle and reduce him into a bag of nerves. Even though he was convinced he looked decent in the suit he'd bought, it seemed that he had been wearing it too much over the past week as there were toothpaste and chocolate milk stains on the legs and sleeves. He couldn't even pull the fly all the way up as it was stuck. However, he realised this too late, so he had no time to take it to the dry cleaners.

"Excuse me. Have you seen a Carol?" Max asked the bartender. He had just shuffled inside the Bottle Bureau, a popular two-bit establishment on Stapleford high street. "She's my date. Yes, *my* date. I just thought I'd emphasise that part to avoid confusion."

"Huh?"

A dubstep song thrummed in the background, making him feel awfully queasy with its lyrics about twerking. Besides the low cost, he'd chosen the Bottle Bureau because he knew it was a "hip" place for young people to go, and he didn't think meeting Carol at his apartment—with all his puzzle and reference books—was a good idea. Besides, he was not opposed to being "groovy" and "radicool" too. He hardly wanted Carol to think he was some stodgy crossword addict.

However, he started to doubt that this had been a good choice for a meeting location when his attention landed on somebody he knew: Eddie Tomlinson.

In the corner of the carousing bar, Eddie stood with a soused expression as he chewed the fat with his rugby friends. He was Max's second-greatest archenemy. Max had once bumped into him around here, but that'd been years ago, and he'd heard that he had since moved to London to pursue a career in rugby.

Max gritted his teeth as he hurried out of the pub and circled around the Bottle Bureau to its back garden. He determined that he would wait there for

Carol and hope they could get dinner elsewhere.

As the background chatter of bar patrons chugging beers droned on and the dim candlelight on cheap tables illuminated the frigid night, he hopelessly stared at the last update he'd received from Carol: a poorly written report that she'd left for Nottingham hours ago.

He was past being sceptical of her story by this point. When he asked where she was again, it took thirty minutes until she replied with the absurd claim:

`Soz. I bin kidnapped otw there. Wanna £5000 ransom. Send moneys to mai paypal.`

After he read this, he finally gave up all hope of ever meeting Carol. If that was even her real name.

With raving mad finger taps, Max messaged back:

`Pray tell, has our entire star-crossed dalliance just been a hoax of your scabrous imagination?`

No answer came. Nevertheless, shortly after this, "Carol's" profile disappeared. He took that to mean that she had deleted her account in utter humiliation. Perhaps it was for the best given Max's history of restraining order threats. His last date had gone so poorly that his lover-to-be ended up excusing herself to go to the bathroom, where she'd climbed out the window to get away from him...and broke her arm in the process.

While he nursed the sherry he'd ordered, he peered up into the endless black firmament and questioned whether he'd ever find true love. The ebony night enveloped him in a shroud of gloom. He imagined the twinkling stars as the Jewelled Chalice crystals, so close yet forever out of his reach.

Chilled through and despondent, he got up to walk home when he sensed someone else facing him.

"Heh. Look who it is."

Eddie Tomlinson was almost as short as he had been at the Children's Society, less than five foot, five inches, but he was no longer the plump boy he once was. Max wouldn't have been surprised to hear that he spent every spare moment at the gym. As Max eyed the new lion tattoo on his neck, Eddie's three rugby buddies were having a smoke and prattling on behind him.

Perhaps Max should have left the bar as soon as he had spotted Eddie, but of course, it was too late now. *What if I get beaten up? I've got nothing to lose. I'll never solve The Crystalline Crucible. Rosie doesn't even like me anymore. I'm like the Crusaders at the Battle of Hattin: doomed.*

"Nice to see you too, Eddie," Max said simply.

"I didn't say that," Eddie grumbled.

"Me neither. It's what they call in my encyclopaedia a phatic expression. I guess this is the point where you make demeaning pejorative comments about me. I'd appreciate it if we could get it over with quickly."

Eddie responded with a snaggle-toothed, hateful grin. "But why should we hurry up the fun? You haven't grown up since we were kids in that crappy children's home, Maxy. You still need a haircut more than ever, and that suit looks like you've pulled it out of a dumpster."

"Funny. So does your face," he shot back.

"Heh, heh. Touché. Someone's got bolshie in recent years, eh? Why're you even here? You do realise this is not the library, right?"

"I didn't know the local pub was your personal territory. For your information, I have just been stood up by my date, so I really don't need you to rub salt in the wound."

Eddie exchanged gleeful smirks with his rugby friends. "Who in England would go out with a freak like you? Oh, wait. I *get* it. You mean a hooker."

"Not quite. We'd never met in person, but I believed heretofore that Carol was a charming sixty-two-year-old lady who was to become my beloved wife," he revealed. "Alack, I now suspect she was a con woman."

Eddie and his friends let out a great outburst of chuckles.

"Didn't know you were into cougars, Max," Eddie ribbed. "What a dirty rascal."

One of Eddie's cronies asked him, "So, what's your beef with this guy? You know him from school?"

"Yup. Don't be fooled by him, boys. His dad, Terrence, is a real dangerous criminal. I reckon Max here inherited his twisted nature. His mother would've aborted him if she knew what he'd become."

Max scowled. He barely heard anyone comment about his deceased mother these days, but she was on his mind every day.

"She would not!" he cried. "That would incite a universe-threatening temporal paradox."

Eventually, Eddie and his friends mumbled that Max was "out of order" and started to bear down on him like gangsters in a film.

"You can't just beat me up!" Max exclaimed, realising what was about to happen. "This isn't school. That's *assault*!"

"No problem," Eddie imparted. "My uncle is head of the local police. He'll believe anything I say. Besides, this is payback for all your father did to those ladies."

"Hold on. Your uncle is a police officer? He's not Constable Tomlinson, is he?"

"Hey, so you've already been acquainted."

At this, Eddie and his wannabe gangsters grabbed Max and dragged him behind the Bottle Bureau's alley, his shoes scraping against smashed bottles on the grimy pavement. With a sense of impending doom, Max's resistance was non-existent.

The first punch came, and a volcano of pain swiftly erupted in his every limb.

His mind randomly returned to Khalil's offer of partnership. It would certainly have been helpful to have him on his side in a situation like this. Maybe, Max considered regretfully, he'd been too quick to decline his Co-op co-worker. But as his vision faded to black, he wasn't convinced that he would *ever* be returning to the Co-op after this.

CHAPTER 7

THE STALKER'S RETURN

"AND IMPERIAL COMMANDER STORMS TO VICTORY!"

On the wall TV, Imperial Commander raced by Black Caviar and galloped over the finish line. Khalil kicked the table leg and cursed to himself. It was just past midday, and he was somewhere he knew he shouldn't be—the local William Hill—doing what he really shouldn't be doing: betting on horses. Regrettably, he'd put fifty pounds on Black Caviar.

To his left, a cluster of potbellied elders cheered and gave him the side-eye while they watched the rest of the results come in.

To his right, a man grinned at a slot machine. "Yes, yes, yes!" he cheered as coins fell out of it like a waterfall.

Khalil groaned. He'd quit gambling years ago. It was Aaron's recent threat that had driven him back into the habit. He sipped the last drop of whisky from his flask and slammed it back down on the counter. *Can I sell an organ? My lungs are ruined, but what about a kidney? Thieving from Ms Johnson these past weeks isn't a permanent solution. She's too doddery to notice, but I still feel bad.*

"Not having any luck, mate?" the guy at the slot machine asked.

He leered over while collecting his winnings into a bag. He was a tight-faced, middle-aged fellow with filthy nails. He also had the most unrealistic wig Khalil had ever seen.

"Not yet," Khalil said with a roll of his eyes.

"I am. I just won over fifty pounds!" the man boasted as plastic-looking blond strands swayed over his shoulders.

"That's nice. Why don't you go tell your mother? I'm sure she'd be really proud."

"I can give you a tip if you're struggling with the horses," the guy crowed before starting back on the machine. "Pick the one that comes first, buddy! Or just sell that old Polaroid camera."

"Can I give you a tip since you're obviously struggling with hair loss? Get a realistic wig!" Khalil hit back.

The man blushed bright pink and turned away.

Inferring his money problems, Max had made a most helpful suggestion for him to get some cash last week: "If you are desperate for money, why don't you stop stealing and become a professional juggler? I'm a juggler extraordinaire, haven't you heard? I would make a career of it, but I'm used to the Co-op at this point and can only do regular balls and not flaming chainsaws, which isn't really good enough professionally."

Khalil glanced down at his silver bracelet, a gift from his mother for his eighteenth birthday. Briefly, he considered hawking it and the colour drained from his face. On it was a picture of young Fatima, Khalil and their parents standing by Captain Seadog, the pirate mascot of an amusement park they'd visited one summer a lifetime ago. It was one of the only mementos he still had of his childhood.

As he admired the photo, he remembered how Mother always used to tell him off for having long hair and forced him to go to the hairdresser. It had been so annoying back then, yet it now seemed so inconsequential. It appeared he'd never learned his lesson because his hair was even longer now—the length of a biblical prophet.

No, Khalil refused to sell the bracelet. Never. He threw away his betting card, grabbed his camera and left for work.

It was somewhere between when Khalil had trooped out of William Hill and when he'd got into his car that he first sensed something was awry.

He wasn't sure if it was paranoia at first; he'd lost track of how many times he had thought someone was spying on him. All he knew was that it was possible that anybody—absolutely anyone around him—could be one of Aaron's men. This meant he had to live in a constant state of caution. Of course, Aaron's spies were unlikely to try anything until the payment deadline arrived. But still, the Black Dog Disciples were known for their harsh intimidation tactics.

In his rear-view mirror, Khalil noticed the faint reflection of a man whose face was hidden beneath a balaclava. He sat in a Mini Cooper and—by the looks of it—was gazing furtively in his direction.

Khalil accelerated out of the parking space, keeping an eye on the Mini behind him to see if it would leave the car park along with him. It did just that. The balaclava man was definitely following him.

Khalil ran his hand through his hair, and then checked for his Swiss Army knife. Could this balaclava man be the same one who'd chased him that night just before he'd run into Max?

Evading a vehicle in pursuit was a novel experience, even keeping in mind his perilous dealings with the London criminal underworld. As Khalil turned the corner by the Stapleford Library, he tried to form a coherent plan.

After he'd driven enough to assume that his pursuer would be getting lax, he made his move. He parked at a local Argos on Stapleford high street, got out and walked down an adjoining crooked, sooty alleyway. Nobody was in sight, and the only sounds were the distant whoosh and honking of passing traffic. He ducked behind a skip and waited for a few seconds, readying his knife.

As soon as the balaclava man appeared, Khalil leapt out from behind his cover and wrapped his left hand around the skinny man's mouth, while his right held the Swiss knife over his neck. As the man struggled senselessly for release, Khalil dragged him behind the skip.

"I know you've been following me. I'm gonna ask you some questions. You'd better answer honestly, and without screaming," Khalil spat into the side of the balaclava. The man's ragged breath was tense against his hand.

Khalil carefully released his hand from the man's mouth.

A meek voice broke out with a frantic cry, "Help! Help!"

"Shut it," Khalil ordered. He covered the man's mouth again and dug the knife into his neck. "Answer me. You think I couldn't kill you if I wanted to? I could do it now and dump your body into the skip. It'd be easy."

"Just let me go, man! Please!" the man cried out, his voice muffled by Khalil's hand. "It was Aaron who sent me, okay? He said to keep tabs on you at all times."

Irate, Khalil shook his head. It was just as he had expected. Why couldn't Aaron just leave him alone? "So, you were the one who was chasing me that night. What were his exact instructions?"

Hardly taking in air, the man croaked, "Just to keep an eye on you and make sure you don't rat to the police or anything like that."

Khalil adjusted his grip on the man's throat. It made no sense whatsoever. Why would Khalil rat to the police when it would get him in trouble, just as it would Aaron? Aaron must be trying to intimidate him.

"Tell me this, have you planted any bugs in my apartment?" he asked.

"No…" the man said, hesitating slightly. "Nothing like that."

"Why did you hesitate?" he said aggressively. He pressed the knife so tightly against the man's neck that he inadvertently drew a slither of blood.

He could easily tell how petrified the man was, if only by the drumming pulse in his neck. Even with the balaclava, the guy seemed rather youthful. Though Khalil reckoned he'd got rather good at intimidating people and acting like a tough guy over the years, he didn't enjoy it. Most likely, this was just one of Aaron's vulnerable, juvenile recruits.

Much like what Aaron had tried to turn him into.

"Not a bug exactly," the young man confessed. "A GPS tracker on your car."

"Oh, great." Khalil rolled his eyes. "So, that's how you guys can tell where I'm going. What's your name?"

"T-tommy," he stuttered, and gasped for breath.

Khalil swallowed, realising abruptly who was really to blame. "All right. Don't worry, I'm not gonna hurt you. How old are you?"

"S-seventeen…"

"And you own a Mini Cooper?"

"Casablancas let me borrow it."

Khalil knitted his brow and put the knife away. *Who sees all beings in his own self and his own self in all beings, loses all fear.* "Aaron really does have no limits. You don't want to get involved with him, mate. Take my advice and get out while you're still young. D'you know where he is now?" he asked.

At that moment, the teenager made a sudden last-ditch effort for freedom, elbowing Khalil's gut and lurching to escape his chokehold. Momentarily taken aback by the pain, Khalil lost his grip. Tommy scrambled to his feet and dashed towards the alley's entryway.

CHAPTER 8

AN UNLIKELY COLLABORATION

When he came to, Max was convinced at first he'd ascended to Heaven. But sadly, he slowly realised that it had only been a vivid dream. Rather than fishing in sunny Ithaca, sipping lemonade and waving to dolphin-riding mermaids, he was in a bed, tangled in sweaty bedsheets. His throat ached as if he had swallowed hot coals. He couldn't recall crawling home after the events of the prior night, though it seemed by the scrapes on his knees that he must have.

Ten minutes later, he gathered the self-awareness to reach into his pocket and look at his rubber watch. As the sting in his groggy head gave a particularly agonising throb, he gasped at the time. It was almost noon, meaning he had been lying in bed all morning and would be late for his afternoon shift. Yet he was sure by the crack of his ankles when he attempted to get to his feet—as well as the blood smeared on his hands as he tried to clean his face—that Ms Johnson wouldn't be particularly happy to see him in the condition he was in. Time to call in sick.

"Salutations, how are you this fine morning?" he asked after he had dialled her.

"Is that you, Maxwell? What the dickens are you calling me for on the store line?" her irritated, scratchy voice said over the phone. "I haven't got long to talk. I'm about to head to bingo and then a cardiologist appointment. Don't be late to work, or I certainly won't be pleased."

"That's the issue. Lamentably, I can't come to the Co-op today. I've got, uh"—he spotted his Ithaca poster—"Ithaca-itis."

"What?" she said blankly. "Never heard of it. What kind of condition is it?"

"Uh… It's a, er…" he muttered, grasping at straws. "An infection of the Ithaca."

"The Ithaca? Is that an organ? Well, whatever it is, you do realise you're on thin ice with me already? I'm not sure about my Ithaca, but my heart has been giving me trouble lately, and it's not helped by your senseless antics. Now, get to work, and no more silly excuses."

"I'm sorry about that, but I just can't come," Max said pleadingly. "Really, I can't."

She grunted. "If you do not even have the get-up-and-go to show up to work, let alone do a good job, then please tell me why I should continue to keep you in my employment?"

"I don't know. But I'm genuinely not feeling well. Honest. I have sick days, don't I? And—"

"In fact, if I'm being *honest*, I have an interview with a lovely young woman next week to whom I am seriously considering giving your position. This may be the last straw before I take the plunge and give her a shot over your atrocious job performance!"

Max sat up. The revelation that Ms Johnson was actively looking for his replacement engulfed him with an unexpected rush of energy. Yes, he might be battered around a bit, maybe even on the verge of death, but there was no good reason why he couldn't still get to work on time and keep a cash register.

"Don't worry, Ms Johnson," he affirmed with determination. "I'll be there faster than you can say Jack Robinson…a hundred times."

Max hung up, clambered onto his feet, laboriously changed into his uniform and braced himself for the arduous journey to the Co-op.

Everybody on Stapleford high street stared at him as he hobbled along. He distracted himself with nursery rhymes, "Jack and Jill" and "Humpty Dumpty", as a group of senior schoolboys with fidget spinners sent offensive jokes and outrageous slurs his way. It was normally a short walk to work, but by the time he arrived at the front steps, he felt like he'd just run a marathon. It took over two minutes longer than his average commute. A catastrophic loss of productivity.

When the automatic front doors opened, he slumped in and dropped onto all fours, half-consciously crawling behind the counter. "Behold, I'm here…" he muttered faintly. "Ms Johnson…salutations and greetings…I've escaped the scythe of the Grim Reaper yet again…"

After lying there for a moment, he opened his eyes to find two socks standing parallel to him. A second later, he looked up and spotted the befuddled face of Khalil, his eyes wavering over him like he was a pariah dog that had just wandered in.

"What happened to you?" Khalil asked, looking uneasy.

"Various events and circumstances," Max replied. Every inch of his body seared with pain, and he realised he was soaked in icy sweat. "It seems my exocrine system is malfunctioning. How troubling."

"You look like you've just been mauled by hyenas. Should I call someone?"

"No," he said as he tried to get up. But he tripped and knocked over the sour onion crisp stand. "I just need a drink. D'you happen to have any chocolate milk? That's a panacea for all maladies."

Yet as he proceeded to the cash register while Khalil gazed at him with an open mouth, the weight vanished from his feet. He fell forward and tumbled to the floor.

In a delirium, Max was not entirely sure what happened during the next few minutes. After a while, his head cleared and he discerned where he was.

Two things were immediately apparent: his wounds had been bandaged, and thanks to the audio-visual stimuli around him, he deduced he'd been transported to the backroom of the Co-op. Khalil stood in the doorway, a Co-op first aid kit in his hands and an oddly solicitous look in his eye.

"Am I dead, Hippocrates?" Max asked, pulling himself up with the radiator.

"Unfortunately not," Khalil said gruffly. He folded his arms. "Do you have any idea how shit you look?"

"The thugs didn't consult me as to when to stop pummelling. Sure would've been nice of them."

"Yeah, yeah. Don't be so sarcastic. I was half-minded to call an ambulance, mate. But seeing as I don't exactly need any police attention, and I have some medical experience myself, I decided to see what I could do."

"Much obliged. I'm right as rain now," Max said, but he stumbled as he made his first step, tumbling with arms akimbo onto a stack of boxes. "Oops-a-daisy."

"More like wrong as rain. You have a black eye, a crap ton of bruises and about ten different scrapes and cuts. And you're lucky nothing worse. What happened?"

"Oh, no! What is the prognosis, Dr Ahmed?" he asked as he tottered over to the water dispenser and drank from a plastic cup. "Well, I got beat up, if it's not self-evident. But I'm not going to the police or the hospital, so that's that."

"For your information, I went to med school for three years before dropping out, so maybe I'm not as foolish as you seem to think," Khalil revealed. "You really ought to be thanking me for helping you at all, mate."

Max stared perplexedly at Khalil, but he found it difficult to keep his attention focused and to stop himself from keeling over. "Either way, I just remembered," he said out of the blue. "Last night, in the midst of being beaten to death, I reconsidered your offer."

"What offer?"

Max gulped. "The Crystalline Crucible. You wanted to team up."

Khalil gaped. "You said you'd rather be stoned to death!"

"I reconsidered. In light of recent events, I am open to making a deal," he said, wondering if what he was saying was a result of brain damage.

"Now is not the time," Khalil snapped. He kneaded his fingers. "You gotta rest, mate. I don't think you have any serious injuries, but still, you're not in good shape."

"Time is a game played beautifully by children," Max said, stifling a yawn. "That's what Heraclitus always said. I'll be fine."

But within seconds, it became clear that Khalil was quite right. It was rather difficult for Max to stock shelves when he could hardly walk, and customers hurrying out of the store when they saw his face wasn't good for business. Maybe he would have been more inclined to soldier through if Khalil, in the subsequent moments, had not provided verbal evidence of the medical expertise he claimed to wield.

In an authoritative voice, Khalil advised Max that it would be wise to keep an ice pack on his sprained ankle and to rest in bed as much as possible. He also said he would dissimulate to Ms Johnson that Max was, indeed, too sick to work.

As Max traipsed apace home, hardly able to keep himself upright, he was struck by Khalil's change in character. He found himself swamped with an uncomfortable guilt that he had been so doubtful of him and wondered if Khalil was a decent guy at heart. Yet it was hard to trust anyone in Stapleford these days, and to be fair, Khalil had been best friends with Mr Knife not long ago.

After successfully floundering his way up the Norman Court staircase, entering his apartment and shoving a pack of custard creams and a bottle of Calpol down his mouth, Max passed out on his bed.

He awoke late that evening to the sound of his *SpongeBob* ringtone.

"What's going on, Max?" Rosie asked through the loudspeaker. "I just got a call from Ms Johnson. She told me your colleague said that you were too sick to work and that you had to take the week off."

Fantastic. A week will be plenty of time to recover from this Slough of Despond. Max knew he'd been foolish to make Rosie his emergency contact. Ms Johnson rang her up constantly to tattle on him. "Veritably," he stated, not particularly keen to inform Rosie about his date disaster. "I'm so glad she has informed you about the current state of my medical situation."

"So, it's really true. Are you, um, okay?"

"Yes, splendid. It's just that I've contracted an incredibly rare and likely deadly disease. Personally, I would recommend steering clear of me for the next two, three, maybe four weeks, or you would inevitably suffer a painful and slow death."

"Wow. Really? Maybe you caught it at the football game," she replied in a concerned voice. "I'm sorry for giving you such a hard time there. It's just that you and Brad fighting irks me. Do you want me to drop by to bring you some groceries while you recover?"

"What?" Brad yelled in the background. "Max says he's sick? But he's obviously lying! Don't talk to that jerk at all. He assaulted me with *How to Win Friends and Influence People.*"

"It'd be far too reckless. Any contact with me would result in a agonising, excruciating demise," Max said, ignoring Brad's shouts. "You could get the illness and pass it onto Bradley too. I would just hate for him to painfully and slowly die."

"Hmm, I bet," she said. "So, there's nothing I can do?"

"Just pray to sweet baby Jesus and all the other false prophets for my swift return to health. I'm afraid I will obviously have to miss quiz practice this week, though. How exceedingly tragic."

After Max hung up, relief soaked through him. He was off the hook, for now at least, although he remained ashamed of his continued lies. *With every lie, the human soul dies a little bit. I read that somewhere. If so, I'm practically a vampire at this point.*

Sure enough, the next few days were largely a period of slow and painful recovery for Max.

In accordance with Khalil's expert medical advice, he stayed in bed all the time. He used the upturn in his free time to count the number of strands of hair on his head, 95,341; to recount how many frosted flakes came in the average box—the figure was going down by several flakes each year—what despicable shrinkflation; and to record every single thought that came in his head—which was surprisingly difficult. But he mostly occupied himself with the incredibly dangerous, action-packed, life-threatening art of treasure hunting, in particular disassembling his Crystal vacuum to look for real crystals. There weren't any.

Legally speaking, he was not in the clear at all. As much as he tried to ignore it, his upcoming court hearing was a constant source of dread-filled nightmares, in which he dreamt of a hard-faced judge sentencing him to the electric chair or death by some form of shark-lion hybrid.

By the time Friday arrived, Max was getting claustrophobic, maybe even suffering cabin fever. So later that day, he sneaked out to the library. Khalil had actually agreed to pick him up from there after work to discuss their treasure hunting partnership. By this point, they had exchanged phone numbers and had a call the previous night about the best way to proceed. He still wasn't anywhere near trusting Khalil though, not even a tad.

The instant Max stepped inside the library, Sofia's eyes met his and she burst out in a little scream. While he knew he still had a bit of a black eye, he'd rather hoped that nobody would be able to tell the extent of his injuries. Walking to and fro places still wasn't exactly easy, but he was getting back to normal.

"Max, you dinnae look bonny!" Sofia exclaimed. Her overhanging belly jiggled under her pink tracksuit as she ran over to him with the book trolley. She pulled her headphones off, which indicated some real concern.

"Incorrect. I'm right as rain," Max muttered. He blushed slightly, remembering his excuse. "Fell down the stairs, you see."

"Oh, I gotcha. Ouch." She nodded incredulously. "So, did yer date go well?"

Max's stomach turned at the memory. "Negative. It didn't work out."

She bit her lip while Snoop Dogg continued to boom through her headphones. "Pish posh. Sorry, pet. Remember, there are plenty of fish in the sea."

"I'm aware. About three trillion." He gazed at the shelves. "How're the books?"

"Laddie, 'ave you nae heard?" she asked as she adjusted her thin bottoms.

Alarmed, he shook his head. "What?"

"I'm gonna bubble! We're shuttin' down even sooner than I'd anticipated, pet. Ach, I'll have to start destroyin' the bookies in no time. I'll lose my job an' all! The library simply cannae go on." She gazed down with grief in her eyes. "You see, some feckin' eejits from the government want to turn the library into some sort of immigration office!"

It was as if Eddie had just impaled him with a pike. Max had thought that he would have *some* time to come up with the funds to save the library. But now…

Crestfallen, he asked Sofia for more details about what had happened. While he listened, hopelessness grew inside him like a black hole. Imminent closure was now inevitable as the library just wasn't popular enough to justify more government funding.

"I see… What a nightmare," Max said, feeling chastened by endless failures, nonstop misfortunes and the general unfortunate nature of the human condition.

It seemed as if everything in his world had turned askew.

While Sofia went to fetch a Snickers bar, he shuffled over to take a gander at all the books. From Samuel Beckett to Herman Melville to Elisabeth Beresford, Max's favourite, the library had everything one could possibly want. As he passed scruffy orphans in tattered clothes reading picture books on the beanbags, empathy for them surged through Max. A deluge of memories of the many years he used to come here with his mum to blow off steam after preschool hit him. It was going to be like saying goodbye to a second home.

Seeing all the books' depressed, moribund spines and visualising them decaying in graves like corpses, he knew he had to do something.

Even if it brought some awful news, Max's trip to the library resulted in a brand-new clue. On one of the back shelves, he found an ancient book called *A Traveller's Companion to Georgian England.* This book was published around the time Wordsworth would have been alive. All the pages were musty and yellowed, and the text was printed in an old-fashioned, sometimes unreadable typeface.

As he leafed through the old book, he made an ingenious connection between the guidebook and the poem. A feverish rush of excitement stirred in his gut.

By the time Khalil's second-hand Hyundai rolled up to the library curb,

Max had deliberated for over an hour about his book loans: *The Fine Art of Small Talk*, *Advanced Origami*, and, most importantly, *The Biography of William Wordsworth*. As he jumped into the car and closed the door, the scent of nicotine and whisky clung in the air while the news on the radio hummed softly.

"Recovered yet, mate?" Khalil, who was still dressed in his Co-op uniform, asked as he looked him over. "You look a bit better. I've been working with Poppy instead."

"I'm just agathokakological," Max said, before he recalled that most other humans don't memorise dictionaries. "That means good and bad. So, how far is it to your place?"

Khalil crinkled his nose. "We're not going to my place. That's off-limits. Just because we're teaming up on this, uh, whatever, contest doesn't mean we're mates, does it?"

"Whatever contest? Holy moly. You don't even know what it's called."

"Crystal. Anyway, why were you at the library? You can just get eBooks, can't you?"

"EBooks?! I'm not a Segway-riding, iPhone-using degenerate slave to ephemeral technological trends," Max snarled. "My mum used to work at Stapleford Library, and I've been going for years."

"All right, all right. You don't need to yell at me for a simple question."

Max huffed. "It just shouldn't be of interest to you. I am oh so keen to avoid the enemies-to-friends trope that's so common in films yet so foreign in real life. Let's just stick with enemies-to-enemies, okay?"

Khalil's eyebrow levered. "Of course. I don't know why I'm even acting like I care, to be frank."

"I'm certainly glad that we have established that our working relationship will continue to be purely professional."

"I agree, but I wouldn't even call it a working relationship. A working acquaintanceship."

"Let's make it absolutely clear now then: we will make team decisions unanimously and keep our private lives to ourselves. Personally, I can't think of anything less appealing than being your mate. Maybe drinking strychnine." Max let out a small chortle. "But not by much. Our only mutual interest is the prize."

"Fine with me. Let's get down to business, shall we?" Khalil proposed. "You suggested that you have some idea about the next clue. I wanna hear it."

And so, Max told him all about the idea he'd just got, which he was honestly buzzing to get off his chest. In *A Traveller's Companion to Georgian England*, he'd found a map to an old inn called the Olde Crown Hotel, which was described as being surrounded by ruined cottages.

A treasure map of sorts!

Thus, it seemed quite likely to Max that Wordsworth could've passed by one of these cottages, as the poet did stay in Bath multiple times in his life. In that case, it could well be that The Crystalline Crucible clue makers had hidden the next clue inside one of the ruined cottages near the Olde Crown Hotel.

"That sounds like a wild goose chase," Khalil replied.

Max made an outraged face. "I thought it through. You will go to Bath and keep me updated through Morse code. An epic adventure the likes of which England has never seen before beckons!"

Khalil's eyes drifted downwards. "What do you mean keep you updated?"

"I can't go. I've not left Nottinghamshire for years!"

"You want me to go *alone*? For Chrissake, it's not like your last hunch went amazingly. And I thought you wanted to get out of this damn town anyhow!"

"Unless you know any other treasure hunting experts to team up with?"

Khalil scratched his arm and gazed out the window. "Honestly, I was half-joking about teaming up. And I don't want to trek all the way to Bath for nothing."

"Very well," Max said, trying to sound as uncaring as possible. "I'm not going to sit here and persuade you. If you say no, I can easily find someone else to go for me. I'll call Lara Croft when I get home."

Khalil hemmed and hawed. Max was not truly expecting his colleague to agree. Yet somehow following more questions, his lips jerked as if on the edge of saying yes.

"Fine, fine. I'm in," he said. "But only if you come too."

Max gathered his courage. He seriously disliked new places, but he didn't want to mess up this free ride. "I'm already dreading working with you when MI6 hires us. I hope I get all the good secret agent missions!"

They worked out the logistics of the trip. Max and Khalil would leave tomorrow, Saturday morning, for Bath, and get rooms at the same Olde Crown Hotel—which, remarkably, was still in operation—even though it had apparently been completely rebuilt. The journey there would be about a three-hour drive.

Feeling that something may come of his years of treasure hunting escapades at last, Max was in an unexpectedly good mood as Khalil agreed to drive him home. His mind whirled with all the book and sock packing he would have to do tonight. But his good mood was interrupted when he noticed something abhorrent during a traffic light stop: a man bumbling along the road with excessive pomade and horribly done tattoos.

Unfortunately, Brad frequented this part of Stapleford for his job at the Lemon Dragon Tattoo Parlour. Every instance Max ran into Brad motivated him to never leave his flat again.

Yet before he could crouch, Brad spotted him. Almost in slow motion, Brad's eyes fixed on him and enlarged.

Max swallowed a considerable amount of saliva. "Go, go, go!" he bawled, reaching over with his foot to try to force Khalil's shoe down on the acceleration.

"What the hell!" Khalil shouted, blinking at Max as if he'd lost his mind. "We can't. The light's red."

"Just go!"

Brad stomped toward Khalil's car with a menacing grin on his face.

Max managed to get Khalil to drive through the red light with the predictable effect of getting beeped at by all the surrounding cars. They zoomed back to Norman Court. Heart thumping, Max gazed in the rear-view mirror and discerned that Brad was in pursuit of the car. He'd never seen such a malicious countenance as the one on his face.

Max had to get home before Brad caught him. Bradley was no doubt determined to prove to Rosie how not sick he really was and ruin their relationship—an evil scheme of sorts. Eyes wide, Khalil looked nonplussed as Max appealed for him to drive as fast as possible. There would be time to explain later.

As soon as they arrived at the gates of Norman Court, Max slammed the car door shut and raced up the steps to his apartment, crying, "Cheerio!"

He swore to himself that he wouldn't let Brad and his evil scheme win. *Everything* was on the line.

CHAPTER 9

THE EVIL SCHEME

Rosie Shaw couldn't say exactly when her boyfriend had taken such a dislike to her best friend, but it was becoming increasingly clear that his hatred towards him had reached unhealthy levels.

She sat next to Brad in his BMW, scribbling in her notebook and glancing up occasionally as he ranted on and on. The veins in his forehead bulged further out like tree roots. Rosie knew first-hand that Max wasn't the easiest person to get along with, but it wasn't like he was fundamentally a *bad* person.

"I tell you that Max of yours is the devil incarnate," Brad said, baring his buck teeth. "How did you two *ever* get along? He's *nothing* like me. He's a complete, well, I don't even know what."

"A nerd? God, why do you act like he's your competition all the time?" She drew a beaver and a raccoon in her notepad as he steered around the corner of Brentwood Avenue. "This isn't a soap opera. Max is like Owl. At first, he seems horrible, but when you get to know him, you realise he's a total sweetheart."

"I don't!"

When she'd first met Max in Stapleford Senior School, they hadn't been immediate friends at all. Indeed, she had first thought he was a pretentious ass and maybe even slightly insane. A few years had passed since then, and now Max was probably her best friend. Because of her long relationship with him, she could sympathise more than anyone that her friend was flawed. Still, she had no idea why Brad was hamming it up like Max was the Antichrist of England.

"Cor blimey, I've never met someone quite so intelligent and idiotic at the same time as Maxwell," Brad fulminated. "His total lack of social skills and his obsession with the Knights Templar and fishing and crosswords and Disney films and treasure hunting and cheese sandwiches and encyclopaedias and Tetris, and whatever else. It's all so, so odd. You'll see when we get to his apartment just how much he lies, too."

"I'm a maths teacher. You think I don't know what's odd?" Rosie joked, and exhaled. "Look, I know you and him haven't got off on the right foot, but you don't have to be so vindictive about him. He's not neurotypical, you know. And I have been friends with him much longer than I've known you."

"Whatever. If you want to talk about something else so badly, tell me, what are you doing?" he asked, pointing down at her notes.

"Working on Theodore Tabby," she said, finishing her sketch of Billy Beaver. She gestured to the backseat, where unopened bill notices sat. "A distraction. My landlady is driving me up the wall about rent. Sorry if it's morbid, but if she got hit by a bus I would feel major *schadenfreude*."

"Uh, yeah. What was that you said? Timmy Toby?" Brad asked.

They pulled up to Norman Court's car park.

"Theodore Tabby. The cat detective of the children's book I've been writing for years."

"You've been writing a children's book?"

"Of course. I've told you about it a hundred times," she retorted, showing him her sketches of Gabby the Goose, Leo the Lion and, of course, Theodore Tabby. "The story is set on the idyllic Lemondrop Island and follows the adventures of the tabby cat detective, Theodore, and his roguish Great Dane assistant, Count Ferdinand, to find the thief of Mrs Mole's candy corn, Billy Beaver." She goggled at his blank face. "You don't remember? The love interest is Jenny Jaguar. Still not ringing any bells?"

Brad scratched his armpit as he reversed the car into a spot, almost squashing a child he hadn't spotted against the wall. "Uh, I think you mentioned it. That's really nice." He patted her leg. "Sorry. I've just been distracted lately. We're doing trials at the club, trying to get new members for the summer."

"You don't care since it's not football or Max, the only two subjects you seem to give a damn about," she grunted. She got out, feeling deeply patronised. "I'm sure there's an explanation for this Max thing, and I don't think surprising him at his apartment is the mature response."

"Mature, shmature!" Brad thundered, and ripped the car keys out from the ignition.

Rosie adjusted her bead necklace. She imagined herself growing wings and flying away like a dove. *Brad might as well be deaf most days. Right now, I wish he was mute too.*

As they both paced up Norman Court's magnolia and maggot-scented drive, she wondered when Brad and Max's relationship had started to go so downhill. The last thing she had expected when she'd met Brad and introduced him to her quizzing teammate was that they would turn into archenemies.

She reached into her handbag and sprayed herself with a puff of her favourite strawberry perfume, steeling herself for the embarrassing scene that was undoubtedly about to unfold.

"So, what're we doing? Barging in with the spare key?" she asked as Brad practically dragged her up the apartment stairs by her hand. "I think we ought to knock. Max might be indisposed."

"Nope. Absolutely not. He'd be able to get in bed and act sick!" Brad ran up the staircase ahead of her. "If you don't want to get involved, just give me the spare key and I'll deal with it. I can always say I needed a piss."

"Fine," Rosie muttered sourly. "I'll do it, but you are *way* too worked up about this."

As soon as the door was a millimetre ajar, Brad stepped forward and knocked it wide open as if he were a police officer conducting a drug bust. She had to suppress the image of him getting caught in a violent booby trap like in *Home Alone*, just like the ones Max used to set up for the teachers in school.

"Maxwell! Maxwell! Where are you, you twat?!" Brad screamed as he stomped by Max's Ithaca poster, his DVD collection and his Wii. He marched through each room, calling Max's name so loudly that someone passing in the corridor looked nervously in, surely thinking they were burglars.

Yet it quickly became clear that Max wasn't there.

Brad turned to Rosie with a grin. "See! I said he wouldn't be here. Now, are you going to start believing me? I *told* you he's lying. Just like he does about everything else. He's been doing that treasure hunting shit this whole time, I bet."

She stared at him, at a loss for words. Nothing seemed harsh enough. Nevertheless, something was strange about Max's absence if he truly was suffering from such an infectious disease. Had she been foolish to trust him again after he had broken his promises so many times before?

"Don't jump to conclusions," she said, and pulled out her mobile. "I'll give him a ring. He rarely answers though—prefers that I text him in binary or semaphore."

As Max's phone rang, she watched Brad stamp around some more and check behind the bookcase as if Max was hiding a secret hidden passage.

"What does he need all these encyclopaedias for?! And these books about William Wordsworth?!" he yapped, reaching under Max's bed. A grin hitched onto his face. "Aha! Books about secret codes! How are you gonna get away with this one, Grouch?"

Finally, the ringing ceased, and a voice that did not belong to Max answered.

"Good day," a stranger's voice greeted.

"Er, hello?" Rosie said, her stomach twisting.

"Is this Ms Shaw?" The man's voice was distinctly mature, whereas Max's was much more youthful and flatter.

Who could it be? A frog rose in Rosie's throat as Brad's face came around the corner.

"Um, yeah. May I ask what you are doing with my friend's phone?" she asked.

"This is Dr Khalil Ahmed from Stapleford Hospital. Maxwell gave me his phone and asked me to take his calls. I'm afraid he has been admitted to the hospital for an acute and deadly case of the swine flu."

"What?!" she exclaimed. "I heard about that on the news. Is he okay?"

"What's going on?" Brad demanded, yet she just ignored him.

"It's been going around," Dr Ahmed said gravely. "Unfortunately, Max is not in a suitable condition to speak now. I don't want to worry you, though. He is set to make a full recovery, but he isn't allowed visitors at the moment as he is in quarantine. It is a rather serious situation."

Doctor Ahmed went on to tell her all about Max's condition. It was certainly alarming to hear. Brad became curious about what was going on. By the time Rosie said goodbye, he was trying to listen in by jamming his ear right up to the phone.

"It was the hospital. Max's been admitted. In other words, he wasn't lying, after all," she explained after she'd put her mobile away. "And before you try to convince me I was talking to some actor or whatever, don't bother! I've had it up to here with you today."

"But, Rosie, I swear it can't be true," Brad cried exasperatedly, hands in the air. "I saw him as healthy as can be the other day besides a few bruises! Maybe that twit hired a voice actor or something. And I found all these books about secret codes under his bed. Isn't that a bit fishy?"

"*You're* the twit. You need to get a life and stop obsessing about Max."

As she glared at his tattoos, in particular the dragon and trident that looked more like a stabbed dead cat, she found herself agreeing with Max: they were about as good as a child's scribbles.

And then, before Rosie could stop herself, Brad turned into Billy Beaver. His buck teeth sprang out even further from his mouth, his feet turned webbed and he grew a thick layer of shaggy fur.

"Come on, Rosie. Don't be so gullible," Brad Beaver said, grotesque teeth jutting out. "You're better than that."

She stared at him, and rubbed phosphenes from her eyes. *Gosh, I have to get my maladaptive daydreaming under control. It's getting ridiculous. But no more ridiculous than Bradley.*

"Why are you looking at me like that?" he asked, his coat of reddish-brown fur bristling as he stepped forward.

"No reason," she said sharply. "I think I'm going to walk home alone. Nice to see you haven't got the balls to admit you were wrong. And even if he is lying, you're acting worse right now. This whole thing is just a complete joke."

As Rosie turned, Brad's buck teeth gritted and his tail swished. He chomped angrily on a log that had just materialised.

"I can't believe Max has fooled you! I bet he's laughing his head off right now!" Brad shouted. He punched the wall with his beaver paw. "Well, I won't let him get away with this!"

CHAPTER 10

THE MYSTERIOUS TREASURE HUNTRESS

About halfway across the country, Max and Khalil were on the motorway, already well on their way to Bath. Max wore a *Blue Peter* shirt under a wrinkly green parka and Wombles socks, while Khalil was garbed in a grey cap, a black linen shirt and trainers. They'd set off early that morning to get a head start on their thrilling treasure hunting exploits and adventures.

Max had just been regaling Khalil with the commandments of chivalry, namely, "Thou shalt be everywhere and always the champion of the right and the good against injustice and evil", as well as the funny story of how he gave his therapist a nervous breakdown. Then he'd told him all about his favourite episode from *The Twilight Zone*, and why he identified with William Shatner's character in the episode "Nightmare at 20,000 Feet" when he's besieged by a gremlin on an aeroplane. That was all before showing him his score on his *Tetris* app—the top of the whole country.

But right now, they were both in hysterics.

"We shouldn't be so mirthful," Max warned, trying to control himself as he watched cars speed along the motorway. On his lap lay today's copy of *The Guardian,* which was heavily crumpled by now. The quick crossword that he'd solved twice was splayed open. "We might have fooled Rosie, but Brad will still be suspicious."

"Come on," Khalil said, and sniggered. He handed Max back his phone. "That was fun."

"Remember Luke Skywalker: 'your overconfidence is your weakness'.

We don't want to end up like Sheev Palpatine. Our priority is making sure we don't get spotted. We can't let throbbinhood420 win!"

Khalil rolled his eyes and flicked his wrist dismissively, his bracelet jingling. "I guess you're right. But I don't think you have to worry about being spotted. It's a big country, mate. When was the last time you even went out of Nottinghamshire?"

"It's hard to say. A school trip to Essex a few years ago, I guess. I was attacked by vicious, man-eating swans and swore never to leave again unless absolutely necessary," Max muttered, and stroked his chin. "For me, Nottinghamshire is all I've ever known, for better or for worse."

"Shit. You know what my mother says? Birds born in a cage think flying is an illness."

Max cringed. "That may be applicable if only I were a bird, but I've always related more to moles."

"I don't understand why you never applied to university. As soon as I finished school, my father gave me three options: study engineering, study medicine or join the army. If I didn't do any of those, heck, he probably would've disowned me," Khalil revealed. "My parents escaped the war in Afghanistan, so I felt a big responsibility to be a success, especially after they fought so hard to get settled in the UK as refugees. They had to stow away on a boat to get here. Well, too bad I was never interested in university. I chose medicine, mostly because being a doctor sounded cool."

"I couldn't find any university that taught treasure hunting," Max said offhandedly, and fiddled with the door lock as he gazed out the window for rest stops. "As for me, my mum died when I was young, so my teenage years weren't that fun. Helpfully, I became skilled at acting like I was sick during those years. In any case, I think we'd better get something to eat, no? I am truly the antonym of sated."

"You mean hungry? Me too. Looks like there's a place here."

Max was not sure of the last time he'd visited a motorway service station, if ever. His first impressions were not one bit positive. The overwhelming scent of petrol clogged his nostrils, and the blaring thrum of all the shipping lorries racing by made him dizzy and nauseous. A baby crying in a stroller nearby sounded like it had a megaphone, and a schizophrenic man, who seemed convinced he was Jesus Christ, felt centimetres near, despite standing metres from him. Everything was just far too loud and overbearing. Slumping his shoulders, he decided he definitely did *not* like this country.

But this has to be done, he told himself as he walked alongside Khalil inside the rest stop. *Or I'll never get out of Stapleford—for good.*

They both ordered lunch at a McDonald's. Max was very aware that he had left Benjamin and all his things in his new "partner's" car. An anxious twitch spasmed across his face at the thought of what would happen if Khalil decided to ditch him at the rest stop and find the clue himself. Getting a taxi home would bankrupt him, and Brad would surely be champing at the bit to get his hands on him if he called Rosie for help.

While Khalil and Max waited for their food at the counter in silence, Khalil's phone rang. He refused to answer it, but the caller wouldn't stop redialling. Khalil adjusted his weight.

"Aren't you gonna get that?" Max asked, studying Khalil. "It could be a Nigerian prince about to offer you a fortune."

"Suppose I should," Khalil said as he cast a sidelong glance at Max. He pulled out his phone and strolled away.

At the same time, a peculiar sense of paranoia gripped Max. After that heartbreaking incident with Carol, gone were the days where he would blindly trust strangers. As it was, he barely knew a thing about Khalil. *What if he isn't who he claims? He might even be a Russian spy with that peculiar black bag I saw him throw away. Dear God, Kal-El? Superman!*

The food arrived on a tray seconds later and derailed his suspicious train of thought.

After he picked up the tray, he proceeded to the seating area through a spot where a teenager was mopping. This turned out to be a mistake. Somewhere along the way, his feet lost their connection with the ground.

Within moments, Max was prone on the floor, coated in fries and soda. Laughing at him on all sides were about thirty small children, who had arrived that very instant while on a school trip. As he scrambled to his feet, they would not stop staring and guffawing at him. *Ugh. Friction strikes again. One day, I will defeat you.*

Leaving the ruined food behind, he hurried to the toilets to wash himself. But try as he might, his *Blue Peter* T-shirt remained filthy. As he attempted to get the stain off his crotch, a voice spoke nearby. Khalil. He must have gone into the toilet stall to take his call.

Max wasn't the type of person to eavesdrop, besides perhaps on Brad, but it was one of those situations where he couldn't help it. Khalil was talking loudly and, by the sound of it, heatedly too.

"Mother, for the hundredth time, I'm not coming back to London," Khalil declaimed. "You need to accept my decision. Now, I have no idea how you or Fatima found this number, but I want you to delete it as soon as I hang up."

Max's heart pumped. Why didn't Khalil want to talk to his mother? And where was he not coming back to? Was he on the lam? Was he in a debacle? What about on a lam that was also in the debacle?

As Khalil stopped talking and flushed the loo, Max hastily slid into another stall and locked the door. Khalil let out a frustrated groan, stepped outside and washed his hands before he left the bathroom.

"Where's the food?" he asked, glancing at Max as he returned. "Oh."

"Yeah. I'm going to skip the burger and just buy a sandwich. Please tender my apologies to the cleaner," Max said, while all the children resumed laughing.

After both of them had eaten lunch, they set off again. Max was ready to bet that Khalil was some kind of serial killer at this point, so he sat trembling in the back seat and occupied himself with a crossword while plotting his escape. As he read and reread the crossword clue, he couldn't help but think that he should be extremely careful. He rested his sweaty fingers on the car door handle while his skin tingled.

The guilt of deception was starting to get to Max, too. It wasn't long ago that he had sworn to Rosie that he would give up The Crystalline Crucible for good. *Deceiving and lying to my best friend… All based on what? A hunch? It's like that story, "The Tell-Tale Heart"; I'm worse than Judas!*

"Are you stuck on a clue?" Khalil asked, giving Max a shock. "Maybe I could help. I used to assist my mother with crosswords. Well, I tried to. I barely ever actually contributed to be honest."

"Oh, your mother, you say? Uh, sure. It goes: 'any state or process known through the senses rather than by intuition or reasoning'," he said, tapping his foot violently.

"Let's see… What about *phenomenon*?" Khalil suggested, and pressed hard on the gas.

Max traced his pen over the crossword boxes as his pupils dilated. Ten letters. It fit.

"Wow." He gaped. "I should've thought of that."

Khalil grinned back at him in the mirror. "I'm not just a pretty face, mate. I have a brain."

"Really? I haven't got a brain...only straw," he said, and reflected on the unpleasantness of his current phenomena. He would vastly prefer to be playing his kazoo and rewatching *The Wizard of Oz*, one of his favourite films. "What about this? 'A frivolous, flighty or excessively talkative person'. Fifteen letters. I know the answer, but you'll *never* get it."

"Flibbertigibbet? My favourite word."

"Correct, again! Wait. You have a favourite word too?"

"Evidently. What's your favourite one?"

"Collywobbles," Max said without hesitation, and in fact, he had the collywobbles presently.

Hours later, as Khalil parked at the Olde Crown Hotel Max stared at the tree-lined, mossy façade of a building that he recognised from the website. The hotel was not far from the city centre of Bath but suitably separated so that there was a lot of sparse countryside available for dog walkers and hikers. He wondered if Wordsworth had ever come by the area as his scheme necessitated. Max had gone through so much of the former poet laureate's works in the past few weeks that he had dreamt that he was wandering through a ruined cottage himself last night. He even spotted a lonely, crying woman, just like Margaret.

"Right," Max said, straightening his chafing back. "Let's check into our rooms, and then we'll start the search for the cottage. What name is my reservation under?"

"Your reservation?" Khalil remarked. "What do you mean?"

He grimaced. It felt as if he had just been kicked in his genitals by spiked cleats. "Didn't you book us rooms?"

"No. I booked *myself* a room. Why would I book one for you? You're an adult."

"I thought the plan was for you to book the rooms for both of us," he replied, as he got out his phone and scrolled up through the short history of his texts with Khalil. "It says here: 'I'll book room'."

"Yeah. I said it pretty plainly there, didn't I? Book a room. Not *rooms*."

"No. That's not plain at all. You forgot to say *my* or *a*. Don't you understand the indefinite article?"

"But I didn't say *rooms*. Don't you get what plural is?"

"That's no excuse. Let's say it was a quarter my fault, three-quarters yours."

Max had never booked anything in his life besides doctor's appointments for odd lumps on his private parts, so he'd just assumed that Khalil was taking care of it.

"Nope, I'd say four-quarters yours," Khalil said. "A hundred percent."

"Look, they'll probably have a spare room," Max said sotto voce.

"I wouldn't count on it," he pooh-poohed.

"Well, we're certainly not *sharing* a room."

"I didn't offer."

The receptionist at the front desk proved deeply unhelpful. But Max believed the man when he said that the hotel was full because the adjacent bar was so teeming that the waitress was visibly perspiring, racing from table to table.

"Why can't I sleep in the boiler room?" Max asked worryingly.

"That wouldn't be possible," the receptionist answered. "Sadly it would break health and safety regulations."

Though the Olde Crown Hotel had been completely rebuilt since the time Wordsworth had lived here, it still had the air of an ancient building. The wall plaster was cracked, and the floors—varnished cedarwood—gave off an antiquated, mouldy scent. As Max gazed at the wall painting, an impressionist watercolour of West England's heathland, he felt as if he were Dorothy on the yellow brick road.

"It's fine. I'll sleep in your car, then," Max said dejectedly, after Khalil had collected his room key. "Or the pavement. Maybe it will be an interesting experience."

Khalil snorted. "Interesting?"

"Diogenes liked it. He was an ancient Greek philosopher who lived on the streets with the dogs and said it was the best life. And Heraclitus said the soul is dyed the colour of its thoughts. Reading the encyclopaedia isn't such a waste of time, huh?"

Khalil squinted at him. "Okay…?"

He sighed. "Since I've no room, I may as well start looking for the ruined cottage right away. No point shilly-shallying and dilly-dallying. Time doesn't grow on trees."

"Don't you want to get a drink first?"

"*Tempus fugit,*" Max said zealously, and looked down at his cheap watch.

"What? Understanding what you're saying is a chore. Anyways, I'm going to have a beer."

He looked down at his tapping foot and forced it to stop. "Get chocolate milk for me for later. Ta-ta," Max said, turned and plodded out of the door.

Minutes later, he realised he had left his wallet in Khalil's car, and to make matters worse, his phone was out of power too. He felt more foolish than ever as he stood in the centre of a heath, surrounded by nothing but a million mole holes. Which would have been very helpful—if he only happened to be a mole! He was stranded in the middle of nowhere with no maps, no money and no way to contact anyone, shivering as the evening's darkness descended over the rolling hills of rural Bath and brought the biting cold with it.

As he surveyed the environment, he couldn't see one single ruined cottage! Why was treasure hunting so hard? Discouraged, he picked up a twig and furiously practised lunge, parry and riposte, imagining himself in an epic duel with Brad over the fair maiden, Rosie.

Afterwards, Max aimlessly waded through the mud, gradually getting fed up with being a bipedal organism. Shifting one foot in front of the other was such a chore. Quadrupedalism would be superior by far.

Wishing he'd brought a better parka, Max scowled as he meandered back down to the hotel, soaked in dirt. The only option now was to locate Khalil and pray to God he wasn't a serial killer after all, but he couldn't help but suspect Khalil was a mass-murdering Hannibal Lecter copycat.

As he re-entered the Olde Crown Hotel, he glanced at the grandfather clock and saw it was nine p.m. The yawn he'd been stifling forced itself out. He was starving, the sandwich from earlier barely having sated him. The hotel's atmosphere had a soporific quality, the lazy murmur of Bath's high society dinner conversazione filling the air. He reasoned it was time that Khalil would be getting a bite to eat, and as he stepped into the dining area, his suspicions were confirmed.

But Khalil was not dining alone. Quite the contrary. He was with a woman. She was a petite lady with red hair, diamond earrings and olive-green eyes.

"Ah, there you are, mate," Khalil said over a cinnamon-scented candle. "You look like a right mess. Did you have any luck?"

Famished, Max was glad to see they had not yet started their mains. He slumped next to Khalil at the four-chair table, feeling a piercing sting in all his joints. He doubted he would've felt much worse if he had just fallen off the top of Mount Everest and landed on a bed of spikes.

The Olde Crown Hotel's restaurant exuded fanciness, with embroidered folded napkins on all the tables and suit-wearing couples who leered over at him and his soiled garments.

Max helped himself to a chunky chip and dipped it headfirst into the pot of ketchup. "I had luck, not the good kind though. So, who's she?"

"Do you want to introduce yourself? She's also into treasure hunting, supposedly," Khalil said, glanced over at the woman and took a sip from his beer. "I'm surprised so many people care. I thought it was too niche."

"Why not? I'm Amelia Henderson," the woman introduced herself. She looked somewhere in between Max's and Khalil's ages, her mid-twenties. "I work in taxes, and I came to Bath for the weekend to see if I could figure out the clue. Nice to meet you. Hehehe."

Max covered his ears; her laugh was so shrill that it hurt his head. "It may or may *not* be nice to meet you. I couldn't say yet, thanks to the linear nature of the spacetime continuum. I must ask why my associate is fraternising with competitors."

"Wait a minute. You're like six years younger than me, and you're calling the shots?" Khalil jibed, smirking.

The waiter came by to deliver some complimentary breadsticks. Max ended up ordering from the children's menu. Chicken and chips were the only things that looked remotely edible to him among the long list of ratatouille, bruschetta and so on, whatever those were. It was often quite difficult going to restaurants as he had a limited palette or, as Rosie put it, was a pickier eater than a toddler.

"So," Max said somewhat bitterly, "what were you twenty-first century Homo sapiens vocalising phonemes and morphemes about?"

"Khalil was just telling me about you actually," Amelia said. She took a sip from her glass of chardonnay.

"Oh, was he? Do tell. I'm sure it was some highly rib-tickling anecdote from our historied partnership of one week."

"I was telling her about our lead," Khalil revealed.

"You've been telling her our team secrets?" Max asked, tapping his foot under the tablecloth.

"Secrets are hard to keep," he said.

Amelia giggled nervously, and ran her hand through her auburn hair.

Khalil frowned. "I think you must have trust issues, Maxwell. Besides, stop acting like you're goddamn Indiana Jones."

"Actually, they used to call me Indiana Jacobs," Max informed him. "Or I did at least."

"Who cares? Will you stop attacking Amelia? You're making her uncomfortable."

Amelia shrugged. She treated herself to a breadstick. "It's totally fine. You're entitled to be suspicious. But I can promise you that I have no intention to steal anything. Except these breadsticks, perhaps! Hehehe."

Max dropped the subject, and the topic changed to their dinner guest's line of work. Apparently, she did taxes for celebrities, such as Stacey Solomon and Holly Willoughby.

"So, Khalil, do you like Nottingham?" she asked, resting her chin on her hand.

"I've never been, although I know ibuprofen was discovered there."

"Meh. It's okay," he judged. "I miss London. I actually grew up there."

"I miss London too, and I *still* live there."

"Don't be so generous, Khalil," Max cut in. "I think we can both agree that Stapleford is a town-disguised trash heap, eviscerated of anything slightly okay. And not to digress, but Khalil, why did you leave London?"

"That's kind of a personal question," Khalil said, brow furrowing.

"It just seems strange if you like it so much."

"Maybe I'm strange."

"I'd say so," Max said bluntly. "Personally, I would sell my lungs and brain to live somewhere without staples in the name. Maybe even my *Miss Marple* box set."

"Who's Miss Marple?"

He gasped and jumped to his feet, flabbergasted. "WHO'S MISS MARPLE?!" Max had never been so embarrassed on someone else's behalf. "Only the best character on TV. The elderly sleuth from the genius mind of Agatha Christie with the brains of Sherlock and the wit of Poirot, combined in one white-haired, handbag-clutching package?! The role the ravishing Geraldine McEwan was born to play?"

"Uh, right," Khalil commented. "Personally, I think it's bizarre that a twenty-one-year-old man watches a show for old people and has a teddy bear, but who am I to judge?"

Max froze. "How the *hell* do you know about Benjamin?"

He had been careful to ensure that Khalil didn't find out about his teddy bear, tucking him deep into his rucksack and covering him whenever he reached inside to get something. The only explanation was that Khalil had been digging through his things. It struck Max—Khalil would've had the opportunity to do this when he had been trudging over the Bath fields, developing calluses on his feet that were no doubt thickening right now.

But at that moment, the waiter interrupted them again to bring everyone their food.

"Forget it, Max. So, Amelia, what do you do in your spare time?" Khalil asked, tucking into his roast duck.

"I adore going on the TreasureNet forum and chatting with the treasure hunting community," she said excitedly. "Other than that, I *love* music. They're a bit nineties now, but I'm still *such* a big fan of Boyzone."

"Maybe you've heard of me," Max said, cutting his chicken nuggets into animal shapes. "I don't post much anymore on TreasureNet, but my username these days is thecrystalhunter."

She choked. "That's you?! The famous Dreadnought Chevalier, eh? I've been reading your treasure hunting posts for years. Did you ever find the Holy Grail? You sure have some really interesting theories."

"Would I lie?" he said, and rolled his shoulders back proudly. "What's your name then?"

"Boyzonefan42," she said, savouring her crab.

He gasped. It couldn't be her. The user who had *stolen* his lead.

"Oh my God. We messaged online, didn't we?!" Max exclaimed.

"That's me!" Amelia enthused, her diamond earrings glimmering above the candlelight. "How wild. We already know each other. What happened to your face by the way?"

"Oh, that? Fell down the stairs," he said shortly.

"It happens! Hehehe." Her laugh was as squawky as a crying parrot. "I'm as clumsy as Miss Marple in season three, episode four when she had to carry the melons to church in high heels!"

"You watch *Miss Marple*, too?" Max asked, eyes enlarging.

Could she be my soulmate? But my soulmate wouldn't have such an annoying laugh, would she?

The conversation went on, and it seemed Max and Amelia had more in common than he'd first assumed. She was almost as omniscient about treasure hunting as he was, and as he got to know the mysterious treasure huntress, he wasn't as opposed to her as he had been.

By the end of the evening, Max had that lovely, drowsy feeling that he associated with finishing an especially tricky book of crosswords, consuming several gallons of chocolate milk and playing Pokémon for ten hours. Khalil had even ordered him a beer, which contributed to his light-headed, tipsy state.

However, the issue of where his bed would be tonight still remained.

After about an hour more of Khalil and Amelia's banter, Max decided it was high time for him to hit the hay before he ripped his ears out. "I'm going to sleep now," he said, interrupting them. He turned to Khalil. "Can I have your keys then?"

"You really want to sleep in my car?" Khalil asked. "It'll be freezing!"

"I'm a polar bear in the cold," Max said with a monotonous undertone. "The Children's Society had no heating for several winters. Besides, I am rather a sinner for lying to Rosie and getting you to lie also. I deserve punishment."

"A sinner? Your friend's not God, is she?" Amelia chimed in. "Hehehe."

"To the Mayans, sinning means following one's own lower nature. So, in a sense I've been sinning by misleading her. I told her I wouldn't continue with the contest, and yet here I am."

"Good thing you're not a Mayan," Khalil said, getting to his feet. He looked toward Amelia. "Can you excuse me for a moment, Amelia? I'll just let Max into my car."

"Toodle-oo, Max!" she said kindly.

Max waved bye to her. "Ditto, Ophelia."

"Er, it's Amelia. Hehehe."

"Oh. Sorry, Cornelia."

They left.

As Max trudged to the car beside Khalil, he realised he had let himself momentarily forget about The Crystalline Crucible situation. It wasn't looking good.

"So, what's the plan for tomorrow?" Khalil asked optimistically. "We can look for the ruined cottage at first light."

"It's simply woebegone," Max admitted as he opened the car door. "I looked for hours today. Couldn't find a thing except bugs. The only treasure we'll ever find is the sweet release of death."

Khalil shrugged. "I'm gonna have a look with or without you."

"Why bother?" he asked morosely, and slipped into the passenger seat.

Khalil sat next to him. "Why so negative?" he remarked, words slurring.

Max didn't know what to say. It was usually him telling Rosie not to be so negative. He rubbed his hands for warmth and got out the novel he'd brought, Henry James' *The Turn of The Screw*, from his rucksack. He might be used to the cold, but it was freezing and Stygian black in here, only a faint light coming from the radio screen.

"Trying with no chance of success is failing in denial," Max said, opening his book.

"Failing in denial is *better* than just failing," Khalil counselled bracingly. "Let's just have a search and do our best. I mean, what's the harm?"

"Why are you nice now? Bring back the old Khalil!"

"Man, I need the prize money. That's the only reason I'm doing this. But I just think, you know, we can be quasi-mates as well. It's not exclusive."

Max stared at his lap. Had he been too cynical about the enemies-to-friends trope? "I'm not sure I can be mates with a serial killer. Or a con man. I know about Frank Abagnale."

"Max, I'm not going to tell you all about my past. If you don't feel comfortable with that, we can easily disband our partnership, or whatever this is. I just need you to trust me about one thing: I'm not a serial killer, and I'm not a con man either."

"Exactly what a serial killer and a con man would say."

"Pot, meet kettle. I have to get back to Amelia," Khalil muttered. "How about this: we wake up early to hunt for the cottage tomorrow morning, and if we find nothing, cut our losses and head back?"

A brief pause swept between them.

"Ms Kensington used to say 'damned if you do and damned if you don't'," Max reasoned. "Or was that Bart Simpson? I have to say, taking arms against a sea of troubles is mighty exhausting."

"Good. I'll leave the keys in the car, so you can use the heating. If I were a con man, I wouldn't be foolish enough to trust you with my car, would I? We'll meet up first thing tomorrow in the lobby."

"Excellacious and wondertastic," Max said, fighting off his drooping eyelids.

"Why did you get that book out?" Khalil asked, and reached for the handle. "Is it a ghost story? Wouldn't be reading that in the dark. You'll have a heart attack."

"I can handle it," he replied. He gestured to the starry night. "This is perfect."

"To each his own," Khalil said, and opened the door. "By the way, I only knew about your teddy because you left him on the backseat. Let me guess, you're the type who keeps a spare key under the doormat?"

Max sighed. "No. Okay, yes."

With Khalil gone, Max collected Benjamin and prepared for snuggling. Yet before he could read his book, he needed to charge his phone if possible. He opened the glove box to look for a portable charger, and his fingers stumbled across two curious things.

The first was just an anthology of the Persian poet, Rumi. The second was more concerning: an electronic device. He examined it and found a label: TruTrak GPS Tracker.

He stared at the GPS tracker in alarm, turning it back and forth in his fingers. At that instant, Max's phone vibrated with a text:

`You might've fooled Rosie, but not me. I know exactly where you are, and come hell or high water, I'm gonna prove you don't have ruddy swine flu.`

CHAPTER 11

MORTAL THREATS

The first thing Khalil saw when he woke up the next morning was a text message with a low-definition image of a severed hand. He threw himself out of bed, put on a polo shirt and jeans, grabbed his camera and strode out to the Olde Crown Hotel gardens. Once he had found a quiet spot by a patch of greenery, he sat on a rotting mahogany bench beside a primrose flowerbed and dialled the number.

Aaron picked up instantaneously. "Hello! How's things, Khalil?" he asked in a jolly voice.

Khalil's forehead burned like an ablaze fire. "Just great," he replied gruffly. "What do you *want*? And can we skip the protracted speech you've no doubt prepared?"

"I want what I've always wanted: my money. But it seems to me that you're not going to deliver it, especially since, for reasons unknown, you're in Bath."

Blood rushed to Khalil's cheeks. He had disabled the GPS tracker, and yet somehow, Aaron still knew his location. Who was to say somebody wasn't following him right now? He peered around cautiously.

"I'm in Bath to get you your damn money, Aaron," he said through gritted teeth. "It didn't just randomly occur to me that I'd love to waltz over here and take a spring holiday. How does that relate to somebody's hand?"

"That somebody's hand is someone you've had dealings with yourself," Aaron remarked. He let out a silvery laugh. "Don't worry. Just that teenage birdbrain I asked to watch you in Nottingham, Tommy. Good job cornering him in that alley and scaring the living daylights out of him. He's still alive. I just took his hand as punishment. He's messed up a lot else, too. I even caught him stealing from me."

Relief and horror soaked through Khalil's mind. Mother and Fatima were fine. As cruel as it was for Aaron to take that poor kid's hand, he preferred that to one of them.

"That wasn't necessary," Khalil snapped. Splinters stuck into his hand as he tightly gripped the bench. "Well, you don't have to worry. I'm working on the money."

"I'm glad to hear it. But I'm afraid, due to your suspicious actions, I've decided to move the first payment date up to March third."

He couldn't believe his ears. "But that's in no time!"

"I think you can cope. Now, remember this: we'll meet at the Costa Coffee on Frederick Street, just you and me, and you'll bring the cash in a bag. It better be exactly the amount we agreed. Not a penny less. After the delivery, I'll get back to you when I've counted it all to let you know whether you've been a good or a bad boy."

"No way. I need more time."

"Fine. I'll give you the original time if you need it so badly. However, for my kindness, I'll round the total money up to one hundred thousand pounds. How's that sound?"

"For God's sake!" Khalil bit his lip as a granny, who walked through the park with a cute little poodle, idly glared at him. He lowered his voice. "That's ludicrous. I've never had that much dough in all my life. Do you think I have a butler and a chauffeur or something?"

"You'll manage. And parenthetically, who is that funny fellow who you've been spending so much time with?" Aaron asked with a snicker. "He wore some kind of Cookie Monster garment first and a Tweenies shirt on another occasion."

Khalil exhaled, wishing Max would buy some clothes that weren't decades old. "Don't you worry about that guy. He has nothing to do with this."

If Aaron knew about Max, that was very, very bad.

"He's below your usual calibre of girlfriends is all," Aaron continued. "I mean, not exactly a stunning replacement for Noora. I wouldn't be surprised if he's next to lose a hand. Or Fatima. I've been building a nice collection of fingers, haven't I? May even start a museum."

"I said I'll get the money, even if it's the rawest deal ever, so stop harassing me. Tell the drug barons I sent hugs and kisses."

As the conversation ended, Khalil recalled a Bible verse. It is mine to avenge; I will repay. In due time their foot will slip; their day of disaster is near and their doom rushes upon them.

He hadn't considered it before, but was he being selfish to involve Max in his dangerous life? Whatever the case, he resolved he would focus on The Crystalline Crucible for the rest of his time in Bath and worry about the money later.

While he breathed in the fresh air, and the early morning chill eased off slightly, he took out his flask and drained the last few drops of whisky. He gazed at the colourful bed of fragrant tulips beside him. Their sweet scent turned his mind back to his childhood, and he decided to take a picture of them on the spur of the moment.

It seemed so long ago that his mother had planted tulips around the garden of his childhood home in London. He used to play cards with Father and Fatima under the fig tree there, the sun bright and heavy on his youthful face.

His parents used to tell him about the days in Afghanistan when the idea of war was a distant possibility. Yet the war had broken out suddenly, and within months they had to emigrate to Russia, the only place that would accept Afghan visas. Then came the treacherous process of travelling to the UK with Fatima in a shipping container before claiming refugee status. Of course, Khalil was a mere foetus during that time, but he'd heard about it in great detail.

When Khalil's parents had arrived in England, they had barely had a penny to their name. It'd been in his sixth form years that Aaron had started recruiting Khalil for minor jobs, on the verge of being illegal. In med school, when his family had struggled to pay the bills, Aaron hadn't hesitated to offer to take care of Khalil's fees under the condition that he work solely for him. Khalil had almost always said no, but Aaron wouldn't stop harassing him.

The worst thing was that—no matter how much he tried to cling to his humanity—Khalil feared he was becoming more like Aaron. *Didn't Max say the soul is dyed the colour of its thoughts? If so, mine is desperately in need of a good wash.*

He shook his head as if all his thoughts would come falling out, pulled out and examined the Polaroid of the tulips. Khalil had always believed photography was the best art form. Unlike others, it didn't distort the subject. It was the most objective, realistic and even democratic art.

But he couldn't stay there forever taking photos. As he left the garden to have some breakfast and to meet up with his teammate, he swore to himself that, no matter what happened with Aaron, Max was going to keep *both* of his hands.

"How're you doing this fine morning, Max?" he asked brightly when he spotted Max in the hotel lobby.

Max looked like he'd just survived the longest night of his life, his skin white as paper and his eyes blood red. "Tell me, how in God's name did you neglect to forewarn me that your car was haunted?!"

CHAPTER 12

FAILURE AND VICTORY

"Somehow, our trip to Bath might be even more of a train wreck than my floundering romantic life," Max said, moments after he had tripped over a foetid pile of horse manure.

Once he'd met up with Khalil, Max suggested they drive a little further out to where ruined cottages might be lurking, and Khalil—seemingly out of indifference—had agreed. However, their search had uncovered nothing of significance even after several hours. They'd already plodded over the vast majority of the area around the hotel. The whole time, Max had wondered out loud what Brad's sinister text message had meant. The GPS tracker was also still on his mind, yet he didn't know how to bring it up without sounding like he'd been snooping.

"I can't say my romantic life is much more successful," Khalil admitted. He took out a pack of cigarettes and lit one. "I broke up with my girlfriend, Noora, shortly before I moved. I had no real choice as I couldn't do long distance. I believe true, pure love is when two souls are perfectly attuned, and it can spring up in the most surprising of places. Although, whether it can ever stay intact in this anarchic world is something I have always questioned."

The mid-morning air felt sub-zero, drying Max's throat and forcing him to take shallow breaths. As he stepped over a lightning-struck willow tree that had collapsed, and skirted around a railing mouldering in rusty decay, Max recalled a wise man's words: "So nature wars with all the works of man."

"Maybe we're destined to be eligible bachelors like Nikola Tesla," Max replied as he tore off a branch from the fallen tree and pierced the air with it, still raring for a proper sword fight. "So much the better. Love is nothing but oxytocin-conditioned primal attachments. And sex is just, ew. Overrated."

"It can be amazing, though. I'm not sure you know much about birds."

"In fact, I know a great deal about ornithology, despite being a fisherman. I have memorised *Bird Watching 101*."

"I mean, females. Are you on any of those modern dating apps, mate?"

"Oh, yeah. OkCupid. But I don't seem to get many love letters on there, even after updating my profile."

"Maybe I can give you some feedback on it."

Max opened the app and handed over his phone, but was soon galled at Khalil's poorly concealed snickering.

"Look, mate. This needs a bit of work," Khalil carped. "Nobody cares about how many hairs are on your head, or that you're the universe experiencing itself so technically you don't exist."

"Maybe not, but I'm sure any prospective partner would be interested in my MBTI and blood types. INTP and AB negative, incidentally."

"Interesting. I'm ESTJ I think, and O positive."

As the pair ambled along, chaffinches tweeted melancholy songs on branching twigs and sensuous purple violas blossomed out of the long grass.

"The ironic truth is," Max started to say, "the damsel I want can't be found on dating apps. There's a girl I like, but she's in love with Louis Tomlinson and has a tattoo exhibition dickhead of a boyfriend."

"Is it that girl I rang? Rosie?"

He nodded.

"That's too bad," Khalil murmured. "Maybe she'll break up with her boyfriend someday. Brad, right? But the most important thing is honesty. If you have feelings for her, just tell her."

"Honesty—I'm just an exemplar of that particular virtue, aren't I?" he reflected.

As lunchtime drew nearer, Max was sick and tired of trudging through these desolate fields with only the meagre prospect that they were about to find treasure.

By the time they got back into Bath rain was pelting down, so Max and Khalil stopped at a local deli to get something to eat. Feeling ready to give up and go home, he ordered a croque monsieur without ham while Khalil got a gorgonzola sandwich. He sat at a table and then received a message from Rosie asking how he was and if he'd got any calls from the quiz posters, which he had, but only prank calls.

"I overheard those codgers over there chatting about The Crystalline Crucible," Khalil whispered, and pointed towards a trio of white-haired seventy-year-olds who were sipping tea. "They said they'd trawled well-nigh all of England to find a clue and got nowhere. What do you think happens when you win? Is it really true that nobody knows?"

"I think," Max said in a contemplative tone, "you get to join the Knights Templar and become the Grand Master. I could finally meet my people and become a real knight! I've waited so long."

"Anyway, we'll have to decide how we split the winnings. Fifty-fifty?"

"More like seventy-thirty. Still, I don't see how we'll split the answers to the mysteries of the world."

"You can keep that. As for myself, I'm going to buy a mansion with a swimming pool, a Ferrari, a football field with one of those ball shooters and a home cinema to boot. Oh, and my own photography studio."

"Me too. Except instead of a football field, I'll have a game room with every Wii game ever made, a robot assistant, a private water park, a jet pack and a—"

"Heya! Khalil, Max! Hehehe. How funny seeing you here!"

The two men jumped. Amelia had just entered the cafe. She pottered over to their table, face pale from the cold. Her tweed coat was drenched, and her ginger locks glistened like she'd been swimming.

"You look wet," she said, rubbing her hands on her coat. "Did you have any success?"

"Yes. We won the contest," Max said hotly.

She giggled. "It's as simple as X marks the spot, right? Boy, I've been treasure hunting so much that I'm miles behind on Hugh Grant's and Emma Thompson's taxes."

"I'm just about to go check myself out of the hotel," Khalil said. "We found nothing but dirt. Lots of dirt."

"Oooh, can I come with? We can be losers together and console each other. Hehehe."

"Fair enough," he said, and reached for his pocket. "I need a cigarette. Do you think they give a shit about smoking in here?"

But as he lit the cigarette, the deli owner shouted, "Hey, douche canoe! No smoking indoors!"

The three braved the bucketing rain. Max's doubts that Amelia was his soulmate intensified when she started singing her favourite Boyzone tunes on the way back to the hotel. The trip had been a giant failure. He hadn't failed so badly since he had attempted to run the Nottingham Marathon in a venture to prove to Rosie that he wasn't a "navel-gazing lazybones", but ended up collapsing during the first one hundred metres because his feet ached.

Depressed enough to read the guest book for a distraction, Max stayed silent as Khalil gave his debit card to the receptionist at the front desk. Amelia had just headed to her own room to pack her things.

"Out of curiosity, did there used to be any ruined cottages around these parts?" Khalil questioned.

"As sure as eggs," the elderly man croaked. "But all of those were torn down decades ago by the council, so you won't have much luck there. That is, if you're on The Crystalline Crucible prowl."

He shot Max a knowing look. "Um, I see."

"You might be interested to know that Wordsworth did stay here once though," he said, with the tone of someone who did not have a particularly high bar for what was interesting. "Yes, he was a guest just like you. I have that information on the authority of my grandfather. Part of this building used to be a ruined cottage, but was entirely renovated and rebuilt."

"Cool, cool. You wouldn't think so, would you?"

As Max glanced at the guest book's signatures, he had a sudden moment of clarity. Maybe the receptionist was giving them a sign. He skimmed through the guest book.

Sure enough, on the last page was the symbol of The Crystalline Crucible: a crystal—a jade one this time. Below it were images of three planets. A note of congratulations was written above it, instructing participants to identify the planets on an internet link.

Max wasn't sure what he was looking at initially, but it hit him all at once: he'd found the next clue! This must mean that the ruined cottage Wordsworth mentioned in the poem was the hotel *itself.*

He glanced back to confirm that Khalil was distracting the receptionist before slyly pulling out his phone and taking a photo of the page. He almost ripped it out yet recalled how that could get him disqualified. When The Crystalline Crucible was first announced, there had been advertisements for it in every newspaper, so it was clear that the contest runners must be powerful enough to have the resources to detect cheating.

Straight away, Max retrieved the car keys from Khalil and ran towards the car. A balloon of elation swelled in his stomach. But before he arrived at the Hyundai, Amelia tootled into his path by the revolving door. Talking on her mobile with her back to him, she rolled her Hello Kitty suitcase behind her.

He was about to interrupt to ask her to budge, when he overheard her saying something suspicious: "Sorry I missed your hen party, Amy. My trip didn't go well. I even tried to see if I could get anything out of these two nutjobs last night out of desperation. Don't know why I bothered. They had nothing, and I could've spent the valuable time researching alone. At least one of them was smoulderingly sexy! Now I'm about to head home for my meeting with Julie Andrews about her tax—"

She revolved abruptly, and her cheeks turned vermilion red.

"Eek, M-max," Amelia stammered. "Hehehe. Nice to see you again."

Max frowned. He could tell by her giggling, which seemed more nervous than usual, that she knew he'd overheard. "Kindly locomote eastwards," he said shortly.

"It was good meeting you," she replied, stepping out of the way. But then she interrupted his stride. "Before you go, would you like to, uh, exchange phone numbers? Just in case, er, you want to get in contact regarding, uh, going out sometime."

"Going out?"

"Yeah! Y'know, a date."

"No, I don't particularly. Treasure doesn't hunt itself."

As Max was about to bolt out the revolving doors, she grabbed his shoulder with a claw-like grip. "Since you heard what I had said, I might as well tell you this," Amelia said maliciously. "Though you are undoubtedly swelteringly handsome, I don't find you one bit amusing, Crystal Hunter, and your treasure hunting theories are complete rubbish." She prodded his chest with her finger. "I'm going to win this contest, and you should concede now. You don't stand a chance against me, you pathetic, foolish, arrogant treasure hunter wannabe."

"Let me tell you something," he said, taken aback. "You can…you can…take a running jump. And stop being so mean, meanie!"

Chagrined, Max returned to the car. He tried and failed to dismiss Amelia from his brain as he studied the cryptic planet clue. By the time Khalil returned to the car, he couldn't decide how to explain what he'd discovered. Due to his excitement, it came out in a string of confused gibberish, and he had to repeat it three times.

"Incredible!" Khalil gasped, and grinned with childlike joy as Max showed him the clue. "Kudos to you for checking the guest book. I never would've thought of that."

"I thought it couldn't hurt," Max said under his breath.

"Welp, we're one step closer to winning, mate! I'm extra glad I didn't stab you now."

"Foolish of you to assume I couldn't defend myself. I know karate, tai chi and kung fu. As a matter of fact, if I still had Fleshrender you'd be terrified."

Both of them were in high spirits as they began their journey back to Stapleford.

On the way, Max told Khalil some anecdotes about the prior, equally thrilling treasure hunts he had gone on. A few years ago, for instance, he'd gone on a quest to find Excalibur. Unfortunately, it had concluded when he fell into a puddle and mortally bruised his knee. On another occasion, he'd been hunting for the Holy Grail and even bought a pricey metal detector subsequent to saving for a full year. Regrettably, Eddie Tomlinson brought this fledgling treasure hunt to a close by throwing the detector out the window when Max came home from school—just when he was sure he was on the verge of discovering the Temple of Doom, too!

"Hopefully, this clue will be easy," Khalil said, his earlier excitement tempered a bit. "There is a lot about astronomy in encyclopaedias, isn't there? You *must* know about it!"

It was seven p.m. when the two of them arrived back in Nottingham. Max was grateful to Khalil for parking near Norman Court and scouting the corridors for any sign of Brad, and his landlord who he hadn't paid rent to for three months.

"Just don't share the clue with anyone," Max firmly instructed as he forwarded the image to Khalil and stepped out of the car. "I bet there are loads who would pay millions for it. Well, thousands. Fine. Hundreds."

"What about Amelia?" Khalil suggested to Max's displeasure. "I got her number last night. Maybe she can join our group for the rest of the contest."

"Absolutely not."

"She could be helpful."

"Maybe at being unhelpful." Max grimaced, and waved through the car window. "I don't trust that Boyzone zealot. Sayonara."

"Whatever. See you, Max," Khalil said tiredly. He drove away.

It was good to be home. After spending half an hour in the heavenly warmth of his shower, he changed into his pyjamas and binged his box set of season one of *Miss Marple*, as if he hadn't already seen it over ten times. His favourite episode was season one, episode three. He played it at double speed, fearing he might burst with anticipation otherwise. It was so exciting that he could barely eat his popcorn; he just kept dropping it.

"May I have some final words?" Miss Marple said mincingly, clutching her purse.

"Very well. What would you like to say before I shoot you and finish my dastardly plan?" the villain said as he aimed the revolver at her.

And then Miss Marple smiled daintily and said, "My dear, I said final words. I didn't say my own!"

Nonetheless, the fact he'd been ignoring calls from Rosie continued to needle him. Max had got rather used to his phone's vibratory thigh massage but decided that after the credits of his third film of the night, *Finding Nemo*, preceded by *The Aristocats* and *A Goofy Movie*, he couldn't disregard Rosie anymore or she may call the morgue to see if he was there.

He muted the television and mentally rehearsed the intricate web of lies that he'd threaded. He would have to be more convincing than Mata Hari.

"Jello?"

"Max! Where have you been? I've been calling *all day*," Rosie asked, her voice tense.

"I'm on the mend. Don't worry," Max reassured her. His stomach lurched with guilt.

"What's that supposed to mean? The doctor I talked to made it sound like you were on death's door. Let me guess. That wasn't really a doctor. Brad's been going on and on about how he saw you out and about and how you aren't really sick. He's visited virtually every hospital in Nottinghamshire to try and prove it. It's ridiculous. What's going on? Really, this time."

Huh… That was Brad's big evil scheme? I needn't have been so worried. "It's been an outré couple of days, to be sure," he mumbled, and made a tiny fake cough. "But in sum, I have made a miraculous recovery, and I was released yesterday. Bless the NHS."

"Really? That soon?" she asked, sounding surprised and doubtful in equal measure. "All of this is starting to sound real weird to me. You know what? I'll come over now."

Before Max could reject her self-invitation, the line went dead.

Adrenaline rushed through him. He tried to redial Rosie, but she didn't pick up. If she was on the way, she would see his bruises. They weren't fully healed yet. Twenty minutes later, a knock echoed at the door, and he still didn't know what to do. Was it finally time to make his confession?

Can't go on with this forever. The guilt will ruin me. I'm not Pinocchio.

"Max, open up!" Rosie called, thumping on the redwood. "I brought questions. We can do a late-night weekend practice session."

Max took his time to open the door, deciding how best to break it to her.

"God! What happened to you?" Rosie exclaimed as she scanned his face in the doorway.

"I've got a confession to make," he muttered, and gazed down at the floor in shame. "A frightfully terrible one. I wasn't sick at all. I lied. I went to Bath with my treasure hunting partner, Khalil."

A painful sense of his own wickedness spread through him like he'd drunk cyanide, as Max explained what had happened. He didn't tell her the full story of getting beaten up; he didn't want her to pity him.

"You are the worst friend in the world!" Rosie screeched.

"I know what I did was bad, but no need to be a drama queen. I'm sure worse friends exist in the world's magnitude…"

Her mouth fell agape. "You think calling me a drama queen is the right way to apologise?"

"I just meant, there are seven billion people on this accursed planet. There must be worse! What about Lando in *The Empire Strikes Back*?" Max appealed.

"I'm pretty sure you must rank among the worst. Trust me."

And with that, Rosie stormed out of the flat—and perhaps out of Max's life too.

Closing the door, he rested his back against the wall and sighed, praying that there may be *some* way for her to forgive him.

As important as Rosie and treasure hunting was, he had much higher priorities at the moment: his woolly mammoth theft hearing. He picked up the court letter from the floor. It had come while he'd been away, and he prayed that he was only going to get a fine. He could not help but think that he hadn't been worrying enough about this. The court might be lenient on him, but there was just as much a chance that he could end up rotting in prison. He certainly didn't think he could survive behind bars, unless maybe they were the bars of a nice Scandinavian prison equipped with plenty of video games and encyclopaedias.

Despite being worn to a frazzle, Max still didn't sleep well that night. Moonlight poured in through the curtains, coating him and Benjamin in selenic glimmers of pale white and grey. Every time he dozed for a few moments, he jolted awake from terrifying nightmares in which the ghost of William Wordsworth had invaded his apartment and taken him hostage, demanding he find Margaret for him. Wordsworth had also visited him that night in Khalil's haunted car.

Sleeping in fits, he could neither stop his racing heart nor shake the feeling that something was off. By dawn, he'd slept for three hours at most. Yawning, he leaned over for some water and drowsily observed the notification light on his phone. He read the message, and his arms and legs lost feeling in an instant.

It was from Mr Johnson, and it was not good news—at all.

CHAPTER 13

A BATTLE OF WITS AND HALFWITS

Rosie had a feeling that today's quiz practice would not be productive long before it had started.

"Frankly, I don't get why you're doing this quiz championship anymore," Brad bleated, annoyance in his voice as they strode down Worrin Road. "Why spend any more time with Grouch?"

"We've been practising for the championship for months. Years even," she purred dismissively. "I don't get why you insist you have to come, like I need protection or something."

"You know what his dad did! The four women he viciously tortured and killed?"

"Three, to be precise," she corrected, although she didn't feel that made it much better. "But Max is nothing like Terrence. As it happens, if Max were an animal, what d'you think he would be?"

"I dunno. He looks kinda like a raccoon. Stop changing the subject!" Brad yapped. "Maxwell is bad news, plain and simple."

Rosie scowled. Brad had been acting ridiculous, gloating left and right, ever since he'd found out about Max's lie. She hadn't even believed that Max was sick after a few days, but she'd gone along with it primarily because Brad was being intensely annoying.

Last night, Brad had woken her up. He'd been in a sweat, shaking and sleep-talking, saying, "Max, take that, little punk!"

What was more was that she found herself increasingly devoid of answers every time she asked herself why she was still with Brad besides habit. He was about as likeable as an old toothpick and only marginally attractive. These days, she often felt like her life resembled a bizarre daydream that she just couldn't snap out of.

They stepped inside the Costa Coffee.

"WHAT IS HE DOING HERE?" Max erupted.

He said *he* as though he were referring to the Slenderman or a ten-foot-tall werewolf.

Rosie's ears went red as customers eating lunch glared disapprovingly over at them. *Why does nearly every meeting with Max have people either screaming, sobbing or staring at us?*

"What ever happened to 'good to see you again', Grouch?" Brad said.

Max's face scrunched up, and he would not stop tapping his foot. She'd noticed that the tempo of his stimming foot tap was an excellent barometer for how stressed he was, and currently, it was so fast that his shoe was almost blurred.

While Brad went to get them drinks, she sat across from Max on the settee, planting her baguette bag by her side. They said nothing for a few moments as he gave her the evil eye.

"You just love bringing Brad along uninvited, don't you?" he whined.

"Oh, now come on. He didn't give me a choice," she muttered, her necklace feeling tight around her neck. "He's *obsessed* with you. Even seems to think you're dangerous."

"I *am* dangerous. I could defeat the Mongolian army single-handedly if I still had Fleshrender. Not sure about Owl though, Ms Eeyore."

Rosie's insides seemed light as she spoke to him. She was still furious with him for lying, and yet no matter how much she told herself off for it, Max remained one of her closest friends in her heart for reasons she hardly understood. Rosie had been half tempted to not turn up to practice or to kick him out of Agatha Quiztie—but seeing as he was the only other member, that probably wouldn't improve their odds in the championship.

"Are you doing okay, then?" she cooed, emptying her voice of emotion. "How's your lawyer search going? And work?"

"Splendiferously marvellacious," Max boasted. "I'm defending myself in court, so that problem is solved. Though I must admit, work is not great. Ms Johnson had a heart attack. Her son is now the temporary manager. I just hope it didn't happen when she found the foxes I had let into the shop to sleep. They looked so cold."

"Oh my gosh. Your boss had a *heart attack*? And you're self-defending?!"

But at that moment, Brad returned with a scornful grin. "So, how's life, Grouch? Or shall I call you liar, liar, pants on fire?" he snarled, and handed Rosie a latte.

He sat next to her and wrapped his dragon-tattooed arm around her shoulder. She flinched, finding it hard to stop herself from pushing him off her and slapping him across the face.

"Fine, fopdoodle," Max brayed, crossing his arms.

Brad chuckled. "*Fopdoodle*? For someone who's memorised the dictionary, you'd think you have better insults, Mr Bean."

"Act like adults, both of you," Rosie ordered as she raised her question cards and shuffled them. "Max, shall we get started?"

"Sure," he said at once, raising his chin. "I didn't come here to be mocked."

"Let's get on with it. I printed a load of new questions last night, some really tricky ones too. What are the two planets in the solar system with one moon?"

"Trick question. It's just Earth," he said without delay. "Incidentally, my least favourite planet in the universe."

"I bet I know your favourite," Brad said wryly with a whinny-like laugh. "Uranus!"

"Brad, grow up!" she hooted. "Next question. Who is the—"

Yet before Rosie could stop it, Brad grew buck teeth, and a tail sprang out of him. This time, Max also underwent a metamorphosis and transformed into a little raccoon inside an imaginary trash bin.

"Who is the captain of Arsenal?" Rosie continued, striving to distract herself by staring at the ceiling.

"A sports question?" Max Raccoon snapped as his little head peeked out from the trash. "My greatest weakness."

"Don't you know anything?" Brad Beaver quacked. He gnawed on some spare lumber. "It's so obvious. I thought these questions were supposed to be hard."

"Christ, Brad," Rosie barked. "You're not competing in the championship, so if you don't mind, pipe down." She turned back to Max. "What banker died in *EastEnders* last month?"

"And now a soap opera question? Why has the God of questions forsaken me?" Max Raccoon squeaked, his face in his grey palms.

She slammed the question cards down. "Max, you're showing a lot of weak areas."

"Apologies," he said, licking his underlip. "In days of yore, this was a real quiz team and not just you and me."

"I'll check the enrolment deadline," she said and pulled out her phone. "It's in April. Getting close."

"Too bad nobody replied to my posters. I spent two hours designing them in Microsoft Paint, and I thought they looked exceptionally professional."

"Why don't you show one to me, and I'll be the judge?"

Max Raccoon pulled out a poster from his bin and handed it to her:

Agatha Quiztie, Stapleford's most illustrious and distinguished quiz team, is on the hunt for new members. If you have an IQ over two hundred; don't enjoy any form of competitive physical activity; dislike chocolate (not including the milk), ice cream and pizza; speak three languages or more; consider William Hartnell your favourite Doctor in Doctor Who; and can memorise pi to at least the one-hundredth digit, call this number for consideration.

Below those words was a crude drawing of Max and Rosie that looked like it'd been done by a toddler.

"Max, this is terrible," she admitted, sighing. "Nobody can meet these strict specifications. You don't even speak two languages and your IQ is average, if that."

"Yes, but do you want just any Tom, Dick and Harry?" Max Raccoon said, and disappeared again into his bin. "We could find the Einstein of Stapleford! Ooh, I ought to create my own Crystalline Crucible to assess potential members."

"You'd have to pay me a lot to join," Brad Beaver said, tail giving a wag.

His snout covered in dirt, Max Raccoon re-emerged. "Let's just finish up with a few more questions. Frankly, these quiz practices have been deteriorating into an execrable breeding ground of impropriety and iniquity."

As the end of practice drew near, Rosie was increasingly sick of Brad Beaver and Max Raccoon's crosstalk. They were *insufferable*. She somehow couldn't manage to get rid of their animal alter egos. It was so bad that at one point, her mind created a dragon that swooped in and ate them both whole.

"What is the brain of the cell?" she asked Max Raccoon after a string of correct answers.

"Nucleus. Potentially the only type of brain some people have."

Brad Beaver erected his furry posture and glared at him with his forepaws raised. "One more comment like that, and I'll let you have it," he threatened.

"Simmer down," she woofed. "Next question. Butch Cassidy and Sundance Kid died in which country?"

"Bolivia," Max Raccoon cawed breezily, doing a little jig in the bin. "A Wild West question? Easy-peasy. If not a knight-errant, I've always said I'd be a cowboy."

And then, Theodore Tabby made an elegant entrance into Costa Coffee while donning a top hat, accompanied by the loyal presence of Count Ferdinand, who leisurely puffed on his pipe.

Rosie flipped to the next card, finding it increasingly difficult to discern reality. "What is the angle that is over ninety degrees and less than one hundred and eighty degrees called?"

"Obtuse." Max reached into his bin and threw a 7Up can at Brad. "An adjective that also applies perfectly to a member of this room."

"Okay!" Brad Beaver roared, turning back into a human. "That's it."

Before Rosie could grasp what was happening, Brad blew his top and leapt on Max to get his hands around his neck.

Meanwhile, Max lost his raccoon nose and cute face and slipped away just in time, dashing off. His last words echoed. "Adieu and arrivederci, scoundrels!"

"Oh, bother," Rosie said, facepalming.

CHAPTER 14

THE YOUNG KNIGHT IN COURT

Being a walking flesh bag was getting on Max's nerves. Lately, he frequently wondered whether he'd been abandoned on Earth by aliens as a baby. There had been far too much cortisol buzzing about his brain for his liking lately and not nearly enough dopamine and serotonin. He longed for the days when the biggest thing to worry about was his next crossword fix.

But he certainly couldn't do a crossword on a day like this.

Max's pulse thudded as he hastened toward the courthouse, his breath coming quicker with each step. Having forgotten to wear his suit for the big day, he was dressed in his Pingu the penguin T-shirt and Crocs. The clouds filtered spangling daylight over Nottingham's trashy pavements, turquoise sky passing in patches. It was a rarely pleasant morning that day, but he had neither the time nor the desire to enjoy it.

Nottingham Court appeared around the corner: a stony, intimidating building with an exterior carved from granite and a shadowy overhang under which pasty-faced smokers loitered.

Max tensed as he entered and was shown to the waiting room. Around him, people sat talking in low tones about TV licence fees, parking fines and benefits issues. He didn't suppose anybody else was likely to be in trouble for attempted woolly mammoth theft.

In due time, the staff led him into the courtroom and guided him to the defendant's dock.

At the front of the chamber on a raised leather chair sat the district judge. He was a great, grizzled lump of a man whose angular frown gave the distinct impression that he hadn't smiled in decades, much like Rosie and Ms Johnson. He glowered over the courtroom from his varnished rosewood desk, casting an incredulous glance at Max. A stern-faced usher faffed about with his black gown at the back. The prosecution sat nearby, sorting out a huge folder of files. And then as Max looked over the courtroom seating area, he spotted her.

Rosie.

Dressed in a green cardigan, she was perched in the middle of the benches, biting her nails. *Didn't think she'd show up. So, she hasn't entirely given up on me. Nice to know. I wouldn't have blamed her.*

After establishing he was self-representing to the court and receiving several patronising looks as a result, the trial began. The defendant's dock didn't have seats, so he had to stand bolt upright, feet aching.

"Please could the defendant state his name, address, date of birth and nationality," the district judge of Nottingham Magistrates' Court, Mr Thomas Beaton, ordered in a stately voice. After Max did, the judge continued. "Mr Maxwell Jacobs, you are charged with illegally entering the premises of the Nottingham Natural History Museum with the intention of stealing a mammoth tusk. In doing so, you broke a window of the lobby, damaged the skeleton from which you were trying to extricate the tusk and threatened the police with a sword. Thus, you are charged with breaking and entering, vandalism and intent to steal. Ah, and criminal possession of a weapon. Despite it being offered, you have elected to forgo professional defence and represent yourself. How do you plead?"

"Guilty as charged, Your Honour," quoth he.

"Very well." Judge Beaton glanced down at the papers in front of him. "It says here you are the son of Terrence Jacobs… Interesting." He clicked his tongue in his cheek, steely eyes wavering over Max like he was a wayward adolescent. "May I ask, what are you wearing?"

Besides Rosie, only a couple of spectators were present on the benches, but all stared at Max following Judge Beaton's prior statement. Such was his dad's reputation that almost everybody in Stapleford knew his bad name, and that was one of the reasons—other than only really being liked by pigeons—why Max avoided socialising.

The courtroom gave off the stale stink of paper and sweat. Max sweated bullets and found it increasingly hard to breathe as the peach walls stared him down. On them hung staid portraits of lawyers with bob wigs, robes and self-satisfied expressions.

"I'm his son. Yes," Max said, his foot rapping against the floor. He glanced down at his shirt, where Pingu was smiling and waving. "And it's just my Pingu shirt. You know, Pingu the penguin?"

"Pingu? A cartoon character? That is obviously completely inappropriate attire for court, Mr Jacobs. Consider yourself lucky that I will not make an issue out of it, as I'm eager to get this over with. Out of curiosity, when was the last time you had contact with your father?"

"My dad? Dunno. That's about as relevant as Pingu," he mumbled.

Judge Beaton's frown deepened. "Mr Jacobs, we are in *my* courtroom, so I decide what's relevant. Now, please forget Pingu and answer my questions. Tell me, have you ever shown any signs of psychosis akin to your father's mental illness?"

Forget Pingu? I could never. It's my favourite show after Miss Marple.

"My dad's nothing to do with this," Max avowed. "I'm perfectly sane. You can test me if you want. I can recall every Doctor in *Doctor Who* by reverse alphabetical order, and the same with their companions, in less than a minute!"

"That would not suffice as a benchmark of your sanity, I'm afraid," Judge Beaton said with gravitas, scratching his nostrils. "Of course, you are a different person than your father, and his actions are legally inapposite to yours. Nevertheless, you can surely understand that the son of a murderer engaging in delinquency doesn't bode well for his future."

"I only broke into the museum for treasure hunting. That's all. Not anything delinquent."

"Treasure hunting?"

Max knew he shouldn't have brought this up. Everybody ridiculed him when they found out about his favourite profession. "Yes, I'm a famous treasure hunter, The Crystal Hunter. Maybe the best one in England, too. I'm desperately trying to win a contest, so I can become a true knight, get rich and find out the answers to the mysteries of the world. I'll readily admit that my father was a sick man, but what I did…I mean, it's a bit different."

"If only it were that straightforward," the judge asserted poshly. "A history of family crime is important, even if it is not considered evidence. It suggests your misdemeanour may well lead to a bigger incident down the road." He fingered his gavel on the desk. "And all this about treasure hunting… Mr Jacobs, you may need psychiatric help."

I don't like this guy. Why didn't I get a jury? I'd easily win.

"Uh, no, Your Honour," Max disagreed. "My last psychiatrist said I don't belong in therapy. Rather, a zoo. Oh wait, I just got what she meant. Anyhow, I don't plan to go from mammoth tusks to murdering people. Pingu—"

"Mr Jacobs, if you mention Pingu *one* more time, I shall sentence you to the maximum possible sentence!" Judge Beaton scowled and asked the prosecutor to speak.

As Max glanced over at Rosie, she shot him a seething look and made a gesture that plainly told him to shut up. She probably wouldn't be that upset if he ended up in HM Prison Belmarsh after their tiff.

The prosecutor went on to make up all sorts of exaggerations about him, which made it hard for Max to keep silent and not defend himself. The worst was when he called Max "a threat to Nottinghamshire's moral order" and a "troubled, lost youth", and attempted to evidence this by showing his broadsword, the photographs of the window he had broken and the power box he'd poured chocolate milk on.

Surprisingly, the rest of the trial only lasted about forty-five minutes. Prickly cactus-like anxiety crept over his body when the time came to announce his sentence. He envisaged himself being put in the guillotine and tried to work out how long it would take for him to lose consciousness after his head came off. Hopefully, it would be lengthy enough to call Judge Beaton a scoundrel.

Finally, Judge Beaton cleared his throat. "Mr Jacobs, you are hereby given a community order. The terms of this order are as follows: you must complete three hundred hours of community service over the course of the next five years, report to a probation officer on a weekly basis and pay a fine of three thousand pounds. Should you fail to abide by these terms, you will be resentenced, with the possibility of serving prison time. Once the fine is settled, the terms of the community service may be subject to amendment."

"Cheers, Your Honour!" Max exclaimed as relief swept over him.

With a buoyant smile, he looked at Rosie, who unexpectedly grinned back at him.

But Judge Beaton wasn't quite done. "Lastly, as your interest in the subject has patently been driving you to crime, you are from now on forbidden from pursuing any actions related to—what was it?—oh yes, your alleged treasure hunting. If it is discovered by your probation officer that you have engaged in treasure hunting, the price will surely be prison."

It couldn't be. It was too tragic for words. It made the ending of *Titanic* a happy conclusion in comparison. The worst possible outcome besides prison, and he hadn't even anticipated it.

And to his horror, with a whack of the gavel, it was law, and the court was dismissed. A magnitude ten earthquake rumbled through Max's heart, and a category five hurricane opened in his soul, sucking into it all his earthly hopes and dreams.

"But that's not fair!" he shouted over the scuffle of everyone getting to their feet. "Treasure hunting is my life!"

With a grimace, Judge Beaton turned to face him one last time. "If I were you, I would just be grateful to not have ended up behind bars today," he snarled and strode away. "*Treasure hunting.* A load of old tosh."

Max stomped out of the defendant's dock, both furious and sorrowful. It had all been going so well, and now everything had gone oh so catastrophically and irreversibly wrong. As he met up with Rosie outside the courthouse doors, he didn't feel their moods matched.

"So, that went well!" she said in a chipper tone.

He could guess why she felt that way. The result meant that Rosie would be getting her wish at last. He would never be able to treasure hunt again, a fact that must be revenge for her. But she had no clue how far he and Khalil had already come in the contest.

"Oh, yeah. Amazing," he grumbled. "Stupefyingly, mind-numbingly goodtacular."

To his surprise, she offered to give him a ride home, which was good as he was far too blue to walk all the way to the bus stop without collapsing.

"Cheer up. Why are you upset?" she asked as she started the car and drove them away.

Max bit his lip. Chances were, Rosie could easily work it out and was playing coy. But one thing was certain to him now: he couldn't break the law anymore for any reason. It was just *too* risky.

"The only things that could make me more unhappy are if *Miss Marple* gets cancelled or Santa Claus puts me on the naughty list," Max bemoaned. "I have a huge fine to pay and months of community service on my plate, and not to mention, I've no way to save the library and get out of Stapleford. Where are all the orphans going to go? I've failed them completely."

"Look on the positive side for a change; this could be a new start for you. Why won't you just forget treasure hunting and try a new hobby?"

"Like what?"

"Maybe sudokus rather than crosswords for a change. Or you could go to the gym and get fit!"

"Ew. Sudokus are just crosswords for desperate hobos. And the gym? My body is already a well-oiled machine, sculpted to perfection. I won't even dignify that with a response."

"You just did. Let's see, what about chess?"

"Not likely. I'm banned from the local chess club for suspected cheating. It's not my fault they're so unimaginative with the rules. Knights should be just as good as queens."

"You're impossible. I know. I'll pick up Brad, and we can all go out for a celebratory meal," Rosie declared. "That'll cheer you right up."

"Are you losing your marbles?!" He glared at her with flared nostrils.

"I'm joking," she said hastily.

"I'd prefer to be a prisoner in a torture chamber with Stalin, Idi Amin and Vlad the Impaler and their worst torture methods than spend another minute with Bradley. I'm a knight, not his doormat."

Rosie absent-mindedly coiled a tendril of her hair around her index finger. "Maybe this will cheer you up. I guess I should get it over with and admit it. I'm going to break up with him this week."

Max's eyes popped out and he gasped. "Huh?"

He was in disbelief as she went on to tell him that she hadn't been happy with Brad for a long, long time and that she was hoping Max would be mature about it and not make any jokes.

"It's not funny," she said seriously. "You don't understand what breaking up is like. I just thought there was something good in Brad, despite all the general badness. I was wrong."

"What? Jokes? I'm appalled you think so lowly of me," he proclaimed. "Don't worry. The singles market isn't so bad. Perhaps I can even give you some dating tips."

His mobile buzzed. It was a text from Khalil:

```
Heading to the hospital now to visit Ms Johnson and see David.
You should join if possible. Room 69. Let's chat after.
```

"Ah, I've just been invited to visit Ms Johnson. I hope she's all right."

Rosie shot Max a side-eye questioningly.

"It seems Mr Johnson wants to talk to me and my co-worker, Khalil, about arrangements for him to manage the Co-op without Ms Johnson," he added. "I don't see how anyone thinks David can possibly do a good job though, seeing as he can't even keep a basic library afloat."

"Fine," she agreed, as if she were his mother giving approval. She paused. "Is this *the* Khalil? Your treasure hunting teammate?"

Max dared not meet Rosie's fiery eyes, not much wanting to bear the brunt of her boundless wrath again. "Kinda. He's pretty cool actually. A photographer."

"A photographer and a fisherman teaming up, eh?" she said, and she pulled up to the bus stop. "God knows how he was foolish enough to trust Maxwell Jacobs. You couldn't make it up."

She dropped him off and he took the bus to the local hospital.

The hospital wing of Queen's Medical Centre was chock-a-block, bustling with nurses rushing through its narrow halls to shrieking women in labour and perishing old people.

As Max walked past the cancer wards, a sudden morbid urge to grab a needle of morphine and sedate himself swelled through him. He remembered the heavenly feeling of morphine pumping through his veins from the time he had tried to roller-skate blindfolded to prove a point. He'd been successful, too, until that stupid open manhole appeared out of nowhere.

He walked into room sixty-nine and spotted Ms Johnson's sickly figure, her almost paper-white arms covered with IV lines. A bulky oxygen mask obstructed her colourless face. As Max had more or less expected, she still wasn't conscious.

Khalil and Mr Johnson sat discoursing in the corner with mugs of coffee in their hands, both reclined on high-back blue hospital chairs.

"How's it going?" Khalil asked as he turned his head and spotted Max in the doorway. "Nice shirt."

Max sighed deeply. "If *it* is going anywhere, it's to the darkest depths of hell. Lately, I'd say it's transformed into a relentless Demogorgon, hell-bent on thwarting my ambitions, tormenting my very spirit, crucifying my mind and sealing my untimely fate."

"Uh, right. So, not well."

"Nice to see you, Maxwell," David said coldly. "Come and take a seat."

In his mid-forties, David had indigo eyes and a bald egg of a head, not a hair in sight. Max had only ever seen him in a suit and tie, and if only going by Mr Johnson's utter disdain for anything that wasn't conducive to profit—which unfortunately often included Max—he had always understood that he didn't like him much.

Max sat across from Khalil and David and intuited a serious mood in the air.

"I've just been telling Khalil that things are going to have to change at the Co-op now that I'm in charge," David stated. "My mother has told me lots of horror stories that made me blush. I love her dearly, but she's been far too old to run the shop for some time now."

"What exactly did she say?" Max asked, starting to wish he hadn't come at all.

"All sorts of funny things. Like the time when you set the hot dog machine on fire, and when you locked her out of the store for hours while juggling in the staffroom," David said murderously. "*She* said it was funny. I don't suppose it takes an accountant to work out why our profits started declining the month you were hired. The apple doesn't fall far from the tree."

Max groaned internally. Why was *everyone* giving him such a hard time today?

"Correlation doesn't equal causation. But how nice of her to tell others about the peaks and valleys of my long, fruitful career at the Co-op," he said, straightening his back. "So, how is Ms Johnson?"

"Not good, sadly." David glanced over at her. "The doctor says she's had a STEMI heart attack, the worst kind. She hasn't improved in the past few days since she was put in an induced coma. She's on life support, and to be frank, it isn't looking hopeful."

"Well, I'm sure she'll be back to normal in no time. Swings and roundabouts."

"So, here are the plans for the shop in the interim. In short, I'll be the manager. But since I also have to keep working at Stapleford Library until it shuts down, you two and Poppy will have to work more hours and contribute to other tasks. This may even include some financial matters like taxes, advertising and ordering stock. How does that sound?"

David put on a fake smile that looked like a robot mimicking human emotion.

"Fine!" Max said with intense bitterness, and turned to Khalil to surmise if he felt the same way. "Simply terrific. Trickle-down economics, yada yada."

"Same," Khalil said.

David beamed, his bald scalp shining under the hospital light bulb. "How about we treat this as a brand-new start for the Co-op? A new leaf. I'm sure Mother would have wanted the shop to go on while she's ill," he said, and gazed soberly at her again. "Life goes on."

My old new leaf didn't turn out so well.

"Until life is killed in an eventually inevitable mass extinction event," Max corrected.

Ignoring him, David proceeded to give Max and Khalil their extra tasks for the week, such as cleaning the toilet, completing insurance forms and locking up the shop after closing time. When the conversation came to an end, Max and Khalil wished Ms Johnson a strong recovery and said their goodbyes.

Inside the hospital room, it had almost seemed that what had happened earlier that day at Nottingham Court might have been a vivid nightmare. However, as they walked outside, Khalil reminded him of its unfortunate reality.

"So, how did court go?" Khalil asked, shuffling along beside him.

"Astoundingly wonderful," Max said shortly. "Don't really want to talk about it, though. I need to move on. Blame is for those stuck in the past."

"Okay… Have you made any progress on the planet clue?" he asked, broadening his shoulders.

Max perked up. "Ah. Yes, I solved it last night. I'd been working on the clue tirelessly and finally figured out the planets. You'd be surprised how many exoplanets have been discovered. The three in question were Gliese 504 b, the pink planet, HD 189733 b, the planet that rains molten glass and 55 Cancri e, the diamond planet."

Khalil grinned. "Great! You could've told me before. So, you've got the next clue?"

"Affirmative. I received it on the website for inputting the correct planets. It's a number grid," Max explained. "It has left me rather discombobulated. The trouble is I'm terrible at maths, my Achilles' heel.

"Really?"

"We're not all Rain Man."

As he spoke, guilt ensnared Max's mind much like the feeling of the days when he neglected to brush his teeth. *What am I doing? I'm banned from treasure hunting now. I must've forgotten for a moment.*

"Hmm… Me too," Khalil admitted, frowning. "Show it to me then."

Max reluctantly showed him the new clue on his phone. Khalil scrunched his face.

"Looks confusing. So, we're stuck?"

"Afraid so. If only I knew someone who was good at decrypting maths clues, who could help us out with it… My friend, Rosie, is a maths teacher, but she would never ever, ever."

Khalil gave Max a look and rubbed his chin as they passed by a cluster of seniors in hospital gowns. "Why don't we ring Rosie and see what she says? Can't hurt."

"You've forgotten how hard she was on me when she found out I went to Bath. Not that I'm innocent. I'm a rotten liar."

"Don't be so paranoid. I think I'll ask her right now," Khalil said, and got out his phone. "I remember her number from when I acted like you were sick."

Max ground his teeth and grasped for Khalil's mobile, only for it to be jerked out of reach. "You can't just make a team decision," he lashed out. "That's…that's unilateralism."

"Huh? We need to make some major progress already."

"Rosie and treasure hunting are Coke and Mentos. Besides, I think I've almost cracked the clue. All we need are plane tickets to North Korea, a Smooth Cayenne pineapple and a great horned owl!"

"Makes total sense," Khalil remarked. "I just hope you're not this unbearable while we're working at the Co-op together over the next few weeks. It's gonna be hard enough with this David prick. Might even ask to switch shifts to work with Poppy for a change."

"I'm curious whether you're going to keep stealing now that Ms Johnson's unwell," Max said, shooting him a baleful glance. "I have to come up with three thousand pounds for a fine after my hearing this morning. More than a limited-edition *Miss Marple* action figure!"

"Three thousand? That's nothing compared to what I need," he snapped, and swept around. "And why do you watch all those old lady shows? Try football like a normal person."

It was as if someone had sieved his mind of words as Max watched Khalil stomp off, disappearing around the corner. *What's he mean by "what I need"? Is Khalil in arrears?*

Seconds later, Max received another text. It was from Sofia, and it reported that the library was going to shut down even sooner once again due to a council decision. He shivered as he imagined *The Famous Five*, one of his favourite series of all time, being dumped in the bin like it was nothing. Julian, Dick, George, Anne and Timothy—he simply couldn't let them down. And yet he was almost too late, as there was even less of a chance now he could win the contest in the time left.

He returned home with a gloomy demeanour, scanning the pavement for a genie's lamp or billionaire's lost wallet.

Over the next few days, Max experienced first-hand just how torturous it was to work at the Co-op without Ms Johnson. David proved far worse than she'd ever been, making every minor mistake Max made into the end of the world. Despite Khalil saying it was too much, Max felt that Dr Evil comparisons weren't exaggerated, and he often craved to take a spoon, whack it against David's scalp and see if yolk would pour out of his head.

When a child ordered a 99 Flake, Max had to use the ice cream machine, which he always dreaded since he had the hand-eye coordination of a handless and eyeless man. The ice cream would either flop onto the floor, or he would add far too much or too little. He found it even more challenging with David's vitriolic eyes stalking his every move.

"Maxwell, that's the fourth ice cream you've dropped today! It's not an Olympic sport!" David howled. "You'll have to pay for all those wasted scoops. I'm taking them out of your wages."

Fortunately, Max managed to make the next ice cream without an incident. Even when David was working at the library, he had the surveillance cameras tied to his mobile, so he would call Max up on the store phone and complain without physically being there.

"Max, playing on your Game Boy isn't stocking the toilet rolls. Get to work!" he clucked.

As Max went to have lunch on his usual bench, his encyclopaedia in hand, he was seized with regret that he had taken Ms Johnson for granted. He pined for the days when he could work without being monitored the whole time, and called a liability, a walking disaster or a blundering fool. For some strange reason, the cheese didn't taste as delightful and the captivating encyclopaedia entry on pine cones didn't seem to engage his interest on that particular day.

As for Khalil, David had given him new tasks that he wasn't trained for. Nowadays, Khalil was often busy working in Ms Johnson's office rather than at the till.

"I'm so fed up with Mr Johnson," Khalil complained as he and Max briefly passed each other in the corridor. "David has me doing all these things I don't know how to do and is watching me *constantly*. Probably has me wiretapped too. I'm thinking investing in a mannequin and a wig might not be a bad idea, mate."

"Don't worry," Max said heatedly. "I've been setting up some absolutely lethal booby traps. Just wait. He will rue the day he asked me to clean the toilet."

"I don't think that's a good idea, Max."

But Max had already left to look for sticky tape.

Even if his booby traps did work, Max was getting so annoyed with David that he wasn't sure they'd be enough. Max was used to being able to do what he wanted when no customers were around; now, he had no free time to think about what to do with his train wreck of a life.

Later that week, while David was on the loo, Max sneaked a look at the classifieds of *The Stapleford Herald* for ways to make some of his fine money. If he relied on his current wages, it would take him until roughly 2052 to save up his bail, yet it would be too risky to time travel there in case of a paradox. The dismal reality was that the most he had ever saved up was about a hundred pounds for his sword and his metal detector.

He'd even applied for *Big Brother* and *I'm a Celebrity...Get Me Out of Here!* the previous week—the prize money being just what he needed. But unfortunately, after he sent them his detailed profile, they'd just replied asking whether it was a bizarre joke. Somehow, he didn't qualify as a celebrity, even though all the local pigeons knew him.

The Crystalline Crucible prize money would presumably cover it all, but he was barred from treasure hunting, and there was not much he could do about that. And, of course, he hadn't forgotten the Stapleford Quiz Championship's five-thousand-pound prize, although splitting the reward between the other teammates ensured his share would be virtually nothing.

Coming into work for the morning shift one Monday, Max found Khalil in Ms Johnson's office. He reckoned that today was the day he had to reveal what had transpired in Nottingham Court, as he'd been avoiding that, and Khalil had been bugging him to ask Rosie for help.

Khalil sat slumped at the desk, scratching his neck over an avalanche of paperwork. Covering the desk was a barrage of empty beer cans and Crunchie wrappers. As he bit the lid of his pen, his forehead puckered and he muttered cusses.

“Mate, do you think I could ring up Amelia for assistance on these damn taxes?” he asked as he hit his palm against his brow. “How does David think I’m qualified for this? Why don’t you have a go?”

“You think David would let me have a go with something as complicated as that?” Max asked. “He won’t let me use the Crystal vacuum cleaner. Is Ms Johnson not getting better?”

Khalil released a world-weary sigh. “Doesn’t look like it. We’re gonna be stuck with David indefinitely.”

“That’s just wonderful. Speaking of wonderful, I’ve got a shockingly unwonderful secret I need to admit to you.”

“How dramatic. Go on.”

Max braced himself for an uproar. Throughout his explanation, Khalil’s expression exhibited signs of textbook anger: his lip curling and his eyebrows shooting right up.

Khalil crossed his arms. “So, you’re going to quit, right when we’re on the doorstep of winning? You’ve lost your mind. Who cares about what the court says?”

“Did you not hear?” Max said, shoulders drooping. “I could end up in prison if I continue. Besides, I wouldn’t say we’re on the doorstep of winning quite yet.”

“So what? It’s a risk we must take!” Khalil got up and stepped closer to him, fist shaking. “Anyways, you couldn’t quit at this stage even if you wanted to. You don’t have my permission.”

“What?” Max asked in disbelief, blowing out his cheeks.

“You can’t make a team decision unanimously,” Khalil stated. He stood at arm’s length from Max and raised his left eyebrow. “That’s what you said to me. It applies to you too, and leaving is a team decision, isn’t it? You forget the eighth commandment of chivalry: thou shalt never lie and remain faithful to thy pledged word. Yeah, I remember.”

“I’m as much a knight as you are now,” he said off the cuff. “The court didn’t even return my sword. I need to become something else. A…a cowboy or something.”

“The same goes for cowboys.”

“Rubbish. What’s it even matter? You’ll find some new way to make money.”

“Don’t be so spineless. We’ve come too far to give up now. Giving up is the birth of regret.”

"Where did you get that from?" Max asked, bemused.

"My father was really spiritual. He died of an aneurysm, but before he passed, he gave me *The Complete Works of Rumi* and told me to read a page every day," Khalil murmured, grazing his neck with his finger. "Besides, can't I read poetry of my own accord, or do you think I'm just a fool?"

"No. *I'm* the fool. I screwed everything up. And I am happy to birth a little regret. Maybe even regret twins. You can change your shift, and in time, we'll forget this ever happened."

"I won't forget, and neither will you."

Despite still not being convinced, Max could see that Khalil was adamant. And didn't he have a point? A knight's foremost responsibility was to uphold rectitude, with obedience to the law coming as a secondary consideration.

"I'll tell you what," Max asserted, "I'll *think* about continuing on one condition."

"Good," Khalil said as he narrowed his eyes. "What's the condition?"

"You join Agatha Quiztie. We need another member for the tournament, you see."

"Huh? I'm crap at trivia and stuff. I'd be no help," he said. His face contorted.

"We just need another head," Max explained. "You don't even have to come to practice."

Khalil thought it over for a second, tilting his head. "Fine. I'll join your quiz team—on one condition of my own. You ask Rosie to help us out with the contest. We need some assistance with the new clue, and she's all we've got," he retaliated. "What would you prefer? To waste time until some treasure hunting expert finds the next clue? I went on TreasureNet the other day, and the contest is really heating up. Somebody even told me they're almost on the final clue."

Max thumbed his chin.

"Maybe," he finally resolved. "Although, I make no promises."

Despite this being a snag, one thing was accomplished in this exchange: Max had found a third member for Agatha Quiztie. Now Rosie just had to find someone, and they'd be a real team again.

He got back to work post-haste and barely spoke to Khalil for the rest of the day, although it was clear to each of them what the other was thinking about.

That evening, while Max was looking high and low through his apartment for a book he'd bought years ago on cryptography, he was amused to discover something unexpected: old Halloween costumes that he had once worn in the Children's Society. They had been buried deep in the corner of his cupboard.

Other than Bugs Bunny, he had both a knight and cowboy costume in pristine condition. Obeying his instincts, he took out the cowboy hat and put it on. It fit surprisingly well, and examining himself in the bathroom mirror, he thought it suited him rather well too. Maybe it really was time to retire from the treacherous knight lifestyle.

Am I too old for this? I guess Wordsworth said the child is father of the man.

Someone's knock drummed on the door. Rosie's signature strawberry perfume seeped inside, and yet what reason could she have for visiting him without calling first?

"Max, great news! I've got someone for our team!" she exclaimed, and stepped inside with a letter in her hands. "I've been asking everyone at school, and *finally*, somebody agreed to join Agatha Quiztie!"

"So great that you didn't think to call first?" he replied. He didn't like surprises at all. "Or even ask if you are welcome in my noble abode?"

"Come on, Max. You're the one who lied to me for weeks. Wait." She paused, shifting her gaze. "What the heck are you wearing? Oh, it doesn't matter. Listen, her name is Lauren, and she's a teacher of my class at Kiddy Winks. She's kind of annoying, but she'll do."

"Huzzah. In fact, by great coincidence, I've found someone too."

"You have?" She hopped in excitement. "Just perfect. Now we have enough people."

"What the heck is that, Postman Pat?" Max asked, pointing at the envelope.

"It was in your mailbox. I don't mean to pry, but I spotted it sticking out," she said, and handed it over.

Max gazed down at the sender's address: Jebb Avenue, Brixton Hill. London. SW2 5XF.

He stopped dead on the spot. *Wait a second. Isn't that the prison where my father is?*

This letter had to be from his dad. He nearly opened the seal, but as he thought briefly about it, he decided for now he'd rather be tasered again than read it. He tucked the letter into the deepest pocket of his rucksack instead.

Yet his concerns about the letter were superseded by a frightful clamour. Something loud crashed, followed by glass smashing.

"Wh-what was that noise?" Rosie asked as they gazed around with bewildered eyes.

"I dunno," Max said, mind racing. "Sounded like a—" He stopped himself. The word he was about to say—*gunshot*—was too preposterous.

"Must be an engine backfire," Rosie replied, her voice aquiver. "Right?"

"Let's look outside."

Both unconvinced, the duo ambled over to the window, and then they saw it. The glass was shattered. A smoking bullet hole marred the opposite wall.

CHAPTER 15

THE ASSASSIN OF STAPLEFORD

Rosie had seen Max act like a senseless person many times—from the occasion he arrived at school in his pyjamas when he'd forgotten to get dressed, to the time he went on a hunger strike at school over the discontinued production of cinnamon roll Pop-Tarts, which lasted two days—but finally, the day had come when he might have lost the plot completely.

Still wearing a cowboy hat, Max had been lying on his stomach on the cold floor for an hour, humming the *Super Mario Bros.* theme song over and over in between recalling every word from the dictionary in order. He had just reached the letter *I* and showed no sign of stopping.

"They're gonna put you in a mental institution if you don't stop acting like that," she said, and shot a glare down at him.

They were alone in the questioning room of Nottingham City Police Station. Apparently, the police were working out what to do with them.

On the questioning room's stainless-steel table before them was her notepad, where her Theodore Tabby sketches sat splayed open. Everybody teased her when they heard she was writing a book about a talking tabby, but the beauty of the story was in Count Ferdinand and Detective Theodore's unlikely fellowship and their goodness on an island tarnished by conniving fairies and corrupt elves. And so, it wasn't some silly pet project. Much like Brad, Max had never shown a crumb of interest in her book, even going so far as to call her a furry in denial. He wasn't much of a writer, with the exception of a short story he'd once written about an anthropomorphic cheese sandwich who had superpowers, Cheese-man.

She'd been doing sketches while they waited, but now, she put her pencil down since she couldn't concentrate. *Don't think Max's always been this barmy. Ever since the museum break-in, it's been a downward spiral. He would make a great mad scientist. Shame his only ambitions are cryptic crosswords and Tetris high scores. Why does he call me Eeyore when he's negative about everything?*

"Judge Beaton also glibly suggested I was insane," Max recalled. "But I could *beat* him in a duel any day. That chair, or should I say iron chair, would give any reasonable person sciatica. I've always been of the view that bipedalism is overrated. Horizontality is much more comfortable. I may stay like this indefinitely."

"The cement floor is better? I agree with Brad sometimes: you're a nut."

"That's ad hominem."

Seconds later, funnily enough, Brad texted her:

```
Where are you? I thought you'd be cooking me dinner tonight.
I had to eat cereal. You know I love Coco Pops, but not for
supper. Why are you so unreliable lately?
```

Rosie tucked her phone away as Max continued reciting words. Brad remained somewhat of a problem. She'd decided to separate from him a while ago but had not yet found the right moment to do it. Every time she began to tell him, he would start going on and on about football or tattoos, and she would get distracted. *I wonder if I could just do it over the phone. Is that too mean? Or pay a pilot to write it in the sky.*

It had been four hours since the gunshot, but it felt like it had only occurred four minutes ago. Every time she remembered that somebody had tried to shoot them dead, a surreal sense of unreality pierced her. It was just too horrifying.

Max speculated that the assassin had climbed onto the roof of Poolway Shopping Centre across from Norman Court, pulled out a sniper rifle and aimed at them. They had *many* reasons to want to kill him in particular, such as the threat he posed in the quiz championship and on the Tetris scoreboard. She didn't know how much weight to put into his suspicions though. For a month, he'd once become convinced that Stapleford had been invaded by murderous clowns following a chilling nightmare about Stephen King's *It*. Unlike Rosie, Max didn't handle horror well, having projectile vomited when they went to see *Saw* and cried at *The Phantom of the Opera*.

As she doodled absently, she remembered seeing her life flash before her eyes—her perennially unfinished children's book, Theodore Tabby; her invariably unpaid student debts; her disaster of a love life. If the bullet had fired just inches differently, she would be six feet under right now.

Rosie played with her pencil and stared at the ceiling pensively. *Life is so fragile. And I take everything for granted, don't I? Maybe I should become one of those people who say carpe diem. Carpe diem. No, it's not me.*

"Oh, fine. I'll sit in the blasted chair," Max said, and plopped himself onto the seat. "I lost my place in the id words. Do you think *idiot savant* counts as a single word?"

"You should know," she muttered.

It was at that moment that a familiar police officer came in. Constable Tomlinson clomped into the questioning room, his grumpy face wrinkling like cracked cement.

"Nice to see you again, Maxwell and Rosie," Constable Tomlinson uttered with a self-assured inflexion, nodding to them. He sat. "I've just been informed of what happened. You have had quite a day, haven't you?"

"Yes, we have," Max agreed. "And it's not at all nice to see you, if I'm being honest."

"Max! Be polite," she said brusquely, slapping his wrist. "Nice to see you too, Constable."

This feels just like an Agatha Christie novel. If only Miss Marple were here, Max would have a field day. Theodore Tabby would be better, of course.

"I heard you got off scot-free for the museum incident, Maxwell. How lucky for you," Constable Tomlinson continued, shooting him a scornful look. "I wouldn't have been so generous. I just hope I don't hear anything about you and treasure hunting for the rest of my life."

"I don't suppose a huge fine and community service could be considered lucky by any metric, even in an infinite multiverse," he replied haughtily. "Unless you consider lucky as referring to abominably unfair and extreme punishments. I may well be the modern Jean Valjean."

"Shut it. Should I even ask about that, cowboy?" the constable quipped, pointing at his hat.

Max tipped its rim. "No, I wouldn't if I were you. It's beyond your understanding."

"I'll get straight to the point. My colleagues and I have evaluated all possibilities, and come to the conclusion that the gunshot was a simple stray bullet. Thankfully, that means I can assure you both that there is absolutely nothing to worry about."

"Really?" Rosie asked, on the edge of her seat. "Can't you give us some more details?"

"Yes, mam," Constable Tomlinson said, looking sure of himself. "A hunter called the station shortly after the incident and confessed to misfiring while passing through town. Unfortunately, he called anonymously and left no contact details. We will investigate this individual concerning the removal of his gun licence, but as for you two, the police should be gone from your residence tomorrow, and you'll be free to return. I believe that in a few months you will see this as a funny story."

"I see," Rosie said, running her fingers through her hair.

Max stared at them both, mouth hanging open. "I can't deny that I find your deductions elementary, my dear Constable Tomlinson. Are we to believe that some random person misfired by complete chance in exactly the direction it smashed through my window? And I suppose John Wilkes Booth just happened to shoot Abraham Lincoln by pure coincidence, too? I do hope this is all an elaborate joke, and you're not really so shockingly incompetent."

"Stray bullets are not particularly uncommon for your information, although they don't usually go through windows in the middle of town, I'll admit," the constable divulged pointedly. "I think it's something like fifty-seven people die from them every year."

"Wow. Fifty-seven?" she repeated. "How? Guns are illegal in this country."

"I meant globally. But guns can be attained here for hunting purposes with a firearms certificate."

Max blinked distrustfully. Rosie could tell by his disapproving expression and his history of diehard scepticism in regard to the Nottingham Police Department that he wouldn't let this go easily.

"Maybe it was the gun fairy, then!" he said resentfully. "I'll tell you a titbit that may be of relevance. There's this abandoned shopping mall across from Norman Court, and weird noises from there always wake me up in the night. That's also exactly where the bullet came from."

A stray bullet... It does sound somewhat odd. Max has a point. It's too convenient.

She nodded. "Yeah, Max was telling me this. Honestly, I agree with him. A stray bullet seems incredibly improbable."

"I wouldn't pay any attention to the twaddle Maxwell says. You're kinda smart, aren't you, son?" the constable sneered at him. "Have you heard of Occam's razor? It means the simplest explanation is the best. Regardless, I'd be happy to support a larger investigation should you present cogent evidence or conceivable suspects."

"Very well. It's clear to me," Max said, peering seriously at Rosie. "Brad must have done it."

A flummoxed pause fell over the questioning room.

"Brad?! Have you lost your mind, Max?" Rosie lashed out, shell-shocked. "He's never even touched a gun."

"You've certainly got some cheek, Maxwell. Whoever this Brad fellow is," Constable Tomlinson scorned. He rose. "I've had quite enough of this. The case is closed."

"Thank you so, so much for doing nothing in the laziest way possible!" Max shouted, as he kicked the table over and charged out. "I will write to the thesaurus right now and request they put your name down as a synonym of the word *incompetent*."

"Hey, I'll do the same for your name for the word *insane*!" Constable Tomlinson retorted.

"I'm so, so sorry about him, Constable Tomlinson," Rosie said, threading her fingers before following him. "He's rude to everyone. It's not just you."

"That pompous wise guy should thank his lucky stars he's not in prison for that tongue of his. I could keep him here and charge him for his disrespect, but I think I'd lose my mind if I spent any more time with him. My nephew, Eddie, knew him in school and told me he was always a bad egg. He's fortunate to have a friend like you. Keep an eye on him."

Not sure whether to be more embarrassed or relieved, Rosie caught up with Max as he stomped out of Nottingham City Police Station and to the bus stop. He wouldn't stop complaining about Constable Tomlinson for a second.

By now, night had fallen on Nottingham, and the lights from suburban houses shimmered like fires in the dark. Clubbers who smelled of dodgy drugs surrounded the bus stop, drinking liquor and snogging.

Rosie glanced at them as she and Max came to the stop. "You don't want a lift?"

"I'll survive," he said, carelessly passing by the kissing partiers as he slouched over and looked at the bus schedule. "I can't wait for Khalil to hear about this. He's gonna be well impressed; I survived an assassination! A new box ticked off the bucket list."

"Huh, you've got a few ones this year. Where're you gonna sleep tonight?"

"Sofia told me where the library's spare key is," Max revealed. "The books will have to be my pillows."

"That sounds *totally* legal," Rosie said, and inspired a deep breath. "Listen, I've been thinking about this whole stray bullet thing, and even if it's not true, whatever happened really puts life in perspective, doesn't it? We could have died. We could be rotting in graves right now. I don't want to waste time from now on. I'm going to do things sooner rather than later."

"How profound, Guru Rosie," he quipped. "Next, you're gonna start preaching about the power of now and chakras. I wouldn't be in a grave at any rate; I have a feeling that when I die, my corpse will be stuffed and displayed at the British Museum."

"Oh, stop taking the mickey! You acted ridiculous enough in there."

"I'm convinced that Constable Tomlinson is corrupt. He's the uncle of that pillock, Eddie from the Children's Society. I bet he *knows* it wasn't a stray bullet and is covering for someone," he explained fiercely. "But I am sorry about my behaviour. I'm just getting so sick of everything. I wish the vagaries of life would start going my way already. They've been heading in the completely wrong direction for so long now. It's probably all my fault."

The bus arrived, and as the drunken crowd boarded it, one of them pointed at Max, barking, "Nice hat, nonce!"

"Whatever. We'll meet up later this week, and we can discuss this further," Rosie said, a yawn arriving in the back of her throat. "And I probably shouldn't say this but...if you want to be a treasure hunter, *be* a treasure hunter. Ignore what anybody else says, even Judge Beaton. There's no way he could realistically find out. I realise I can't stop you anymore. It's your dream."

"Wow... Seriously? I'll get started tonight on the Ark of the Covenant and Blackbeard's Gold!" he said, grinning. "Thanks. That means the world."

As Max boarded the bus and it vanished into the night, Rosie felt like a kettle that had just finished boiling. Everything she'd ever wanted to say—but had stopped herself for whatever reason—bubbled inside of her. She knew what she should do first.

CHAPTER 16

A ROGUISH RUSE

It took Khalil a full thirty minutes to count all the fifty-pound notes on the carpet of his apartment. He had organised them into batches of a thousand, secured with elastic bands. Every penny was intended for Aaron's initial extortion payment.

He crouched over and gazed at the stacks of cash, stress-eating from an open pack of Jammie Dodgers and a bag of Percy Pigs. His stomach writhed as he recalled what he'd done to acquire the money. He'd been short of money plenty of times before, scrounging just to afford dinner. It'd been difficult for him to reject Aaron's work offers in the past. However, he couldn't remember ever resorting to such desperate measures for cash.

When I was a child, this would've seemed like a fortune. Now it's just paper and ink.

"D'you think treasure hunting just exists in films?" the radio thrummed, a dirt cheap one he'd bought from an Argos when selling some of his things. "Apparently, you're one of the normal people in this country who hasn't heard of The Crystalline Crucible, a mystifying treasure hunting contest that's been puzzling jobless basement dwellers this year. It's said to be run by an organisation that's recruiting intelligent individuals. They could've just hired me! Word on the street is that a cunning treasure hunter is getting close to solving the final clue."

Blinking, Khalil wiggled his eyebrows before turning the radio off. He focused his attention on the payment situation. The regrettable reality was that he hadn't been able to come up with all the money he needed, even after gambling and stealing from the till.

Nonetheless, he had a trick up his sleeve.

The week prior, he had discovered a website selling counterfeit cash on the dark web and, following extensive consideration, made a large order. He knew all about the dark web from some assignments Aaron had given him back in the day. A batch of extremely realistic fake notes had come three days ago, and he hoped to God that Aaron wouldn't notice the difference. The money he *had* stolen and won from gambling was now sitting in his safe, hidden under the bed.

It was an extremely roguish ruse, but could it work? Khalil wasn't convinced. But he knew one thing: he didn't want to be a coward anymore, always running away from his past. It didn't work the first time in London, and so for now, he refused to leave Stapleford. If he could play a minor role in the fall of the Black Dog Disciples, he'd do it. To trick Aaron into using counterfeit cash had a small chance of leading the police to his gang, or if nothing else, it'd feel good to cheat him. In addition, Khalil had decided he wasn't going to take a penny more from the Johnson family.

It'd just passed eight-thirty a.m., less than half an hour before the meeting time. Khalil wasn't entirely sure where the Costa Coffee was. One by one, he picked up all the note batches and deposited them into a recently purchased blue duffel bag. He left his apartment and leapt down the exterior spiral staircase, grateful not to have been stopped by Mr Brooks's ravings for once as he got in his car and drove away.

Twenty minutes later, he locked his car and strode into Costa Coffee. He looked around for a few moments before concluding that Aaron hadn't arrived yet. He ordered a tea and sat to wait.

An hour dragged by. Aaron still hadn't shown up. Eventually, Khalil's phone rang, yet it wasn't Aaron.

"Yes, Max?" he greeted with a sigh.

"Khalil, you won't believe it!" Max screamed through the speaker. "It's the most shocking thing that's ever occurred in the universe's history!"

Stunned, Khalil jolted forward. "What?"

"They are discontinuing lemon cream pie Pop-Tarts. First, it was cinnamon roll, and now this! What is the world coming to? I am going to write a strongly worded letter to the Queen to see if there's anything she can do about this. Kellogg's is a total disgrace."

Khalil grunted and sipped his tea. "That's great, Max. But I'm kind of busy. I'll see you and your, uh, rosy friend in a couple of hours. Thanks for inviting her."

But Max wasn't finished. "Wait! One more thing. An assassin tried to kill me and Rosie!"

"*What*?!" he exclaimed, spitting out his tea.

Khalil couldn't tell if Max was joking at first, but then he remembered Max barely had a sense of humour. He couldn't believe it. Aaron, or one of his men, had tried to shoot Max and his friend, Rosie. They must have. Who else could it be?

Khalil hung up as Aaron strolled in, right when Max asked him if he knew anywhere that might have spare stock of lemon cream pie Pop-Tarts. He watched Aaron order an Americano and recline on a cushioned armchair across from him, smug face behind the steaming cup.

"Aren't you going to say hi?" Aaron asked. His teal eyes pored over Khalil like a surgeon over a patient.

What a guy. He arrives an hour late and still acts like a diva to me. The gall...

"You're late," Khalil said, lowering his voice in fear of idle ears.

"I'm so very sorry," Aaron stated flatly. He joined his fingers, and Khalil noticed his expensive, freshly dry-cleaned suit. "I got caught up with some work. This place is a dump, isn't it? I only chose a public venue so that you'd feel reassured. In London, I always dine at the finest restaurants available."

It seemed like a perfectly nice cafe to Khalil, in spite of a few leaves blowing along the floor and some dirty tables. "High standards? Do you eat caviar for breakfast nowadays?"

"I suppose I do like luxury. But it's not my fault the hoi polloi of Albion are content with living in borderline squalor," he said in a disdainful tone. "So, have you got the money?"

Khalil's eyes narrowed to slits. "Yes. But before I give it to you, how can I trust anything you say if your gang is shooting my mates now?"

Aaron forced a laugh. "What?"

"So, you're going to try to convince me that it's just a coincidence that a bullet crashed through my mate's window the other day? Not long after you threatened to chop his hand off?" Khalil said. "I'm not buying it."

"Very well. I'd hoped this wouldn't come out," Aaron averred. "It's a bit embarrassing. In short, it was just an accident. I asked one of my newest men to watch that wacko you've been hanging out with. He mentioned that he was testing a sniper rifle with no intent to actually shoot, and it accidentally misfired. I made him ring the police and anonymously give a phoney excuse to avoid a large investigation."

"So, he was testing guns on *people*?!" Khalil asked in disbelief. "Try a gun range!"

"He told me he was just excited to try it out," Aaron stated, waving his hand impatiently. "It was a M2010 Enhanced Sniper Rifle that he'd ordered off the dark web. Accidents happen. I won't deny that I've been having him follow your eccentric new buddy to see what you've been doing with him."

"Is this the Tommy guy whose hand you chopped off? That one I met?"

"No, of course not. A highly experienced assassin. I only hire the finest. He's excellent at disguises. Even the pros make mistakes sometimes. Don't they say that about football, too?"

Highly experienced? And yet he accidentally shoots rifles? That's not even an easy thing to do. Khalil thought back. Aaron knew about his aptitude on a football pitch because he had first met him when he was still playing for his school team. Aaron had even come to his matches and cheered for him on occasion, which Khalil had realised later was to manipulate him into stealing for him. The Black Dog Disciples were primarily involved in drug-related activities, but they also engaged in robbery in certain cases, such as the theft of the rings that Khalil had sold.

He hesitated. "That's ridiculous, but whatever. I have another question. Why are you making such a big deal out of this jewellery? Surely, it costs you way more to have your men stalking me than to just forget it."

"Well, the truth is—and don't laugh at this—it's not all that much about the money. The fact is I sometimes think of you as the son I never had. I hate to see you wasting your life on this photography nonsense. I want you working for me. I always have, but you're leaving me no choice but to take this route. Besides, I'm not in Nottinghamshire solely for you. I'm always trying to expand the business," Aaron said, and sucked in his right cheek.

"A son? I think I'd rather be the son of Satan than you," Khalil snapped. "You need to go back to drug lord school. You could've saved both of us a lot of time. I never wanted to be a drug dealer. I have ambitions."

At that, Aaron frowned. "Your *photography* ambitions? Yeah, right… I've had enough. Hand over the bag. Or have you made me come to this hovel of a town again for nothing? Stapleford is so miserable I'm surprised all the locals haven't already shot themselves. That bullet would've been doing that Maxwell a favour."

Khalil gulped. Aaron knew Max's name.

Either way, Khalil found it unexpectedly easy to give Aaron the money, knowing it was all fake. Indeed, he had to stop himself from smiling.

Aaron made sure to dramatise the handover; he petted the blue bag like a poodle before slipping it onto his shoulder. He proceeded to ramble for a period about how things with the Black Dog Disciples were going in London. Apparently, business was booming as of late after a little gang war with the Lambeth Lads over some contested territory.

“Pleasure doing business with you,” Aaron concluded at last, extending his hand.

Khalil promptly declined to take it.

“So rude,” Aaron said, sneering. “I’ll let you know if the money’s satisfactory in due time. If so, see you soon for the next payment. But I am going to ask my associates to examine every single note, and if I find you’re trying any funny games, the next shots won’t be accidents.”

“There is no such thing as accidents. They are fate misnamed,” Khalil said.

Aaron didn’t respond. Instead, he paced out with an eye-roll and disappeared into the rush-hour crowd.

CHAPTER 17

THE CODE CRACKER

It had been over two weeks since the assassination attempt, but as Max turned the corner and almost got eaten by a feral flock of swans, he reminded himself that he couldn't let his guard down for a moment. He'd noticed an awful lot of sketchy people stalking him recently. *Someone* was following him. He hadn't yet worked out whether it was the Mafia or the Yakuza.

Having taken a break from building a Lego Taj Mahal, he was on the way to a meeting. Although, it wasn't any normal meeting. Both Rosie and Khalil had been invited.

Since the information they were going to discuss was more than a little confidential, Khalil had wisely suggested they meet at an unfrequented park, The Arboretum. It was a local botanical collection that was open to the public, decorated with endless allegedly interesting trees and supposedly pretty lichen-covered rocks.

After a few minutes of searching, he spotted Rosie sitting on the grass, her hair falling over her shoulders like a chocolate fountain. Her back rested on the moss-swallowed statue of a dead worthy, the spot where they'd agreed to meet. Rosie's nose was buried deep in a maths book titled *Gödel, Escher, Bach: An Eternal Golden Braid.*

"How's things, Buffalo Bill?" she asked, looking up as she put her book aside. "Forgotten your chaps?"

Max pouted arrogantly. He loved his cowboy hat, no matter what anyone said. Being a cowboy was so much fun; maybe next he'd become a Viking. Besides that, he sported cheap plastic sunglasses, odd socks and an old T-shirt that had a faded imprint of Thomas the Tank Engine, having thrown out his Pingu one following the negative feedback from the English judiciary.

"Outstanding, thanks," he answered, a frown tugging on the corners of his mouth. "Mortally afraid for my life, but aside from that, top-notch. Excuse me if my head explodes in the next two minutes and a skull fragment gets in your eye. I hear stray bullets are exceptionally common this time of year."

"If you say so. We might as well relax then while we wait for your friend," she said, and lay back.

Max followed suit and reclined on the grass, letting the warmth beam down as he squinted up at the sunny skies. The instant a dog barked in the distance, he slid over onto his belly and pulled out his new weapon following the loss of Fleshrender.

"Are you still alive?" Rosie asked placidly. "That was a dog. You've heard of them, right? The ones that go woof? Like Gromit?"

"I'm familiar. I prefer bearded dragons though," he muttered and displayed his laser pointer. "See this? I bought it for self-defence, along with invisible ink, a spy microphone pen, hidden camera glasses and walkie-talkies. It's a high-powered laser pointer. You're blind for at least a week if the laser hits your eye for even a second. I tried to get a bow and arrows, but they were sold out on the weapons website."

"Maybe you should get a silver hammer instead," she said as he juggled it in his hands.

But when Max pointed the laser pointer at a blade of grass, and smoke started to rise, she did not appear quite so sceptical anymore.

"Wow. That is cool," she said in awe.

"It's a discontinued model because it blinded children. Desperate times call for desperate measures," he said, highly strung. "I would've just got a taser, but turns out they're prohibited."

He practised drawing it from his pocket like in a Wild West gun draw.

"Well, I'm glad you're no longer the English Don Quixote. That phase went on for over a year. You have enough interests for ten people. Remember when you used to be a ninja?"

Max lolled back and tried to enjoy the ebullient sun again, but frankly, he did not see what was all that enjoyable about exposing himself to an increased skin cancer risk and, in the meantime, sweating unpleasantly. Besides, he had something he needed to talk about.

"Rosie, listen. I, uh, need to beseech you about something," he vocalised.

"Oh, great," she grumbled. "I can just tell I'm gonna *love* this."

And so, he told her the story of all that had happened after he found the mammoth tusk clue until everything was off his chest.

"Ergo, that's when I realised the clue was hidden in the Olde Crown Hotel guest book," he explained like he was dictating his autobiography.

"Why didn't you tell me?" Rosie cried.

"Your irascibility. The point is, well, we need your help to solve the next clue—if you'd be so kind."

She sat up. "Because I know about maths?"

"Yes. It's a numerical sort of clue. A number grid. So, what do you think?"

"What do *I* think?" she repeated, cheeks reddening. "What did you expect me to say? *No problem! I'll help you break the law*. I don't want to get in trouble with your probation officer. Forget what I said at the bus stop. I was exhausted after being in that police station for hours, okay? Do you really want to risk prison for this?"

Rosie's point was undoubtedly a good one. However, before Max could reply, Khalil appeared on the horizon.

"Sorry I'm late," Khalil huffed, out of breath. He sat on the grass next to them, looking harried as if he'd just come from a particularly stressful morning. Max couldn't imagine why since neither of them worked that day. "Lovely day, eh?"

It was more than odd for Khalil to meet Rosie at last, akin to a Detective Poirot and Miss Marple crossover. Max wasn't entirely sure he liked it.

"Delightful," Rosie said uncertainly. She and Max twisted around and sat cross-legged, facing Khalil. She reached over, and they shook hands. "So good to meet Agatha Quiztie's newest team member. Khalil, right? Or should I say Dr Ahmed?"

"What? Oh, Agatha Quiztie. How could I forget?" Khalil replied as though it'd completely slipped his mind he'd agreed to join. "Thanks for having me. Rosie, is it?"

"That's what my parents told me."

"Sorry for lying to you about Max being sick and all," Khalil apologised.

"I'm just astonished you believed Maxwell enough to go all the way to Bath," Rosie said.

"Please don't refer to me in the third person. I've just told Rosie the scandalous truth," Max revealed. He turned to her. "So, are you up for helping to solve the clue?"

She shot him a look both outraged and nonplussed. "Of course not! Why would I?"

"But Rosie, when we win, think how much money we could get. We'd be instant kajillionaires."

"You don't know that!" Rosie hit back. "It's all speculation."

"You could quit your job, pay off your student debt and move to wherever you want. Didn't you always want to go on a world cruise? And remember, after the gunshot, you said that you had decided to support my treasure hunting career." Max exhaled, becoming inflamed. "I've really had enough of this, Rosie. You're the most cynical person I know, a complete and utter negative Nancy. *Eat food other than Brussels sprouts and cheese sandwiches, or you'll get ill. Quit stealing from the library because ten books at a time is enough. Don't put your hand into the lion cage, or you'll get your fingers bitten off.*"

"I was right on all those occasions!" she rebutted, infuriated.

"I still have all my fingers, don't I? The truth is you're a no-man, or no-woman. Just a general no-person. And you never smile. Not the Duchenne smile. The real kind."

"Rosie, have you heard about the prize?" Khalil, who Max had almost forgotten was present, interrupted. "Besides, we may be the only people who know this clue. Just think how cool it would be if we win."

She stayed silent for a few fraught seconds. Her nose twitched and she bit her nails. "I do need money. I'm way behind on rent. Let me have a look at it."

As soon as Max showed her the number grid, Rosie's eyes glinted with intrigue. She requested a pen. She then jotted down some notes on the back of her hand, and started to speculate that the grid must be a cipher. "I mean, it *has* to be. Maybe some kind of encrypted address?"

"What's a cipher?" Khalil asked. He leaned over her shoulder.

"A way to convert numbers to intelligible letters."

Max didn't want to sound like a know-it-all, but the question was not whether it was a cipher but which *kind.* Over the past few weeks, he'd spied on Amelia's TreasureNet account to see what she was getting up to. In suspicious fashion, she had posted recently:

```
Do you guys know any good books about ciphers? Just asking.
It's for a personal project.
```

Throbbinhood420 and wombraider69 also seemed to be doing well in the contest. They kept harassing Max with private messages—telling him that they'd won ages ago and that he should give up. He didn't understand where they had found that picture of him that they had cruelly photoshopped to make him look like he was a bedraggled tramp.

"I know what it could be. Wait. What's it called…" she mumbled, mulling it over. "A Caesar cipher, the code cracker. It's a type of substitution cipher in which the numbers are switched for letters, and then the letters should be replaced by other letters that are some number of positions up or down the alphabet."

"We'll have to go to Khalil's apartment to try it out," Max asserted, and sprung to his feet. "Thanks so much for that, Khalil."

"I kinda feel put upon, mate, but I guess," Khalil said, lip twisted like a corkscrew. "Haven't cleaned though. It is a bit of a mess."

"Fine," Rosie said darkly. "I'll come, but I don't want you to get the wrong idea, Max. Don't let this make you think I approve. *I* can legally do this, not you. *You* could end up in prison. Maybe you should just stay away."

"Don't worry, Mummy. I'll be a good boy," Max joshed. "I just have to make my probation officer think I believe that treasure hunting is out of fashion and uncool. As if. I must see her in an hour actually. Such fun."

Judging by Rosie's increasingly positive attitude, Max was starting to think that Khalil could have been right to let her in on the clue. That said, questions now surfaced about how his partnership with Khalil was to work if there were a third member. Would she want to help them beyond this clue?

When they arrived at Khalil's apartment, he could, for the first time, appreciate how much his co-worker must be struggling with money. Hamlet House was perhaps the most unpleasant tower block in Nottinghamshire. Half of the building work remained unfinished, shifty thugs lurked around the corners and a thick miasma of cigarette smoke lingered everywhere. Max didn't have high standards. Norman Court was nothing to write home about either, but at least the building wasn't falling apart.

As soon as Khalil opened his door, his neighbour's one swung forward too, like the doors were roped together. Out of it stepped a musty, ancient man with pupils that appeared magnetised together.

"Excuse me, Muhammad. You have to get my permission to have visitors!" he complained, spit flying out of his mouth. By the look of his woolly jumper, which was covered with tea stains and full of holes, he hadn't changed clothes in weeks. "The rumpus you've been making these past few days has been giving me a headache!"

"What are you talking about, Mr Brooks? I haven't been making any bloody noise," Khalil grunted, flinching. "And my name's not Muhammad. It's Khalil."

"Balderdash! I've had enough of your ruckus with you alone, and now you're bringing along these hoodlums. Here I am innocently trying to enjoy my retirement and watch reruns of the lovely angel, Mary Berry, on *The Great British Bake Off*. And you disturb me!"

Max decided to intervene. "Excuse me, sir. What's your name?"

Mr Brooks glowered at him and raised his walking stick like a sword. "What was that, you little lout?"

"He asked for your name!" Khalil shouted, before turning to Max and Rosie. "The old fogey can't hear a thing unless you yell. His hearing aid is broken, and he never bothers to fix it. Pretty sure he's just lonely. He's gone on and on about a fictitious ruckus as well as people watching him for months."

"I'm Mr Albert Brooks, a veteran of the Falklands War! Not that it should be any of your concern!" Mr Brooks yelled. "I bet it's you and your fellow hoodie-wearing yobs who come around here in the night with your van to stalk me. Bog off!"

"I WAS JUST GOING TO SAY, MR BROOKS, THAT MAYBE YOU HAVE SCHIZOPHRENIA. AUDITORY HALLUCINATIONS ARE A SYMPTOM ACCORDING TO MY ENCYCLOPAEDIA!" Max shouted so loudly that everyone went quiet for a few seconds. "OR PERHAPS MORE LIKELY JUST PLAIN DEMENTIA!"

Mr Brooks' temper sparked. He stomped his walking stick on the floor. "I've not lost my mind, if that's what you're saying, you scallywag! You have!"

"OH, THAT'S MATURE!" he howled at the top of his lungs.

Utterly incensed, Mr Brooks struck him across the shoulder with his cane.

"Ouch!" Max cried.

"How dare you speak to your elders like that? How many wars did you fight in for Her Majesty?" demanded Mr Brooks.

"INCLUDING PREVIOUS LIVES? TWO."

"You don't need to be that loud, Max. Come on, you guys," Khalil said, gesturing Max and Rosie inside his flat. "Let's leave Mr Brooks alone."

"Pay attention, Max," Rosie warned as Max rubbed his aching shoulder.

"That'll be you in a few years if you don't change things: a crazy old man."

"You mean man-child."

They dodged Mr Brooks' cane and entered the flat.

As soon as they stepped inside, Khalil began to apologise about the dirtiness of his place. "It's in such a state… I would have cleaned…"

Despite the beer bottles, cigarette butts and dirty plates scattered pell-mell, Max found the place kind of cosy.

The first interesting discovery he made was a bill addressed to someone whose name sounded both different and yet oddly similar to Khalil Ahmed, a so-called Charlie Almond. It was sitting on the kitchen table.

However, by far the most intriguing thing in the apartment could be found in the bedroom, which contained a vast collection of photos that had been taken all over Stapleford on the walls. It was an incredibly diverse gallery, and a lot of them looked pretty good, too.

Max gasped. "Wow. These are all yours?" He stared at the hundreds of Polaroids. "There's a photo for everything: the Co-op, the library and even that horrible spot where all the drunks piss! How did you get so talented?"

"Max, get out of my bedroom!" Khalil shouted, and herded him away. "I'd appreciate it if you don't treat my apartment like a museum."

"It's cool is all. I'm a bit bamboozled, though. Why do you take so many photos of this dump?"

"I dunno. I think a photographer should find beauty in the mundane," he said, glancing shyly up at the ceiling. "Would you prefer I take photographs of stunning models or your beloved Ithaca?"

Channelling his inner cowboy, Max told them that there was no time for more wrangling, the imperative clear. Khalil lent Rosie his laptop, and they all gathered around his table, watching her analyse the code. Max's and Khalil's eyes were transfixed on the screen as she undertook Gordian knot-esque and Grigori Perelman-esque calculations to decipher the numbers.

It speedily became obvious this was going to take a while. Max noticed the clock. It was nearly time for his first shift of community service and meeting with his probation officer. Cursing, he got to his feet. It was looking to be a deeply unpleasant afternoon, but he had to do it, or he really would end up in prison.

"Keep me updated about how you get on," he said blankly. "I pray you triumph like Wyatt Earp at the O.K. Corral."

"Cheers," Khalil said, hardly paying attention.

"It does seem like you've made me look like something of a hypocrite, Maxwell!" Rosie added, glancing over the screen.

"Huzzah. I'll take that to mean you've changed your ways for good," Max said, and left before she could protest. Once he was out of the door, he muttered, "Goody two-shoes."

When Max arrived at the Stapleford Community Centre, which incidentally was the venue for the rapidly approaching Stapleford Quiz Championship, he first had to talk to his grouchy probation officer. She was a short, squat middle-aged woman named Janet Cooper, who had stale breath and a lethargic, insipid voice. It was quite clear that she was just a pencil pusher; Max was not looking forward to seeing her once a month for the next year.

"Have you consumed any illicit drugs in the past month, Mr Jacobs?" the probation officer drawled, turning a page of her bulky sheet of notes.

They sat in a tiny, fresh paint-smelling office, surrounded by folders and staplers. The questioning was taking forever, and Max was increasingly famished for a good puzzle.

"Drugs? I don't think so. Unless the intoxicating methamphetamine of crosswords count," he quipped. He didn't usually joke, but was bored out of his mind. "Sorry. That was just a facetious bon mot!"

"This isn't the time for comedy, Mr Jacobs," Ms Cooper said disapprovingly, brow rising. She looked down at her papers. "I almost forgot. Have you pursued any treasure hunting activities in the past month? I certainly hope not."

"No, no," he said hastily. "I would never brook myself to get involved in that awful treasure hunting business ever again! Once bitten, twice shy. The only thing I treasure hunt for now is a life of virtue and probity."

"A simple no is sufficient," she replied petulantly.

The rest of the questioning didn't go too badly, but Ms Cooper did complain about several of Max's "choice remarks", such as when he suggested Stapleford should be renamed to Stapehellford.

Soon enough, it was community service time. Max was put into a group of ten and given a yellow vest and a rubbish picker, and they set off down the streets of Stapleford. It was about as much fun as working in the Co-op under Mr Johnson, who had been particularly awful lately, constantly threatening to fire him unless he "got his act together." The incident that had most enraged David was probably when Max had sold a hundred-pound lottery ticket for one pound, not to mention when he spilled hot coffee all over the open cash register and broke it.

Max longed to be fishing on the coast of Ithaca as he shuffled along the cracked pavement, poking crisp bags and dropping them into the orange bin bags. The first ten minutes passed like ten hours, and he was already fed up. He had accidentally stepped in somebody's sick more than once. Trudging up and down the road for hours on end while being treated like a walking rubbish bin by the supervisor—a surly elderly lady in the vein of Margaret Thatcher—wasn't a ball. While he was desperate to see what if any progress Rosie and Khalil were making, it was also eating into his precious conlang creation time.

The morning's bright weather didn't last past noon. Dreary clouds emerged and spat down on them all as if God was trying to say, "Bwahaha. Maxwell, this is what you get for continuing to treasure hunt! Just wait for what's to come!"

Max gazed around at the undead-like faces of his fellow volunteers, who looked like they'd forgotten what happiness was. Life *had* to be better than this. As he lost himself in a dream of stepping into his Ithaca poster, drooling at the images of deck chairs, lemonade and a beautiful beach sunset, the rubbish bag slipped out of his grip and all the trash tumbled out.

Four p.m. neared, and Max felt as though he had travelled several parsecs and climbed more than one stairway to Heaven to boot. The other volunteers were muttering indistinctly that they were getting sick of this too, and he seriously considered mounting a Cromwell-style rebellion.

As he picked up a flyer for *Britain's Got Talent* auditions, which he had gone to once but didn't get past the auditions, he decided rubbish was better off in the streets. What harm did it do there? The pavement didn't mind at all. Dropping the flyer into the bag, he noticed something out of the corner of his eye that made him wince and gasp at the same time.

The Children's Society.

As his eyes fell over the aluminium gates, the mortar chimney and the buff renovated church itself, he felt as if the assassin had just shot at him again—hitting his lungs. It was in this building that he had spent much of the first eighteen painful years of his life. He only had a few fond memories here: where he'd undertaken his earliest efforts in treasure hunting; where he had read his first ghost story; and where he had learned what a crossword was. Many of them included being called a "spaz" and other not so charming names. Merely the sight of the building evoked bilious dread in his gut.

Someone stepped out of the building with the trash. Max's hands and feet got pins and needles as he recognised who it was. Ms Kensington. She looked significantly older than when he had known her, her hair greying and her ageing skin textured like sandpaper. But it was definitely her. She glanced at him, put the trash bag in the bin and returned inside.

Words escaped Max, even though nobody was there to speak with him. He had not seen Ms Kensington for three years, the woman who had essentially raised him after his mother's death. Despite only a relatively small amount of time having passed, she didn't recognise him at all. Was it the cowboy hat? Or had *he* changed? How sad to think.

I need to get a grip on myself! My mind and molecular constitution should be an indomitable fortress, and yet I'm besieged by the spectres of the past. It's as Khalil said: I'm still a bird born in a cage.

And then, an astonishing, life-altering thought struck Max: he was a grown-up!

In two shakes of a lamb's tail, Rosie interrupted his epiphany as his phone beeped with a text:

`Come to Khalil's flat ASAP. We cracked the code!`

CHAPTER 18

THE ELABORATE DISGUISE

Khalil glared at the tattoo exhibition of a footballer facing him. Maybe he was imagining it, but ignoring the endless tattoos the man's face and buck teeth distinctly resembled a beaver. Either way, he was acting like a total prick. The two stood in the middle of the local stadium's mud-caked pitch, a blanket of clouds bathing them in shadows that coagulated like curds below the temperamental sky.

"So, you wanna join the team, eh?" the team captain, who'd moments prior told Khalil that his name was Nobody, asked. He had an undeniably supercilious air to him, and glared at Khalil as though he was a cat auditioning to play a dog. "What experience do you have?"

"Once in the London Seniors Tournament, my team came third out of several hundred, if I remember correctly," Khalil mumbled, juggling the football with his foot. Max would be so proud.

"Third? You think that's good?" Nobody remarked. "No offence, man, but this isn't just a random club. It's a *professional* football team."

One other teammate, seemingly Nobody's friend, stood on the pitch lines in a football uniform. He'd followed them like a third wheel and made football comments every now and then.

"Did you see that ludicrous display last night?" he shouted over unrelatedly.

Now that Khalil had made his first payment to Aaron—real or not—and was on his way to settling into Stapleford, he'd decided it was high time to join the community and get to know more people than Maxwell. The local football club had seemed like a good place to start. Khalil had always had a fondness for the game and used to support Arsenal.

The need to order more counterfeit notes for the next payment to Aaron was still pressing on his mind. Maybe it was far-fetched, but Khalil hoped he and the others would win the Jewelled Chalice and the prize money before the due date, in which case it wouldn't be an issue. Upon winning, he could theoretically catch the next flight to the USA. That was why he, Rosie and Max were heading to London imminently to investigate the next clue.

"What do you mean it isn't just a club?" Khalil asked, bemused. He scratched his neck. "I read it was a club…"

"Maybe technically. But Stapleford Men's Football League doesn't just let any person with legs in, no sirree. We only accept the best."

The other player, a middle-aged moustached man, heckled, "Yup! Only the very best!"

Khalil's eyes darted between them. Both Nobody and Nobody's friend looked oddly familiar, but he supposed he was just having déjà vu.

"Oh, right," Khalil said. "I just haven't had much time to practise in recent years, mate. Been real busy. But I'm a real good forward and a decent dribbler."

"Are you nearly done?" the man on the pitch lines yelled.

"Stop butting in! No one cares!" Nobody howled at him. Rubbing the nape of his neck, the tattooed man turned back. "Sorry. I have no idea who that guy is and why he's following us. Anyways, I think we're done here."

"You haven't given me a fair shot. How about I show you my skills with some penalties?" Khalil grunted. He was at the end of his tether.

"Ah, do you really want to bother?"

"Why not?"

"I can just tell it's not going to change anything. To be honest, you just look a bit naff, mate, and I really don't think you're cut out for this."

Khalil wasn't sure it was possible for him to look more naff than his interlocutor. Besides his beaver face, his tattoos could've been done by a drunk. Be that as it may, he didn't have long to hang around before he had to meet up with Max and Rosie.

"Sorry. What's your name again?" Khalil asked, dribbling the football back and forth between his feet.

"Uh, I didn't actually say. It's Brad."

A realisation hit Khalil like a bucket of bricks dropped on his head. "I know you!" he exclaimed. "So, that's why you're acting like such a prick!"

Max had told Khalil about Bradley Thompson in the most hyperbolic way possible on more than one occasion, once referring to him as something like, "Rosie's demented, Caligula/Pol Pot/Hitler-cocktail psychopath of a partner and possibly the human incarnation of Lucifer." Max had also informed him the aforementioned spawn of Satan was an enthusiastic but untalented footballer.

"Yeah," Brad grunted, and gritted his teeth. "And you're Max's photographer co-worker, I guess."

"Yup," Khalil said, trainers sinking into the sticky pitch. "How's things, mate? Wake up on the wrong side of the bed this morning? Seems like the wrong side of the house too."

"What's going on?" the other man hollered.

"I suspected it was you. You're the reason Rosie called things off between us. You and Max!" Brad yelled, ignoring the football fan as he stomped his cleats into the turf.

Baffled, Khalil stared at the man with a hung lip. "How do you figure that, Brad?"

"I spotted you with Grouch when he was claiming to be ill. He even admitted it. And yet, despite the fact I was right all along, Rosie *still* split up with me, going on and on about how I was obsessed with him and how it wasn't a healthy relationship."

"Listen, Brad, it's none of my business, but can I say something?"

"Uh, no."

He continued regardless. "You need to forget Rosie already. Move on. Clearly, you were never going to let me join your dumb league. I don't want to anymore. You're a tosser, and I've had enough."

Khalil strode away towards the changing rooms.

"You were too crap to join, Paki! Why don't you go back to Iraq, along with the rest of you towelheads?" Brad screamed.

"I love staples too much."

"Say, why do you even hang out with Max, anyway? You do realise he's an Aspie? That Frankenstein monster had more of a soul."

"At least he's not racist like you. And my parents were *Afghan*. Not that it matters," he shot back over his shoulder. "I guess you're the type of person who thinks Africa is a single country, too. How about you read Rumi once in a while? 'Stop acting so small. You are the universe in ecstatic motion'."

"Afghan? What's that? Some country nobody has heard of?"

"Did he get in?" the other man shouted cluelessly.

Having changed back into normal clothes—a brown corduroy jacket and faded jeans—Khalil headed straight for his car. It was afternoon already; the sky was as grey as cement, which meant he ought to be off to meet Rosie and Max any second now.

He and Max had been working like dogs in the shop all week. Khalil was starting to relish the weekends like he was back at senior school, and he'd noticed David's voice had got hoarse from yelling at Max.

"Ahmed, over here!" a rough, earthy voice shouted.

Turning from his car door, Khalil recognised him at once: the player who'd been watching him from the side of the pitch. The key difference was that now he was wearing a fedora.

Khalil's face became hot as he squinted at the man. Where did he know him from? He was a tall guy with a stern face, sunken cheeks and callous eyes. Not to forget, that moustache. He didn't look one bit happy, nothing like the footie fanatic he'd been with Brad. He had his hands in his pocket as if he were reaching for something.

It likely wasn't for anything good.

Finally, Khalil recognised him: the jewellery deal's moustache man. The very one he'd met months ago, who'd paid him to throw his mysterious bag into the river.

"Did you believe my elaborate disguise?" Gerald taunted snidely, unveiling a pistol. "Truth be told, I don't give a shit about football. Hello again, Khalil."

Ignoring him, Khalil jumped into his car. He slammed the door. A millisecond later, a gunshot rang out. More shots followed, booming like crashing lightning. His tyres sputtered.

Disbelief etched onto his face, Khalil crouched low under the steering wheel and reached into his pocket for his car key. As his fingers fumbled around, he rammed the key into the ignition. Another shot boomed from metres away. Glass from the car window rained down. When the engine came to life, he smacked his foot down on the pedal.

Bullets thundered. Shouts echoed. Glass crunched.

CHAPTER 19

THE FALL OF KIDDY WINKS

"So, what's the goss?"

Rosie looked up from her treasure hunting notes and at the face of Lauren Collins, who'd just sat next to her. It was playtime at the school, and a staff meeting was about to begin. Anxious staff members filled the staffroom, sipping from tepid cups of stale coffee and trying to balance on wobbly chairs. Some shared rumours about why they had all been called here and the strange notice that had been hung on the noticeboard that morning:

Announcement in staffroom at lunchtime break. Attendance is mandatory for all staff.

"Nothing much," Rosie said, closed her notebook and tucked it inside her baguette bag. "What's the goss with you?"

"I went out with Frank last night, and he was just the loveliest," Lauren said giddily. She was a stout lady with bright hair, thigh-high black boots, a green skirt and a duck-themed blouse. "It hasn't been long since I broke up with Mikey, I know, but I feel it's high time for me to get back in the game. Find a man who really appreciates me for me. Do you know him? Frank Robbins. He said he used to be the janitor here. He's a real stud."

Rosie stared at Lauren for a second and pondered briefly how a person could be quite so annoying without trying. *She reminds me of Angelina Emu from Theodore Tabby. They both have really big heads.*

"Uh, I don't think so," she said, stroking her chin. "So, do you fancy him?"

"Those ocean eyes, that five o'clock shadow and the six-pack—of course! The date was amazing. We went to the Bottle Bureau and ended the night at… Oh, well…I won't kiss and tell." A toothy grin formed on Lauren's lips. "But let's just say, there was snogging! And a lot else."

"That's nice," Rosie said.

She tapped her foot against the red carpet. *Max always does this, doesn't he? I hope I'm not becoming him. Yesterday, I even caught myself saying huzzah. He'd tell me I'm being too negative.*

"Yeah. It was damn *nice* for a first date," Lauren enthused, placing her baby blue manicured nails on Rosie's shoulder. "Frank's such a guy, a man's man, and he makes me laugh. Like, seriously laugh. I was chuckling so hard that I snorted the whole evening. I hope he'll text me back soon. It's been a few hours since he left me on read, but I'm sure he'd never ghost me!"

"I'm sure you and Frank will be great together"; "He sounds really nice"; and "A good kisser is so important" were some of Rosie's uninspired responses as she tried to be as good a friend as possible. The reality was that what Max had said the other day about her cynicism had got to her, so she was making an effort to be positive, without overdoing it.

One of the many things that was irritating about Lauren was that she didn't know when to stop. She went on and on about the ins and outs of Frank, her newest romantic interest after the past three she'd had so far this year. Eventually, Rosie grew tired of hearing about the quality of Frank's kisses, so she changed the subject.

"Are you still up for joining Agatha Quiztie? I can tell you the practice times if you want to come to one," she proposed. "The championship is coming up relatively soon."

"Huh?" Lauren asked, brushing her fringe.

"Y'know, you said you'd be part of our quiz team, Agatha Quiztie, for the upcoming championship?"

"Oh, yeah. That bizarre, uh, I mean, interesting hobby of yours. As long as it's just one day and all," she said vacantly. "Will Brad be there?"

"No. Just my best friend, Max and Khalil, his mate," Rosie explained, struggling to stop herself from saying some cynical things.

"You have to tell me more about you and Brad. The power couple of Stapleford, eh? Do I hear wedding bells? How many kids are you gonna have? Sorry. That's rude of me. You could be sterile."

"Excuse me?"

It was not on Rosie's agenda to tell Lauren that she and Brad were no longer an item, or that she'd broken up with him after she and Max had almost been hit by an allegedly stray bullet. Similarly, she had no desire to inform her that Brad had come over to her house, had thrown a huge tantrum and now continued to ring her ten times a day. Maybe she ought to be flattered, but it was just too funny.

At that moment, Headmaster Wilson stepped into the staffroom. A permanently peeved and yet simultaneously fragile man with stubby fingers and leathery skin, he displayed a drab, misanthropic expression as he looked over his staff.

"Hello everyone," he said, periodically gazing at the ceiling. "I'll get on with the announcement. As you might've heard, there has been a lot of hubbub in the paper lately about Lovell Unlimited expanding its operations and making some building acquisitions across this area of the country. Recently, the company has even made a generous offer on our very own Kiddy Winks property. Since this is a privately owned preschool, it is naturally up to the headmaster, who is, of course, me, whether to accept. Sadly, the opening of the Building Blocks Preschool across town has had a destabilising effect on the number of sign-ups for next year. Given the school's current dire financial situation and the fact we simply cannot go on in this climate of increased competition and economic recession without a significant turnaround, I have decided to accept the offer. Accordingly, Kiddy Winks will be terminating operations as of the end of term. The next few weeks will be, therefore, the perfect time for you all to start researching new pedagogical opportunities. Let me know if you have any questions."

A disbelieving silence permeated the staffroom for ten intensely tense seconds. Then, it erupted with outrage.

"In other words, you're laying us all off for some lousy corporation!" the English teacher wailed. "And you have the gall to act like you're doing us a favour?"

"How do you expect us to react?!" the art teacher, who looked just as apoplectic with rage, wailed. "You've just said we're all getting the sack!"

Rosie stared into the distance, struggling to take in enough air as she registered what had just been said. She imagined rumbling tremors breaking out, forming a chasm that consumed the headmaster. He might have dressed it up in a fancy speech, but Wilson had just made her redundant. It was surely going to take months to find another job. What was she going to do about her rent and student debt in the interim?

Lauren leaned over and whispered in her ear. "This is outrageous, isn't it? Utterly OUTRAGEOUS! Wilson's betraying us just so that company can have one more office! What do Lovell Unlimited even do?"

"They're primarily a vacuum company owned by the billionaire, Anthony Lovell," Rosie said disapprovingly. "He invented the first suctionless vacuum or something. Max and I have never liked him."

"Oh yeah, what a bastard!" Lauren spat. "I saw Lovell on the news one time. That grumpy, out-of-touch old billionaire."

It was quite difficult to hear Lauren over the pure indignation spreading across the staffroom. An onslaught of furious teachers yelled at Headmaster Wilson: "I promised my kids we'd go to Disney this summer!"; "I can't afford my rhinoplasty surgery without this job!"; "How will I pay my labradoodle's vet fees now?" and so on. Headmaster Wilson tried ineffectually to placate them.

Rosie raised her hand. "Sir, what about the children for whom Building Blocks is too far? Are they just going to have to be homeschooled?"

"I'm sorry. Kiddy Winks may be a school, but it's certainly not a charity, and if we don't have enough students, we simply can't keep going," Headmaster Wilson sniffed, seemingly close to tears. "Besides, I can assure you all that you'll be getting severance pay for one month."

"One month?!" several people shouted almost in unison.

The furore continued until he back-pedalled. "Make that, er, two months. I mean, three. Four? Four and a half?"

Rosie was dumbstruck with disbelief. It felt as if someone was tickling her body with a feather.

Playtime had come to an end, and Headmaster Wilson seemed to have had enough of being yelled at. He ran out of the staffroom in a fit of tears, leaving behind an awkward silence. Rosie and Lauren got up and trudged back to class.

"So, whatcha gonna do to pass time while you're on the job hunt?" Lauren asked hotly, while the children flooded into the corridor from the playground.

At that moment, Lauren turned into an emu, sprouting a long neck and a soft-feathered brown coat. *Ah, so that's what animal Lauren is! Well, I predicted it. She has emu eyes.*

"Not sure yet," Rosie muttered. "I'm already on a treasure hunt apparently."

"You'd better start thinking about it before summer. I'm sure Wilson is getting a lovely payout after this. At least he and that Lovell will be happy!" Lauren Emu exclaimed, and stretched her velvety wings.

"Indeed," she said, watching Lauren Emu peck at some bird feed on the floor as kids ran along beside them. "It's really sad, isn't it? They don't care about the kids at all."

Anthony Lovell was unquestionably her least favourite public figure. She'd heard that Lovell Unlimited made use of lax child labour laws abroad to employ five-year-olds to build their vacuums. They were also rumoured to have utilised dog bones as parts in their hoovers.

Rosie bridled as she reflected on how easily they could get away with all of this and, in the meanwhile, did her best to ignore that the kids in the corridor were successively metamorphosing into barnyard animals.

Lauren threw her long furry neck back, beak shining with lipstick. "I've said it before, and I'll say it again: it's OUTRAGEOUS, SHAMEWORTHY and DISGRACEFUL!" she squawked. "Totally OUTRAGEOUS!"

CHAPTER 20

OLD ENEMIES AND NEW THREATS

Max was waiting for others—highly unusual for him, as he tended to be the late one. He sat on the dirty pavement outside Kiddy Winks, trying to scrape gum off his shoes, thinking idly about whether his landlord would allow him to adopt a chimpanzee and if he should change his name to Axel, Hieronymus or Salvador. Rosie and Khalil were taking far too long. Having had quite enough, he rose and paced up to the preschool, realising that he'd never seen Rosie at work in all the years they'd known each other.

The coloured number and alphabet sticker-decorated automatic doors opened automatically for him. He knew that she taught the first years, so he found her classroom without much difficulty. He knocked on the door, and a woman with silky blonde hair and lustrous fingernails stepped out, glaring at him. She had clown-like makeup on every inch of her face.

"Who are you?" the woman asked, blowing out her puffy cheeks.

"A boon companion to Rosie Shaw, and cowboy in training," Max introduced himself. He peered in to see toddlers fiddling about with Play-Doh and Rosie daydreaming in the corner. "There she is. I don't suppose you could fetch her for me."

"You're *not* allowed in here. Friend or not."

"Why not? Please. Pretty please with a cherry on top."

"You could be a child predator. Leave the school now!" she exclaimed, and shooed him away like a cat.

"She told me Kiddy Winks closed at three," he said, but he couldn't stop himself from staring at the woman's countenance. "Holy smokes, I can barely see your face behind all that makeup. It reminds me of that time I pretended to be a girl, so I didn't have to use the horrid bug-infested boys' bathroom at school."

"What?" the woman exclaimed. She raised a palm to her face and pushed him out. "It's three-thirty, not three. Now, will you leave, or do I have to call the police?"

"Calm now. I'll sling my hook, if you insist," Max said reluctantly, slouching away. *Great. Looks like How to Win Friends and Influence People has failed me yet again.*

He had nothing else to do but wait. He wandered back out, occupying himself by practising parkour like he used to do on a postbox, but it wasn't the same since he fell off the roof of Town Hall and landed in that bin. Sword fighting didn't scratch the same itch lately either.

"You find new ways to embarrass me every day," Rosie said firmly. She appeared behind him with her arms crossed tighter than a padlock.

As Max caught sight of Rosie, he was struck by her effortless beauty. He couldn't help but wonder if it was time for him to finally "make a move" now that Brad was out of the picture. If he was being honest, he didn't really know what making a move meant. He had heard the phrase before and had concluded it was the thing to do, yet he didn't know in what cardinal direction that move should be: north, east or maybe even north-east. At the same time, making a move in any direction was surely a ridiculous notion. She would never want anything to do with him and all his baggage romantically!

"Not only did you get the time wrong, but you've alienated someone we need on our good side," Rosie added. "You know who that teacher was? Lauren. The lady who's gonna be on our quiz team."

"Oh, really? She seems lovely, albeit somewhat tetchy," he said.

Rosie jostled a small suitcase by her feet. "Let's get going. I'm done for the day. I've packed things for one night away," she said, and looked around. "Where's Khalil?"

"Beats me. I just hope he's not too long since he's our wheels to London."

As Rosie ingeniously worked out, the Caesar cipher had turned the number grid into a word grid, and one containing a host of London tourist attractions. But where exactly they ought to go in London was still a puzzle to be solved: Parliament, Buckingham Palace or Madame Tussauds. The phrase *needle in a haystack* seemed apt.

They waited outside Kiddy Winks for half an hour, getting progressively more irritated with each other as they both tried to get in contact with Khalil in between bouts of bickering. Finally, after about a billion unanswered calls, Max's phone rang back. He put it on loudspeaker.

Before he even uttered a sound, Max could tell something was off. He shared a look with Rosie and thought her eyes suggested that she felt it too.

"Hey, guys," Khalil said briskly. "I'm so sorry. I can't come to London today."

"Is it David's orders?" Max asked. "Last week, he made me fix the coffee machine. I don't even know how to make coffee, let alone fix a machine that does!"

The static crackled.

"No. My car broke down while I was on my way. It's being towed," Khalil disclosed. "I'm stranded. It'll take me hours to get this all sorted out. Why don't you go to London alone? You can get the train. You'll be fine without me, I'm sure. Just trust your intuition."

"Let's be honest: this is bilge, claptrap and malarkey in equal measure," said Max judgmentally. "We're partners!"

"Geez. Give me a break, mate."

"We need a guide to help us in London. You're the only one who's from there. Otherwise, we'll end up kidnapped and butchered by cannibals. Do you want that on your conscience?"

"For Chrissake, I'm not your babysitter."

Before Max could protest further, the line went dead. He turned to Rosie, feeling very much like something bad was afoot. "I wonder what's up with him. I guess you'll have to be my babysitter."

Another reason Max had wanted Khalil to come so badly was because he could perhaps intimidate Amelia to stop bullying him. She'd been sending him incessant mean messages, calling him a "Tetris-addicted manbaby" and gloating that The Crystalline Crucible prize was just chump change to her due to her fabulously well-paying job. She even invited him to The Queen's Head pub by King's Cross station to catch up when she heard he was heading to London, but he wasn't planning on attending without Khalil.

Going to London for the first time in his life seemed like enough unnecessary newness to Max for one day. Throw in getting the train through England for the first time, and it was like going to Ithaca and Tokyo on the same day. Still, he supposed leaving Stapleford was something he had proved more than capable of doing. He had even bragged to Rosie that he was the

Stapleford equivalent of Marco Polo, having gone all the way to Bath and back. The next destination after today would be Ithaca.

Rosie and Max dashed away from the school and got the bus to Nottingham Train Station. When they arrived and proceeded to the ticket machine, he frowned at the cacophonous rumble of luggage being hauled along the marble floor and the thick, eye-watering funk—plenty of unnecessary stimulation already. The ticket machine proved rather too byzantine for his liking, too.

"That's the receipt printer. Not the card reader," Rosie said tiredly, slapping his hand away and pointing at the right slot. "You're twenty-one, aren't you?"

"To be precise, as of this moment I'm seven thousand, eight hundred and sixty-two days fresh out of the womb," he responded. He glanced at his watch. "And three hours and five minutes."

They found their seats on the train and, in moments, were watching the familiar streets of Nottingham blur into the rugged landscapes of rural England. The interior of the train was much less chaotic than the station, calm and unexpectedly relaxing. Cattle grazed and swine rooted peacefully on cultivated pastures that hastened by the window; Max was convinced he even spotted Peppa Pig herself.

Saying this might be an excellent opportunity to practise for the Stapleford Quiz Championship, Rosie reached into her baguette bag and pulled out her question cards.

"Have you made the application yet?" he asked, watching her shuffle the cards. On the pull-out table, he placed his heavenly pre-prepared white bread cheese sandwich (no crusts), Cheestring, Dairylea Dunkers, Babybel, platter of rare cheeses and succulent Capri-Sun. A feast fit for a king.

"Yup. We're in. All we need to do is make sure Khalil and Lauren show up."

"I'm afraid Khalil might be in trouble," he said as the train sped along the tracks. "He cancelled so suddenly. He was always secretive about where he came from. I even found a GPS tracker in his car once."

"We all have secrets. He's probably fine. By the way, I got some bad news today," she revealed abruptly. She explained with contempt that Lovell Unlimited was buying her preschool building.

"That damn company," Max grumbled, his shirt covered in crumbs. "I loathe Anthony Lovell. Maybe I should figure out some way to protest. Oooh, I've never tried self-immolation or hara-kiri."

"No, don't do that. Your protests never go anywhere," Rosie discouraged caustically, and shrugged. "It is what it is. I'll find a new job. For now, let's get practising."

Rosie had put them on a strict quiz preparation regime over the past few weeks. She'd even made Max come to the local pub quiz with her last week to scope out the teams they would be facing. Universally Challenged proved skilful. They were a competitive group of university-educated elders who looked like they had been watching *University Challenge* since Bamber Gascoigne was the host in the eighties. Another strong team was Quizzy McQuizface, a book club turned quiz club of housewives with an encyclopaedic knowledge of footballers' wives, celebrity deaths and the Royal Family.

Alas, Rosie and Max had not even placed in the pub quiz, but to be fair, that was only because they got disqualified after he accidentally spilled chocolate milk all over their answer sheet.

The day's quiz practice served as something of a wake-up call.

"Rosie, have you even been revising?" he asked, sighing. "By Jove, you will need to ramp up revision sessions in the next couple of weeks and go on a strict regime of ten *University Challenge* episodes a day. I'm not sure we stand a chance of being in the top ten at this rate."

"You didn't even know who Maggie Smith was. She's like the most famous actress in the country," she said heatedly. She ripped the cards from his hands. "Here's a good one. What's the capital of Switzerland?"

"Too easy," Max affirmed in a braggadocious tone. "Zürich."

"Nope. Bern."

Annoyed, he dug out his phone. "How ludicrous! I was so convinced The Governess on *The Chase* said it was that… She must have lied."

"We can't afford to make rookie mistakes like that. I reckon the quizmaster will be as tough as Jeremy Paxman."

"Give me a break. I don't have a fancy university degree or toff parents like all the contestants on that show. I'm a polymath autodidact."

"A what?"

The quiz practice ended with Max promising to work on his football and popular culture trivia, and Rosie promising to work on her politics and history.

"I just hope Khalil and Lauren can make up for our blind spots. Khalil's quite a fan of football," he said.

"And Lauren is a big soap opera buff. She loves EastEnders and Corrie," she said. "You should hear how annoying she is. My wonderful boyfriend is dazzlingly handsome, brilliant and funny. We've only met twice, but I'm already sure we're going to have two beautiful kids named Darcy and James."

"She seemed a class lady to me, Ms Cynic. Maybe I'll ask her out sometime."

"She *is* sweet," Rosie said quickly, as if trying to correct herself, "in a sort of *I'll throttle you unless you shut up right now* sort of way. Kind of like you."

By the time the train rolled into London, Max had almost forgotten the fact that he was about to see the capital of his own country for the first time. Rosie remarked that living in England and never having been to London was comparable to being a bee and never having entered the hive. But he felt he might have a better understanding of London than a good percentage of its citizens, having memorised *A People's History of London* to prepare for this trip and having watched every Disney film the city was featured in.

At about six p.m., they disembarked from the train at King's Cross station and idled beside a red telephone box, not far from The Queen's Head, as they decided their next step. Max fidgeted. The Queen's Head was where Amelia had invited him, and now was the right time for the meeting.

"Where do we need to go first? Only have a whole city to search," he said breathlessly, intimidated by the intense sights and sounds. "Why don't we start with the Sigmund Freud Museum? I'm keen to have my dreams of being buried alive by Barney the Dinosaur psychoanalysed."

Rosie's normal frown loosened into an infinitesimally small grin. "I have an idea: the London Eye."

"Why?" he muttered, shivering at the idea. Heights weren't his cup of tea.

"I had another little look at the decrypted word grid." She displayed the clue on her notepad. "Did you happen to notice any absences in the tourist attractions? It was doing my head in trying to get any more information from it, but then I noticed there's one missing. It has practically everything else."

"Aha!" Max said. He enjoyed letting Rosie do all the treasure hunting busywork.

"The Millennium Wheel. It might be a leap in the dark, but I think it's a hint. A trick clue."

"Makes sense to me. Let's have a drink before doing anything. I'm parched," Max resolved, and pointed to The Queen's Head. Since Amelia had said she'd be here, he might as well see whether she had the guts to turn up. "Maybe they even have Brussels sprouts. Although honestly, so far I don't doubt these Londoners are more inclined towards ice cream, chocolate and pizza, their Taylor Swifts, Justine Biebers and Cold and/or Hot Plays. I shouldn't be surprised; people with tastes as good as mine are the most endangered breed."

"Your taste in Britney Spears and the *High School Musical* soundtrack?"

"THAT WAS A GLITCH IN *JUST DANCE*!"

They entered the pub, ordered drinks and sat on stalls at the back of the pub. The air was redolent of whisky and roasted nuts, and abuzz with the din of ongoing banter. They shared a packet of sour onion crisps, which made Max reflect sadly on Khalil's absence.

Amelia's ginger hair was hard to miss. She stood in the corner of the pub, chatting with a bunch of glamorous women in dresses who were presumably her girlfriends. Moments after Max's eyes landed on her, she clocked him too, got up and paced over with a wide smirk.

"My, my, Maximilian the Great. Hehehe. What a coincidence. Although, not really a traditional coincidence," Amelia said, eyes twinkling. She turned to Rosie. "Oh, and is this your girlfriend? What a beaut. Hehehe."

"Er, who are you?" Rosie asked.

Max frowned, ignoring Rosie. "Cut the pleasantries, Delia. We both recall what happened in Bath." He recoiled from her. "Why don't you go back to your friends and stop denying them the pleasure of your hyena laugh?"

"How dare you insult my beautiful laugh," she remarked, undeterred. "Hehehe. And my name's Amelia, for the tenth time. It's not exactly a hard name to remember!" She looked around. "Wait. Where's Khalil?"

"None of your business. I know you have a crush on him. Sorry. He's not interested."

"It's not him I have a crush on. Believe me. *You* are practically the Marlon Brando of treasure hunters. But fine, if you're gonna be like that, I'll go," she said, untangling her red strands. "I thought you'd want to have a chat, though. That's why I invited you after all."

Max puffed out his chest. "Not interested. I didn't come for your invitation. I just, er, like this pub."

"Hello?" Rosie said.

Amelia lifted her chin. "That's a shame. You may have noticed I'm not alone. I'm celebrating with my friends. I suppose I may as well tell you that I've found the next clue."

He suppressed a gasp. "You have?"

"What're you two arguing about?" interjected Rosie. "Stop ignoring me."

"Yup. And you're never, ever gonna work it out. Frankly, I'm surprised you even got this far." Amelia's eyes flickered to Rosie. "Sorry about this, honey. Max and I have history."

"Why do you even care about this contest?" Max asked. "I thought you said that you make *so* much money that The Crystalline Crucible prize is worthless to you."

"It's true, but we all have fascinations and mine is the sweet taste of treasure. Nothing compares, not even the strongest cocaine. I've been treasure hunting since I was a little girl and I've found hundreds of priceless artefacts. They used to call me the Ginger Genius."

"I've found loads of treasure too. Way more, I bet," Max dissimulated. "Shouldn't you be busy completing Stephen Fry's taxes or something?"

"Right, because the only thing I love more than Ronan Keating and Co is my precious taxes! I'll tell you something and don't forget it—I'm the shark of treasure hunters, and I can detect my prey's scent from miles away." She glanced back at her friends. "I'd better get back. Toodle-oo, Crystal Hunter. Or should I say Crystal *Loser*?" Amelia said evilly. "By the by, the guest book clue just came out publicly. You ought to hurry up and find the next one!"

With a mischievous, simpering grin, she wandered back over to her friends and resumed gossiping.

Max grunted, enraged. *Grrrr, if only Khalil were here she wouldn't be acting like that.*

Taken aback, Rosie stared at him. "Thanks *so* much for introducing me. Who was that crazy lady?"

"It doesn't matter. Crackers and honey with cream cheese on top of a blasted pickle," Max said uneasily. "I'm starting to think we should go to the London Eye right away."

"I was gonna say the exact same thing."

The guest book clue being made public was, Max realised as he tensely sipped his orange juice through a straw, the worst thing that could've possibly happened. They had one night to find the next clue before a gigantic swarm of treasure hunters would be on their way to the London Eye.

CHAPTER 21

A DEATH AND AN INJURY

Khalil raised his binoculars to the bridge of his nose and trained them on the door of his apartment. He was crouching low in the bushes of Hamlet House, stinging nettles pressing into his back.

It's getting so cold I can barely feel my hands. Better make a move soon.

Inhaling sharply, he evaluated that he would need to be in his apartment for a half hour to pack his things. In the event anybody came while he was there, his only escape would be the window. That option was not ideal unless breaking his legs was on the menu. He had dumped his bullet-shattered car on a squalid side road by a gay strip club, meaning he had no means of a quick getaway either.

After the shooting, he'd spent the whole day in hiding, biding time while ignoring incessant questions from Max about London—like how he could make an appointment with Fergie.

A grim wave of courage coming over him, Khalil put his binoculars away and darted toward his flat. It was time to get this over with.

He reached the winding stairs. His breath shallowed from the chill as he ran up to his floor, bearing left to his flat. As soon as he arrived, he put his ear to his door to listen for intruders. He only heard the dull hum of electricity.

While Khalil reached into his pocket for his key, a rasping sound resonated behind him. He grabbed his Swiss Army knife and whipped around.

"Muhammad, what the gadzooks are you doing out now?" Mr Brooks asked. He had just stepped out in a patchy dressing gown brandishing his cane. "You woke me up! I was just having a lovely dream of dancing with my late wife on *Strictly Come Dancing*. Craig Revel Horwood gave us ten points!"

Khalil sighed. He lowered the knife and tucked it in his pocket before Mr Brooks spotted it. He was as relieved to see his elderly neighbour as he was irritated. Mr Brooks with his *Grand Designs* and *Bargain Hunt* rambles was a lot less of a threat.

"For God's sake, go back to bed," Khalil ordered.

"There are a lot of hoodlums around Stapleford. Haven't you noticed?" Mr Brooks said, nostrils flaring. He looked so run-down and out of it that he easily could have just crawled out from his grave. "They've been stalking me. I'm not a spry young gentleman like yourself. I have to look after myself. Protect my back against ruffians."

At this, he extended his cane as if threatening to thwomp Khalil with it.

Khalil gave a derisive snort. However, perhaps Mr Brooks' paranoid claims about disreputable people hanging around Hamlet House might hold more water than he'd initially thought. Had he really been hallucinating all of it?

"Go to bed. You look like a ghost," Khalil ordered, hunching his shoulders as he unlocked his door.

"A what?"

"A ghost? You know, like Casper the Ghost!"

"Jeremy Corbyn?" Mr Brooks repeated, eyes hardening. "Is that what you said? I despise that snivelling communist! Speak up, you roughneck tearaway. Do you even know who the monarch of Great Britannia is, the country that has so kindly let you in?"

"Let me think. Henry the Eighth? Go to sleep!" Khalil shouted unintentionally loudly.

He entered his flat and started to pack immediately. He stuffed every single possession he had that would fit into his suitcase. From his records to his favourite photos, everything had to go in or he would never see it again. He made sure to take every penny from the safe under his bed. There was something quite melancholy about leaving home again. First it was London. Now Stapleford. But he no longer had a choice.

Living on the move is exhausting. Maybe I'll always be a bird of passage from now on. I sure hope not. I'd like a family one day. I wonder what Noora's doing right now.

Out of breath, Khalil gave himself a brief moment's rest. He gazed regretfully through the window at the moonlit silhouette of Stapleford, pondering where he'd go next as the stars shone down like fireflies. For now, he'd return to London and keep a low profile. Aaron would find out he was back there if he wasn't heedful enough. And after that, where to? Who was to say that Aaron wouldn't find him again in the next place? As the lurches of doubt got stronger in his stomach, Khalil forced himself to get back to his current mission.

He was trying to fit his Polaroids of the River Trent into the suitcase when a voice pierced the silence outside.

"Buzz off, you yob scum. Right now. Or I'll call the coppers. I'm fed up with Muhammad's friends!" Mr Brooks snapped. "You interrupted another dream. I was being knighted by Her Majesty for my heroism in the Falklands War."

Khalil froze on the spot. Was this just another neighbour Mr Brooks was addressing or a person far more concerning?

"Listen, old man. I don't want any trouble," someone replied, their voice flat. "Go back into your flat and forget all about this. I'm just going to visit our good friend, Muhammad."

The man in the disguise. Gerald.

A painful dilemma hit Khalil: run or hide? If he made a run for it, he'd have to try and dodge Gerald and bound off as fast as possible. But without a car, that didn't sound appealing. The second option was to hide in his apartment, although equally, he didn't much like the sound of being stuck in an enclosed space with no way out.

He had no good choice.

"What was that claptrap?" Mr Brooks fired back indignantly. "My hearing aid is on the fritz. You'll have to speak up, you nincompoop."

"I said fuck off, old codger, and forget this. Or else."

"How *dare* you speak to a senior like that?! Who the bloody hell are you, you chav?!"

"Don't call me a chav. Would a chav have this?"

There was a sudden pause.

"Hey, what's that?" Mr Brooks asked. "Oh my God. Get away from me, you deuced—"

An enormous boom sounded outside the apartment. A gunshot. Gerald, Aaron's assassin, had just shot Mr Brooks.

Not twenty seconds after the shot rang out, a key slid into his apartment door. Aaron must have given the man the master key.

Khalil looked around frantically. The wardrobe. He had no other place to go.

He bounded in and pulled the door shut. His heart thumped like a bass drum as footsteps plodded into his flat, slow and steady. The shooter must be looking for him.

Five minutes passed, each one seeming to last longer than the one before. Meanwhile, Khalil reached around blindly for something blunt to use as a weapon, though it was rather tricky in the wardrobe. His hand eventually landed on an iron.

Before long, voices spoke in hushed tones outside.

"Any luck, Gerald?"

A second person. Khalil immediately recognised who it was by the Machiavellian guile in his voice: Aaron.

"Nope, boss," Gerald replied nonchalantly. "Weird. Could've sworn I saw him heading up."

There was a sharp intake of breath. "What the hell! Who is this old man?"

Khalil leaned forward in a bid to spy through the door crack, but inadvertently sent a mop toppling. He caught it just in time before it hit the wall and made a clatter.

"Meh. Just an old grump who was making a ruckus. I had to deal with him," Gerald said, not sounding nearly as carefree as he had on the football pitch. "Dragged him in here afterwards."

"You must be the worst hitman I've ever done business with," Aaron grumbled. "Not only have you failed miserably at intimidating Khalil, you attracted police attention by trying to kill him in broad daylight, and now you've murdered an innocent. Don't you understand what assassins do? Be *covert.*"

"I get the job done, boss. At least, I will. Trust me."

Gerald struck Khalil as a man who was a dangerous mixture of overconfident, incapable and an ass.

"You blew your disguise in the most bovine way!" Aaron spat. "The only good thing you've done was inform me about Khalil's whereabouts, and that was months ago. What about that Max fellow you were following and misfired at?"

"He was unharmed, wasn't he? I made Ahmed think I was some dummy football player and got the jump on him. It was just bad luck that he got away. And as I said, I didn't have a choice about this mister. He was threatening to call the police."

"The police are definitely on their way now, smart-arse. We'd better vamoose before we end up behind bars tonight." Another pause. "Look at all these pretentious photos. Khalil should have given up this photography business long ago. It won't make him any money."

"Yeah. What a waste of time. He told me about it back when he sold me your jewellery, and I said the same thing. Little did he know what was in that bag I got him to toss."

"Uh, wait. Hold on, Gerald. I just noticed something."

"What is it, boss?"

A lump rose in Khalil's throat. Being stuck in this tiny closet was far more uncomfortable than the bushes. It forced him to stand with his back inches from the water heater, which was scalding hot. Even worse, the mop fell once again and landed on his shoulder. He couldn't risk moving.

"Look. A suitcase," Aaron observed. "His things are half packed. What if he's hiding in here?"

Khalil strengthened his grip on the iron handle. *They know.*

"You think? I've already scoped out the whole damn apartment," Gerald said.

"Of course!" Aaron said, peeved off. "You saw him come up. Why else would his suitcase be like that? Right. Let's check it out and get out of here."

"Sure, boss. You check out his living room. I'll do the bedroom."

Khalil's frame coursed with anxiety. The suitcase was lying metres from the wardrobe, and everyone knew that a closet was both the most obvious and worst possible place to hide.

Sure enough, the door swung open mere moments later.

Seeing light for the first time in fifteen minutes didn't give Khalil's eyes enough time to adjust. Visually impaired, he stepped forward and swung the iron. It made contact with a sickening whack.

Gerald screamed. "Casablancas, he's here. Help!"

Khalil dropped the iron and scrambled towards the door. He briefly turned back to glance at Gerald lying supine on the floor, blood smeared across his forehead. Mr Brooks' lifeless body lay next to him.

Khalil gulped. *Looks dead to me. I can't stick around to give first aid.*

Aaron shouted something, but Khalil didn't hear what or see him. He sprinted into the misty night. Minutes later, his phone pinged in his pocket. Winded, he pulled it out and read an odd message from the drug lord himself. Aaron was open to making a deal.

CHAPTER 22

THE LONDON EYE CONUNDRUM

Max's foot tapped extremely fast. So quickly, in fact, that Rosie warned him it was going to fall off. They were standing inside an unbearably cramped London bus heading over Westminster Bridge. Max's face turned apple red as the shoulders of businesspeople in suits closed in, surrounding him on all sides. He desperately attempted to astral travel to Ithaca.

So far, his first impression of London was that it was the worst place in the world, just narrowly beating Stapleford. To be fair, he'd only been in the city a few hours, but his first impressions had proved in the past to be unfailingly accurate. London was simply a terrible combination of boring, ugly and just plain unpleasant. Simply nothing like its portrayal in the seminal film, *One Hundred and One Dalmatians.*

"The city looks beautiful at night, doesn't it?" Rosie said as if making an effort to be positive. She gazed out at the cityscape's refulgent flashing lights. "I mean, the stars look nice and all. Kinda."

"Maybe to Helen Keller. I wonder if the same people who built Stapleford designed London. There are no dalmatians *at all.*"

"You watch too many Disney films."

"Oh, bother. This big red bus is certainly making me claustrophobic. They really should put oxygen masks in these death traps."

As they passed by a member of the Queen's Guard standing at attention, he knitted his fingers. *The Queen never replied to my letters. Maybe they got lost in the post. Claudius founded London, didn't he? He ought to be ashamed of himself, maybe even more so than Kellogg's.*

"We still don't have a game plan for when we get to the London Eye," Rosie reminded him. "The clue could be lurking anywhere, and we sure don't want to miss anything. It's not like it's gonna be displayed in plain sight or else any old person would have found it already."

"I've heard it said that all heroes on an epic, inspiring, heartrendingly touching adventure can always turn to the gods for help," Max proclaimed. "Although it has to be said, no gods have intervened quite yet. Not even Zeus."

When the bus finally stopped, Rosie and Max spotted the London Eye, a circle of oversized light bulbs contrasting with the dingy evening sky in front of the Thames.

The queue stretched around crowd control barriers. He hadn't expected it to be quite so long. Queues were one of Max's least favourite things in the world, along with raindrops on roses and whiskers on kittens, so it wasn't going to be a fun night. As they joined the back of the queue, he gazed up at the rotating pods and hoped that Rosie hadn't made a mistake. Maybe his worst phobia was acrophobia, so he didn't want to go up there for nothing.

His stomach squirmed as though ants were crawling inside it. There was also a ravenously hungry-like pressure at the thought that if they didn't find the clue tonight, it was essentially the end of the road.

The queue lasted a tiresome half hour. When they finally boarded the pod, it took ten minutes for the vessel to rise to a position where he could see anything. London spread out before them from a giant's point of view, a panorama of shimmering lights reflecting over a vista of grand and nondescript buildings, all merging into one. Max's immediate impression was that being this high was absolutely detestable.

"We can't stargaze forever. Let's get looking," Rosie reasoned, turning around.

If she wasn't a teacher, Rosie would make an excellent commander in the British army. Too bad they kicked me out after I shot that major general in the foot during training.

"Yes, ma'am," he said nauseously. He wished he'd brought a sick bag.

Nevertheless, problems quickly became apparent. For one thing, the pod was no bigger than Max's living room. For another, the only thing inside of it to examine for clues was…pretty much nothing.

Once the pod had risen to around the nine o'clock position, he could see far and wide over London, from Parliament to the Gherkin. It was undeniably pretty, and even Max said so. Rosie had once pointed out that he had the ability of a stale turnip to appreciate beauty, not to mention the charisma of a broken pencil. But the fact remained that they were literally clueless and running out of time.

Rosie paced over and fretted. "Max, we've got to think of something. The pod is about to descend."

"There's no point in stewing," he said, remembering how courageously Khalil had acted when hope had seemed lost in Bath. "A cowboy never despairs. Or was that a knight… Let's go back over the original clue. See if we're missing anything."

"Mummy! I want to get off!"

A scrawny, moon-faced toddler made a fuss as he tugged at his pinched-faced mother's leg, mucus dangling from his nostrils.

"Eek! It's too slow!" the child shrieked. His voice resembled the screeching of a train grinding to a halt.

Max shot the child a death stare, reminding himself to never have kids.

"This is like trying to ascend a mountain while only using a knife and fork." Rosie sighed and dug out her notepad, where she had written the deciphered grid. "There's nothing else there. Just the grid. Thirteen rows and thirteen columns."

"IT'S TOO HIGH. I DON'T LIKE IT. LET ME OFF!" the young boy yelled.

He punched the glass walls, then got on his back and slid under the centre bench, kicking at it.

"Aha! Thirteen rows and thirteen columns!" Max exclaimed. "Oddly random numbers. What if that's some sort of clue?"

And that was when it hit him. He'd read prior to this trip that there were exactly thirty-two pods on the London Eye, but the thirteenth was not labelled as such because it was considered unlucky. It could only mean one thing.

"Got it." Max paced forward through the crowd to get a better look at the sign at the top of the pod. "It says there we've got on the fifth pod. We need the thirteenth one, which is called the fourteenth."

"You think? Well, we do have one more ticket in Khalil's name," Rosie pointed out.

"AAARRRGGGHHH!" the boy screamed once more, half under the bench. "IT'S TOO SLOW!"

"Will you shut up, loathsome rascal!" Max shouted, eliciting a bitter scowl from the boy's mother. "Sorry. My eardrums don't agree with loud noises."

He had a good feeling about his idea, not least because his hunches had an outstanding track record of success. Apart from that time he became deadly convinced a Martian impostor had replaced the Prime Minister, or the one occasion he thought he was developing occult powers and could perform telekinesis.

When the pod had completed its rotation, they ran to the back of the queue. The problem was going to be arriving at the front of the line when capsule thirteen/fourteen arrived. In the end, they did something clever yet dishonest. They acted like confused tourists who didn't understand English and, keeping an eye on the pods, carefully bumbled through the queue until they'd skipped it.

As pod thirteen/fourteen finally came, Max abandoned Rosie and hastily jumped on board the pod.

Rubbing his hands in relief, he looked around as the pod languorously began to ascend. However, the search didn't go any better. Ten minutes passed, and he made about as much progress as on the first ride.

Max sat on the centre bench. He dropped his face into his palms as he despairingly wondered what to do. *Come on, Zeus, if you're real and listening, give me a clue. Anything. I can't let Amelia win.*

Like a bolt from the heavens, an idea struck Max. That boy from before—he'd crawled under the bench he was sitting on. Max followed suit. Disregarding the glares of onlookers, he got on the ground and dragged himself beneath the bench. He spotted a piece of paper stapled to the wood. It had an anagram:

Ti si tawh? Ti leef orn ees eithern anc ti sesu how speron het. Ti rof seu on sah ti yubs how ersonp het. Ti fo eedn on sah ti akmse how eronsp eht.

Max reached for his phone and took a picture of the code. As he got up and scrutinised the photo, he spotted something curious at the bottom of the page: a crystal. It looked like a red beryl one, too. One of the rarest.

They had done it!

While he disembarked from the pod, he bounced up and down with joy.

He couldn't wait to tell Rosie. *Feels like I've almost found the treasure of Monte Cristo. Soon, I will start plotting my grand revenge, and England will be mine. Bwahaha.*

"Guess what I just got," he said to Rosie, a grin emerging.

As he explained, her face slowly filled with disbelief and delight alike.

"Wow. An anagram?!" she exclaimed feverishly.

"Seems so," he said, and yawned as fatigue began to wear him down. "And red beryl is really valuable. See! Treasure hunting isn't so bad, is it?"

"Hooray. Let's go check into the hotel. I'm knackered."

Max had been called many things in his twenty-one years—bookish, self-absorbed, idiotic, tiresome, ugly, unbearably pretentious and shockingly delusional—and no matter how true those may be, something that nobody could fairly say about him was that he didn't learn from his mistakes. In this way, he had taken great care to book a luxurious room for himself at Premier Inn, doing so over a day in advance. He had even printed the receipts as proof.

One thing that had slipped his mind in the painstaking and fastidious process of booking was double-checking the location of the hotel. That turned out to be a grave error.

"We've got no record of you in our computer, sir," the receptionist, an old roly-poly woman with cratered skin, droned at the check-in desk. She looked like she would rather be doing anything else in the world other than working here tonight. "Are you sure you didn't book a room at a different location?"

"There's more than one Premier Inn?" Max asked.

Rosie wagged her eyebrows. "Of course, there is! It's like the biggest hotel chain in the country, you numpty!"

He sighed. This day seemed to be one of the longest in his life. He desperately longed to be tucked in bed with Benjamin and his Game Boy.

"Oh, bother," he said as he glanced down at his booking receipt. "Seems I booked a room at Stapleford Premier Inn. You don't have any spare rooms?"

"We usually do but not tonight, I'm afraid, sir," the receptionist said.

"Why do all the hotels in this infernal country have fewer spare rooms than Bethlehem?" he asked, a jolt of panic piercing him. He had nowhere to sleep. Again. The streets of London didn't sound like fun, and there was no car as a last resort this time. He turned to Rosie. "Would you, uh, let me—"

"Sure. If you don't mind sleeping on the floor," she said, stifling a yawn.

Max nodded at once, having slept on the floor at the Children's Society for several months after Eddie Tomlinson put spiders in his mattress. They bought ready-made sandwiches from the bar just as it was shutting down for the night and headed up to their room on the second floor, buzzing from their success.

As he removed the lettuce from his cheese sandwich, he made a make-do bed with a spare pillow and bedsheets on the floral carpeted floor. They didn't even have a sofa bed for him.

Rosie jumped on her bed and sipped a glass of vermouth she'd ordered.

"I've not been so wiped out since PE back in school," she mused, nibbling on the crusts. They'd put a repeat of *The X Factor* on the TV, but Max didn't like the show when he recalled Simon Cowell's hurtful, simply unfair comments on his juggling ability. "What a day. So, tell me the anagram again."

Reclined on his makeshift bed, Max tried to read it out loud. "Gibberish. And there's also a URL in which to input the right answer. We can solve it tomorrow."

Louis Walsh softly babbled in the background about the commercial viability of a boy band, sending Max briskly to the arms of Morpheus.

"By the way, I'm sorry if I seemed grouchy today," Rosie said with a note of regret. "I feel kinda bad. For months, I'd been telling you off for participating in this damn contest—until a hint of money came into the picture. I still can't believe I've lost my job. I probably should be looking for a new one right now instead of damn treasure hunting."

"I forgive you, GrouchyMcGrouchFace," he said, feeling strangely sympathetic. "We're both treasure hunters now, sticking it to the Man. When we get recruited as spies for MI6, I promise I'll let you borrow my helicopter and holiday in my secret underwater base."

Max reached for Benjamin in his rucksack. In doing so, his fingers brushed his father's letter, and his heart faltered. He had yet to open it, but he found himself digging the letter out now. As he lay there and stared at it, he wondered why he didn't just read it. A part of him simply didn't want to hear from his father after all these years and all he'd done. They hadn't seen each other in a lifetime. Despite the terrible crimes his father had committed, Max couldn't help but hope his dad had miraculously changed.

Either way, Max opened the envelope. It ran:

Hi, Max!

It's been a few years. The last time I saw you, you were about thirteen years old, visiting me in prison with that crabby Ms Kensington lady. You wore some babyish Cookie Monster hoodie and had your nose buried in a comic book the whole time. Back then, only crosswords, knights and video games interested you. Still doing that treasure hunting shit?

I'm just joking. I bet you have a solid nine-to-five job and are married with kids. Tell me, what kind of woman are you into now that you're a grown man? By the way, I read you went to court for the first time for museum theft. Harsh luck, but good job trying! We won't let the fat cats in Parliament tell the Jacobs what to do!

I'm mainly writing because my bunkmate and I are trying to start a new smuggling operation here in prison, and we need some help. I was wondering whether you could get some cigs and cheap phones for us. If you would visit me and hide them in your shoes or something sometime soon, that'd be great. I had to sneak this letter out of the prison, so don't let me down!

Cheers, Terrence (or Dad)

P.S. Oh, and how's that Rosie girl you like doing? Did you ever get out of the friend zone?

Setting the letter down, Max felt a surge of determination wash over him as he swallowed hard. The reality was that he'd been nurturing the idea that he might visit Terrence here in London. Maybe even leave the door open to some kind of reconciliation.

The next moments found him getting to his feet, opening the hotel window, ripping the letter to shreds and dumping them outside. Rosie stared at Max as he watched the shreds of paper drift away into the gusty, nocturnal air and disappear into the fathomless black.

"What was that, Max?" she asked, finishing her vermouth.

"Something I ought to forget about in a jiffy," he said blankly. He got back under the covers and gave Benjamin a tight squeeze.

"Was it that letter I gave you? Well, what did it say? Who was it?"

"Nothing much. It was just Carol, desperately trying to get me back."

CHAPTER 23

A DEAL WITH THE DEVIL

It was an unpleasant, drizzly day as Khalil stepped through the automatic doors of Nottingham Bowl. He wasn't here to bowl. Aaron had texted him the prior night and offered to make a peace deal with him here. Khalil had thought it through for a long while before giving an answer. One part of him was certain it was a trap, and yet another part, the side of him that was eager to bring down the Black Dog Disciples and stop running from his past, had eventually been persuaded to hear him out.

The situation was something of a Hobson's choice. This was a concept Max had taught him, which referred to an illusory decision where only one option was actually legitimate. In Maxwell's case, the excruciating dilemma of whether to add mayonnaise to his daily cheese sandwich.

Glimpsing at his phone, Khalil grunted when he spotted that he had eighteen missed calls from Max. A spike of guilt poked him somewhere near his oesophagus. He felt like he'd abandoned both him and Rosie over the past couple of days. Still and all, he'd come to the rather unfortunate conclusion that it might well be the case that he could never see Max again, if it put him in danger.

As Khalil stood around, adjusted his bracelet and watched a picturesque family of four tallying up their bowling scores, his mind cast over the friends he'd made in Stapleford and whether he could truly leave them. He'd only just met Rosie, and she seemed nice enough, but it was Max who had become his, well, mate. He didn't think he had ever met someone quite like Max. He had good enough pals at senior school in London, but they were the type of people one acted tough with, bantered with and chatted about girls with. Max was more of—in a strange sort of way—a brother.

By the time Khalil spotted Aaron entering the bowling alley, he had almost fallen asleep in the alley bar. Aaron had arrived tardy, almost an hour after the arranged time. The delay caused Khalil to be overtaken by a fog of drowsiness during the interminable wait.

"Good to see you," Aaron said slyly, doing a double take. "God, you look like shit. We didn't leave things amicably last night, did we?"

Aaron was not alone this time. Tommy, the teenager who had been stalking Khalil and now self-evidently only had a single hand, was right next to him. With a hangdog look on his face, he would not meet either of their eyes for a second. Now that Khalil could get a proper look at him, he saw that he was a short lad with a stick figure and teenage spots. He certainly did not give the impression of being a criminal or a drug dealer, and Khalil wouldn't be surprised if he was still in school.

"The skin is just a window to the soul, mate. Anyway, I'm not in the mood for games," Khalil said, standing straight. "You're late, again. Tell me what your offer is right now."

The moment they made eye contact, the voice in his head told him to get out of here while he still could. Yet he supposed he was more instinctual than someone like Max, who once told him he spent a whole day evaluating the pros and cons of buying an electric toothbrush. His legs were resolutely telling him to stay put.

"You're at a bowling alley, and you're not in the mood for games?" Aaron quipped, glancing at Khalil's bowling shoes, which he'd been forced to rent to wait inside. Aaron patted his back. "Hem, hem. So you *are* ready. I'll just get some, and we can start! I brought Tommy along with me. One hand should be enough, right?"

"Yes, sir," Tommy said at once. He cast a nervous smile at Aaron that didn't conceal the terror lurking underneath.

"Just kidding. You're not playing."

Khalil felt physically sick as Aaron trudged over to get some bowling shoes. *How can anyone be so jovial after last night? Mr Brooks is dead. Batty though he might be, he didn't deserve that, did he? And what ever happened to Gerald? I might've killed him. Don't know if that's a good thing.*

Khalil had never bowled in his life. Subsequent to inputting their names in the game machine, it was apparently his turn first. After he picked up the ball with three fingers, his first throw landed with a clumsy thump on the lane and drifted into the gutter.

"If only you were as good at this as you are at football," Aaron remarked. "Gerald told me you're still not bad at it."

"Nice of you to send him to kill me," Khalil said. He looked at Tommy, who twisted his lip while sitting alone and struggling to use his phone with one hand. "I guess he's recovered from the iron, then."

"More or less. Gerald's rather like you. Though unlike you, he's proven extremely incompetent. It's not as easy to find a competent assassin as you see in the films," Aaron explained, and chortled. "There's no assassin test like a driving licence unfortunately. I may even end up taking his hand too at this rate!"

"Yeah. I noticed he's not great," Khalil said grumpily. "So, I guess you're training Tommy just as you did with me?"

"That's true. But I'm afraid Tommy's as terrible as Gerald. He might be loyal enough, but he's a bit lacking upstairs and a hand short now as well. I mainly brought him here because he can't be left alone." Aaron glanced over at Tommy. "Aren't you useless, Tommy? Like a dog on a leash."

"Yes, sir," Tommy said again, blushing.

Khalil swept his fingers through his lengthy hair. *He looks terrified. I bet Aaron tortures the poor kid. The cycle continues. After Tommy, there'll be another one. The Black Dog Disciples need to be stopped. Too bad I'm probably about to be arrested for murder. They'll think I killed Mr Brooks. Shit.*

"I wish you'd just get it over with and tell me why I'm here," Khalil hit back as he sat on the moth-eaten leather seat and watched Aaron take his turn. "Mr Brooks died yesterday because of you, and yet you couldn't seem to care less. And now that I know you're working with Gerald, it's even more obvious that your money threats were merely a pretext for stalking me."

"Oh, Brooks. Was that his name?" Aaron said, scoring six points. "Gerald and I left the body of that codger rotting in your flat. A shame. No doubt it'll only take a week at most for the police to bash down your door, and before you know it, you'll become Stapleford's most wanted. Maybe less if he has a worried family."

"Cheers," Khalil said, hoping nobody was eavesdropping. "I already worked that out. Your point?"

Aaron straightened his back. "You need a fresh start, a *fresh*, fresh start.

And after all you've done to me—steal my jewellery, run away and so on—I'm willing to give you just that purely out of generosity. I admit, I was leaning towards doing you off after your rudeness the other night, but I've decided to give you the benefit of the doubt. I'll forget about the fake money and everything else too!"

"Yes, sir," Tommy, who was sitting slouched with half-lidded eyes by the ball machine, drawled.

"I wasn't talking to you!" Aaron shouted, striding over and slapping Tommy's cheek.

Khalil simmered at Aaron's smug, sanctimonious tone as he threw his ball and got another gutter ball. It was as if Aaron believed he was doing him a great favour when he was threatening to frame Khalil for murder. He certainly had a twisted way of looking at the world.

"How gracious, Your Majesty," Khalil spat, seething. "Am I supposed to prostrate myself?"

Aaron cast him a sidelong glance. "What I really need is someone I can depend on to do dirty work. Sales in Nottinghamshire are going fantastically, but there's a lot of area in the Midlands left for expansion as regards crystal meth. So, my proposal is that I forgive your debt if you move to Birmingham and help me get business off the ground there. I can give you a new identity, a disguise of sorts and even enough time to take as many of those inane photos as you want."

"Inane, eh? You wouldn't understand art, Aaron. It's not something that you can snort or sell. It is the only way to make the chaos of this absurd life into a form that's beautiful, and it's permanent, or at least as permanent as things can be."

"As for me, I find women beautiful. Not the old photographs you call art!"

"I've realised lately that history is an infinite, self-repeating exercise in futility," Khalil declared. "Art may be the only way for us to break the cycle. Ultimately though, life is all there is, and it's a gift."

"What big words that ultimately amount to nothing. I bet you consider yourself a real hero, eh?"

"Not at all. A hero is someone who gives their life to something bigger than themself, even something tiny like saving a library. I believe I recently met a true hero, actually. He's not the normal kind. Sort of the opposite."

Ruminating, Khalil kept schtum for a few instants while Aaron scored a strike.

"Wow. Looks like luck is on my side!" Aaron exclaimed. "Well, enough equivocating. What do you say about my offer? I don't suppose you would be foolish enough to turn down such generosity."

"I think," Khalil said, dragging out the words as he retrieved a ball, "you can suck a dick. I don't want any part of your business anymore. I'd rather eat nails."

"That can be arranged."

He chucked his ball. It gracefully glided along the lane but drifted to the left at the last second and only poked a single bowling pin over.

"You're as ungrateful as you are a terrible shot! Do you need the bumpers?" Aaron said in affected outrage, blinked at him and twitched his cleft lip. "I have to say, I'm not particularly surprised after everything. Despite your apparent lack of bowling skills, I've always nursed an admiration for your determination and sharpness. In other words, you've always been my favourite lackey. With that said, I admit that I vastly preferred your skills when they were being put to profitable use in the Black Dog Disciples. That's why I've always wanted you to join our organisation formally, and have been ever so persistent."

Khalil winced. "Yeah? How come? It can't be that hard to find drug dealers. I simply never wanted to be part of that lifestyle."

"It's not complicated. You were a good worker—clever, street-smart and mature. And to be blunt, I've yet to find anyone quite as reliable as you. All the lads I hire these days don't have half the brains. Most can't even hold their heads upright. You could even be my successor someday, if you wanted."

"Trying to kill me isn't a good way of persuading me to work for you!"

"You're right. To be quite honest, I only told Gerald to intimidate you. He took it to the extremes. Yes, he's proven to be a disappointment. Maybe you don't have much textbook knowledge, but you make savvy decisions. At least, you used to." Aaron took his shot and scored another strike. "Yes! Two strikes in a row! Watch and learn."

Khalil knew Aaron far too well to believe him. He'd never seen Aaron be nice to anyone without wanting something in return. The offer must be a ploy.

A surge of anger boiled up inside him, his rage rising to levels he had never felt before. "Selling drugs doesn't exactly require a degree in quantum mechanics," he said cuttingly, losing his temper. "I shouldn't have come today. What a joke!"

He strode over and picked up one of the bowling balls from the machine. Instead of throwing it down the lane, he hurled it towards Aaron. It hit his crotch and fell on his left foot, before rolling with a whirring thrum across the alley hall.

Aaron's shrill, childish scream was laughable.

"How's that for a strike?" he said, and turned away for the exit.

"You'll regret that more than you can imagine, Khalil Ahmed," Aaron said, grunting in pain.

"Good. Regrets never hurt me." Khalil shot a compassionate glance at Tommy, who was doing a poor job of concealing a grin. "Get out of here, kid," he advised. "You don't want to be around Aaron any longer."

"He said I c-can't, or he'll take my other h-hand," Tommy floundered.

"Forget what he said."

Just as Khalil was about to leave, he found himself charging back and pummelling Aaron's face. He punched him again and again until Aaron was barely conscious, squealing for him to stop.

Khalil froze and stood stock-still, breathing heavily. Aaron's features were all bloody and bruised. He couldn't just kill Aaron here, no matter how vile he was. The Black Dog Disciples would have to be brought down another way.

As Aaron gasped for breath with blood gushing from his nose, Khalil knew he had taken it too far. Tommy and all the other bowlers were staring. After taking a last glimpse at Aaron's battered form, he ran outside. For all he knew, the police were already on the way.

In Nottingham Bowl car park, his phone rang—Max on his nineteenth call of the morning. He hesitated to answer before deciding he couldn't ignore him any longer.

"Salutations, Khalil. How are your phenomena going?"

It was the first time Khalil had heard Max's voice in days, and he found it oddly comforting.

"My what?" he asked in a strained voice.

"The observable circumstances and occurrences of your embodied existence. The constant stream of experiences that constitute what you perceive as reality."

"Oh. My phenomena are just fine. Beat your high score on Tetris, lately?"

"Egad, I don't have time for small talk," Max said quickly. "Where the hell have you been? And I don't want any more of that car breaking down codswallop. We're on the train home right now."

Max never buys my excuses. I think it's high time to reveal everything.

Khalil wasn't paying much attention as he speed-walked down the road, keeping an eye on the circumambient windows in case Gerald had a sniper on him.

"Answer me!" Max demanded. "You didn't steal my time machine and get stranded in medieval times, did you?!"

"Uh, no. Listen, I need to meet up with you guys tomorrow, and then I'll explain everything." He grappled for a location where Aaron and his cronies wouldn't think to track them down. As far as he knew, Aaron still had no idea about Rosie. "How about Rosie's place?"

They arranged to meet at Rosie's house the following day at lunchtime. He hung up before Max could ask any more questions. The last thing he heard was Max saying he was acting like a textbook tomfool and a loggerhead lummox. Whatever they meant.

As he turned the corner of the street, he was so wrapped up in his haywire thoughts that he hardly noticed a fellow in a trench coat pacing towards him.

"Spare cigarette, buddy?"

Khalil turned. It was only after saying, "nope" that he spotted the person's hat. A fedora. Seconds later, his eyes took in the man's moustached features. Gerald. He had a huge bandage across his face.

And two feet from Khalil, he reached into his coat pocket and pulled out a pistol.

CHAPTER 24

UNEXPECTED DEVELOPMENTS

Rosie was quite certain she'd never met a grown man with such an annoying knock as Maxwell Jacobs. It would have been perfectly sufficient to simply knock once and wait the time it took for her to get to the door, but instead, he had to bang his damn fist against the beechwood twice a second while shouting, "I'm here!"

"I heard the first ten times," she snapped as she tore the door open.

"How was I to know?" he asked shortly, paced in and took his soaked rucksack off. "Oh my. It does smell sublime in here. Like ambrosia."

She glanced outside before slamming the door shut. It was an overcast, murky morning. Puddles formed in the uneven driveway and rain leaked from the broken gutters of her semi-detached house. She lived in a small, cheap property that she rented in one of the shadier areas of Stapleford, which was saying a lot because most of the town was pretty shady.

She held her quiz book, *Collins Quiz Master,* and the answers she'd just read were still revolving in her mind. *Jupiter: the planet with the strongest gravity. Fleming: discovered penicillin. First American President: George Washington.* Rosie had spent the morning practising for the championship, desperate as she was for Agatha Quiztie to finally triumph and take the grand prize.

"It's Brussels sprouts," she revealed. "I was considering making brownies, but I remembered it's you. I've been revising for the championship while I cook."

"Then you *are* making ambrosia!" Max said, licking his lips.

"Anyway, we ought to practise before Khalil gets here. Who were Henry

VIII's wives in order?" she asked, reading a random question from the quiz book.

Max made a do-you-think-I'm-that-much-of-a-dunce face and recited, "Aragon, Boleyn, Seymour, Cleves, Howard and Parr, but it doesn't matter. The reason I was knocking so much was because I need to tell you something in equal parts big, significant and momentous: I've solved the anagram! It was in reverse; that's why it took me a while. The solution's actually a riddle!"

"What in tarnation?"

"I figured the riddle out too, on the way here!" He removed his drenched parka. "I was riding the bus, past the Church of Scientology where I used to go worship Hubbard, around the park where I undertook gnostic, Dionysian dance rituals to summon Beelzebub, under the bridge where I busked with my kazoo in 2007 when I saw a hearse and it just dropped into my head!"

"A hearse? Right. Make yourself comfortable. I need to turn the oven off, but I'll be right back," she said before she dashed to the kitchen.

Rosie fetched the tray of Brussels sprouts, put a few on a plate and brought them to the living room. She wasn't much of a cook, and they smelled revolting to her, but Max was always bugging her to make them. She'd once made a chocolate sponge cake to get him to try new food, and he ended up feeding it to the pigeons—one of those frequent incidents that made her wonder why she was still friends with him.

"So, spit it out." She placed the plate down on her cocktail table and sat on her cretonne sofa to face Max. "Uh-oh. Don't get any sprout leaves on the sofa. My witch of a landlady said it's an antique. She'd kill me if I ruined it."

"Get out your laptop, and we can try the solution," he said, helping himself to his first sprout and handing her a piece of paper. "Exquisite. I wrote the decrypted riddle down here."

She paced over to a drawer, pulled out her laptop and set it down between them. She read the deciphered anagram out loud:

The person who makes it has no need of it. The person who buys it has no use for it. The person who uses it can neither see nor feel it. What is it?

"And the answer is…" Max said, gorging himself with sprouts. "Hold on. It just slipped my mind."

"Oh, great." Rosie bit her nails. "You remember every single thing in the world except the one thing we need to know."

The door knocked once more—a slightly less aggravating knock than Max's, to be sure, but still a somewhat annoying rhythmic one to the beat of "We Will Rock You" by Queen.

"One sec," she said. "Must be Khalil."

It had now been a while since either of them had seen Khalil, and Rosie was almost as curious as Max about what had happened to him, although she didn't agree with his hypothesis that he'd been transformed into a voodoo doll by malicious pagans. Nonetheless, as she opened the door, she frowned as her eyes met someone who was certainly not Khalil and who wasn't even entirely human.

"Brad, what are you doing here?!" she demanded.

Brad Beaver stood in a football jersey, his fluffy chin marked by a new goatee. "I need to talk to you about something. Can I come in?" he asked, trying to waddle past her.

Oh, dear. Max and Brad in close proximity is a disaster waiting to happen. I can't deal with this today.

"I don't know if that's such a good idea," she said, blocking his stride. She stepped outside and left the door very slightly ajar to minimise the chance of Max and Brad coming to blows. "Would you please leave without a fuss right now?"

Brad was still not taking their separation lightly. "I miss you. Please give me another chance"; "I promise I won't go off about Max ever again"; and "But we were meant to be together" were just a few of the whiny, inebriated messages she had in the backlog of her voicemail. She thought it was amusing more than anything, not because she was cruel but because Brad was such an arse. It'd taken the threat of a restraining order to get him to quit calling.

"No, not yet." Brad Beaver dug his paws into his pockets and stared down stiffly at the porch's mosaic tiles. "I've just got something to say that I think you ought to know. I mean, you probably already do, but I thought I'd better come just in case."

"What?" she asked, disconcerted. "I'm in the middle of something."

He made a pensive, furry face—which was odd to see as he never seemed to think much. "You're familiar with Max's co-worker, Khalil?"

She nodded hesitantly, arms crossed.

"The other day, he came for a trial to join the league. He didn't get in as he was kind of shit, but that's not the point. Shortly after he left, there was this, well, shooting."

Rosie stared at him, words escaping her. "A what?"

"Nobody got hurt, but I think he might be involved. The point is—and don't say this is a jealousy thing—I'm not sure it's a good idea for you to be hanging around with Max after this."

"Why?"

"Because he's associated with such a dangerous terrorist."

"What are you on about?" she asked, open-mouthed. "Khalil's not a terrorist."

Yikes. A shooting in town. The stray bullet that almost hit us. They can't be connected, can they?

Stapleford was so dull that it was certainly not the type of town to have a shooting, let alone two in such close proximity. The most exciting and famous thing in Stapleford was the so-called Hemlock Stone, which was basically just a really old rock.

"Have you heard of that terrorist group, ISIS?" he speculated, his buck teeth coming into view. "I've been thinking…maybe Khalil's a member. He said his parents are from Afghanistan. I did some research on it, and that's where they're based. It could just be he's a convert or—"

"Rosie, you don't have any maple syrup, do you?" Max Raccoon called from inside the house. "I thought it may taste good with the sprouts."

"Maxwell? Is he here?" Brad Beaver asked furiously as blood surged to his face.

Rosie thought she must have just been transported to a poorly written sitcom. *And here's the big plot twist before the commercial break…*

Max appeared at the door, caught Brad's eyes and slapped his hands against an imaginary trash bin. "Oh, no. Not Bradley."

"So, now you're seeing each other, I bet!" Brad Beaver roared, his shaggy temples forming lines. "I don't know why I even bothered to come, Rosie. It's your choice if you want to spend your life with that conniving oddity and his criminal friends. Just don't say I didn't warn you."

"At least I'm not a wretched mooncalf," Max Raccoon sneered, whiskers stirring.

"A mooncalf? Is that still the best insult you can come up with?" Brad Beaver's downy face contorted with scorn. "I don't even know what it means."

"You should know. Takes one to know one," Max Raccoon said, his snout raised.

"Be quiet, both of you," Rosie said, and turned to Max with her fingers intertwined. "Apparently, Khalil might have been involved in a shooting. I have a feeling he's not going to show up at all."

"A shooting?" Max Raccoon repeated, baring his pointed teeth. "Of what? Nerf guns?"

"Yeah, exactly..." Brad Beaver barked with a hiss. "Why don't you invest some of that endless time you spend reading encyclopaedias into developing common sense?"

"Brad, will you please just leave before I call the police?" Rosie asked.

"Fine! I'll go!" Brad snapped so loudly that it seemed to set off a burglar's alarm down the road. "But I just wanna say, Rosie, that it's your loss. I was into you solely because I thought you were kinda good-looking. But I deserve better. I really do. And frankly, I never really dug your thing for quizzing and your bad maths puns and"—he glared at Max Raccoon—"him. Have a nice life."

With the most dramatic gait he could manage, Brad Beaver stormed off, his tail flapping behind him. Rosie turned to Max, who in the meantime had lost his rummaging bin and his furry grey ears as he turned back into a man.

"Something abominably insufferable is going on," he declaimed. "I'm sure of it."

"You don't say," she said. "I don't believe Brad would make up something so random without a good reason. He's not smart enough. Once he even told me he thought eggs come from cows."

"How about we go to Khalil's? We can pick up *The Stapleford Herald* on the way."

She hastily stepped over to her bowl to get her car keys. "Oh, but what about the riddle?"

"I solved it already. The answer was coffin. And the next clue is pirate themed! The website told me so."

"Good job. Wait. Where are you going?" she asked as he ran off to the kitchen.

He soon reappeared, carrying the platter of Brussels sprouts as well as something else. "I found your maple syrup," he mumbled, and poured it into his gullet along with a sprout.

In the middle of their frantic drive to Khalil's place, they stopped at the local newsagents. Max jumped out of the car, ran in and bought the latest newspaper. As he read out a headline about a black bag filled with severed hands that someone had found in the River Trent, Rosie stiffened in her seat. A foreboding feeling that one of *them* would soon be requiring a coffin settled over her.

CHAPTER 25

MURDER MYSTERY

Bundled in parkas, Max and Rosie dashed up the stairwell to Khalil's flat. When they reached his floor, they were greeted by a line of blue and white tape with police gathered behind it. Several locals, mostly residents and some members of the local press by the looks of it, huddled behind the tape, twiddling their thumbs and gossiping amongst themselves.

Tapping his foot at near light-speed, Max cleared his throat and said softly, "You don't think this has something to do with his neighbour, uh, Mr Brooks?"

"Seems possible. Mr Brooks' door is also behind the tape, isn't it?" Rosie observed, pointing forward. "Did Khalil ever tell you why he left London?"

"No. He was always unforthcoming," he said. "I once overheard him speaking to his mother. I couldn't understand what he was saying, but it was something about not being able to come back home. That said, ages ago I did spot him dumping a black bag in the River Trent just like the one in that article."

A little frown came upon her face. "Really? Hmm. I bet the police don't know who his flat belongs to. I saw bills addressed to Charlie Almond when I was here. Maybe it's his pseudonym."

"I did too," he said sullenly. "Or maybe Khalil is the fake name, and Charlie's the real one!"

Rosie just groaned, and in the middle of that groan, a person whom Max disliked almost as vehemently as Brad appeared. Constable Tomlinson had stepped out of Khalil's apartment and stomped towards the crowd with a surly, displeased expression.

"Move it along, folks. Absolutely nothing to see here," he barked.

Max thought this day had to be cursed to run into Brad and Constable Tomlinson within the same hour. He hid his face and tried to become invisible so that Constable Tomlinson wouldn't spot him, but unfortunately, in his crimson *Fireman Sam* T-shirt, he was not easily concealed. He couldn't wait till he won the contest and could buy some new clothes.

"Well, well, what do we have here? The dynamic duo," Constable Tomlinson said. He trod over. "Care to explain? Last time I checked, you're not from this neck of the woods."

The others dispersed and left them nowhere to hide.

It's disturbing how incompetent the Stapleford police are. Maybe when this all blows over, I should become the town vigilante: Max the Almighty. Can't let that Judge Beaton ruin my whole life.

"Why does it matter to you where we betake ourselves, how we acquit ourselves and when we indulge ourselves in this rusty mailbox of a town?" Max proclaimed shrewdly. "The fact is we heard about that football shooting and now this similar incident. Let me guess—another stray bullet?"

Constable Tomlinson grimaced. "Don't be a ruddy smart aleck. Y'know you could get arrested for speaking to a police officer like that. This homicide is none of your business," he said, his beetle brow furrowing.

Homicide? Oh, no. The next worst type of -cide after pesticide.

"And the other incident was what?" Max riposted. "The shooting outside Stapleford Stadium?"

"A suspected gang shooting," Constable Tomlinson said, eyes flitting downwards. "Aren't you the man-child here? Why are you so interested? Shouldn't you be playing your Game Boy instead of worrying about police matters?"

"Better to be a man-child than a policeman-child."

"Pipe down, Max, before you get us into trouble," Rosie hissed, elbowing his side and eliciting a yelp of pain. She faced Tomlinson. "I'm sorry, Constable Tomlinson. You see, we're just worried about the recent spate of local crimes. Did something bad happen here?"

"I can't reveal many details, but it's a tragic case," the constable said, his face drained of colour. "We got a couple of calls the other night about a loud noise and came to investigate. Seems a beloved elderly local has been killed in cold blood by his neighbour, a new arrival in town. We're still trying to work out his identity, but whoever the psycho is, he'll be lucky to get less than life." He clicked his tongue. "Nothing to concern you two, though. Maxwell, why don't you get back to your Old MacDonald nursery rhymes and whatnot?"

As a chilly gust of wind swept over him, Max saw his own shock reflected in Rosie's eyes. No matter how annoying Mr Brooks might be, he couldn't fathom a set of circumstances that would incite Khalil to kill him. The only explanation was that Khalil had been framed.

And on his farm, he had some cows. E-I-E-I-O. Damn song stuck in my head at a time like this.

Worry swilled through Max's mind. "How ghastly. Why do you think it was his neighbour?"

"The old man's body was found in his neighbour's flat with a bullet through his brain. Instant death." The constable scowled. "At any rate, I don't buy you're just lollygagging around here out of interest. Really, why are you so curious?"

And on his farm, he had some pigs. E-I-E-I-O. Get out of my damn head!

"With an oink-oink here," Max said.

"An oink. Excuse me?" Constable Tomlinson asked, bewildered.

He flushed. "Yes, and an oink-oink there..."

"I just like true crime, okay?" Rosie interjected, saving the day. She grazed Max's hand. "Come on. Let's go to my place and have a cup of tea. Good luck with your investigation, Constable."

She grabbed Max's arm and practically pulled it out of its socket as she tugged him away. While they sprinted down the stairwell together, words spilled out of both of their mouths.

"I know Khalil didn't murder Mr Brooks," he asserted, panting. "He's not a killer."

"I don't doubt it, but who on Earth did?" she asked tensely. "Old MacDonald?"

"Maybe Mr Brooks shot himself and decided to frame Khalil as revenge."

Max didn't particularly know why they were going so fast as they arrived at Rosie's car. Neither had a clue what to do next. He thought hard about what Khalil would do if he was in his shoes, ceased his foot tapping and turned to her seriously.

"We have to split our energies. I'll focus on finding Khalil while you work on the pirate clue. As I mentioned briefly, I got it on the website this morning along with an alexandrite crystal," he said, showing her the clue. "I'm sure he's somewhere in town."

"Fine." Rosie put her car key in and reversed out of the car park. "And another thing. I know it's not that important in the grand scheme of things, but what are we going to do for the championship's fourth member now?"

Max thought for a moment. "How about I ask Sofia, my librarian friend? She may say yes with some persuasion."

"As long as we have four heads, we can participate. That's all that matters."

With a sense of being in the final stretch of a long, epic war, Max glanced out the window as the rain began hammering down. The pitter-patter of the droplets against the car roof was like a war march drumroll. Despite summer having more or less arrived, the sky was not tinged with the faintest trace of blue, the greyness extending for miles on end.

Distracted by treasure hunting over the past few weeks, Max could barely believe how long it had been since he had last gone to the library. Yet when Rosie dropped him off, and he stepped inside, his heart sank. Rows and rows of shelves were empty, which must mean they'd already started massacring the books. He found Sofia vacuuming with a Crystal vacuum by the wardrobe, her belly looming larger than ever.

"What's going on? Where are the books?" he asked, making her jump.

What am I going to read now? The toothpaste ingredients? I already know two: hydrogen peroxide and sodium bicarbonate. It gets dull if it never changes!

Max could tell something was not well by Sofia's doleful eyes. What's more, not only was her stomach bulging, but her double neck was growing increasingly chubby. Over the years, he'd frequently seen her indulge in her cravings when she was going through a rough spot. He'd once seen her devouring a Tesco bag's worth of packs of Smarties and M&M's in a single hour when she'd been having marital problems.

"It's not good news, pet," she lamented. "Pish posh. This is gonna be my last week ever."

He gasped. "Why? Have some books already been euthanised? I mean, thrown away?!"

Max glanced around at the tearful orphans in hand-me-downs inside the children's section, crowded around the only remaining copy of *The World of Moominvalley*. (He currently had the other one checked out.) He had failed them all!

"Some bookies 'ave already been sold," Sofia explained, her voice thick with woe. "The rest are goin' to be shredded or incinerated. Or both."

Faintness enveloped Max. This was egregious news but not quite as bad as it could've been. There was time, albeit barely.

He surveyed the vacant shelves, feeling that today might have just breached worst-day-of-all-time territory. Prior to today, he'd not thought anything could come close to the day he had won the lottery grand prize and accidentally dropped the ticket down the waste disposal.

"Why not just donate the books if the library has to close?" he asked, indignant.

"Mr Johnson insists. Och. We're as bankrupt as a Scotsman's fiddle," she explained briskly, wolfing down a Yorkie bar. "My ma said this to me when I was a wee bairn: don't fight battles ye cannae win."

He bristled. After everything—all his eccentric, serio-comic misadventures—could it have all been for nothing? He scanned all the bookies that he would never see again. Spotting the amazing Nancy Drew and Mr. Men series, his despair converted into burning rage at who was *really* to blame.

"I'm going to talk to Mr Johnson right now," he avowed gruffly.

Before Sofia could protest, he swept around and headed straight for his office.

The problem was that Mr Johnson had obviously never been fond of Max. Needless to say, since he'd become caretaker manager of the Co-op, his opinion of Max seemed to have sunk about as low as the Earth's core. Nonetheless, Max knocked on his door.

"Is that you, Sofia? I'm desperate for a coffee," Mr Johnson yelped. He pulled a face when he spotted Max in the door crack. "Oh, it's *you*. Well, whatever it is, trust me, I haven't got time for it. I'm busy organising the book disposal."

"I j-just need a m-minute of your time," Max said, stepping inside. Somewhere along, his rage seemed to have turned into nerves.

Mr Johnson was the only person he knew who could compete with both Brad and Constable Tomlinson in terms of unpleasantness. In the short lulls between screaming fits, he could be found typing on his BlackBerry or reading history books about World War II.

"As Dickens said, procrastination is the thief of time," David grunted.

"Actually, it was Edward Young who said that."

David got up to pack some more files into a box labelled "Recycle." His office was as messy as a teenager's room, with files scattered and cabinets dangling open. He certainly hadn't inherited Ms Johnson's tidiness.

"I don't care," David said. "I can't imagine you saying anything remotely helpful to me. Balancing my mother's hospitalisation, running a business, orchestrating a library closure and dealing with my wife who's filing for divorce absorbs every minute of my focus."

"What about a few seconds then?" Max queried. "I can talk fast. How many words per second can you comprehend?"

Pouting, Mr Johnson glanced at his watch. "A second in your presence feels more like ten years. The answer is no."

"Come on. Hear me out," he urged. "I've just heard about our imminent bankruptcy. I truly think I could get together the money to save the library if you could just bide a little time. I'm extremely close to winning The Crystalline Crucible and being recruited into a secret immensely powerful organisation that's gonna solve all my problems and make me richer than Bill Gates. Like really, really, really close."

David gave a great, uppity sigh as if he was being deflated. "What do you mean our bankruptcy?" he said in a dismissive voice.

"According to the Oxford dictionary, bankruptcy is an insolvency process for individuals, which commences on the day the bankruptcy order is made and releases a debtor from their debts in exchange for the realisation of their estate by a trustee," he explained.

"No, no. I meant, what do you mean by *our*?" David snapped.

"The possessive pronoun. Sofia said you're about to start burning our books."

"Give me a break!" Mr Johnson rolled his eyes. "Now, listen here, Maxwell Jacobs, if you're even capable of it. I've been meaning to tell you the truth about what I think about you for years. For the past decade, I've seen you traipse in here with your sword and your encyclopaedias, drink from the water dispenser willy-nilly and stomp around the corridors like you own the damn place. Not to mention, eat all my digestive biscuits. You're a complete nutcase! This is a library—not your private holiday home!"

"What?" Max exclaimed. "But you knew my mother, didn't you? I figured you don't like me much, but I always felt like… I mean, after she passed…I was part of the team here."

"How dare you! You're not part of any bloody team, and you never have been," he bellyached. "Yes, your mother worked here a millennium ago, but she wasn't a good employee, and I barely knew her. Even if we were best friends, I certainly wouldn't expect her orphaned son to develop an obsession with the library she worked at subsequent to her death, a bizarre saviour complex that you are the knight in shining armour of this star-crossed institution. And I mean that literally. Since we're shutting down, I suppose it hardly matters now, but I'm convinced it's imperative for both my mental stability and yours that you forget Stapleford Library ever existed. And see about getting yourself a life, too. How about not giving my mother heart attacks! God, it's tiresome enough seeing you at the Co-op every day. I'd fire you if not for her."

Stunned, Max spluttered, "I've just b-been trying to h-help out around here. And the bookless orphans—where else will they go?"

"We don't need *your* help. This place is like the Titanic three hours after hitting the iceberg, and it's time you accept it!" he roared. "I still can't fully understand why in God's name you've developed such a bizarre fixation on this library, but I do know that I never want to see your face here again. Nobody even uses libraries anymore! Get an e-reader! Move on! Now, for the love of Jesus, leave me alone."

And with that, Mr Johnson rounded on Max, shoved him out, and slammed his office door with a bang so loud that it resembled a sonic boom.

Max was used to his trips to the library cheering him up. He certainly didn't feel like that this time. There was no getting around the fact that he was no longer welcome here, and here wouldn't even exist for much longer, either. He turned around to say his final farewell to Sofia, but she seemed to have disappeared to get some crisps. It was a miserable affair bidding farewell to all the precious, insightful books—from *The Culture of Narcissism* to *The Conspiracy Against the Human Race*, and, perhaps most important of all, *Milly-Molly-Mandy Stories*.

After he left the library, he sat on the curb outside and stared into space, heartbroken. The next priority on his to-do list was to start looking properly for Khalil, who was no doubt soon to be a wanted man. Yet he was far too depressed for that. He'd not felt this bad since he ran for Nottingham MP with his manifesto to ban all schools and for Tamagotchi rights. Only Rosie had voted for him out of the whole district. She'd called him way too sensitive many times, and he had once been in tears for a full week after Eddie had called him ugly. *This library was my home. Now, I'm as homeless as Diogenes. I just need to start pleasuring myself in public as well.*

A sympathetic voice broke out from behind him. "Are ye doin' all righ', Max? You look propa gutted."

He looked around. Sofia. She approached him, took her headphones off and sat next to him.

"Deplorably unsatisfactory," he wailed. "I feel terrible about the books. I'm *so* close to getting the money. I can feel it! All the books are gonna be destroyed; it's so sad. And the poor kids who come here… Alas, I've let them down. I'm just too late."

"Pish posh. How come yer so close, pet?" she said, munching on a packet of sour onion crisps.

"On account of The Crystalline Crucible. I don't want to give away any unnecessary details as it could risk your safety, but my team and I have nearly won."

Max sighed; he wished he could be working on the new clue right now.

"Hum. Possibly I could get ya a week or so," she said, engrossed in thought. "Aye, I'll make up somethin' real daft for Mr Johnson like the government changed its mind. He's nae exactly Stephen Hawking."

"Veraciously? You'd do that? Thanks so much!" he exclaimed, his heart warming. "You're my Tinker Bell, Sofia."

"Nae big deal," she said, licking her fingers of crisp dust. "I wanna keep my job too. Just don't waste it, laddie."

Max thanked Sofia again. Another favour may be asking for too much, but the championship was, after all, the original reason he'd come to the library. He felt he had to bring it up.

"Not to push my luck," he said, "but I was wondering if you may be able to help with my quiz team as well. We are competing next week in the annual Stapleford Quiz Championship, and we've just lost our fourth member. I thought you could take his place."

"Me?" she said, and pointed to herself. "I cannae help ya there, unless they're nosh questions. If anythin', I'd lose you points, pet. I'm as thick as a plank."

"We just need another player. It's not paramount that you're good," he reassured. "To wit, all you must do is show up on the day. That's all. There's also prize money. Five thousand split."

She paused. "If all I 'ave to do is come, an' I get a cut when we win, I'll be there, Maxy."

Max was not the type of person to give hugs. He tended to recoil on the rare occasions anybody had offered them or any physical affection. But, for whatever reason, he was overcome with the instinct to reach over and give Sofia an affectionate pat on the back, the most it seemed he was capable of.

"Much obliged, Sofia," he said. "I daresay you may just be a morbidly obese angel!"

He smiled in relief. *Rosie will be so happy. Maybe hope lingers yet in Stapehellford.*

"Cheers," Sofia said, grinning as she patted him too. "Aye, I may be a bit on the chunky side, but that's just me. An' now I'm peckish for another snack. Ooh, I fancy Haribo Starmix!"

She struggled to her feet. Exeunt Sofia. And with the problem of the Stapleford Quiz Championship solved, Max set his sights on finding Khalil.

That night, when the sun had fallen and when the only light was coming from the Challenge channel playing in the background on his TV, he sat deep in thought in his armchair. Instead of doing a crossword or playing with himself (on his Wii) like he would've done on any normal evening, Max got his scheming notepad out and wrote down a list of all the places his mate could possibly be hiding. Unfortunately, even after an hour had passed, the list remained as empty as the list of physics professors who'd responded to the letters he'd sent containing his physics theories. The only plausible idea he had come up with so far was that Khalil had been abducted by aliens, in which case he hoped they were just Vulcans probing him and nothing worse.

As he was completing this task, Max heard shouts coming from outside.

He got down on his knees and crawled under the windowsill, keeping low in case a bullet was about to crash through. After a strained moment, he peeped over. Across the road stood a moustached man in a fedora. He was pulling a large rectangular package out of a van. His shouts seemed to be aimed at another handless man who looked much younger, as they picked up the package and took it inside the abandoned Poolway Shopping Centre. Max couldn't hear a word they said, but something about it was odd to him. He could've sworn that he'd seen one of those men following him around town a few weeks ago. Besides, he had long been convinced that the abandoned shopping centre was a drug den. He wrote it down on his list in the remote chance it had anything to do with Khalil and that peculiar black bag he'd read about in the paper.

Over the next few hectic days, Max and Rosie met up every afternoon for quiz practice at Costa Coffee, where they updated each other about their progress on their respective missions. The pirate clue was nothing more than a photo of a pirate with a parrot and an eye patch. Rosie had tried scanning it and searching for the image online, even posting it to various forums and seeing if anyone recognised the name of the pirate, but she'd made no strides in working out his identity or meaning. The worrying thought that they were stuck crossed both of their minds.

Meanwhile, Max was forced to keep working as usual.

"Maxwell, you haven't heard from Khalil, have you?" Mr Johnson asked on Wednesday's shift.

"Er, not in local spatiotemporal coordinates, no," Max murmured.

Poppy was at the till today while Max was cleaning. He was almost done pouring bleach over the newspapers and magazines, having just finished washing the pastries. Poppy had largely taken Khalil's place following his disappearance, and Max had been avoiding Mr Johnson like the black plague ever since their explosive fight at the library.

"If he doesn't come into work by the end of the week, he'll have to get the axe," Mr Johnson stated, arms crossed. His stony eyes hovered over Max, and then he paced over and grabbed the bottle. "Will you stop pouring bleach on those! For God's sake! You've ruined at least fifty of them!"

"Humblest apologies," Max murmured. He raised his hands defensively in case David was about to wallop him. "I was trying to disinfect them of pathogens."

He'd been so deep in thought about where Khalil could be that he'd forgotten one didn't *need* to clean magazines and newspapers. Khalil's absence had wreaked havoc on his acuity, among other things.

"Good job on ruining more products," Mr Johnson hurled abuse. "I haven't forgotten when you juggled the croissants and dropped ten! Count those up. They'll be deducted from your pay."

He stormed away.

Max tallied them up, and his blood went cold. *Twenty-two ruined magazines and sixteen ruined newspapers. So, that means I'm working for negative eight pounds an hour today. Huzzah.*

The front page of *The Stapleford Herald* this week was about Mr Brooks' death, which was all Stapleford had been talking about. The story had reached some national tabloids. It appeared the police were in the dark about Khalil's identity as they were yet to reveal a suspect. It had been clever of him to rent his apartment under a fake name. But Max couldn't help but feel that it was only a matter of days till they realised who he was.

Max could scarcely tell where the time went, yet before long, a whole week had passed, and the Stapleford Quiz Championship was only one day away. Not only had he made essentially no progress in finding Khalil, but he hadn't been able to focus at all in *Wii Sports Resort*, where his scores—especially in canoeing and frisbee—were getting worse and worse. This sharp drop in performance might have been exacerbated by Amelia's messages on TreasureNet:

boyzonefan42: heya, max. just wanted to let u know i'm days away from getting the last clue!!! I feel sorta bad about being so nasty in london. when i win, maybe I'll buy u a year's World of Warcraft subscription as a peace offering, and to get you off Club Penguin

thecrystalhunter: Trust me, the only one of us who will have time for WOW is most certainly you, as I will be far too busy building the crossword library and theme park on my private island.

boyzonefan42: lol. so, tell me, who was that pretty girl with you in London? ur first gerlfrend? ;)

thecrystalhunter: Just a friend. Knights don't take lovers. We are married to the principles of honour and chivalry.

Other forum members had been messaging him lately too, either to ask for help with clues or to cyberbully him.

Ifureadthisurgay had sent a particularly nasty message:

Why don't you start calling yourself The Crystal Hunter after you win? Everyone on this forum thinks you are a troll.

It was on the eve of the quiz that Rosie decided to bring Lauren along to practice. And so, for the first time in months, Agatha Quiztie had a quiz practice with more than two members, just like when Fred and Bob used to come.

Max entered the Costa Coffee and shortly found Rosie and Lauren sitting around a table with steaming coffees.

"Nice to see you, Ms Collins," Max greeted.

Lunchtime had arrived, and the air was thick with the mingled aroma of caffeine and Rosie's strawberry perfume. Lauren's face was laden with even more layers of makeup than before, like a child who had found their mother's cosmetics drawer. Her nails were painted bright cerise to match her plump lips.

"What are you wearing?" Lauren asked, glaring at him. "First the cowboy hat and now this? You've truly outdone yourself."

His gaze fell to his garments. He wore a furry suit with long, floppy ears. "Oh, bother." He sighed. "I was in a daze this morning, and I must have put on my old Bugs Bunny Halloween costume by mistake. It's no surprise I'm distracted. Rosie's made me study non-stop for the past two days. I can't believe there's only one night left until the championship."

"Can you go home and change, like, now?" she asked, and sipped her coffee as she glanced around at the staring strangers. "People might think I'm your friend or something."

"You think this is embarrassing? One time he came as Mr Blobby," Rosie pointed out.

Max bowed over and tied up his shoelaces. They'd been undone over the past decade, and he kept neglecting to tie them up. "I'd better stay. I need to go to community service after this, and I can't be late. I now have two strikes for dumping my bin bag on a flowerbed and telling my supervisor to stop being such a Draconian tyrant," he said, ears dangling. He sat down. "Welp. Let's get cracking."

As he got the question cards out, Rosie leaned over and whispered, "Any success with Khalil?"

"If only," Max said in a frustrated tone. "When Agatha Christie disappeared for eleven days, there was a huge search for her but then she just turned up out of nowhere. I hope something similar will happen."

Rosie groaned and clasped her hand to her forehead. "I've been staring at that pirate for what feels like years. It's starting to infiltrate my dreams," she said uncertainly. "What kind of clue is a simple pirate? I'd prefer if it were another riddle. I don't think he's Captain Hook or Blackbeard."

"Um, did you bring me here to practise or to, like, gossip?" Lauren interrupted.

She was quite right that they ought to not waste this final practice session, so Max started reeling off his questions.

"Who was the first emperor of Rome?" he asked.

"Augustus," Rosie answered, quick as a flash.

"Correct. What is the capital of Kyrgyzstan?"

"Bishkek."

"Correct. What is the largest fish?"

"Whale shark. And the smallest is Photocorynus spiniceps."

It seemed she'd been practising hard. Rosie no longer confused the Montagues and Capulets, or thought that tomatoes were really vegetables.

In the interim, Lauren had taken to texting and was yet to answer any questions correctly besides "Who killed Archie Mitchell?" So, apparently, she was an expert on the Mitchells. Whoever they were.

"Very well done, Rosie. I don't know how, but you've improved remarkably," Max said, after she correctly answered that there were twenty-six counties in the Republic of Ireland, a question even he would've got wrong on account of Northern Ireland. "Work on your knowledge of ancient Egypt and Asian rivers, and we'll be golden."

"It's nothing," she said, blushing slightly. "I can just never recall the difference between Akhenaten and Tutankhamun, or the Yangtze and Yellow rivers."

"Why do they only quiz about useless stuff?" Lauren asked bad-temperedly. "If there were more questions about real things, I'd get them all right."

Rosie folded her arms. "What's real stuff to you?"

"You know, the Royal Family and *Big Brother* stuff. Things that actually affect me. Oh, and Katie Price trivia."

She jutted her chin. "Fine. Here's a Royals question: who won the Wars of the Roses?"

"Um, George Bush?" Lauren mumbled. At the sight of both of their mystified expressions, she corrected herself. "I mean, Hillary Clinton. Sorry. I was thinking of the Civil War."

"Precisely. Hillary Clinton slaughtered King Obama on Bosworth Field with a robust blow of the sword, shortly before becoming senator of New York," Max ribbed.

Rosie rested her hand on Lauren's. "Henry Tudor. But don't worry. There'll be plenty of celebrity gossip questions as well," she said.

"I'm smart enough for the other ones," Lauren said, flustered. "Don't patronise me. But I can't quiz any longer. I have a fish pedicure at four and a date with you-know-who tonight at Bistrot Pierre, the five-star French restaurant that just opened in town. I wouldn't be able to afford it now without a job, but Frank always volunteers to pay. He's a gent."

"La-di-da," Max said under his breath. "Would you mind if I tagged along with Benjamin the Bear, my stuffed animal companion?"

"Maybe in your dreams," she said insolently.

Lauren departed, leaving Max and Rosie to discuss their plans before the championship.

"I have to go too," he said grimly. "It's time for community service, which, much like school, they should really call legalised torture. I'm pretty sure my probation officer is getting suspicious. During our last meeting, I stupidly wore my 'I love treasure hunting' T-shirt."

"And I've got to work on the clue to no avail," Rosie groaned as she packed up the cards. "Please don't be late tomorrow. We all need to be at the Stapleford Community Centre by nine, at least an hour early. It begins at ten, and the quizzing schedule is packed." She said the next part very pointedly. "In other words, they won't wait for us if *you* are late. Did you hear that? Don't be late!"

"No need to worry. However, I do have an engagement with David, Ms Johnson's son, at the hospital shortly before. He wants to tell me something apparently. It's only a ten-minute walk away."

"Bad idea, Max. You'll lose track of the time."

"Don't worry. It'll be fine."

"Famous last words. Just don't be late."

"You already said that," Max said, tying his bunny ears into a knot.

"I'll say it again till it gets through your thick skull. Well, good luck to both of us," she said sternly, turning away. "And one more thing: don't be late!"

He pined amorously as he watched Rosie leave, her long, beautiful brown hair flowing behind her. No matter how much of a grouch she might be, no matter how cynical she'd become and no matter how subpar her Brussels sprouts had been lately, without her, he always missed her melodious voice, her passion for maths and, perhaps most of all, her strawberry aroma. Was he too much of a coward to tell Rosie how he really felt? Would she simply laugh at him?

That night, Max slept in fits and starts. The past months had been leading up to the following day, and now all he wanted to do was get the championship over with. As he awoke from a horrifying dream where Wordsworth cannibalised Miss Marple, who had been Margaret all along, he realised with dread that the day was finally here. After a bowl of Coco Pops, he spent a few fleeting minutes on TreasureNet messaging Amelia, who reported with glee that she was about to set off on a journey to find the final clue. Subsequently, Max zipped up his parka and set off for the hospital.

For once, it was a sunny morning, the first blush of dawn burning down on his skin like a hot water bottle. As he arrived at the hospital, he recalled when he had walked down these halls with Khalil. The truth was—he realised at that moment—he didn't just want Khalil back as a teammate. He missed him as a friend, a fidus Achates.

The problem with getting attached to people had reared its head once again. When he got too close to Rosie, she didn't reciprocate his feelings. Khalil had gone the more extreme route and chosen to extricate himself from his life completely without any explanation. Unless he was dead, in which case Khalil had a strong excuse.

As Max entered Ms Johnson's hospital room, he was half-expecting to find her bed empty with David standing beside it while waiting to inform him that she'd passed away and that he was sacked. But there she remained. In fact, he could've sworn she was looking much better.

"Max, how nice of you to visit," Ms Johnson greeted, leaning up in her bed.

He stared at her. Ms Johnson had just addressed him. It was like something from a nightmare.

Dear God, no. She's patient zero. Don't step any closer.

"I thought..." he muttered. "They said you were... Please don't bite me."

"You're not hallucinating. I woke up two days ago," she said, giving him a tranquil smile. "Isn't it good to be alive? Don't be angry at an old woman's fun, but I asked my son to let me tell you. Thought I'd give you a little surprise."

"Thank Zeus," he said. Max paced to Ms Johnson's bedside, dumbfounded. "Apologies. I thought you were the origin patient of an imminent zombie apocalypse. How do you feel?"

"Not great. I've got a terrible itch on my back under my hospital gown, and I can't reach it," she said, tittering. "But you don't want to hear about my aches and pains. Tell me, how's the shop been? I trust you've kept it shipshape."

"Same as usual," he mumbled, still taken aback. "Actually, that's not the truth. The Co-op has been really empty and miserable without you. We all miss you a lot. I suspected your son was going to fire me today; he's had a lot of spleen lately."

"Sorry to disappoint. I'm afraid I am going to be sticking around for a little while longer," Ms Johnson said, her silver strands curling around her neck. "I hope my son's not been too harsh. I just want to say thanks for keeping the Co-op going while I was out of action. Indeed, I've got something I want to give you for helping out. A thank-you gift."

She reached across to her bedside table, picked up a small felt box and deposited it in his hand.

"What's this?" he asked. He raised the box up to his eyes.

She smiled and then opened it for him. "It's yours. My late husband's Rolex. I was going to give it to David, but he has a perfectly good one already. I thought you deserved it."

"I couldn't," Max said, pointing at his cheap plastic watch. "I have a perfectly good one too."

He hastily put the box back down on her bedside table, but she wouldn't have it and forced the box back into his hand.

"Nonsense," Ms Johnson insisted. "You must've been wearing that cheap, childish thing since you were five. I insist. As I'm sure you've noticed, David's a bit of a grump; he wouldn't appreciate it. Why don't you try it on now?"

Max didn't see the point of protesting, so he put the watch on and gazed down at his wrist. The strap was chromium gold, and the bezel glistened brightly like a crystal.

"I can't thank you enough, Ms Johnson. It's the nicest gift anyone has ever given me. I don't deserve it after how asinine I've been at the Co-op," he said, his face hot.

"You've been my loyal employee for years. Yes, I never denied you're not the best at your job, but you're not the worst either."

"Are you sure about that?"

"Your heart has always been in the right place, and that's what matters. How's Khalil been lately?"

"Oh, he's doing exceedingly well," Max said, stumbling over his words. "Out-of-this-world good. The paragon and quintessence of wellness."

His phone chimed. It was a message from Rosie:

`It's nine. Are you on the way yet?! Don't let me down.`

Although turning up an hour early seemed excessive, he supposed there was no point in unnecessarily worrying her, given how uptight she was about the championship.

"You will *definitely* get into Heaven now in the essentially impossible chance it exists," Max said tenderly. "But I've got to skedaddle. It's the Stapleford Quiz Championship today. My team wants me to get there early."

"Ah, of course. I'm sure you'll do splendidly with all the encyclopaedia reading you get up to on your lunch breaks."

"We can only hope."

"Make me proud. But before you go, can I ask a small favour?" she asked, and her stomach gave a rumble. "They have these lovely sausage rolls in the hospital cafe. Would you mind getting me one? And a tea, while you're at it?"

"A sausage roll?" He winked and pointed to his new watch. "I'd get you a hundred and one sausage rolls after this!"

In addition, Max's borborygmus told him that he could do with a nice cheese sandwich before the competition to maximise recall, so there was no reason to say no to Ms Johnson. He left the hospital room and found his way to the cafe, where he joined the back of an unfortunately long queue.

As he tapped his foot and waited, he occupied himself by making a crossword in his mind. He chuckled to himself when he thought up an incredibly witty clue about an obscure phenomenon that only he'd be able to answer. But the man in front of him was painfully distracting, talking on his phone loudly. He found himself incapable of not listening in.

"Just be patient. I'm in the hospital queue presently getting a cuppa. Aaron has almost fully recovered," the man revealed. "I'm about to take him to the shopping centre to decide what we're gonna do with our little prisoner. I don't think it's gonna be anything nice, to say the least."

That was when Max realised what the man was wearing—a fedora. It was the same fellow he'd seen outside the abandoned mall with the younger man. Could he possibly be talking about Khalil?

Trying hard to look indifferent, he gazed intently at the glass pastry display and continued to eavesdrop. The fedora man seemed to be speaking about picking up a superior who would make a decision about someone's fate. Though it may only be a short while until the championship, Max knew he couldn't let this slide. He had to follow the man and see what he was going on about.

After the fedora man bought himself a coffee, Max abandoned the queue and Ms Johnson's sausage rolls, resolving that he would make it up to her later. He paced around the hospital corridors in pursuit, staying several metres behind the fedora man at all times. It helped that he wasn't dressed like Bugs Bunny or a cowboy today.

Every turn of a corner led to an exceedingly stressful moment in which he came all too close to losing him or being spotted. Finally, the fedora man wandered into a hospital room while Max waited outside. He hung around the corner to listen in.

"How are you doing, boss?" the man asked with a distinctive, gravelly voice.

"Doctors say I survived by the skin of my teeth," another person said. "I just got the bandages off yesterday, and I look like some sort of mutant, don't I? Khalil is gonna pay; I can tell you that."

Max stopped dead. They'd just mentioned Khalil directly. He wasn't imagining it.

"I'm glad," the fedora man affirmed. "My head still hurts like hell too after he hit me with that iron."

The fedora man's voice was slightly younger with a working-class accent, while the other's, that of the alleged boss, was deeper and hoarser. Max racked his brains to try to recall if Khalil had ever mentioned them.

"Well, Khalil's tied up in the shopping centre right now," the fedora man continued. "I've given him some water but haven't fed him anything much. He's really out of it after the past few days of beatings, yet still alive. Do you want to head there now?"

"Hmm. Is someone watching him and making sure he's staying put?" the boss asked. His voice quivered as he spoke, as if he was still slightly unwell or recovering from an injury.

"Of course. That useless Tommy kid. I just spoke to him. But it's not really necessary. I tie a mean handcuff knot." He sounded pleased with himself about that. "Khalil's not going anywhere."

"We'll go in an hour. I'm lusting to take his hand, but first, I need something in my stomach. Hospital food makes me gag. Let's have lunch somewhere fancy. Know anywhere good?"

"Sure. Bistrot Pierre is nice. It's this new French restaurant in town. I had a date there yesterday with this girl I was seeing in disguise. Name's Lauren."

"Perfect. And then the fun will begin."

Footsteps headed toward Max. He jumped behind the wall and drank from a water fountain for cover. He didn't dare move a muscle as the men passed by for the exit.

They were gone. Whoever they were, it sounded very much like the two men were keeping Khalil in the Poolway Shopping Centre. Max didn't think the "fun" they were planning on having sounded like Tetris. Chest heaving, he swept around to the hospital's back exit and bolted straight for Khalil.

CHAPTER 26

TOTAL, UTTER DISASTER

Rosie had been annoyed at Max on many occasions. From when he borrowed her quiz book and returned it with the pages covered in notes about his perpetual motion machine design, to when he'd said the tattoo that Brad had done on her ankle of her childhood pet looked inside out—there had never been a shortage of reasons to be angry at him. But even with all of that, Rosie had no doubt that this was the worst thing he'd ever done. It was perhaps even indelibly unforgivable.

The championship was about to start, and Max was nowhere in sight. Her phone in one hand, she hopelessly pressed redial on his number for the umpteenth time. Still no answer. She turned to Lauren, who was also staring down at her mobile. Yet in her case, she was hypnotised by her social media follower count. She'd been in emu form since this morning.

"I can't believe it. Max's missing, and Sofia's not here either," Rosie said, as she groped in vain for a possible solution. "I mean, I can't tell if she is or if she isn't. I've never met the damn woman. All I know is that she's Scottish."

"I guess she didn't bother to turn up to quiz practice like I did," Lauren said with a squawk.

"We simply can't compete without them. We'll have to submit our withdrawal. What a total, utter disaster."

In truth, Rosie didn't know whether she ought to be worrying instead of raging. *Could this have to do with Khalil? But why wouldn't Max just wait until tomorrow? I told him to be here so many times!*

"Maybe we should just ditch this place and go out for some drinks," Lauren Emu suggested in a grumpy tone. She fluffed her feathers. "Now that it's the summer holidays and we're jobless, we don't have to worry about hangovers. Y'know, I barely showed up, too. I'm just so pissed at Frank after he broke things off between us yesterday."

"Drinks, now? It's a bit early," she said. "Where do you think Max is, then?"

Lauren's eyes hadn't left her phone for hours; she was texting with her emu beak.

"The insane asylum. Who cares? Realistically, we weren't gonna win. Looks like the only things the people here ever do here is read newspapers and watch *Countdown*," she remarked. "Fine, then. If you're gonna be a prude about it, how about we go shopping instead?"

"No way. We can't let Universally Challenged and Gertrude win so easily," Rosie asserted.

They sat on Monobloc chairs while facing the stage, where the first two teams had already started. The quizmaster, a tall, wiry man with a voice like David Attenborough and a face resembling Bruce Forsyth, stood at a podium.

The Stapleford Community Centre was a panorama of old people gathered around battered tables. Hardly anyone younger than forty was in sight. Everyone whispered with their teams as they watched the ongoing quiz, the scent of erasers and unbrushed teeth drifting through the hall. The competitive atmosphere was such that she had seen several bookies in the corner taking bets. Agatha Quiztie's odds were not looking particularly good at a thousand to one.

Universally Challenged, the team Agatha Quiztie was facing first, had revealed themselves to not just be intimidating, but physically aggressive. After Rosie and Lauren had stepped through the doors of the Stapleford Community Centre, Gertrude, a toad-like lady with a round face and snake eyes had nearly injured her. After Rosie had signed the team in, the woman extended her foot to trip Rosie, and she'd landed face-first upon the hardwood floor.

"Sorry, dear," Gertrude had muttered with a simpering smirk. "My foot must have spasmed."

But Rosie had not believed her for a second. The "spasm" had looked incredibly contrived, and she recognised Gertrude from last year when she suspected she'd possibly spiked their drinks.

Face still sore, Rosie studied Universally Challenged from across the room. Next to Gertrude sat Universally Challenged's other fearsome members: Henry, a dour fellow with eyes so dark they were almost black;

Dolores, a little old lady in a pink cardigan whose hands were constantly tilted downwards like she was holding a suitcase; and Gary, a man so wrinkled that she wouldn't be shocked to learn he was some sort of alien with a mask.

It was hard to say which one was more formidable.

"I don't like the look of them. I really don't," Rosie hissed in Lauren's ear. She watched Gertrude conspire with Dolores. "They think they're so clever, don't they?"

Lauren Emu cleaned her left wing. "You're getting more and more weird like that Maxwell of yours. I thought old people only did bingo for fun."

"Max doesn't even care about this quiz. He's only competitive about Tetris."

"Ahem, can I ask you something?" Lauren asked, gazing up from her mobile for a fleeting moment.

Rosie nodded.

"About Max. I saw the way you were staring at him the other day. You wouldn't *ever* consider dating him, would you?"

Rosie's nose twitched. *Weird question. She talks about Maxwell as if he were a rare spider.* "I dunno. If I did, would that be such a bad thing?" she asked, digging her nails into her palm.

"Shh," Gertrude shushed from across the room, looking very punchable in her sequin cardigan and lace shirt. "You distracted the team during the spontaneous human combustion question."

"Sorry," Rosie said.

Lauren Emu just carried on at the same volume. "Not to be superficial, but he's shockingly immature, and you're way out of his league. I don't want you to make a mistake because you're desperate after Brad dumped you." She clucked. "Besides, I doubt he's even gone on a proper date in his life. He's a complete outcast, the type of person you wonder how he even exists."

"Max's a really nice, quirky guy, and he's got a good heart. He used to buy me roses all the time, believe it or not. And he cares so much about those poor orphans who rely on the library that he never stops going on about them. In a hypothetical world, I *would* date him. Maybe I will someday. But first and foremost, I wouldn't want to risk harming our friendship."

Sometimes, it felt to Rosie that she was Maxwell's only defender in England.

"Wow! No offence, but that's really, really sad," Lauren Emu muttered. She made no effort to hide her long-necked cringe.

"It is?"

"You don't date someone like Max. You put them in a mental hospital, and when you spot them in public, you cross to the other side of the street."

"If you're just gonna insult me and my friends, you might as well shut up," Rosie said wearily, her brow furrowed. "Max is a great person. He's just a bit different. But he's kinder than most men, and he's really smart. And he never gets down about having to survive on his own with no parents to look after him. I'm sure he has a reason for not being here. I mean, he bloody well must."

"So sorry I called your friend immature when he goes about town in a Bugs Bunny outfit," Lauren Emu quipped, throwing her wings up in exasperation. "And he acts like he's from the Middle Ages and constantly uses words nobody except dictionary writers have even heard of. How ridiculous of me!"

"He can't afford new clothes. It's not his fault. That's just how he is."

She stomped her three-toed feet. "You're in major denial, Rosie. I don't even know why I bothered to come today. You never thanked me for showing up to this complete bore of an event. *I* have a life."

"We can't all lead lives as exciting as you and the ten thousand pedicures you have every year, can we?" Rosie snapped.

In a minute, Agatha Quiztie's going to be the only team in this hall with one member, isn't it?

"Ho-hum. Here's all I have left to say: I'm going. Quizzing is for old cat ladies and headcases like Max," Lauren Emu groused. She stood up, and her chair scraped backwards, causing a tremendous screech. By this point, Universally Challenged, as well as most of the rest of the audience, were leering at them. "Oh, and enjoy your romance with Maxwell. I swear, it's like *Beauty and the Beast* for insane people."

Not bothering to tiptoe, she strutted out the front doors, leaving Rosie sitting there and grinding her teeth. A roomful of disdainful quiz spectators gave her the stink eye.

Now that Agatha Quiztie had lost Lauren, and Rosie had likely lost Lauren as a friend—no big loss there really—she abruptly realised there was simply no hope left. The team wasn't just missing Max; it didn't exist. Nobody else was here.

The round ended and applause broke out. It was Agatha Quiztie's turn next, and therefore, time to throw in the towel.

She sloped up to the stage to tell the quizmaster that Agatha Quiztie had no choice but to withdraw. She found him on the stage, poring over the question sheet.

Glancing at her, the quizmaster, Harold Lawrence, held the questions close to his chest and raised his thick eyebrows. He was a short, bespectacled man in a vintage tweed suit.

"Can I help you, miss?" he asked. "Are you a member of Agatha Quiztie?"

"Indeed, I'm Rosie Shaw," Rosie said with a nod.

But she paused in despair as she gazed over the room of gabbling competitors.

From the stage, she had quite a bird's eye view and estimated that there must be about a hundred folks in attendance. She closed her eyes and buried her face in her hands, contemplating how unimaginably dreadful it was that Agatha Quiztie couldn't compete after months and months of preparation.

It just couldn't be, and yet she *had* to accept it.

As she struggled to find the right words, she unexpectedly caught the eye of someone in the crowd. But it wasn't Max. It was not any member of Agatha Quiztie, but a person she never would've expected to see here.

Brad raised his hand in a wave, grinning at her. A girl was by his side. Had he brought a date?

Brad can't have come for anything good. I've got to see what he's up to. Maybe he knows something about where Max is.

"Ah, Ms Shaw. I see you here," Mr Lawrence said, gazing down at his clipboard. "Quite a witty team name if I do say so myself! I don't mean to sound rude, but where's the rest of Agatha Quiztie?"

"Yeah, I came up with it. My team… Well, the t-thing about t-that is," she said, turning on her heels. "Forget it. I'll be right back."

"Don't delay. Your team is up in three minutes, and we won't wait," he warned.

Mr Lawrence tested his wrong answer bell as Universally Challenged climbed up to the stage, doing some last-minute practice questions on the periodic table.

Rosie stepped down from the stage and hurried toward Brad, painfully aware of the time ticking away. Biting her nails, she tried to think of what to say, feeling like she was in the middle of her own action film.

When she located Brad, she saw he had his arm around a woman with a skull tattoo on her cheek and poorly bleached hair.

"Brad, what are you doing here?" she asked matter-of-factly, poking his shoulder.

"Oh, hi. I'm just having a good time with my girlfriend. Is that a crime?" he asked. He smiled greasily and gave the woman by his side an extra strong squeeze. "This is my new girl, Destiny. She told me she's into trivia, so I suggested we come here for a date."

"Heya," the girl said in a tone so lifeless it sounded like her voice was broken.

Rosie understood why he had *truly* come. It wasn't to support her. It wasn't because his girlfriend enjoyed competitive quizzing either. No, it was to show off his girlfriend. Rosie had always known Brad was petty, having once spied him throwing a tray of Brussels sprouts on the floor so that Max wouldn't get them, but this was a new low.

"Brad, can I have a word with you in private?" she asked, her blood pressure rising.

He placed a finger on his chest. "Me? Uh, I guess. About what?"

"That's the point of the whole in private part." She signalled for him to join her in an isolated corridor of the community centre.

"Fine. But this better not be about Max. One sec, baby," Brad said to a high-looking Destiny.

"Will team Agatha Quiztie report to the stage for round one, quiz two," Mr Lawrence's forbidding voice resounded over the speakers.

Rosie and Brad arrived at a side hall.

"That's your team's dumb name!" he said, grinning. "You'd better get up there. Where's Grouch?"

"I need your help," she said shortly.

"Wait. Why would I ever help you?" he retorted, throwing his arms in the air.

"Listen, Brad. Did you ever like me? Or *care* about me?"

"Um, you had your good parts. Why'd you ask?"

"Well, if you did, now would be the time to show it," she said. "We don't have to be at each other's throats forever. We can be friends and get coffee once in a while. Wouldn't that be nice?"

He broadened his shoulders as if his masculinity were being threatened. "Hey, hey. I'm an adult. What's the big deal anyway?" he questioned.

"My team isn't here yet. I need you to cause a delay for us."

"How am *I* gonna cause a delay? Why don't you do it?"

"This is the last call for Agatha Quiztie to come to the stage for round one before they automatically forfeit," Mr Lawrence said over the speakers, this time sounding piqued.

"That's why. Just figure something out," Rosie said with finality. She left Brad standing there with a sheepish expression as she sprinted up to the stage.

The quizmaster's lip curled with displeasure when she finally got to the stage, but on the contrary, Universally Challenged appeared chuffed. Gertrude was grinning like a Cheshire cat.

"We have been waiting for you, Ms Shaw. For goodness' sake, where *is* your team?" Mr Lawrence asked with a matter of life and death sort of voice.

"Uh, about that," she said, arching her back. "They're stuck in traffic."

"Can we begin already?" Gertrude asked. She and her team were doing a poor job of concealing their elated snickering. "The members of Agatha Quiztie are certainly taking their time. Is there a problem?"

"Indeed, there is," Mr Lawrence said gravely. "Ms Shaw, what can I say? The championship always recommends participants to arrive one hour early. We can hardly wait any longer. There are many other teams waiting for their turn. As the proverb goes, the early bird catches the worm."

"Uh, wait. I just saw them," Rosie revealed. She squinted as she pointed into the crowd.

"You did?"

It was a bad lie. "I promise they will be here in less than two minutes."

Mr Lawrence cast an austere glance at his watch. "Your passion for quizzing is making me generous. You have two minutes, or it's an automatic disqualification."

She crossed her fingers behind her back. *Come on, Brad. Think of something...*

One minute and fifty seconds passed, and no distraction had appeared. She breathed fast.

"Mr Lawrence? The time is up," Gertrude cut in. She shot a demented smirk at Rosie. "A shame. But it would be completely unfair to the other teams to make them wait any longer, wouldn't it?"

Oh, be quiet, Gertrude. I wish you would spontaneously combust.

Rosie sighed. Brad obviously didn't care an iota about her, not even enough to help her in her darkest hour. It was the end of the road.

"Ms Shaw," the quizmaster said churlishly, picking up his clipboard. "That's the harsh truth about life: in this world, we simply can't always get what we want. Maybe you can reapply next year and—"

WEE-WOO, WEE-WOO. Fire sirens blared and the sprinklers went off.

CHAPTER 27

THE FINAL SHOWDOWN

Max strode down the pavement at top speed, cars honking as he ignored a red traffic light for the first time in his life. The past few months had either made him a whole lot braver or a great deal more foolhardy. It was an incredibly reckless thing to do, but debatably even more reckless was breaking into a derelict shopping centre of drug dealers.

Gulping down air, he arrived at the façade of the Poolway Shopping Centre. The building had no front door, only a sinister gaping hole in the wall where one should be, as if the builders had forgotten to put it there. He had been wondering what was inside this place for years but had never dared to enter. Silencing his last lingering reservations, he checked that he had his laser pointer and stepped inside.

As Max's eyes adjusted, the problem of darkness presented itself. He scolded himself for being foolish enough to neglect to bring his torch, but he wasn't sure whether he could build up the courage to do this again if he headed back to get one. Either way, it'd take too much time. *Holy macaron! What if Khalil has been turned into a vampire? Thank the baby Jesus I didn't get bitten by Ms Johnson.*

Using his phone for a light, Max's first impression was that this place would be the perfect horror film set. A tangled mesh of reeds and ivy covered the unpainted stucco walls, which grew desultorily over barely legible faded graffiti. He couldn't describe what the smell was, only that it made his nose shrivel and urged him to get out as fast as possible.

Taking a deep breath, he squinted through the murky gloom and made his way through a maze of hallways.

But he wasn't alone. Someone else was coming his way. Fast.

He leapt into a shop and hid behind a rack of abandoned fireworks. His hand rushed to his pocket for his laser pointer, his only defence. It came as a great relief when the strange figure turned out to be an ally—a mole, who scrambled down the corridor and gazed in his direction briefly before continuing on its merry way.

He tried to pacify himself and continued. He hadn't been so stressed since he had gone on *The Weakest Link*, and Anne Robinson bit his head off for answering other people's questions. Or that time Eddie deleted his save file in *Pokémon Red* and he never saw Squirtle again.

Though this place might make a good haunted mansion, it was hard to imagine it as a bustling shopping centre. All the rooms that were meant to be shops were bare of anything except whatever dirt and rubbish they'd accumulated. Max entered a handful of desolate, chillingly scary shops to check whether there were any indications of life. All he found were endless cigarette butts, decades-old papers and dust-covered merchandise.

Eventually, Max arrived at an abandoned flower shop. Rows and rows of potted plants stood on shelves, giving off a pungent smell. It occurred to him that these might be the property of a flower store that had never opened. Yet how would they have survived so long without water?

And thereupon, he realised that these must be illegal drugs. Cannabis. Which meant that Khalil could be nearby!

A sudden creaking sound—a door opening—rang out, followed by repeating thumps.

Max dove behind a drug shelf and kept still, forcing his foot to not tap. The heavy footsteps—he deduced as fear buffeted his mind like hail—couldn't possibly be a mole's. They were far too loud and measured.

His breathing stopped as a loud, youthful voice drifted through the darkness.

"Hey, Gerald. It's me. How long until you're back? I'm starved."

Max cursed his foolishness again. By the loudness of the voice, the man must be just around the shelf. If he simply came around the corner and looked down, he would easily spot him cowering down here.

There was no audible reply to the question, suggesting that the man was having a phone conversation.

"Hold on. What do you mean Aaron thinks I haven't earned that yet? I just want some grub."

Max leaned past the shelf for a second, but the only thing he saw other than a silhouette was that the man was lacking something: a hand. It was the young fellow who he'd seen speaking with the fedora man!

"This guy's not gonna get away," the fellow went on. "He's barely even conscious. Besides, to be honest, I think we should just let him go. Like what did he even do that was so bad?"

A pause.

The man grunted. "Yeah, yeah. I'm still in Aaron's bad books, aren't I? Isn't my hand enough? He's such a motherfucker." Another pause. "No, please don't tell him I said that. I'm begging you. Well, hurry up with your lunch and try to bring me something back, if he'll allow it."

With that, the young man retreated into the staffroom from which he had come from. Khalil could be in that very same room.

It struck Max at that moment that he needed to create a distraction. But it couldn't just be a short one. He needed to lure the man away long enough so he could get to Khalil and free him.

He desperately tried to gather his frantic thoughts, and gradually what he had to do came to him.

Max hurried back to the rack with the abandoned fireworks. One by one, he unpacked the fireworks and placed them in a row on the cement floor, his heart pounding in his ears. He pulled his laser pointer out from his pocket.

He pointed his laser pointer at one of their fuses. However, it took him over five minutes to light a single one. In the end, Ms Johnson's Rolex was a great help. He reflected the laser off the silver bezel to intensify the growth of the spark. He stared in satisfaction as a single, tiny flame consumed the fuse.

But he had no time to read the firework instructions. As soon as the fuse was ignited, he made his exit, hoping against hope that it would set off the others. He bolted back towards the opposite shop, an abandoned Clarks.

A sound like thunder erupted. The shop exploded with a chaotic flash of blue and green sparkles that banged against the floor and ceiling. The handless man dashed out of the flower shop seconds later, muttering curse words as he raced over to check it out. Following his cue, Max crept away.

He opened the staffroom door, and his jaw dropped.

There was Khalil, sitting in a folding chair, but not at all as Max remembered him. He was in bad shape, his shirt soaked with blood and his face as white as chalk. He looked fast asleep. As Max strode up to him, he saw that his hands were tied in a knot behind the back of the chair.

"Khalil!" Max shouted. He ran over, lowering his voice. "Awake from your slumber!"

Khalil hardly reacted. He glanced up, eyes half open and hovering over Max. "What? I don't want to go back to Afghanistan. I like it here," he mumbled deliriously. "I'd miss my tea and crumpets."

Max sighed, grabbed his shoulders and shook them. "Rise and shine! Wakey-wakey!"

"Fatima can go instead," he went on, words slurring. "I'm used to the rain at this point."

Max reached over and slapped him across the cheek.

Finally, Khalil came to, and his eyes shot around like flies before landing on Max and enlarging. "What're you doing here? You have to get out. Now."

"I came to liberate you," Max said, "and rescue you, if you so wish."

"Well, don't leave it till the last minute. Untie me." Khalil tore against the rope.

"I'll need to cut the rope. The knot looks too tight. What should I use?" He looked around for rope cutters, but none were visible.

"Gerald keeps my Swiss Army knife in the top left drawer of that desk."

"Righto."

Max swiftly took Mr Knife, now a bit bloodied, and ran around to the back of Khalil's chair. Yet the trouble was that the rope was far too strong, and the knife didn't make much of a difference.

"It's not working," Max said shortly.

"Keep trying," Khalil entreated, hands jerking for freedom.

There was not much time. Through the doorway, steady thuds came closer. Footsteps.

"Someone's coming back," Khalil grunted. "You'll have to fight him off."

"Fight him off?" Max asked, panic-stricken. "With what? Verbiage?"

"Get the jump on him with the knife or think of something. You're smart."

"Am I?"

"Yeah. You can do it!"

Max whipped around and scoured the room for something to use, not keen on Khalil's suggestion. His eyes caught sight of a fire extinguisher on the wall. With hardly any time to think, he ran over, detached it and hurried to the area beside the door. He climbed onto a cabinet shelf by the door, a good position to hide. After that, he held the fire extinguisher above the doorway at a perfect angle to strike.

The moment the man stepped back into the doorway, he leaned forward and smashed the fire extinguisher down. It collided with the man's scalp and made a painful cracking sound. The handless teenager collapsed onto the floor, his unconscious body sprawled on the cold cement.

Max stared down at the teen's figure and the fire extinguisher in a state of disbelief. He couldn't quite fathom it was him who'd just done that.

"Murderer. You just killed a million brain cells," Khalil quipped. "Now, for Chrissake, get this rope off."

Wishing he'd brought an inhaler, Max jumped off the shelf, rushed over and resumed sawing through the rope. It took him a good fifteen minutes to get through it; the rope was just that thick. By the time he'd finished, the handless guy had come to, grunting in pain.

"Aaron," the teenager mewled. "It wasn't my fault. Don't take my other hand. Stop being a dickhead about everything."

"Thank God. I'm free. You're a regular James Bond," Khalil muttered, standing and stretching his arms. "Now, let's get out of here, mate."

"I believe your captors won't be here for a while. They said they were going out to lunch," Max informed him as they strode out.

Khalil looked more than drained, his skin sallow and lifeless. "My captors?"

"These two suspicious men I saw at the hospital, one with a cleft lip and the other with a fedora and a moustache. They said they were coming here. That's how I found you."

"Wow. You figured all that out? I thought you'd barely notice I was gone," Khalil said proudly. "It's Aaron with the cleft lip and Gerald with the fedora. The younger fellow is Tommy. I'll explain when this is over."

"What happened to you?" Max asked.

He pointed at the blood seeping through his sweaty shirt.

Khalil looked down. "Funny thing. I got shot. And then beaten up over and over. Luckily, the bullet seems to have missed any organs, unless I happen to have become immortal. I think it hit my shoulder."

"The skin is an organ," Max corrected.

"Vital organs. Is the definition of organs a priority right now?" Khalil grumbled. "Let's go."

They raced out of the shop and into the corridor. It was only when Max stepped outside the store that he noticed the thick fumes spreading throughout the shopping centre. He hadn't quite realised that the fireworks had set the whole shopping centre on fire. But there it was: a roaring bed of flames in the middle of consuming the entire building, as well as a foggy cloud of smoke billowing out and blocking the way to the entrance—their only escape.

"I may or may not have set the shopping centre on fire," Max remarked.

They stared, aghast, at the sea of fire.

"Good job," Khalil said, sighing. "So, how do we get out now?"

Max didn't answer, as at that instant a bullet passed by his right ear. He and Khalil turned in horrified silence to see two men with pistols trained on their foreheads.

Aaron and Gerald.

"I'm so glad we decided to get takeaway after all," Aaron said, giving a dry chuckle. He winked at Gerald. "What luck? Bumping into you two. Not sure if you knew about the back entrance, but we decided to take it when we saw smoke coming out."

"Put your hands in the air," Gerald ordered, distinctly less amused than Aaron. "Nowhere to run this time, Khalil."

Startled, Max and Khalil raised their hands.

"Listen, guys. Let Max go," Khalil beseeched. "He doesn't have a clue about any of this. He only got involved thanks to my idiocy."

"You know I can't do that, Khalil," Aaron said with a contemptuous sneer. He adjusted his grip on the trigger, coughed and glanced over at Gerald. "I suppose we will have to be quick about it and kill them now. They've imposed a bit of a time limit on us with the whole burning building."

"Sounds good, boss," Gerald grunted. "I'm sorry I didn't manage to do it earlier. Good riddance to bad rubbish, if you ask me. Nobody will miss Khalil and his photographs, will they? And Maxwell and his…"

"Cookie Monster outfits." Aaron grinned. "But I still don't fully understand what Khalil was using you for, Max. From what I've heard, you don't seem like a sane person."

"I am neurodivergent, yes, but that doesn't mean I'm insane," Max explained. "Khalil and I have been teaming up to win a treasure hunting contest. He wasn't using me, though. We're mates."

"Is this true, Khalil?" Aaron asked, tittering with amusement. "A treasure hunting contest? I thought you were twenty-seven, not seven."

"Uh, yeah," Khalil answered. "We *are* mates. We've been doing pretty well at the contest, too."

"A shame that you will never get to find out if you were going to win," he said, and squinted while he aimed his gun at Maxwell. "It'll be amusing to see Khalil's face when I put a bullet through your forehead."

By this juncture, Max's breaths came in ragged gasps, the encroaching smoke pressing perilously close to them. "Hold on." He glanced meaningfully at Khalil. "Can't I have some final words? As a courtesy. You kind of owe it to me, killing me in cold blood and all."

"Max, don't be ridiculous," Khalil said, rolling his eyes. "Look, Aaron. We can still make a deal. How about we volunteer at your crystal meth factory? I got a, uh, B in chemistry at school."

"Ha! The answer is still no," Aaron jeered. "But as for final words? It's cute. What do you think, Gerald? Should we let the oddball have his wish?"

The smoke impinged even further on them, the roof heaving as if about to collapse.

"If he's quick, I don't see why not," Gerald said, a tremor in his voice. "Still, I don't fancy staying here much longer."

"Very well," Aaron said with a chortle. "I suppose the villain usually does offer the Byronic hero a chance to say his final words in action films. We all know which one I am. You have one minute. Let's just hope they're not too tiresome."

"In fact, I only have one or two words," Max said.

His hand glided stealthily downward, taking advantage of the billowing smoke to conceal his movement.

"And what would that be?" Aaron snarled.

"Flibbertigibbet."

Gerald snickered. "What was that? Flibbertigibbet? You really want to make that your final word?"

"Yes. And collywobbles. They're excellent words, aren't they?"

"Flibbertigibbet? Collywobbles?" Gerald repeated, bursting out in laughter. "What do they even mean?"

"I think collywobbles is a type of soup," speculated Aaron, chortling. "What jabberwocky!"

"My dears, I said final words. I didn't say my own," Max said, smirking. "Scoundrels."

Max whipped his laser pointer out again. Like a shot, he aimed it towards them, curving the beam over Aaron's and Gerald's eyes. Both men screamed and raised their hands over their eyes.

"Argh! What was that?" Gerald shrieked as he fell to his knees. "What happened? I can't see them, boss. Should I shoot?"

"Just don't let them get away!" Aaron shouted back, pointing his pistol into the air.

Khalil lunged forward and tackled Aaron's knees. His gun fell to the ground with a clatter. Max dove over and picked it up.

Swearing, Aaron tried to get to his feet. Gerald repeatedly shot in their direction, missing each time. Max threw Aaron's gun in the direction of Khalil, and a moment later, two bullets were fired.

Max's heart beat so fast that it took him a moment to work out what had happened.

The first bullet had pierced Gerald's stomach. His fedora had fallen to the floor along with his gun. His hands covered his chest in a futile attempt to stem the gushing blood. He gasped for breath, making a disturbing asphyxiated hissing.

The second appeared to have gone through Aaron's groin. He was lying on the floor, cherry-red blood soaking through his trousers. Unlike Gerald, he made no attempt to stop the bleeding, and instead, he gazed up at the ceiling with a vague, philosophical face.

"Khalil, looks like you've won," Aaron said in a peaceful voice. He wheezed. "You have killed me, just as you've always wanted. How does it feel?"

Khalil looked down at him with disdain in his eyes. "I didn't win! There's nothing to win. You caused this," he spat.

"Fair enough. I will say one other thing before I go: I trained you well, didn't I?" he said, staring at Khalil with almost paternal affection. "In another life, you would've been my successor. My son."

Khalil strode over, took Gerald's gun from the floor and chucked it into the smoke. "You do not see clearly the evil in yourself, or you would hate yourself with all your soul. Like the lion who sprang at his image in the water, you are only hurting yourself. Also, rot in hell."

"I'd prefer Hell to where I'm headed," he wheezed, breaking out in a pained coughing fit. "A dreamless sleep is all that awaits me at the end of this tunnel. Wish me luck in oblivion."

Aaron closed his eyes and blacked out. By this point, the smoke had become so thick that it was hard to see. Neither Khalil nor Max had any desire to stick around.

"Are you going to kill them?" Max asked, fighting for breath as the smoke expanded. He pointed at Aaron. "I doubt the groin wound will be enough."

"No! I'm not a murderer," Khalil denied, rubbing his eyes. "But I'm not gonna try to save them either. I didn't mean to hit Gerald in the stomach. He's the one who almost assassinated you."

Gerald had stopped struggling. He now lay prone with no evident signs of life.

An astonished silence halted both Max and Khalil in their tracks for a few moments.

Max couldn't believe this; assuming they were dead, they were the first humans he'd ever seen perish.

Khalil glanced at Max, gesturing for him to go. "Come on. No point waiting to be burned alive. They said there's a back exit. Head that way," he instructed.

And Khalil ran back into the shop from which they'd just come.

"Wait! I don't get it. Why are you going back there?" Max asked, baffled. "This building is about to collapse. We need to get out. Pronto."

"That kid you hit with the fire extinguisher," Khalil said solicitously. "I've got to help him, or he'll die in here. He's not a bad guy like Aaron or Gerald. He just got caught up in this."

"It's your funeral. I've just become complicit in the homicide of two men, *and* I've got to get to the quiz championship in, let's see"—he glanced down at his Rolex, and sudden horror rushed through him—"one hour ago! Oh, bother. Rosie's going to be furious!"

CHAPTER 28

THE CHAMPIONSHIP

Among the crowd of annoyed quiz contestants, Rosie and Brad stood with folded arms and pronounced scowls, a taut atmosphere filling the car park. Firefighters trudged in and out of the entrance to the community centre while rumours milled around about what was going on. Everyone had been shepherded out after the fire alarm had gone off and they'd got drenched by the sprinklers. It wasn't entirely clear whether the competition was going to proceed at all today and, even if it did, whether there would be time for all the teams.

Regrettably, Max was still nowhere in sight. Rosie didn't know what to think anymore. *He's not just fifteen minutes, not half an hour, but two hours late! That doesn't even count as late! It's just not coming.*

Nobody was in a good mood. Mr Lawrence bloviated to some firefighters, waving his arms about with a purple face. Universally Challenged idled by the fire engine, looking deeply annoyed. Gertrude gripped her handbag and loured sourly.

"So, are you gonna thank me?" Brad asked, flashing a grin.

Destiny had disappeared to go home and change, rather displeased by the impromptu shower.

"For what?" Rosie asked.

"The fire alarm. I mean, not that I'm admitting to anything *legally*."

"Thank you so very much." She tried to sort out her hair, which was still soaking wet. "I honestly don't know whether to be annoyed or worried about Max at this point."

"Don't worry. I'm sure wherever he is, he's bound to be doing something as boring as dust," he affirmed, and then chortled. "Speak of the devil."

Rosie gasped as she spotted Max careening through the crowd, shouldering people away. Behind him, an enormous, headphone-wearing woman who must be Sofia plodded along.

"Pardon for my belatedness," he said. His sweaty face was black with ash and dust.

"You look a right mess," Brad said, as Max recoiled at the sight of him. "Why is your face like that? Did you just save a cat from a burning building or something?"

"I'm real sorry, Rosie, right?" Sofia said, out of breath. Her stomach flopped out of her pink tracksuit as she turned her music down. "I somehow got on the wrong bus. I went halfway 'cross Nottinghamshire 'fore I realised it. I dinnae ken how I managed that! I just bumped into dear Maxy as I was gettin' off. Thank the Lord I'm not late."

"What the hell happened to you?" Rosie asked, staring at Max's bloodshot eyes.

"I, er, overslept," he said darkly.

Max looked and sounded as if he had just come from the battlefields of war. Rosie didn't understand what had happened, but he wasn't revealing anything for now.

Several seconds later, the crowd's lazy murmur died down.

Mr Lawrence strode to the Stapleford Community Centre's porch and shouted, "Everyone, quiet! The firefighters are about to leave! I can now reveal this alleged fire was an entirely false alarm. I'm sorry to say that a miscreant triggered the fire alarm for a reason I can only assume is extremely jejune jiggery-pokery. I should assure everyone that, following the quiz, a thorough investigation will be carried out to identify this criminal." Brad flushed. "Unfortunately, due to the disruption, we will not have time for all our scheduled quizzes. I have just spoken to the mayor's secretary, and he has agreed that we can hold the final quiz tomorrow as a morning event. As for now, Universally Challenged and Agatha Quiztie, please proceed to the stage within the next five minutes."

"Wait. Where's Lauren?" Max asked, wiping off some ash with his sleeve.

"We had a fight, and she left," Rosie admitted. Her gaze shifted to Brad. "Could you? Would you mind?"

"Nope. No way in hell," Brad stated, shaking his head forcefully.

She made praying hands. "Come on, Brad. Think about what we were just talking about in there. Don't you want to be men and put an end to this childish feud? You and Maxwell have way more in common than you think. Maybe you could even be friends if you just stopped fighting for once."

"What do we have in common?" Brad asked, rolling his eyes. "Name one single thing, and I'll do it."

She scratched her back, struggling. "I've got it! You both like Coco Pops."

Brad and Max looked at each other doubtfully.

"He does?" Brad whinged. "Well, everyone likes that cereal. That doesn't count."

"I concur," Max said. "It's not a niche thing like treasure hunting."

"Och. Naw, I don't like it," Sofia said, and made a gagging sound. "Makes me feel right sick. I prefer Oreo cereal."

Rosie sighed and grabbed Brad's and Max's sleeves. "And you have *me* in common, don't you? You asked for an example. That's two. Now, let's go!"

With both Max and Brad giving in, they all hurried inside and proceeded straight to the stage of the community centre.

As she sat on the stage alongside Max, Brad and Sofia, it took Rosie a moment to realise that this was it. Something like butterflies—but stronger, more like bees—swarmed about in her belly. Months of gruelling quiz practices and strenuous revision had been leading up to this. She had to force herself to stop staring over the crowd, a panoply of stern-faced adults with third and possibly fourth-level education. All who were no doubt eager to mock their quizzing naivety. Settling down, Gertrude shot Rosie a death stare.

Rosie whispered over to Max and Brad. "As you might have noticed, Universally Challenged are all seniors. They went to Oxford and won *University Challenge* in 1983."

Have I been kidding myself all this time? We're by far the youngest team! I feel like a toddler.

"Don't worry," Max said in hushed tones. "We've got something they don't."

"What?" she asked with a browbeaten expression. "And don't say yourself."

"I wasn't going to," he denied, eyebrows rising. "Well, maybe I was. But we also have teamwork. And love or something, I guess. Although, technically that's just neurochemicals."

"So inspiring."

"Arrogant as always, Maxwell," Brad groused. "I still don't know what I'm bloody doing here."

"I'm terrible at nearly everything except quizzing, but I won't deny I'm pretty good at that. You can help by keeping your mouth shut as much as possible," Max suggested. "Starting now."

"Hey, I'm only here to help you guys out. I can leave at any second," he fired back.

"Yes, and we are grateful about that," Rosie said. "Put a sock in it, Max. You're not helping."

"Sincerest apologies, Bradley," Max grumbled, sounding about a quarter sincere. "Gramercy for your succour, although I do find your redemption arc a bit too cloying for my tastes."

"Gramercy? Come off it. I'm not doing it for *you*." Brad pointed at Rosie. "I'm doing it for *her*. So, don't thank me."

"At last, let's begin with the quiz, shall we?" Mr Lawrence asserted, interrupting their bickering. "Ah, good to see your team has belatedly arrived, Ms Shaw."

It was time. If Rosie had thought for a second that the first round of the championship ought to be the easiest, she had a feeling that Universally Challenged was about to show her just how wrong she was.

The first question was a simple one, but one's speed of answering played a factor in winning. "A DNA molecule is commonly described as being what shape?" Mr Lawrence asked.

His hand like greased lightning, Max slammed the quiz buzzer so hard that it slipped off the table. "A DOUBLE HELIX!"

"Correct," Mr Lawrence affirmed. Instantly, five points appeared on the screen under their name. "But please, Mr Jacobs, there's no need to yell the answers." He clutched the quiz cards firmly in his hands. "Which chamber of the heart pumps deoxygenated blood to the lungs?"

"THE RIGHT VENTRICLE!" Max shouted, having picked the buzzer up.

"Correct. How many bones are there in the average adult human body?"

"TWO HUNDRED AND SIX!" he screamed.

"What is the name of the Jewish protagonist of James Joyce's *Ulysses*?"

"Leo—" Gertrude started.

"LEOPOLD BLOOM!" caterwauled Maxwell, punching his buzzer.

Gertrude's face contorted with rage. To her chagrin, he'd just beaten her hand to the buzzer.

"*Please* refrain from breaking our eardrums, Mr Jacobs," Mr Lawrence retaliated. "But you are, again, correct. Remember to press the buzzer before answering, Universally Challenged."

So it went during the science and literature rounds. But when the pop culture and maths round came, it was Rosie's time to shine.

"Who is the only actor to have appeared in more than one of the three films that have won eleven Academy Awards each?"

"Bernard Hill," Rosie said, interrupting Max's streak of six correct answers.

"Correct. What is the square root of one?"

That's an easy one. "One."

She even did quite well in the history round.

"Which Egyptian pharaoh is widely believed to be the son of Akhenaten?"

Oh, I remember! "Tutankhamun," she said, after she slammed her buzzer in milliseconds.

"Correct. Who was the principal founder of the football team Arsenal?"

A buzz went off to her right. "David Danskin," Brad cried.

"Correct," the quizmaster said, looking up at him as if surprised he had a voice.

"See, I'm not so thick after all, Grouch," Brad hissed in Max's ear.

"What disease is known for commonly spreading on pirate ships?" Mr Lawrence asked next.

"Scurvy!" Gertrude exclaimed, slapping her buzzer like a whack-a-mole.

"That is correct."

Rosie frowned as Universally Challenged congratulated a smirking Gertrude.

At last, the timer ran out, and the first round was over.

The quizmaster turned around to the crowd. "And the final scores are: one hundred and fifteen points to Agatha Quiztie. One hundred and five points to Universally Challenged!"

The crowd erupted in applause.

Despite smiling being anathema to her, Rosie couldn't help indulging in a little grin as she glanced over at Gertrude, who cursed and slapped her handbag against her teammates. Nonetheless, that was only round one of a three-round contest. They had a pretty long way to go.

As the four stood together in the community centre's echoey corridor and waited for their next turn, Brad remained jubilant about the question he'd got right. "Did you see me? Looks like I'm not just an extra head, eh?"

"Yeah. One question right," Rosie mumbled. "Impressive."

"I can't believe how awful I did," Max moaned in self-reproach, slouching in the corner. "To not just miss the Washington Irving question but *also* the Humphry Davy one. I'll never live it down."

"Will you shut up, Max?" she retorted, her hands on her hips. "You know full well you carried us."

"Sorry I wasn't more 'elp, pet," Sofia said meekly. She had not yet got one question correct. "Pish posh, I warned ya I'm no Bertrand Russell or Nietzsche."

"Don't put yourself down. You did great, Sofia," Rosie said, beaming. "If it weren't for you, we wouldn't be able to compete at all."

Not long later, they were called for the next round, in which they faced Quizzy McQuizface. They were the group of middle-aged housewives who had given up their weekly book club for quiz night, and unlike Universally Challenged, they reached for their buzzers at Concorde speed. Max kept getting told off by Mr Lawrence for yelling the answers, so much so that he threatened to ban him from the quiz.

Perhaps Max's most impressive contributions were getting the answers right regarding the date of Franz Ferdinand's assassination and what class of particle a proton was. Rosie felt she did particularly well, scoring almost as many points as him. She was proud of knowing about Euler's constant to the nearest three digits and even more pleased with herself for recalling Peggy Mitchell's job. Shockingly, Brad made a couple more contributions, such as correctly naming the captain of Chelsea. And finally, Sofia got a point for knowing about the number of chocolates in Quality Street boxes. It seemed they didn't need Lauren at all.

Despite how well they were doing, it was hard for Rosie to stop herself from imagining things during the quizzes. She mostly managed to control herself, except when Gertrude turned into an ill-tempered lizard and Mr Lawrence transformed into a grimacing giraffe. Detective Theodore Tabby and Count Ferdinand also made an appearance. It seemed they'd finally apprehended Billy Beaver.

"And the final scores are: one hundred and twenty points to Agatha Quiztie. One hundred and fifteen points to Quizzy McQuizface!" Mr Lawrence announced.

The crowd applauded rapturously. This time, they even gave them a standing ovation.

"Well done, Agatha Quiztie. I am so glad you managed to get your team together. What an outstanding display of quizzing prowess. Frankly, I've not seen such quizzing skills since the 1960s when I myself was a young hopeful! What is your secret?"

"It all comes down to practice," Rosie answered.

"Yes. And reading the encyclopaedia for several hours every day for years," Max added.

That was it for the day. Having won two out of three quizzes, they were on track to compete in the finale tomorrow. Rosie felt they really found their footing in the second round, where they even managed to get a streak of ten correct answers. It was incredible how much they had improved.

Unfortunately, they were to face Universally Challenged again tomorrow due to a quirk in the scoring system. Mr Lawrence chose the final round teams by who got the most points overall, and since Universally Challenged did so well in the second round, it counteracted their prior loss. Still, Rosie wasn't worrying about facing Gertrude again yet, as she was just too delighted by the results of today.

"Wow! What a day. I am so proud of you all. We did great," she said as they gathered outside Stapleford Community Centre. The remnants of the day's sunlight bathed them in a warm, summery sheen. "Like *incredible*. Even if we lose tomorrow, we'll still get the runner-up prize of three thousand pounds. But I'm sure we're gonna smash Universally Challenged again. I can't wait to see Gertrude in tears."

"Oh, now I'm tied into coming tomorrow?" Brad grunted, hands in his pockets.

She nodded. "Afraid so."

In the corner of her eye, a raving mad Gertrude stomped out of the car park, berating her quizzing teammates. She pummelled Henry with her purse. "How on Earth did you pea-brains let them win? They're *children* compared to us!"

"Well, I won't deny it. I didn't have quite as bad of a time as I'd imagined," Brad said. He glanced at Max with a mixture of disdain and reluctant appreciation. "You did pretty well, Grouch."

"Not really. The competition was just really weak this year," Max said with a shrug.

"We'll never be friends, but whatever I think of you and your raccoon face, you're definitely a decent quizzer. By the way, er, tell your friend—Khalil, is it?—that I looked it up, and it turns out Afghanistan is a real country! And he wasn't *that* bad at football. I might have exaggerated."

"I'm blushing. Although you may look slightly like a beaver, your tattoos aren't all bad. I even quite like the one with the, er, pheasant in drag."

"That's a dragon! I'm off to see where Destiny went off to. See you," Brad said disinterestedly.

As he trudged away, Rosie had to admit that she was impressed by how he had acted today. Of course, she still knew he was a pretty horrendous person, but there was something to be said for him where there wasn't before. And the weird thing was that she hadn't felt the urge to turn him into a beaver and Max into a raccoon. Maybe they were both finally growing up.

"Cheers for the day, pet. It was propa fun," Sofia said as she toddled away. "Remember, I cannae buy you more than a few days until the bookies are burned. Dinnae waste it!" She cast a sidelong glance at Rosie. "Oooh, and good luck with the lass!"

"Kudos to you, Sofia," Max said with a smile, flushing. "I'll do what I can."

He waved her off while she put a Snoop Dogg tune on her headphones.

"Turns out quizzin' makes me right hungry. I'm gonna go fetch some sprinkled doughnuts. Laters, Max," she called back.

Now, it was just Max and Rosie.

Peace at last. Wait. Why is he looking at me like that?

"You are doing it," he said.

"What?" she asked, fingering her bead necklace.

"The Duchenne smile. Hmm… I think you might need to get your teeth whitened."

"No, I'm not," she remarked, rapidly forming a tight frown.

Rosie certainly didn't think Max was anything like a role model, but despite whatever Lauren had said, she knew in her heart that he *was* a good guy. He might not be a particularly good influence—one time, he'd even signed up for the adopt-a-younger-brother orphanage programme and ended up inadvertently giving the poor boy a concussion after teaching him how to juggle bottles—yet he would always be her friend. Be that as it may, it hadn't slipped her mind that he had arrived late. He'd managed to clean most of the soot off by now.

“Well, you were,” he said blankly. “It’s nothing to be ashamed of. I won’t tell Lauren.”

“Lauren’s a tool. Are you gonna tell me what happened now?” she asked, staring impatiently.

His foot tapped. “I’m not sure you’re going to like it. How about getting some celebratory Brussels sprouts first?”

CHAPTER 29

A VITAL LEAD

Khalil's ears rang, his shoulder ached like he'd swallowed a jarful of pins and his head was on fire. He'd probably just killed two men. And yet despite all that, he couldn't help but feel sublime. He was free, but more importantly, with Aaron in all likelihood dead, the Black Dog Disciples had finally met their end!

For the past few hours, he'd been lying on Max's sofa, eyes on *Loose Women* reruns but hardly absorbing a word. It was hard to process rational thoughts after all that had occurred. Though he tried to suppress them, the events of the day kept running through his mind.

"In other news, Lovell Unlimited has reportedly just made an expensive acquisition in the tech sector," the presenter announced. "What else are they going to buy? The moon? And it seems they are about to announce a new vacuum with a state-of-the-art processing chip. I'm happy to announce the CEO, Anthony Lovell, is here for his first interview in years."

The sounds of the fire brigade were still audible from outside the windows, sirens having been blaring all afternoon and evening. It was pitch black now, and it seemed they were finally quietening down.

"I still don't get it," someone's muffled voice said from outside the apartment. "How did you figure out Khalil was being kept at the abandoned shopping centre? And how did it catch on fire?"

"I told you, Rosie. I set off the fireworks with my laser pointer and blinded the drug dealers with it too. It's not a complex story." There was the sound of licking lips. "Yummy! Those sprouts were sublime."

Khalil glanced at the front door as dulled voices and footsteps crescendoed. He turned off the TV.

Max and Rosie went on squabbling like an old married couple.

"Your laser pointer? Really?! I don't believe it."

"You'll believe it in a second. Trust me. I told him he could go into my apartment with my spare key and recover. He's probably in here."

As Max unlocked the door, Khalil arose. He wished he wasn't wearing Max's spare *Tweenies* hoodie. It was horribly uncomfortable but was the only thing in Max's wardrobe that would even slightly fit him. As Max and Rosie stepped inside, she spotted Khalil and her eyes widened.

"Yeah, I know. I don't look like Louis Tomlinson right now, do I?" Khalil quipped. For a brief second earlier that day, he'd glanced in the vanity mirror to unpleasant results. "Max said you're a fan of him."

"Not exactly. It's been a few weeks, hasn't it? How're you?" Rosie asked, struggling for words.

"Not amazing," he said, winking. "I've been shot, kept hostage, and barely fed for over a week. You can imagine."

"Oh my God. Sorry for the ridiculous question," she said sympathetically. "Max didn't really tell me about that. Have you had medical attention?"

"My own," he grunted stiffly. "But I can't go to the hospital, and it doesn't matter. I don't think my wound is infected. And I *really* am amazing, actually. You'd know if I was a ghost, wouldn't you, Max?"

Max went pale. "Dunno. You could be haunting us right now. Try and float through my wall, and we'll see. But before that, you have to apprise us of why those men kidnapped you. If not now, then tonight. The truth this time."

"Sure, I will tonight. I promise. Ah, I almost forgot. Your probation officer stopped by. I didn't open the door but she seemed pretty mad at you for skipping community service."

"Not Ms Cooper," Max moaned. "She'd love to see me behind bars almost as much as Constable Tomlinson."

"Wow. So, everything Max said was true?" Rosie asked in a staggered voice.

"I don't know what he told you, but I assume so," Khalil said. "Like I said, I'll tell you everything in due course."

Rosie's eyes locked on him in an unblinking stare. "Holy shit."

"Ditto. That's pretty much an appropriate response. How did you guys get on in the championship?" Khalil asked, and took a sip from his glass of water. "Hope you managed without me."

"Not bad. Only won both rounds. And got to the final tomorrow!" Rosie boasted. "Although, it doesn't seem that important in comparison to what you've been through."

"You should've seen me, Khalil," Max said with a grin. "I got accused of cheating three times! A new record!"

"That's amazing. Good job, guys," Khalil congratulated. "Sorry I couldn't be there. And how did you fare in London? I guess that's a while back now."

They exchanged dark looks and explained what had been going on over the past weeks, including the latest clue.

"A pirate, you say? Let me see," Khalil said, rubbing his head.

"Are you sure you don't want to rejuvenate and exfoliate for a while?" Max asked.

Khalil shook his head. "Nah. I'm up for this. I wanna finish the damn contest already."

"Don't we all…"

Max turned on his Wii, got out his Wiimotes and loaded up the picture of the pirate clue on the screen.

The moment Khalil laid eyes on the jolly pirate, memories of a sunny day by the sea flooded through his mind. It had been years since he'd last seen that pirate. His parents had once told him that they'd gone to the pirate's theme park with Fatima the first week they arrived in England, using the meagre pennies they had to buy a ticket. It might have been a silly thing to spend money on, but he supposed it'd been a treat after the hell that was the journey here. Shortly after that, they had moved to London and would go on to take Khalil there some years later after his birth.

"That's Captain Seadog!" Khalil burst out.

Max and Rosie stared at him. "*Who*?"

"When I was a child, my parents once took me and my sister on a car trip to Blackpool. There was a theme park there they always liked called Blackpool Pirate Park. It had this mascot called Captain Seadog," he explained, ignoring the pain in his shoulder. "I think that's him. Actually, I'm sure of it!"

Wow! That was a lifetime ago. I'd almost completely forgotten about it. Fatima and I had a ball.

"A vital lead! We should repair to there imminently," Max affirmed without a moment of hesitation. "Before somebody else realises the pirate's identity, if they haven't already."

Khalil leaned forward and threw back his long hair. "Really? Now?"

"Absolutely. I've been checking Amelia's posts on the forum every day, and I just know she's getting closer. She even told me about taking a trip to find the final clue this morning."

"But we can't go! It's too late. What about the championship tomorrow?" Rosie pointed out with a dismayed face.

"The riddle won't take two minutes for someone educated to work out. The answer's probably already online. We can come back for the final tomorrow," Max said, lips pursing.

"I doubt we'll have time. Universally Challenged will be thrilled!"

"Rosie, it's just a dumb quiz championship for nobodies. Second place is still good, and I bet you won't give a hoot who wins when we become the winners of The Crystalline Crucible. Learn to prioritise."

They debated for a few minutes, while Khalil stood there, rubbing his hands together and breathing hard. Thank God he was finally free of Aaron and the burdens of his past, but the fact remained that he had no money to his name. He couldn't go back to get his things from his apartment—it was a crime scene now—so, the contest prize represented his only chance to end his eternal nomadism. In a way, there couldn't be a more poetic trip, going back to where his parents had first arrived in this godforsaken country. *The real beloved is your beginning and your end. When you find that one, you'll no longer expect anything else.*

"I don't want to force you to give anything up, Rosie," Khalil maintained. "It's up to you. I can always go alone. In this whole contest, I've not even found one clue. It's the least I can do."

"No, you can't go unchaperoned," Max asserted.

"Why not?"

"You've been shot! Hold on. How long is the drive? If only I hadn't got banned from getting a licence by crashing into the zoo and freeing those Bengal tigers…"

"I'd say it would be about a three-hour journey, but it depends on the traffic. We'd probably get there early tomorrow morning. I could drive. I've been sleeping all afternoon, so I'll be fine."

"But that still means we won't be able to finish the confounded quiz!" Max exclaimed.

There was a pregnant pause.

Rosie paced back and forth, running her fingers through her hair, biting her nails and staring at the ceiling. Finally, she stopped and turned to them. "Fine. We can go…even if it means we'll miss the championship. It kills me, but this is more important. I'll text the others."

"Thank you, Rosie," Max said. "I know how much quizzing means to you."

"Cheers," Khalil echoed.

Max picked up a letter that Ms Cooper must have slipped under his door. It stated that due to his recently missed meetings he needed to report to see her at once, or the police would issue a warrant.

"Huzzah! I think I may just bring my passport too," he added, foot rapping. He strode over to his teddy. "Benjamin, I promise I'll return to get you before I leave for Ithaca."

"But I'll come only on the condition that I drive, at least to begin with," Rosie put in. "Khalil is in no state to take us. And on the way, we have to get him something to wear." She pointed at his *Tweenies* hoodie. "That is hideous."

"I kinda like it," Khalil remarked. "I would've gone for the *Teletubbies* one, but it was a tad small."

And within minutes, they were in Rosie's car, barrelling down the motorway to Blackpool.

CHAPTER 30

ANSWERS, AT LAST

As Max awoke, he wasn't immediately sure whether it was night or day. The sky outside the car window was a pale, misty blend of violet and magenta. He'd fallen fast asleep somewhere along the journey and awoken in confusion to an empty vehicle and the sight of a petrol station. With the click of a door, Rosie opened the passenger seat, and Khalil, carrying fast food bags, got in the driver's seat.

"What ungodly hour is it?" Max asked airily.

He shook his dead arm, which he must have been sleeping on.

"Aren't you a slugabed, Max?" Khalil said, yawned and handed him a burger and fries. "An hour after we got in the car, you dropped off and have been out like a log for like ten hours. It's five-thirty a.m. Now, I'm gonna drive for a little while. Getting shot in the shoulder won't stop me."

"There was an accident on the motorway," Rosie revealed exhaustedly. She had noticeable bags under her eyes. "Aren't three lorry pile-ups great fun? It's been a slow night."

"I feel marginally comatose," Max said, rubbing his eyes. "How close are we to the theme park?"

"Not far," Khalil declared. "It's not so big. When I went there, it had like one rollercoaster and a carousel. I Googled it, and it doesn't even seem to have a website."

Max crossed his arms. "Well, how close to whatever it is?"

Khalil shrugged, the corner of his lip rising. "Close is a subjective concept."

"Oh, come on. Just tell me," Max demanded, flinching. "Is this supposed to be your impression of me? There's not nearly enough subtle social commentary, sesquipedalianism and diverting witticisms."

Khalil faced the road. He straightened his spine as he drove them out of the car park. "An hour, at most."

"No more fighting, kids," Rosie said, rolling her eyes. "Or you won't be getting any ice cream today."

"Kids? I don't think we can qualify as kids in any way, shape or form after what happened yesterday," Max said seriously. "Anyhoo, my bladder is the antonym of empty."

Fireworks. Two homicides. The quiz competition. And now this. What a kerfuffle.

After Khalil turned the car back around, Max headed inside the petrol station and used the grotty bathroom. However, as he was leaving, he bumped into a familiar tangle of ginger hair.

"Would you look at that? Maxwell Jacobs! Lovely to see you," Amelia said, spotting him as she finished her transaction.

She grinned while he frowned at her, astonished by his own bad luck.

"Oh, no. Not you again," Max said, his tone laced with exasperation. "Why do you keep stalking me everywhere?"

"Odd, eh? Shame I keep missing Khalil, though. If you got rid of that girlfriend of yours, maybe we could even be romantic partners! The Ginger Genius and The Dreadnought Chevalier. Think what we could do together. Hehehe."

He gagged. "I think I'd rather be buried alive and eaten to death by fire ants. Then have my body restored to normal before being buried and consumed by them again, in a time loop of infinite agony."

Amelia giggled. "Really? You hate me that much? Hehehe."

He nodded. "Let's just say when I'm boxing in *Wii Sports*, it improves my score to think of your laugh."

"So nice of you," she said, suddenly scowling. "Are you here for the clue, too?"

"Why would I tell you anything, Fidelia?" Max said. "You're only here because of *my* original hint."

She groaned and turned away. "It's Amelia for the hundredth time. And you really think that? I didn't even need your help. I'm a real treasure hunter, unlike some people."

"Not true. I am more of a treasure hunter than you'll ever be. You just do it for the money. I'm in it for the treasure," he affirmed with his head held high. "And I'm going to find the treasure before you do. Just you wait, Celia."

"Yes, I do it for the money. That's the whole point of treasure hunting in the first place! One day I will be the richest woman in England."

"No, it's not. It's for the glory, the majesty…the wonder of discovery. Treasure hunting is the most beautiful thing I have ever known. Other than Rosie, maybe."

"And what is beauty? A big nothing. Nobody ever got rich off childish fantasies. I suppose we'll see who finds the treasure by tonight, Crystal Loser," she said, and trudged off while humming "No Matter What" by Boyzone. "Oh, and I just want to say one more thing."

"What?"

"MY NAME IS GODDAMN AMELIA! GOT IT?!" Amelia screamed. She calmed in an instant and left with one final evil laugh. "Hehehe. Toodle-oo."

With both his bladder and what's-her-face dealt with, Max struggled to control his rage as he returned to the car. Likewise, as they drove along the motorway into Blackpool, he tried to read a guide he'd loaned out about knitting but found it unexpectedly difficult to focus on imbibing the surely fascinating difference between types of sewing stitches.

Max was still in shock to hear all that Khalil had revealed about his past during the drive here. Becoming mates with a former gang member was not something he'd planned to do, so it was rather a revelation to learn that he had already done it, albeit unintentionally. Maybe the biggest surprise of the whole thing was finding out that the attempted assassination of himself and Rosie had indeed been just that—or at least a misfire, and not a stray bullet as Constable Tomlinson had so idiotically suggested.

Max mostly understood why Khalil had lied for so long: he'd been trying to protect him. After hearing Khalil talk about Aaron, he sounded like the most unpleasant person ever, somehow much worse than Brad. It was still hard for Max to comprehend that he'd witnessed Aaron's and Gerald's probable deaths, and had even been complicit. Max didn't like to recall the gory sight of the two men bleeding out. He could not help but feel guilty, no matter how horrible they were. Ultimately though, it was self-defence.

When they finally arrived at Blackpool, Max immediately noticed just how pretty it was. Which was unusual for him, having once called Vincent van Gogh's *The Starry Night* wishy-washy hogwash.

The Irish Sea glimmered under the azure morning sky. A host of seaside cafes and tourist shops were visible along the horizon behind Blackpool Tower, a giant red structure in the centre of the town like the Eiffel Tower but less impressive in about every way conceivable. It was beautiful, but to be fair, Stapleford would make a dumpster look ravishing. The sun had now risen over Blackpool, the glorious weather evoking Ithaca in Maxwell's poster.

Soon enough, they parked the car and began their search. Max let Khalil use his sunglasses as a disguise, in the unlikely event that the police were looking for him.

Strangely, he'd found no evidence of Khalil's so-called Blackpool Pirate Park's existence or address online. Accordingly, they were relying solely on Khalil's memory. The worrying thing was that when they asked around, none of the residents, or Blackpudlians as they liked to be called, seemed to know anything about this theme park.

"Maybe you've had one of those, uh, Mandela effect thingamabobs?" Max suggested.

"No. I know it must be tantalisingly close," Khalil said, and peered around. He'd been slightly limping ever since Max had found him, but other than that, he was much like his normal self. "You see that shop, Waffle World? It's been here forever. I definitely went in there with my sister ages ago. It's really popular around here, I believe. Maybe we should get some breakfast and ask if anyone knows about it."

They proceeded into Waffle World, which was bustling with customers even at this early hour of the day. After queuing, Max, Rosie and Khalil ordered at the till and asked the cashier if they had ever heard of the Blackpool Pirate Park.

Regrettably, the result was a blank face.

"No, sir. Never heard of it, and I've lived here for all my life," the rake-thin, sweaty young teenager in a Waffle World uniform said.

"What a long one you've no doubt lived, but I don't suppose we could ask somebody less pockmarked than yourself?" Max asked impatiently.

An older gentleman appeared over his shoulder. "Can I help you folks?" he asked, elbowing the teenager aside rather roughly. He was a chubby fellow with barely any eyebrows and a receding hairline. "I'm the manager."

"We were just wondering if you're familiar with the Blackpool Pirate Park?" Khalil said brusquely. "I went there as a child but can't seem to find it."

"Oh, yeah. That rings a bell! Cheers for the flashback," he said, all smiles.

"Really?!"

"Yes, sir. I used to love that place. It was tons of fun." He paused, and then his enthusiasm deflated. "But sorry to break it to you, mate. It was knocked down decades ago. I think some business bought the land and built an office. Ah, yeah. Lovell Unlimited!"

"What a shame," Khalil mumbled, brushing his fringe off his cyan eyes. "Do you happen to remember Captain Seadog?"

"Who?"

Khalil showed the manager his bracelet. He'd revealed on the drive that it contained a picture of his family with Captain Seadog.

"Wow! I totally do... Good ol' Captain Seadog," the manager said, chuckling. "The theme park's mascot? Haven't seen him for ages. Almost forgot he even existed, to be honest!"

Max sighed; he had never seen someone be so helpful and unhelpful at the same time.

The three of them looked at one another. So, Khalil was right that Blackpool Pirate Park had once existed, but if the park was gone, where were they supposed to go next? Lovell Unlimited? It didn't seem that they would know anything.

After thanking the manager, they ate their waffles outside the shop on steel chairs as waves rushed in the distance. Max felt more lost than if he were blind and stuck in the Minotaur's Labyrinth. They had no time to waste, especially knowing Amelia was skulking around. Other people were surely on the clue's scent too, as Max overheard a couple of people, who looked oddly like Sherlock Holmes and Watson, confabulating about Captain Seadog. That said, he was acutely aware that surrender was not an option at the eleventh hour.

"Don't panic. I think I have an idea," Max encouraged. He pointed behind Khalil. "Let's go up Blackpool Tower. There may be something useful we can see from up there."

"Well, we might as well try something," Rosie said desperately. "If we were in Stapleford right now, we would've been beating Universally Challenged. I don't want to have come all this way for nothing. How about I head up there while you two look elsewhere?"

"Sounds like a plan," Khalil said at once.

"That phrase is way too cliché," Max said. "Try something like—reverberates as a stratagem."

"That's a bit less catchy, mate."

"So, what exactly am I looking for up there?" she asked. "It's an awfully large town."

"Something clue-esque?" Max said, scratching his head.

"I'll keep a lookout for Clue Mountain and Treasure Avenue then," she snapped testily. "And shall I see if I can spot Atlantis while I'm at it?"

And so, they finished their waffles, Rosie proceeded to Blackpool Tower and Max and Khalil silently wandered down to the pier. Max wasn't sure if Khalil was upset by what had happened the previous day. Max certainly was, but he didn't really want to admit it.

They both enjoyed the breathtaking sights, putting off talking about yesterday.

"D'you like swimming, Max?" Khalil asked. "My sister and I swam at this beach as kids. I love the feeling of sand on my feet."

"I've never gone swimming in my life or even been to a beach, actually. Much like I'd never seen a dead man until recently," Max said, as he admired the sea from afar. "I have thalassophobia, fear of deep bodies of water. And I'm a fisherman…"

"Huh. I'm so sorry for putting you through all that yesterday," Khalil said, rubbing his nape.

"It's okay. I just hope we don't get in trouble for it all. I feel guilty about it honestly."

"We won't. I feel terrible, trust me… But you've got to remember they were bad guys. The world is a better place without them. And who knows? Maybe they somehow managed to get out of the fire after we left and got medical care. Still, I never dreamt anything like that would happen. You saved my life."

"Knights never abandon their brothers-in-arms."

"I bet David's gonna be pissed when neither of us shows up to work today!"

"Being pissed is his default state. He was gonna fire you, and I'm sure he'll fire me too eventually," Max informed him. "Ms Johnson seems to have recovered though. In fact, she gave me this Rolex as a thank-you gift, but I doubt she'll be managing the Co-op again."

"That's good. I've still got to find a way to pay her back for all I took from the register."

"Just think. When we get the prize money, we can go wherever we fancy, do whatever we want and acquire whatever body augmentation superpowers we desire. I'll get X-ray vision first."

"Nice," Khalil said bracingly. "And yeah. We're close. I can feel it. So, tell me, what's been going on with you and Rosie?"

"What do you mean? The standard pursuits of our idiosyncratic, self-aware species of apes: the oral ingestion of nutritional energy; the defecation and urination processes of bodily wastes and fluids; and the verbal and kinesic socialisation that arises from living within the social norms of post-industrial, capitalist Britain," Max said. "Oh, and she made me Brussels sprouts the other day."

"No, I mean romantically. Are you ever gonna make a move?"

"I see. Interesting question. I suppose I'm waiting for the right moment. She recently broke up with Brad," Max said, his cheeks reddening. "I don't know if I should swoop in like that. And I am not sure I'll ever be Casanova or Romeo, no matter what the pigettes think."

At that moment, Max's phone rang. It was her.

"Max, I've just seen something," Rosie said, sounding slightly out of breath. "Where are you?"

"By the beach," he reported, as he watched a bunch of kids scurrying by with floaties.

She gasped. "You may be near where I was gonna tell you to go. Can you see the pier?"

He affirmed that he could indeed see one not far away, about a ten-minute walk.

"I noticed there's this billboard advertisement there, and it has a pirate on it. I'm thinking it might be Seadog," Rosie hypothesised. "It's at the end of the pier, so it looks pretty deserted."

"A spiffingly smashing job, Rosie. We'll check it out," Max reported, excitement colouring his face.

"I'll meet you there," Rosie said. "I've seen all I can see here. Oh, wait. I think I can see you. Max, your posture is terrible!"

Ignoring her pejorative comment, Max and Khalil hurried towards the pier. As they rushed along the oakwood deck and watched boats pull in and out of the peaceful harbour, Max realised this was actually the first time he had ever seen the ocean properly in his whole life. It looked particularly big and scary. He wasn't sure if he liked it, and he wondered whether it was all as blue as this.

Finally, they spotted a billboard that featured the very same jolly portrait of a pirate as the clue on it. The poster was on the large side, but it was concealed at such an angle that no one could see it easily without going right to the pier's end or climbing to the top of the tower. It was a billboard for the Blackpool Pirate Park, and it looked incredibly old and ragged, the bottom half covered in graffiti. Max and Khalil agreed that it must have been left up here since the theme park had closed.

"Well, that's him on the poster. Captain Seadog!" Khalil pointed out.

"Huzzah," Max said flatly, having just caught the sight of something almost as conspicuous as the poster. "Look at him. What's that man doing sitting underneath?"

Directly under the poster, a barefoot man sat on a rug, hawking a wide variety of gems. Max reasoned that the man was homeless unless growing waist-long, ragged hair and wearing stained clothes were Blackpudlian fashion trends. It couldn't be a coincidence that he was selling gems.

"Crystals for sale! Crystals for sale!" the man barked.

The pair strolled over.

"You're not affiliated with this poster, are you?" Max asked, pointing at the poster.

"Depends if you can tell me the pirate's name," the man said with a knowing smile.

"Captain Seadog," Khalil said immediately.

The man nodded and winked as if he'd been waiting to hear that for a long time. "That's correct. Well done. Follow me," he said, and got to his feet.

The past six months flashed through Max's mind as he and Khalil followed the homeless man down the pier. What he really thought, although he was almost embarrassed to admit it in case he was wrong, was that it was over. That they'd done it, and their adventure had all been worth it. Nonetheless, the long-haired, dishevelled hobo remained quiet and would not answer a single question. Was it too good to be true?

By the time they came to their destination—an office building—and had stepped inside, Max was of the opinion that if they didn't get told what was going on, he would have a stress-induced stroke. The homeless man dropped them off at the front desk; the secretary made a call.

"Yes. They're here," she muttered, and glanced up at them. "The winners. They've just arrived."

The instant Max heard the word *winners*, he grinned, euphoria surging through him. It was somehow real. They had actually done it. They'd won The Crystalline Crucible! He'd succeeded in a treasure hunt for the first time in his life, and now all his earthly dreams were about to come true.

It was the best feeling he had ever had in his life.

After the call, the secretary instructed him and Khalil to take a seat in a banal waiting area.

Fifteen minutes passed. So far, there wasn't much celebratory fanfare. It felt like they were waiting for a doctor's appointment rather than having just won the biggest contest in treasure hunting history. Max messaged Rosie where they were, anxious to see her. Soon, she bounded in and dashed over to them with excitement written across her visage. It occurred to Max that this version of Rosie was a far cry from the one she'd been in January.

"Did you find Seadog?!" she shouted, sounding much like him when he'd yelled the quiz answers.

"Seems so," Max said in a disappointed sort of voice.

It was challenging to act like this wasn't a big deal in the midst of urges to jump up and whoop.

At last, the secretary called their names and led them out of the waiting room. At the same time, the door chimed and Amelia sprinted up to the front desk, squealing, "Am I the first one? Did I win?!"

Hehehe, Ginger Loser. You most certainly did not.

Their group was guided to an office and seated in three parallel chairs, facing an elderly gentleman.

"Congratulations," the man said dramatically. "You have embarked on an epic treasure hunt across the country. You have tracked down needle-in-haystack clues and demonstrated your detective skills magnificently. And now, you've found yourselves here as the winners. May I ask your names?"

One by one, they each gave their names. The figure in front of them looked a tad familiar to Max with his sagging jowl, wrinkly skin and skeletal figure.

Max gasped. *Wait a minute. He looks like… But it couldn't be.*

"I'm Anthony Lovell of Lovell Unlimited," the man said, smiling from ear to ear. "Perhaps you recognise me."

"W-what?!" Max burst out.

"Yes, it's really me. You should have worked out by now that this building was constructed on the site of Blackpool Pirate Park, which was demolished over a decade ago to make room for Lovell Unlimited Headquarters. In point of fact, this building is historic as it was the first Lovell Unlimited office."

Max stared at Anthony, at a loss for words. Mr Lovell was one of the richest men in the British business world, even more well-off than Alan Sugar allegedly. Did this mean he and his company were behind the contest this whole time?

"You're the one who invented my vacuum, then," Max said, astonished.

"And your company's buying my school's building," Rosie said, looking almost blue in the face.

Khalil was the only one who didn't say anything. Now that Max thought about it, he'd noticed the Lovell Unlimited logo on this building but had been so exhilarated that he'd scarcely even registered it.

"Well, I don't know about that, but I can reveal I was the founder of The Crystalline Crucible," Mr Lovell said assuredly. "Let me start at the beginning."

"Okey-dokey," Max said.

"Lovell Unlimited has always prided itself on making the best vacuum cleaners in the world. Over the past few years, we've been slowly developing our newest vacuum, the Crystal 2, the first affordable automatic vacuum." At this, Mr Lovell swiftly pulled out a modern-looking, sleek vacuum from under the table. "However, as the design and production came to an end, my marketing team and I decided we needed to revamp the company's image and conceived an ingenious way to launch our new product. The company also requires new faces as we've received a great deal of bad press that claims our company practices are 'immoral', 'despicable' and even 'barbaric'. Personally, I am often viciously calumniated in the news as corrupt, stiff and starchy, and Dyson vacuum cleaners tend to steal the spotlight in the market."

Max hunched over. He couldn't quite grasp the link between vacuums and treasure hunting.

"All in all, we resolved that Lovell Unlimited had to put an end to these rumours and rejuvenate my personal staid public image. Vacuums may seem boring at first glance, but treasure hunting... Now, that's exciting. We created The Crystalline Crucible to begin a marketing campaign for the Crystal 2 and to hire the winners of the contest for Lovell Unlimited! That being the case, I teamed up with the skilled puzzle designers from *The Guardian* to design a cryptic treasure hunt and make it the talk of the town.

I understand you've just met Scruffy. He's the local hobo who we paid to wait by the poster for the winners."

"I have a Crystal vacuum!" Max exclaimed. "It's marvellous!"

"Thank you, Maxwell," Mr Lovell said happily. "Our Crystal 2 improves on it in every way."

"Hold on," Rosie said in disbelief. "You want to recruit us to work for you? Your vacuum company?"

"That is absolutely right," he said in a cheery voice. "You will take senior positions in the department of your choice and will all be given free Crystal 2s. Not a bad prize, if you ask me!"

There was too much to say, too much to ask and too much to process.

"Mr Lovell, I'm not sure I can work for you," Rosie said, clearly trying to be careful with her words. "I don't know a thing about vacuum cleaners."

"But that's the point of the contest: to bring in regular people with big brains and problem-solving abilities, who'll deliver new perspectives and unique ideas to the company!" Mr Lovell dismissed. "And won't it be such good PR too? I was inspired by *The Apprentice*."

"What about the riches beyond our wildest dreams?" Khalil asked dubiously.

"I can assure you your wages will be most satisfactory," he stated, still grinning. "They often stretch to six figures, even seven sometimes. Lovell Unlimited jobs are some of the most well-paid in the business."

"*All their earthly problems will be rendered null, and the mysteries of the world answered*," Max added. "You didn't mention that part either, Mr Willy Wonka. Er, I mean, Mr Lovell."

"Well remembered. I certainly wouldn't want to let you down after all the hard work you've done to win the contest. So, let me get to the best part of your prize," Mr Lovell said, absolutely ecstatic. He reached under the table, pulled out a book and plopped it down on the table. "And here it is! A signed preprint copy of my new tough love self-help book: *Law of Persuasion: The Hidden Secret Power of Success*. I'll get the others their copies later. I think you'll find all your answers in there."

Max picked it up and paged through the book, skimming the words. *Hold on a minute. This is just* How to Win Friends and Influence People *in different words!*

"So basically," Khalil muttered gruffly, "you're saying that we're not getting any money, and this contest was all just a stupid scheme for you to market a new brand of crystal vacuum? What an anticlimax!"

"Excuse me," Mr Lovell said snootily. "It's not just any old new type of vacuum. Lovell Unlimited vacuums are famous the world over."

"I've never heard of them," Khalil retorted. "And I really don't care if they're the world's best vacuums!"

"That they are! And maybe not money, but I forgot to mention, you also get The Crystalline Crucible trophy, the Jewelled Chalice. It's made of the rarest crystals in the world: namely, opal and tanzanite. Here it is!" Mr Lovell pulled out an impressive trophy from under the table. It gleamed so brightly that it looked almost as blinding as Max's laser pointer. "You won't be allowed to take this home with you, of course; it's far too valuable and precious to me. But you can always look at it behind protective glass! I've loved crystals since I was a boy. The Greeks believed they are ice from Heaven, windows to the divine."

Max stared at the Jewelled Chalice, a strange mix of joy and disappointment coursing through him. He put the book down and took the trophy. "Oh, my. It's certainly heavy."

At this, Mr Lovell's phone rang. "I have to get this. One moment."

He stood up and took the call by the room's door. "You can tell the *Daily Mail* that if they even think of publishing that article about Lovell Unlimited using underage workers in sweatshops, and puppy bones to build our vacuums, I will sue them so hard that they won't know what hit them!" he shouted.

A minute later, he wordlessly sat back down with the trio.

"Sorry about that. To sum it up, we created the contest because Lovell Unlimited needed fresh meat for the company and to create a unique media buzz around the launch of the revolutionary Crystal 2!" he explained enthusiastically. "You have to be creative with marketing in such a crowded market, you see, and this contest has been the cheapest form of advertising I've ever encountered."

"Couldn't you have just run adverts? Like a normal company," Rosie said.

Mr Lovell shot daggers at her. "No. In any case, I don't suppose any of you would be so naive to give up such a once-in-a-lifetime chance as to work for me, the business genius, Anthony Lovell. You could all have fifteen minutes of fame. The papers will want to take pictures. I was even planning on redoing this conversation with the cameras rolling, if you would just play along."

"I must be naive," Khalil said, and shook his head. "We thought it was a contest to join MI6 or something. Not a job application. That's false advertising. I want a real prize."

"MI6?" Mr Lovell tilted his head. "Where on Earth did you get that from? It's a contest for a vacuum job, Mr Ahmed. The clue's in the name."

"No offence, Anthony, but why would I want to spend months of my time treasure hunting just to be a pawn in a corporate campaign, to get a free vacuum and a boring as hell job?"

"As for me," Rosie said, frowning, "your company is buying the school I work at. All the staff got the sack. Now, loads of local kids can't get an education as the nearest one is way too far."

"Excuse me," Mr Lovell said with a defensive laugh. "If the owners sold the building, it can't have been put to much use, could it? My God, your rudeness is unparalleled. So, I suppose what you're trying to tell me is that you just expected a quick million-pound payout or something?"

He guffawed as if this was a preposterous notion, but the three of them simply nodded.

"This is highly unfortunate," Max said, peering around at the others' faces. "It's just not what we had in mind. The Knights Templar, the Illuminati and the Freemasons, yes—but never a vacuum company."

"The contest was as transparent as possible without giving the game away," Mr Lovell declared. "I don't appreciate your ungrateful tones, but I'll tell you what. I will give you till tonight to decide whether you'll accept the prize. Then, I'm going to announce to the shareholders that it's time for us to put an end to the contest and reveal the new vacuum to the press. I am ever so looking forward to seeing our stock jump."

"Look, I do appreciate it, Mr Lovell, and I'm sorry if I seemed impolite, but I'll give my answer now," Rosie said without hesitation. "I would never work for a company like yours. I'm a teacher and an aspiring children's writer, and call me whatever you want, but I just don't like your business practices."

"I agree. I'd rather wash dishes at McDonald's than work at Lovell Unlimited, no matter the pay," Khalil spat, patently revolted at the notion. "I've heard about what your company does. My answer is no."

"How callow of all of you! I've never been spoken to so disrespectfully in my whole life," Mr Lovell snarled. "And you? Er, Maxwell? Are you in agreement with your teammates?"

What is he really asking of us? To take a job in the company? It's better than the Co-op, I guess.

"Um, I dunno," Max said apprehensively. He gazed over at Rosie's and Khalil's embittered faces. "I'll think about it. I do like your company's vacuums, although I kind of wanted to join a secret society, become exorbitantly rich and learn the answers to the mysteries of the world."

"Very well. Perhaps you can talk some sense into your friends while you're at it. Despite their disrespect, I'll see to it that you can all eat free of charge at the five-star Felix Hotel restaurant tonight, on me," Mr Lovell said, disgruntled. "However, the employment contract is a one-time offer. Either you join the company this evening, or you get nothing, and we never see each other again. One or the other."

Frowning sinisterly, he stormed out of the office without saying goodbye.

CHAPTER 31

THE UNFORTUNATE END

It was the first time that Khalil had ever eaten oysters, but he wasn't enjoying them much. The only thing he found remotely appealing at the Felix Hotel's restaurant was the candles, which smelled of figs and reminded him of his childhood home. Other than that, the food was all far too fancy for his liking.

By the looks of it, Max wasn't enjoying his caviar any more than he was, and likewise, Rosie her Greek salad. But Max had barely eaten a bite so far, his head buried in the employment contract that Mr Lovell had had his secretary give them.

They'd come here for dinner before tonight's meeting with Mr Lovell, but still, none of them had a clue about what to say to him.

"The jobs come with a lot of benefits," Max inferred, scrutinising the terms and conditions. "You get access to the Lovell Penthouse, a free phone and a complimentary, uh, puppy."

Temper flaring, Khalil shook his head. "No way! I refuse to work for that guy. I heard he uses dog bones in his vacuums. He's worse than Cruella de Vil."

"Same," Rosie concurred. "I don't want to work for Lovell even if he sends us to the moon. He's just awful."

"Lovell Unlimited is rumoured to be investing in space tourism…" Max said and turned a page.

"It's a Hobson's choice," Khalil declared.

The Felix Hotel was one of the best hotels not just in Blackpool but in the country. The restaurant insisted on a formal dress code, so Mr Lovell had provided them with some frilly clothes at the reception upon arrival. Khalil wasn't comfortable in his suit. Max's had been far too "tight", so he'd opted for his *The Flintstones* shirt and spinning bow tie instead. The opulent waiters had been scowling at him the whole evening, and Khalil even overheard them calling him an "indecorous" and "unbecoming" young man.

Khalil wasn't entirely sure if the shock of actually winning The Crystalline Crucible would ever wear off, but the revelation of the prize had certainly done a great job of dampening the sense of victory. It did seem to him that the contest had been misleading with how it had described the prize, or perhaps he'd just let himself get carried away with Max's over-the-top predictions and ridiculous speculation.

Rosie sighed, arms folded over her evening dress. "The nerve of that billionaire. To make up that whole competition just to get a fleeting headline and announce a vacuum cleaner. Who does he think he is?"

"A very creative vacuum salesman, I suppose," Khalil grunted.

She gulped down her vodka, the alcohol painting her features. Khalil supposed it must be far worse for Max, who had all his hopes and dreams invested in the contest. A depressed stillness unfolded between them, which was finally broken when Max banged his head against the table.

"Well, I guess I've been in denial this whole time," he muttered, face resting on the tablecloth. "It's time to accept it. The Crystalline Crucible was a scam, just like Carol and all the Nigerian princes."

Khalil snorted at the absurdity of it all. The cost of winning had not been pretty. Earlier, Rosie and Max had reportedly seen a video of Universally Challenged—their quizzing archenemy—accepting the championship first prize on account of Agatha Quiztie's forfeit, and it'd evidently left a bad taste in their mouths.

Don't regret what's happened. If it's in the past, let it go. The past: a noose around your neck. Dad told me that not long before he died.

"Let's forget about the damn supposed prize for a moment," Rosie said, thumping the table with her fist. "Now that the contest is over, what will we all do with our lives? Without a job, I'll have to go back to Stapleford and find another teaching job. Goodness, I just want to work on Theodore Tabby for a while."

"And if Ithaca is off the cards, I'll have to beg David to not fire me," Max said gloomily.

"I'm never going back to that town. Stapleford has too many bad memories," Khalil said, reflecting on it. "I still need a fresh start. I'll probably move to the US if I can get a green card."

With a groan, Max histrionically threw his cutlery across the room, inciting several gasps and turned heads from suited diners. "You know what, I'm not gonna even bother attending the meeting with that fat cat. I need some air. I want to go out, explore the beach and find out whether the sand dunes are the same as in my encyclopaedia."

"Me too," Khalil said. He stood. "I hate this restaurant. It's way too stuffy and pretentious."

"One of us has to face him," Rosie reminded them. "I guess I don't mind. Maybe it'll even be fun to tell Lovell just how much he and his vacuums, well, suck. I'll see you two after."

Max and Khalil exited the Felix Hotel and headed to the beach again, but this time, they did nothing but sit on the sand together and stare out at the frothy water. It was a spectacular evening, the tangerine-coloured sun sinking as starlings and kestrels twittered above the tide.

Khalil could tell that Max was feeling melancholy. For Khalil, at least, the ocean's calming babble seemed to lighten the weight in his chest.

"What does it really matter if this contest was a waste of time? Hasn't it been a fun ride? You've seen the ocean now, right?" Khalil queried. "You'd normally be at home reading an encyclopaedia otherwise. One can't learn about the real world in books, no matter how many you read."

The temperate night air and the massaging breeze tempted Khalil to close his eyes and drift off to sleep.

"All I'm good for is memorising random nonsense," Max stated after a pause. "And don't give me that it's-the-journey-that-counts line. The journey was miserable."

"Come on. It wasn't that bad!"

"I'm glad you had a nice time. I dunno if I feel worse about losing the contest and not being able to join the Knights Templar, or that I let you down. You were pinning all your hopes and dreams on prize money that didn't exist."

"Don't worry about my hopes and dreams. I thought that it was you who was doing that."

"I mean, I was. But it's over now. The library will close, and I'll never become a spy."

"We'll move on. I don't need a lot to get by, especially now that Aaron is gone. Even if we *did* get a huge payout, I've no clue what I'd do with the prize money realistically. All I need is a roof and a camera."

Khalil absent-mindedly picked up some damp sand and built a little castle, while Max looked fearfully at a crab scuttling by.

"I suppose it was credulous of us to believe all the rumours," Max said with a tight frown. "As Rosie said, I don't have a clue where to go from here. I just can't figure out my life's purpose. Amelia's around my age and she has everything figured out. I never told you I bumped into her, did I?"

"Really? How was she?"

"Not nice. She's a sourpuss, jerkface nasty pants."

"Well put. Maxwell, you don't need to know your purpose by your age. I'd be astonished if you did. Don't compare yourself with Amelia of all people. The world isn't a contest to win. I'm twenty-seven, and I still don't have a clue what I'm doing. I'm sure there are tons of things you could do if you set your mind to it."

"You think? Maybe. The modern crossword puzzle was invented in 1913 by Arthur Wynne. There *must* be more to do if it took humanity that long to work out how to make them. I could invent a 3D crossword. Or I could become a ballet dancer! I'm excellent at Irish dancing."

"Uh, possibly. Or something else."

"They say life is like a game of chess. I used to say it's more like a crossword, but now I'd say it's closest to Tetris: you always lose in the end. I'll never get to Ithaca. Truthfully, I'm not sure I ever even left Calypso."

"The great myths have constantly changed form throughout history. All the same, life is way more complicated than myths or games. It's a kaleidoscopic force that steamroller narratives never manage to keep down, not for long."

"If you say so. I'd much rather be someone like Gilgamesh than Maxwell Jacobs. Jason got the Golden Fleece, Heracles got made immortal, and we...we got nothing. I suppose the true treasure was inside of us all along. How thoroughly emetic."

An unrelated idea crossed Khalil's mind. "Hey, didn't you say you've never gone swimming before?" he asked.

"I might have said something to that effect," Max said hesitantly.

"Why don't we go now?" he said, and took off his shoes and socks. "It'll be fun."

"Uh, no thanks. I think I'd rather be thrown in a tank of termites, black widow spiders and white-lipped vipers before being dropped in a vat of hydrofluoric acid."

"Come on. What about just paddling?"

"I'd still prefer to be hanged, drawn and quartered. Not to mention flayed."

"Stop being so damn dramatic," Khalil grumbled. "Why do you use all those pretentious words?"

"Don't blame me. My mother once told me she dropped a dictionary on my head as a baby, and I've been unbearably verbose ever since," Max explained, twisting his lips.

He took some persuading, but eventually, Khalil managed to get Max to stand right next to the shore.

"I'm not sure I'd much like to be consumed by piranhas on the day I won The Crystalline Crucible, thank you," Max moaned. He grimaced, and his eyes bulged out as he stared down at the water like it was a pit of lava.

"Have some fun," Khalil encouraged. He gently pushed Max in. "It's just H_2O, right?"

"This isn't a coming-of-age eighties film. I'm not sure if I'm more appalled or betrayed," he complained.

However, Max mostly got used to the water in the next few minutes. He *was* a fisherman, after all, among several other occupations.

They paddled around for five minutes, with Max looking quite miserable the whole time and barely venturing a few inches from the shore. Thereafter, they ambled back up to their things.

Trousers soaked, Max removed his shoes and shook them roughly. "Sand—is that what they call this infernal phenomenon? Turns out I hate the damn stuff. Look, it's getting in my bag too!"

Subsequently, he pulled off his rucksack and started to sift the sand out of it. Eventually, he took out something that shimmered like the ocean, catching Khalil's eye. The Jewelled Chalice. Khalil couldn't believe it; he was sure they'd left the trophy at the Lovell Unlimited office!

"I tucked this into my bag when Mr Lovell was on that call," Max revealed disinterestedly. "Miss Marple did once say that stealing is an impolite thing to do, but it's excusable under certain circumstances."

"And you told me off for stealing!" Khalil remarked, hardly believing his eyes.

"I know. Oh, wait… Do you think it's worth much?" he ejaculated, as if suddenly realising this might be important.

"Loads, probably. It sure looks expensive."

Khalil took the trophy from Max and raised it up to the moonlight, watching it twinkle like diamonds. *Wow. Looks like really rare crystals. It seems we've found treasure.*

If this was truly the Jewelled Chalice, it was surely the most valuable object that Khalil had ever held. He hadn't thought that any of them could've taken it out of that office. A colossal cruise liner sailed over the waves in the distance and honked its horn as if saying congratulations.

"I guess it's the only thing about the contest that was true. Eureka!" Max remarked.

Another good idea came to Khalil. "Yup. Do you think we could, uh, sell it?"

"Possibly. I don't think Mr Lovell would like that much," he said, stroking his chin.

Khalil didn't say a word, but at that moment, he thanked England for Maxwell Jacobs.

CHAPTER 32

CONSOLATION PRIZE

The week after Mr Lovell revealed the truth about The Crystalline Crucible on the news, Max anonymously sold the trophy on eBay, the final bid reaching an enormous figure. He viewed the money as something of a consolation prize, although an exceptionally good one by all means. When Mr Lovell had realised they'd taken the Jewelled Chalice, he sent a pointed email requesting it back, clearly annoyed with his mistake. Yet with his billions and the prospect of bad publicity, it was presumably not worth pressing charges, and so, in the end, they were allowed to keep the substantial amount of money they made from its sale.

Subsequent to dividing the sum into three with Rosie and Khalil, the first thing Max did with his newfound riches was post Stapleford Library a cheque that was more than enough to keep it afloat for several years. Sofia sent him a short message of appreciation for the gift and reported that Mr Johnson had resigned in total fury when he found out about Max's good fortune. She was going to be in charge of the library from now on, but more importantly, the Stapleford orphans would get to keep it!

Max also mailed Ms Johnson a thank-you note and enough pounds to buy one hundred and one sausage rolls. In addition, Khalil sent an anonymous get-well card to her with a donation to repay the money he'd stolen.

The news spectacle after Mr Lovell announced that he had been behind the enigmatic contest was immense in all regards—but it only lasted for a few days until people began pointing out that the contest and the Crystal 2 were clearly a distraction from the company's ongoing scandals. While Lovell reported that the original winners declined it due to being "ungrateful nobodies", the lady in second place, that wretched minx Amelia, ended up taking the job. Max even spotted her on the news, boasting.

"I'm so thrilled to become Lovell Unlimited's newest tax accountant," she said heartily into the microphone, giggling twice as much as normal. "What a great prize. I really couldn't be happier! Hehehe."

At first, he was despondent that she'd won by default, but after a week, he realised it really didn't matter. At the end of the day, he and his friends had got more money, and they were the *true* winners. Plus, at least throbbinhood420 and wombraider69 didn't win.

Rosie seemed to have similar disappointed feelings about Universally Challenged and Gertrude, though Max was still looking for a way to make up their loss to her.

Having sold the trophy, Max, Rosie and Khalil stayed in Blackpool for a bit longer, residing at the Premier Inn. Over a heavenly, mostly rainless week, Max went on his first shopping spree. He bought a load of video games, a suitcase full of books, and Rosie took him to buy some clothes too, insisting that now he had no excuse to keep dressing like a five-year-old. It was great to finally wear proper adult garments.

He and Khalil even went on a mates' outing to see a new film at the cinema, which was regrettably so abominable that he yelled at the projector and got them kicked out of the screening. But they didn't just go to the cinema. Max taught Khalil how to sword fight with some plastic swords they had bought from a toy shop, and Khalil gave him some advice on how to talk to girls. They discussed topics like how they'd like their bodies to be disposed of after death, with Khalil opting for a water burial and Max preferring to be cryogenically frozen. Khalil gave Max a book on Rumi, and Max gifted Khalil a how-to guide on juggling. They played football on the beach as well. Max discovered the beautiful game was pretty fun.

Somehow, they'd gone down the enemies-to-friends trope route, after all. And it wasn't just Maxwell and Khalil's friendship that had blossomed. Rosie and Khalil were now good pals too, having swapped book recommendations and discussed their respective creative philosophies.

Max thought the events behind how they half won The Crystalline Crucible would make a good story to tell their grandchildren, but Rosie said it would have to be sensationalised to be even slightly entertaining. Perhaps brave Sir Maxwellian could get into a sword fight to the death with the dishonourable Prince Brad somewhere along the way. Princess Rosie would be searching for the true heir of the crown, the dashing King Maxwell. And lastly, Khalil would be a zen, mystic Bedouin shaman with a troubled past in need of a strapping apprentice—the cunning stable boy, Maxington of the Kingdom of Staplefordius. A much more satisfying and less tragic ending to The Crystalline Crucible would have to be conceived, such as Max, Rosie and Khalil receiving a billion pounds. There would have to be a tense battle on top of a moving train and an urgent quest to save the world from some threat of total destruction, but Max thought they could figure out how to work those parts in later.

It was Rosie who came up with how they could go on with their lives. She spotted a flyer for a world cruise leaving Bristol port the next week—just like she'd always wanted—and it would even stop at Ithaca on the way. The cruise would take them around the world, visiting the shores of Brazil, America, Spain and India.

With no obligations left for them in England, it was perfect. All of them signed up for it at once, and on the July day that the cruise was to set off, they got into Rosie's car and drove to Bristol.

"Max, you're hogging the questions," Rosie griped. "We were supposed to be doing this together."

They both looked down at the latest issue of *The Guardian*, which was splayed open on the middle seat.

"It's not my fault if some people are too slow," he replied. "God, do the crossword makers even try anymore? I suppose the old ones were all hired by Lovell. This thing could have been written by five-year-olds. Just one clue left."

"Let me have a go, mate," Khalil uttered as he drove them past a sign that said "WELCOME TO BRISTOL!"

"Yes, sire," Max remarked. "This is your expertise. Where whisky comes from, ten letters."

He plopped a Malteser into his mouth, having only recently come around to chocolate, pizza and ice cream since Khalil made him try them. Now, he couldn't believe he'd gone so long without them.

Khalil paused for a second. "Distillery."

"Precisely," he said, filling in the last boxes. "But to be fair, an inanimate object could get that."

"Boy, maybe we three should enter a crossword championship next year," Khalil suggested.

"You won one of those in school, didn't you, Max?" Rosie recalled. "Khalil, you should've seen him in school! The teachers all despised him. One time, he came in with a petition to change the curriculum and made us all sign it. Apparently, they were teaching us too much 'childish drivel'. Another time, he graffitied the playground with spray paint, proclaiming that the teachers were 'authoritarian drones'. There was also that one occasion when he called the police and Childline to report on the headmaster for kidnapping and indoctrinating him with 'British propaganda'. Oh, and he was in that wheelchair for months after jumping off the school roof to test if his homemade wingsuit worked."

"I'd stop reminiscing, or I may *accidentally* mention your goth phase," Max snapped.

He was eager to change the subject before she mentioned the time he had got the school shut down for a month by building a functional nuclear reactor in design technology class. Not to forget that incident where he ran away from school to try to make it as a lion tamer.

"So, what are you gonna do with your money?" Khalil asked curiously.

"I just want to see the world," Rosie said with noticeably less cynicism than usual. "I'll probably get back into teaching at some point, yet who knows? I do love children, but I never *really* wanted to be a teacher. The only thing I certainly don't plan to buy with the money is a single vacuum cleaner."

"Reverberates as a stratagem," Khalil said, nodding. "And you, Max? University maybe?"

"Treasure hunting! What else?" Max said. "I watched *National Treasure* the other day, and no matter how unrealistic it may be, I found myself inspired. The way I see it, The Crystalline Crucible was just preparation for something bigger—much bigger. I might've never got the mammoth tusk, but I was thinking of stealing the Magna Carta from the National Archives to examine it for hidden messages."

"Max, I think you need to move on from treasure hunting now," Rosie advised. "With the prize money, you could apply to uni to get a degree in medieval history perhaps."

"Here we go again with what *you* want me to do with my life," he said, and frowned. "Let me guess. You'd love it most of all if I became some boring doctored professor of whatever, boreology."

"I'm sorry. I don't want to be a nag. Do whatever you want. Let's just focus on the cruise," she said and grinned at Khalil. "Did you know the ship has a water park and massage parlour on board? Actually, it has pretty much everything! Are you looking forward to it, Khalil?"

"Oh, uh, yeah. I really am…not," Khalil mumbled. "Sorry to leave it till the last moment, but I'm not gonna come with you guys."

"How come?!" Max yelled with a shriek.

"I just can't. Don't get me wrong; I'd love to. A world cruise sounds like a dream. But despite what *I* may want, I've simply got to go back to London. My family needs me." He stared pensively out at the Bristol roads. "I realised it last night. I don't want to run away anymore, so I can't keep ignoring them…"

"Why can't you just send them money?" Max said adamantly. "God knows you shouldn't stay in this country after everything that's happened. You could still get in trouble for Mr Brooks' death. Plus, for some reason they weren't mentioned in the papers regarding the fire, but in all probability you killed Aaron and Gerald. Not that I judge you for it."

"I know. Regardless, don't you have community service?" Khalil asked.

"I paid my fine so they'll let me have my meetings with Ms Cooper by phone, and my community service no longer has a deadline. Turns out that treasure hunting ban was not legally enforceable. Besides, Rosie's booked all the tickets!"

"Well, it's not that simple for me, Max. I had a girlfriend in London. I want to patch things up with her," Khalil explained. "And other family too. An older sister named Fatima, my mother and loads of nieces and nephews. I'm pretty sure the police won't get me. It seems like they don't have a clue who I am. Still, I'll keep a low profile."

"Max," Rosie said, leaning up to his ear and lowering her voice to a whisper, "the tickets don't matter, do they? Khalil has a family. Maybe *he* doesn't want to come along with us. It's his choice."

"I was thinking about it yesterday," Khalil added hastily. "I shouldn't go either way. You'll be happier if it's just you two."

"But you promised it was gonna be us all, the three musketeers, travelling the world!" Max argued. "Were you lying? You're a big fat liar!"

"Sorry again," he said, the port appearing in the distance. "It's time for me to go. Honestly, I've already refunded my ticket."

"But what about… I mean, you could just—"

"Max, I've made up my mind," he stated with finality.

Max took a moment and then said darkly, "It's your loss. Water off my back."

He didn't say another word as they arrived at the cruise port. After Khalil had parked, they stepped out of the car and awkwardly walked towards the check-in terminal. Hundreds of seagulls swooped gaily above the tide that beat against the cruise ship's hull. The ship was much bigger than he'd expected, a practical leviathan casting a gigantic shadow. The sea around it coruscated like it had been coated in glitter under the scintillating sunlight.

It seemed to Max that there was only a slim chance he would ever see Khalil again. The opportunity would arise if he chose to come back to England, which wasn't likely to happen anytime soon. So, they were essentially going to be bidding each other farewell forever.

Khalil stood with Max and Rosie outside the check-in terminal, the three of them a tad speechless.

"It was lovely meeting you, Khalil. I hope you patch things up in London," Rosie said as she offered him a handshake. "Maybe we'll see each other again sometime."

"You too," Khalil said affectionately. "And good luck with Theodore Tabby. I'm sure it'll be a great read."

"Maybe if I ever finish it." She stepped back and bit her lip as she glanced wistfully between Max and Khalil. "I'll give you a minute."

When she was gone, Khalil and Max stood in silence for a moment. Khalil spoke first. "We've come a long way, haven't we, Max?"

"Yes, you and Mr Knife," Max said, cracking a smile. For some reason, his anger had disappeared. "How is he these days?"

"I'll miss you, mate. Good luck with Rosie. You two may be soulmates."

"I doubt that very much. I'm still not sure she's even interested in me," Max remarked bashfully. "She calls me a man-child. *C'est la vie.*"

"You're not a man-child."

"I dunno. Whenever I talked big or made fun of Brad or whatever, it was only because I thought it'd make me interesting to her. In truth, I know I'm not a knight, a cowboy, a fisherman or even a treasure hunter. I guess I just believed being them would make me, well, cool. Without any of that, I'm the most boring person alive. Even my evil father is way more interesting than me. I never did reply to his letter."

"I will tell you this, Max, and I mean this in sincerity: you're the biggest, baddest badass I've ever met in my life," Khalil affirmed. "Cooler than Brad, Mr Lovell and Miss Marple. You're a hero. And real good at Tetris too. We may never see each other again, so I want you to remember that. You don't need a father in your life to be amazing. Just don't forget to grow up."

"You're not so bad yourself," Max said. "In fact, I'd say you are the real hero. Not me. I never did a heroic thing in my life."

"Of course, you have. Look, I got you something," he said, and pulled a small, wrapped gift from his pocket. He placed it in Max's hand. "A woolly mammoth. I bought it ages ago, and it's been sitting in my pocket. I thought you deserved it after everything. May it bring you luck during your travels."

"Thanks," Max said. He unwrapped the key chain. "Wow! The tusk looks realistic. It's almost as good as Excalibur. Wait a sec." He reached into his own pocket, retrieved an errant staple and handed it to Khalil. "Lucky I have one on me! Something to remember Stapleford by. I'm sure the memories will haunt you, like a ghost."

Max extended his hand for a final handshake. Khalil ignored it, stepped forward and gave him a claustrophobic hug. The embrace lasted for about ten seconds, which he personally felt was rather too long to be pressed against Khalil's large frame and his itchy stubble. Yet it wasn't all bad.

"Well, that was unpleasant," Max said at once, after they'd separated. "In a, er, pleasant way."

"Cheers. Valedictions, Max," Khalil said, and he started to amble away. "And check out the wrapping paper of the tusk. I wrote one of my favourite poetry lines on it."

Khalil wandered off along the pier, snapping a Polaroid of the rippling ocean en route.

Max stayed there for a few minutes after he'd left, doing nothing except listening to the splashing surf. There went the best friend he'd ever had, bar Rosie.

He looked down at the tusk and saw a quote written in cursive on the wrapping paper:

Let us create crystals out of the crucible of our stony hearts that light our path to love. The glance of love is crystalline, and we are blessed by its beauty.

Max read the words thrice, perplexed by them. It occurred to him that his first impressions weren't always good. Sometimes, they couldn't be more wrong. As the sun descended below the skyline, he inhaled the salty air and headed towards the ocean.

He boarded the cruise and met up with Rosie. As it departed, they stood on the deck together with their arms resting on the handrail, looking out at England while it turned into a tiny dot. Their first destination was France. When the country was no longer visible, she turned to him and beamed, even more radiant than the sea. He couldn't help but feel there would never be a better time to make a move than on this trip.

"This is gonna be so much fun!" Rosie exclaimed. "I've always dreamt of going on a world cruise!"

"I just hope Ithaca is as nice as it looks on my poster," Max asserted.

"So, what do you want to do first? The rollercoaster? The climbing wall? The spa?"

He swallowed a lump in his throat. *Oh, bother. I don't think Rosie's idea of a fun time aligns with mine unless the ship has lots of video games and puzzles.*

"Uh, I'm not sure that kind of thing is for me," he said, and rubbed his chin.

"Come on. I'm not gonna let you waste this cruise on crosswords!" Rosie said with a sigh. "Although, I did hear the cruise has its own quiz championship. No team requirements. Agatha Quiztie still has a lot to prove after what happened in Stapleford. Would you be up for it?"

"Maybe," Max said, gasping. "But first, we have to get off the boat. I just realised I left Benjamin behind!"

About The Author

Author Adam Rowan's passion for writing began in childhood, although he admits his early attempts were far from perfect. After a hiatus during his teenage years, Adam rediscovered his love for writing in his early twenties and has been dedicated to improving his craft ever since.

In 2022, MotherButterfly Books published Adam's first novel. His second book, *The Crystalline Crucible*, is published by Spinning Monkey Press and is inspired by his experiences growing up in England.

When he's not immersed in the world of writing, Adam is an electronic musician and avid film fan. With the support of his family, Adam continues to pursue his writing dreams, understanding that patience is key in the journey of creating a book.

Follow Adam on Instagram @shinjutnt

Milton Keynes UK
Ingram Content Group UK Ltd.
UKHW020616030524
441911UK00001B/6